Wiremei

By:

To Mitch,

Best wishes,

Any resemblance to real people, living or dead, is strictly inadvertent. This is a work of fiction!

This book is dedicated to my friend Glenna Turner, a sweet and gentle woman who left us way too soon.

Chapter 1

Bloody froth flew from his mouth splattering the light blue shirts of the two officers. Looking disgusted, they otherwise seemed unaffected by his screams. They stood back a bit, pulling on powdery green surgical gloves. He flailed fiercely at the air; throwing punches, kicks; finally they stepped toward him, bringing him quickly to the ground. It took a few more minutes to get him handcuffed, nothing for them to grab but his naked body.

 Two black lacquered dining room chairs were knocked on their sides. A lamp was broken into several pieces of cerulean blue ceramic with jagged white edges.

"Taliban, Taliban, Taliban, Taliban!"

"What the fuck is he screaming about?"

His brother raised his shoulders in a shrug, shaking his head from side to side, seeming more concerned with the mess that his ordinarily fastidious apartment had become. He bent to pick up a piece of the shattered lamp, held it between his thumb and index finger, staring at it.

"He's been obsessed with the Taliban lately, last month was Al Qaeda."

The cop who'd asked was 6'2" and well over 200 pounds. He was the smaller of the two and it still took all they had to get him under control. The taller cop had straight black hair and a prominent nose. After cuffing Rufus he made notes in his memo book. Jonah Koufax met him somewhere before. He managed to get a peek in the book.

"Wait a second Crean, why write that down?"

"Joint Terrorist Task Force wants stuff like this; they'll probably check him out. By the way - he's a tough little bastard."

"You're joking right? Stuff like what? You can see he's not right in the head, and I told you, he used to be on your job, was a terrific cop."

"Still…"

"He's just being Pacino."

"Pacino?"

"Dog Day Afternoon, outside the bank. When he's screaming Attica, Attica, Attica!

"Don't know what you're talking about."

It occurred to Jonah, these cops were barely thirty, weren't even born in '75, when the film came out. He remembered it though, recalled it being edgy, Pacino playing a down and out Brooklyn character, doing his first bank robbery to finance a sex change operation for his transgender lover.

Down and out, that's what Rufus had become. The tough talking, ruggedly handsome *private eye* and man about town who'd spent most of his life either charming or intimidating people. Now he's an out of control raving lunatic. He hated to admit it to himself, but Jonah felt a sense of relief, that the cops would be taking him away and that some professional would evaluate him. The conversation they'd had a few hours earlier prompted him to call 911.

"Why don't you get dressed, Ruf?"

"What for?"

"For one thing, you're making me uncomfortable."

"What's the other?"

"Never mind… get some clothes on."

"You part of it?"

"Of what?"

"Think I don't know…ha, ha, ha, ha…I know damn well...my clothes have wires running through them…they listen to everything."

"Be careful with the milk…watch it for God's sake!"

He poured the entire quart of milk into the bowl. It overflowed onto the glass table top, spreading like a surging springtime stream, dripping onto the pale beige Berber carpet. He sat eating breakfast - as if nothing had happened.

Jim Crean and his partner dragged him to the waiting ambulance, each grabbing an arm. Once they had him he went limp, like a dead man, feet crashing onto the concrete steps leading from the building's front door to the sidewalk. His slippers disappeared somewhere inside and his heels quickly became bloody messes of scraped skin. Then he cocked his head to the side, laughing, spitting.

"Taliban, you motherfuckers, Taliban, Taliban, Taliban!"

Jonah didn't blame the officers at all…for doing what they had to do.

Chapter 2

Tuesday June 3, 2008 10:11 A.M.

The room was dimly lit. His Smith and Wesson nine, strapped inside its brown leather holster, was out of reach, lying on top of Wanda's mahogany dresser next to a dirty glass vase with two green-stemmed white plastic flowers, bent over like old men. Could he reach it in time? His gray pants and white underwear were draped over a red velvet chair, the end of the belt hanging outside the last two loops. Fortune had himself propped up on one elbow in the middle of the queen-sized bed. Traces of lipstick covered his mouth and neck.

The man looked thirty years older than him and probably wasn't as good with his hands, but Johnny Fortune felt scared. He practically filled the doorframe, his mouth an angry looking knot. Fortune's sphincter tightened. He swallowed hard, like forcing down a half-chewed piece of meat.

He looked at the man's face for a second, then at the very large bone handled knife in his left hand. His right palm protected his groin, as if it mattered whether the intruder saw him naked. The man stared at him, smiling. Fortune smiled back. Him and Wanda had just finished, and he'd been drying himself with a tissue. He looked toward the bathroom, as if he wanted her to come out.

"What the fuck are you doing here?" Fortune said.

He made a move toward the dresser, but wasn't likely to make it.

The call came in at 10:14 a.m. as *a woman screaming.* The first officers on the scene were regular sector car men. Not an unusual call for that part of New Netherland. Violence was part of life in the city, expected and almost looked forward to by some citizens - a distraction from life's dreariness - as long as it didn't touch them or their families. Take a lot of those people out of the inner city and they'd lose their minds, would miss navigating through the obstacle course of urban life.

The radio car arrived, its bubble flashing red and green, the driver angle parking, front bumper touching a fireplug. The light pulsed as the two cops walked through the unlocked decrepit front door of the brown brick building. The lobby's marble floor was the color of a paper bag, with a pattern of darker brown diamonds. A dim yellow light glowed from the high ceiling, incandescent bulbs covered by dirty glass disks. Shadows on the floor showed outlines of long ago stolen furniture. They walked past the elevator to the stairwell.

"You can get trapped in that little box."

The third floor apartment door was open a few inches. Pete Dove pushed the door, his gun drawn. The younger cop wrestled his from its stiff holster.

A woman was tied to the bed, head hanging, blood everywhere. They stared at the saturated carpet, looking for a place to step. Chan, the younger cop, was breathing heavily.

"Careful, Charlie, don't mess up the scene."

"Shouldn't we make sure no one else is here?" Harold Chan said.

Most of the cops called him "Charlie." Dove, sixty years old, was old enough to be Charlie Chan's grandfather. Barely five-eight, built like a barrel, he was the oldest cop in the precinct, close to a legend in Newport West. Their first day together Chan told him that he felt happy Dove was his Field Training Officer. Dove had frowned, shaking his head.

"Cover the door while I look around."

He spoke in a low voice, as if someone was there. A moment later he pointed to the other side of the bed, to a pair of feet. Dove raised his hand and pointed one finger to his eyes, silently telling Chan, who seemed frozen, to keep him covered. He removed his shoes, handed them to Chan, tiptoeing between the dresser and bed until he was next to the body. He knelt, looking carefully at the dead man's face.

"Shit... it's Johnny Fortune".

Fortune, wedged between the bed and the wall, had linebacker's shoulders. His torso was covered with blood, more splattered onto the beige carpet, some onto the headboard and wall. A deep slice ran from a few inches below his right ear half way around his neck, stopping just below his jaw. He knew he was dead, but Dove crouched, putting two fingers on his left temple. Then he found his wallet and flipped it open, looked at the department I.D. photo of John Patrick Fortune's round, smiling face. A mark covered his left eye, from a piece of dirt ground into the laminated card. He reached into his left trouser pocket, felt his leg through the fabric, tried to avoid touching it as he dragged out the leather case that held NNPD patrolman's badge # 912. The holster held a large chrome Smith and Wesson automatic. Both were new, like the badge case. Next to the holster was Mis's cell. That's what everyone in the precinct called Johnny Fortune – because everything he'd handled in his first few weeks seemed to go bad, one misfortune after the other. Dove left the cell alone, too, didn't want to ruin any prints. The doorbell rang. Dove stood up, surprisingly agile, grabbing his shoes from Chan, told him to stay there.

He looked through the peephole then opened the door.

"What the fuck are you doing here?"

"I was about to ask you that, officer," Rufus said. "Problem?"

"You might say that - two dead bodies... and what's this officer shit?"

They'd known each other close to forty years, worked together as rookies, but Rufus Koufax acted like he'd never laid eyes on him. Pete Dove violated

brown twelve-ounce bottle, turned and resumed talking to Heaney and the fishermen. Then the fishermen went to Louie's, for more drinks.

"Come down here," he said.

He'd gone below into the cramped cabin that Heaney slept in when he didn't feel like going home. There was a dirty dark-green sleeping bag with a dark reddish plaid lining spread over the lone bunk. A gray and white pillow without a cover was at one end. Next to the bunk was a rusted pot bellied stove. All sorts of clothes hung from hooks on both side of the cabin. A worn book of charts opened to one of Narragansett Bay was on top of the sleeping bag. Rufus tossed it to the floor.

"What?" she said.

She had a mischievous smile on her face. It was all he needed to see. He told her to take her clothes off. She asked why, hesitated a moment, then complied. When they were done she reminded him how old she was.

"I know that."

"You could be in big trouble."

"Only if you tell someone."

She began to laugh, actually began to tickle him. Rufus didn't think it was funny, worried for weeks about it. Then he did it again, when he'd visited her and her mother one night, and Sissy had already gotten her load on, was fast asleep. It went on like that for years.

He waited for the nausea to pass before searching the rest of the apartment. Soon the street and building would crawl with police, EMTs, detectives, crime scene techs. The furnishings were all wood, with paintings on the walls, too expensive looking for a run-down tenement. The plush white upholstered couch and chairs had muted floral patterns. The bedroom had a bed, a nightstand, a dresser and mirror; a print of a naked reclining Nubian beauty, hands clasped behind her head, a slight smile on her exotic face, tongue barely showing; and a wood and red fabric dining room chair.

Wanda Kelley was bound with quarter inch once white cord, now more pink, tied halfway up the bedposts, the same knots binding her wrists. Her head looked like it might fall off if he touched it. Her long red hair covered her knees. The tattoo on the inside of her left thigh was new – a bright red rose nestled in green leaves. He remembered the one on her back, at the base of her spine, a sort of Celtic design.

His legs trembled, felt again like his breakfast might come up. He no longer felt half as bad about the dead cop. He thought about cutting the bindings, lowering her to the bed, but knew it would be viewed at best as a mistake and at worst as suspicious. Bad enough about the note on the refrigerator, but he'd already forgotten about that.

The dresser was cluttered: a few bottles of different types of massage oil, a pack of Parliaments, several books of matches, some bills and coins, and a small red phone book. A solitary long stemmed purple orchid at one end, in a clear glass vase filled with white gravel, looking out of place.

He grabbed the book, removed gold metal-framed reading glasses from his outside jacket pocket and put them on the tip of his nose. He thumbed through it quickly, thinking - who keeps phone books anymore? He stuck it in his inside jacket pocket. He pulled out his cell, unwrapped the thin black wire coiled around it, fumbling with the earpiece. Rufus had read about health risks associated with cell phones. He opened it, stared at the numbers for a moment, dialed, but hung up when he heard the first ring. Like a *Manchurian Candidate* trigger - the same woozy feeling hit him. He propped himself against the wall. Wanda dead, already cold, rigor mortis beginning; but then she was very much alive, almost like looking at a split screen TV, his thoughts rushing back and forth, between dead Wanda and the one he'd been intimate with days earlier.

"Ever see him before?" he'd said.

"Who?"

"The older guy, the captain?"

"Never."

"Give him your number?"

"He never asked."

"He ever call?"

"I just told you, I never gave him the number."

"Don't get snippy, girlfriend. I'm trying to help you...so explain to me how he ends up here a second time."

"I don't know, he just knocked and I let him in. He's a cop, what was I supposed to do?"

She'd changed into a thin black nightgown held closed with a sash. The neck plunged halfway down the front. Every so often, when one of her breasts came close to popping out, she'd shove it back in. She stood by the stove waiting for the stainless teakettle to whistle. She'd put instant into two white ceramic mugs.

"Black?"

"Hot and black, how I like my women."

"You're bad, Ruf, I ever tell you that?"

"A hundred million times."

The kettle whistled, she poured the boiling water, stirred the coffee then carried them to the table. Her fire-engine red enameled nails stroked his forearm, leaving white marks. She leaned toward him, moved to the back of his neck and scratched it lightly, then put her lips next to his ear so he could feel her breath.

"Come inside."

"Sloppy seconds? I don't think so."

"Never stopped you before."

He slept for a couple of hours. When she shook him awake nothing looked familiar for a few seconds. She helped him sit up, asked if he wanted any more before he left.

"Think I'm good for a while."

"You seemed to enjoy yourself, Ruf," she said.

He grinned a little while he dressed: light blue dress shirt, dark red tie tied with a Windsor, gray pants and navy sport coat with gold buttons. A trail of spots ran from the crotch of his pants toward the knees. If she noticed it she didn't say anything.

She made more coffee, gave him a piece of cinnamon bun she'd gotten at Starbucks early that morning. They sat at the small round table in the alcove off the kitchen, a copy of *People* next to her cup, a picture of Angelina and Brad on the cover. The window was open. Thin yellow curtains with white floral design kept blowing in; the sky suddenly looked dark. He tied his shoes, she reached over and rubbed the top of his scalp, laughing.

"What's so funny?"

"I remember when you had hair."

"That don't bother me."

"What bothers you?"

"Wish I could still go often as I used to…get hard like I used to"

"You do okay."

He laughed now - Rufus, not one for fooling himself.

"Thanks."

"You're always there for me, Ruf."

He bent over, gave her a kiss, tousling her hair a little, told her to take better care of herself, and told her to call right away if they called or came back. She did call…but he got there too late.

He looked at her body, dialed the same number again, this time let it ring four times before a familiar voice answered.

"Lieutenant McCoy."

"Bill, Rufus Koufax. I'm at 310 West 11th, off Moses Brown. Uniform guys are at the scene. You know you've got two bodies here, one of them a cop?"

"I know, I've got one foot out the door."

They spoke for a few seconds. He felt like he was floating in the ocean on a dark night, wondering how deep the water was and what was swimming nearby. That's what his life had become. Rufus tried to avoid getting blood on him, but too late for that.

He walked past Chan, gave him an avuncular pat on the shoulder, then descended the stairs and walked out the front door. Dove was still outside. Rufus took a deep breath of what masqueraded as fresh air in the great city of New Netherland. Waves of heat shimmered off the blacktop, the sun painful. A slight breeze blew in off the West Passage, not masking the city's stench. A white garbage truck picking up a few car lengths away made metallic groans as the San Men tossed full cans into the hopper. A cop gestured, telling the sanitation men to get off the block. The trees on either side of West 11th were stunted, not much more than ten feet. The green leaves provided some shade to the dancers and their friends. Traffic was stopped: taxis, cars, different size trucks, all going nowhere.

The west side of Newport, New Netherland's worst ghetto, was one of the few neighborhoods not cleared out by "progress". The rest of the city had turned into glitzy apartment towers, glass office buildings, Starbucks every two blocks, and multiplexes forcing out the last of the old theaters. Most of those had been burlesque houses a hundred years ago, when the city was one sleazy block after another. All changed now, not even a peep show for the pervs, and only a couple of old housing projects left. The city had become affordable only to the rich, with a few crumbs left for the poor.

Rufus looked at the dancers and the guy with the bongos. They reciprocated with hard stares. Rufus, Dove, the Salsa dancers - now distracted by the wailing of sirens and the flashing of red and green lights as more police turned onto the block. He walked back upstairs to get his last private moments with Wanda.

He pulled Wanda's red phone book out, thumbed through it again, thinking he should leave it for the cops to find. He looked at the name, Grunge, written in neat block letters. He thought of what Johnny "Mis" Fortune had said a week earlier - that he'd introduced the sergeant to Wanda, who in turn brought Captain Benny Fields to meet her. Wanda described them to Rufus that day, after Fortune left. Grunge was a big muscular white-haired guy. Fields was older, "a well-dressed gray-haired gentleman" with a pasty complexion. She described him as very polite, thanked her when she got done giving him a blow job, like she'd just served him breakfast, how she'd described it to Rufus.

Rufus had thought then, just like he was now – *I'm going to kill those bastards.*

Chapter 3

Tuesday June 3, 2008, 10:10 a.m.

He took one long step and was on top of Fortune, the knife slicing at his neck. Blood spurted, spreading onto his face and upper chest. Fortune was dead, but still looked surprised a moment later when he dragged him off the bed onto the floor. He looked at the wound, a little fascinated by the size of it.

Wanda Kelley was in the bathtub, shaking, knees pulled to her chest. A few seconds later he walked in, grabbed a fist full of red hair, dragging her out, white legs flailing to find traction. When she screamed he struck the side of her head with the handle of the knife.

A few minutes later she forced a crooked smile, the smile of someone unnerved. Lipstick stained one of her front teeth and her mascara had run. He forced her up onto the bed, stepping over to the side closer to the bedroom door, climbing up behind her, grabbed her hair and yanked her head back. "Hey!" He took pieces of clothesline from his jacket pocket, tied her left wrist carefully, then the right, tied each end to the corner posts at the foot of her four-poster. He didn't undress, just opened his pants then slid behind her, maneuvering himself inside. In a few seconds she felt the shudder of his climax. He stayed still for a while and she smiled, thinking – thank God it's over, he'll be out of here soon. Then he hit her again, across the back of the head.

When she regained consciousness the man was in front of her trying to masturbate. He laughed while she made muffled moans. No one else could hear her through the gray duck tape covering her mouth. He got more excited the louder she groaned.

He ripped the tape from her mouth and she sucked in a breath, as if it might be her last, and then fell into a coughing fit. He laughed - in low guttural tones.

"Where's Johnny? Is he okay?"

"If you scream again I'll hurt you…even more."

He began to disrobe, slowly, ritual like. He walked to the chair, grabbed Fortune's clothes, tossed them into the nearest corner; carefully placing his own on the red upholstered chair.

"Why the fuck didn't you tell me you were into this. You didn't have to go through all this elaborate bullshit; I'm very good at role-playing. Untie me - I'll take care of you."

This motherfucking freak, she thought. I've got to do something, there's no way I'm done…no way this can be it, oh God, oh blessed mother, blessed mother, please, please…

He took the knife and slid the razor sharp blade across her neck. Blood splattered five or six feet away, made a pattern from the mirror over the dresser, onto the beige carpet and the edge of the bed.

This can't be, can't be…the light is blazing, so white, so white and beautiful and…doesn't even hurt any more…so lovely, the light, the light…something opening…

He pulled while he sliced, as if he wanted to decapitate her. Her last sounds were a combination of gurgles and coughs. Then he just let go. As her head fell forward more blood spurted. He stood, examining himself, using a pillowcase to wipe his hands.

He paused to look at her – both arms raised and tied. She looked poised to perform a swan dive. He cleaned himself as best he could, got dressed, looked around, smiled, and left.

Descending the stairs a neighbor opened her door on the floor below, closing it quickly as he passed. He hesitated a moment, considered knocking then continued and left the building.

Chapter 4

Tuesday June 3, 2008, 10:43 a.m.

It irked McCoy to get the call from Rufus. He practically had one foot out the door when he picked up the phone. He'd already sent Falco and Brito to the scene. He told Falco that this one was his. Once McCoy heard cop, and a double, he wanted him on it, even though he didn't really like him. Falco was always a little too well dressed – almost slick looking – and had an answer for everything. But he was the guy I'd want on the case if one of my kids were a victim, McCoy often thought.

He would have run out with them but Falco took the call from Pete Dove, and then informed the indisposed McCoy, while he sat on the john.

When he got there he parked at the end of West 11th. There were a dozen radio cars in the block, half of them with their dome lights going; an ambulance, the Crime Scene Unit van, several news trucks already setting up cameras, reporters running around shoving mikes in people's faces. Dove and Chan guarded the entrance to 310. As McCoy approached, Dove was arguing with a woman sergeant, a short blond haired woman, not much more than thirty, with a face that needed makeup, about getting two other officers for security. He tried to explain that they were handling the crime report and vouchering the property.

"What do we have, Pete?"

"Bad one, lieutenant - Officer Fortune bought it, and a local hooker, Wanda Kelley. Both close to decapitated...very weird."

"No one gets upstairs unless me or Falco okay it."

"Ten-four, boss."

McCoy took the sergeant aside and whispered something to her. She nodded in agreement. She turned to walk back to her radio car, face bright red.

Upstairs in apartment 3-C, the crime scene detectives were dusting, photographing, and running a handheld vacuum over the entire place. They changed bags for each room, labeling the bag they'd removed.

"Where's Falco and Brito?"

"Doing the canvass...they were nice enough not to get in our way."

Bill McCoy looked at Detective Marie St. Pierre. She looked back.

"Something wrong, Lieu?"

He stared a moment or two more, ignoring the question, clearly distracted; but couldn't allow himself to be, so he stopped, like he'd just turned a switch.

McCoy was considered one of the best detective commanders in the city but at times like these he never quite felt that way. Crime scenes sometimes seemed impossibly chaotic. He managed to hide his insecurity, was very methodical and matter of fact as he went about his business.

"What's it look like?"

"A mess…two victims, lots of blood."

She led him to the bedroom. He stood by the door, surveying the scene, took several moments before walking in and closely examining each victim. He noticed Fortune's weapon on the dresser. Before leaving he glanced at the television – a soap opera playing silently. Then he walked out.

At close to six feet, with black hair and a swimmer's body, and classically pretty Demi Moore kind of face, St. Pierre could have been a cover girl. But most of the cops and detectives saw her black work-shoes, shapeless pants, her standard garb, and presumed - dyke. McCoy didn't.

Brito came walking up the stairs. The detective, almost twenty years his senior, was out of breath. He wore a tan corduroy sport coat and dark brown trousers, his light blue dress shirt opened at the collar, and loosely knotted tie a bit too wide. He looked older than fifty-five, because of his white receding hair.

"Anything?" McCoy said.

"Not yet."

"Where's Falco?"

"Working his way down from six."

"You see Koufax?"

"No… why?"

Brito's eyes widened, as if asking - *why the hell would he be here?*

"He called from the scene, right after you and Falco left. Did Dove say anything?"

"No…want me to talk to him?"

"Yeah."

Despite his feelings about Falco, McCoy knew Brito had a better chance to get the whole story out of Dove. The two detectives had different strengths. In fact, many squad bosses thought of them as amongst the best detectives in the department.

McCoy walked outside. Waiting there were the Chief of Detectives, the Deputy Commissioner for Public Information, a deputy Mayor, and the Supervising Attorney General for Homicide. He wondered where Commissioner Lynch was.

"What's it look like, Bill?" the chief said.

"Pretty bad…a double, one of them one of ours."

"Who?"

"Kid named Fortune."

"Any idea why he was here?"

"My best guess...to get laid."

The chief turned red, his mouth taking a downward arc. The others didn't say anything. The prosecutor, a heavyset man named Calabrese, walked a step toward the entrance.

"Not yet, counselor, not until my people finish processing the scene. Pete, nobody gets up till I clear it."

McCoy knew he'd hear about this from the chief later. But he also knew department rules explicitly stated that the lieutenant of detectives on the scene of a homicide was in charge, regardless of the rank of other responding personnel. And McCoy wasn't shy about telling a boss, diplomatically, that he'd be better off back in headquarters. Though prosecutors weren't subject to police department rules, McCoy, like any good squad boss, also ruled by dint of his personality.

He had a lot to think about. But in the forefront for him, was why Rufus Koufax had been there, and whether he had any role in the murder.

Chapter 5

Wanda

Wanda never knew her father. She grew up in a cramped inner-city apartment, in a neighborhood where a cross-eyed look could at the very least result in a beating. But just like talent can surface in unlikely places, like the afflicted child who might be a piano or violin virtuoso, or the hopeless stutterer who sings flawlessly, Wanda had certain strengths that overcame her circumstances. Or almost did.

"Wanda, come up!"

"Ten minutes!"

"Upstairs, now!"

Shouts from city tenements carried three or four stories, from an apartment window to the street and back. They lived in a railroad flat on the south side of New Netherland, one of the last white families in the neighborhood. Forced busing, the result of Johnson's Great Society and the Civil Rights Act of 1968, had the opposite of the intended result, with residents of city neighborhoods fleeing what they didn't know or understand.

Peter Stuyvesant had intended New Netherland to be a religious and racial sanctuary, a community where prejudice and hatred wouldn't be tolerated. But two hundred and fifty years later the city was a model often studied by sociologists to explain the phenomenon of *white flight.*

They lived in three rooms - living room, bedroom with the kitchen in between. The bathroom didn't qualify as a room, was barely forty square feet, with a tub, toilet and sink squashed together. The paint in the bedroom and living room was a dark off-white. Every wall had cracks traveling the length of the room, with peels coming off in large irregular pieces. The linoleum was a faded red and gray floral design, most of the pattern worn away. The yellow gloss paint in the kitchen didn't look too bad except for the brown stained wall behind the black and white gas stove. The window on the opposite side had been stuck for two years because their mother didn't like the superintendent, a Puerto Rican named Sixto, who didn't smile much. The top window was open a few inches for ventilation.

Wanda and her sister were three years apart and couldn't have been more different. As focused and goal oriented and obedient as Victoria was, Wanda was the complete opposite - flighty, impetuous, defiant, a lot for their mother Sissy to handle. If you asked, they probably wouldn't be able to tell you their mother's real name, always Sissy – the middle child of nine, all the others boys. Wanda and Victoria had different fathers, both bad actors. Sissy was still in her teens when

Wanda was born, had just gotten Victoria out of diapers. She raised them herself, got the apartment on her own, applied for Welfare and food stamps and made what she could doing odd jobs around the neighborhood. She clerked in a bodega, did the same at a dry-cleaners, then answered phones and cleaned the kitchen at the church rectory.

Sissy finally got a break, before the kids were in school. A better than average singer, she could also pick up a dance step after being shown it once. And she'd managed to keep her figure, even after Wanda came along, so she ended up with a steady gig as a showgirl in a Vaudeville revival in the city's theater district. The show lasted a year. After that she got sporadic work, usually as a back-up singer in a nightclub.

That's when she met Rufus. They dated for a few months but Rufus wasn't too comfortable around children, felt inept when it came to doing anything paternal – feeding them or reading stories.

Wanda left home at fifteen to live with a fireman named Buddy Roach in Providence. A year later they had a knock down fight. She got in a few shots but ended up in the emergency room. That's when she found out that she'd never be able to have children.

She and the fireman made up as soon as she left the E.R. They went to Rafferty's old beer hall. It had a sixty-foot long bar, sawdust on the floor, the original tin ceiling that Rafferty had painted brown a long time ago, and a jukebox with only Irish music and Frank Sinatra. Owen Rafferty loved "Old Blue Eyes." The place served beer and ale. If you wanted hard liquor you could walk to a gin mill fifty feet in either direction. Rafferty put out sandwiches and one hot dish on Friday nights, for the regulars. If you weren't a regular and tried to mooch a meal it might not be a good night for you.

Wanda took her first collar for prostitution at sixteen. The fireman was pimping her. Rufus found out, spoke to a friend on the dicks in New Netherland, to talk to someone in the Providence P.D. Word came back – do what you gotta do, but don't leave us a body to answer for - which gave Rufus plenty of latitude.

He found Roach coming out of Rafferty's at 11:30 p.m. on a Tuesday night. He'd been watching him for a couple of days. Rufus was driving a beat up black Ford Fairlane, 1960's vintage, with dents in all four doors, and a gray trunk lid, like someone had begun a paint job then forgot about it. He and the car were unnoticeable.

He got out and followed him; Roach was wearing a maroon sweatshirt with the sleeves cut off, like the old baseball player, Ted Kluzewski. Three blocks from Rafferty's, he walked up the steps of a green triple-decker with white trim, fumbling at the door with the keys. He dropped them, took a pack of cigarettes out and lit one. He was still fumbling around looking for the keys when a hand gripped his right shoulder.

Buddy Roach spent two weeks in the hospital. Rufus used that time trying to get Wanda to see the light. Before long they became an item. Rufus always figured Wanda got all her experience starting with the fireman, but he found out later that Sixto, the superintendent, had more to do with that.

Four years later she disappeared from his life for a while. He still visited Sissy, would ask about her, but all he'd get was *she's doing good.* Once, Sissy told him that Wanda was thinking of trying modeling.

The bar off the lobby of the New Netherland Towers was all glass, chrome and nouveau art. The high-tech sound system had a selection of jazz and pop tunes, designed to appeal to a slightly older clientele. She'd worked the place six months or so, knew the bartenders and bellmen, always made sure to duke them with a few bucks when she left, whether she got business that night or not.

She swayed through the lobby in a tight black dress that reached just above the knees, with matching heels and a string of pearls that looked real, short dyed blond hair, light makeup; all together making her look like a rich man's daughter. Several men turned, including the desk clerk, watched her glide to the bar.

She put her black handbag on the bar, took out a pack of Parliaments and a twenty, shoving the bill toward the bartender. She fumbled with the pack until a cigarette came loose, took it between the first two fingers of her right hand, holding it halfway toward her face.

"Vodka and grapefruit, Mickey."

"You got it, babe."

As she put the cigarette in her lips his lighter flame was under it. She leaned in, the end catching fire for a second. He snapped the silver lighter closed.

Mickey Gannon was the night bartender. He made it his business to know everyone else's, and if you had something going in his joint, how he thought of the hotel bar, he expected his.

"Pretty quiet."

"Tell me about it," he said.

"Any spenders?"

"Not much happening."

Then he motioned with his eyes and head toward the other end of the bar. The thirty-something guy looked like a banker, conservatively dressed, suit and tie.

Up in the room he kissed her and she sensed something wrong. She'd regret later not turning around and walking out – something about the way he kissed, with his lips half closed, his tongue not leaving his mouth. She began to unzip her dress.

"A hundred for a blow job, a buck fifty for the whole deal – your choice."

At Central Booking she no longer looked comely; her hair mussed and mascara soiling both cheeks. The last cop she called a "motherfucker" backhanded her. The mug shot showed encrusted blood at the right corner of her mouth.

A few days later her mother re-introduced her to Rufus. He hadn't seen her much in the last few years. Not a match destined for romance, close to twenty-five years apart, but they genuinely liked each other. Sissy asked him to *Dutch Uncle* Wanda, to keep an eye on her.

He did his best to look out for her, got her a couple of jobs hostessing at middling restaurants. Her temper made them short-lived positions. They got very friendly for a while (very friendly,) but then lost touch again.

A few years later, in '97, he saw her walking Broadway, in a red mini that barely covered her ass, with a tight halter top with wide horizontal black and white stripes, her bellybutton and then some exposed. She no longer had the figure for it - didn't look like a rich guy's daughter any more. Her hair was black and in a way she reminded him of a down and out Monica, the one causing the president a lot of grief.

He pulled to the curb and rolled down the passenger window. She walked towards him, fifteen feet or so, with a heavy sway and a phony smile, then rested both forearms on the door and stuck her head into the car.

"Looking to go out?" she said.

"Yeah, I'm looking."

After she hopped in he noticed track marks on the insides of her elbows. She didn't take a good look at him until the car was in traffic. When she finally recognized him she told him to pull over and let her out; started screaming at him.

Rufus put her in a program, a thirty-day deal out in the country, on an old farm in Burriville. Suddenly acting like she was family, he visited every week, was there to pick her up after the month in rehab. He tried to get Sissy to come, but by then she and Wanda didn't have too much of a relationship. And Sissy was the kind of city person who got a nosebleed if she got too far from the asphalt and big buildings.

Wanda came out large white French doors onto the faded yellow brick patio, wearing a lavender dress with big white buttons down the front. Her hair was blond again, all poofed out, like she'd been to a beauty parlor.

She was twenty-six and Rufus well past fifty, with physical problems beginning to surface. She ran up, threw her arms around his neck, and next thing her tongue was in his mouth. It reminded Rufus of the first time they'd kissed, over ten years earlier - right after he got done with the fireman. Roach never did know what, or who, hit him.

He'd told Roach he'd get Wanda to agree not to press charges for stat rape but that he'd better never go near her again. Roach looked at him funny, kind of suspicious, unsure if Rufus was threatening him or not. But he never did bother Wanda again.

But Rufus did. He thought it might be his last chance, Rufus, never too strong in the romance department. He had a penchant for picking the wrong women, Wanda no exception. Suffice to say, after a couple of months things went down hill, never really recovered, though they remained friendly.

The New Netherland Athletic Club was a thirty-story brown brick building on the lower west side of the city that mostly catered to well-heeled businessmen, politicians, and doctors; one of the last male bastions that still successfully discriminated against women and minorities, and even though Rufus didn't appreciate their policies, he felt comfortable enough taking advantage of the facilities and amenities. And his membership was a free ride – the result of his discretion in a marital case involving a board member of the club. The club manager, Fred Forlini, was also an occasional doubles racquetball teammate when schedules allowed.

At 9:25 a.m. on June 3rd, 2008 Freddy knocked on the door of the racquetball court, dressed in a conservative gray suit and open collared lighter gray dress shirt. Rufus opened the glass portal and stuck his head out.

"Don't you guys hear the phone - young lady for you."

"Thanks Freddy, put it through."

A white phone hung on the wall opposite glass enclosed court#1. Rufus's navy gym shorts and tee were stained with sweat, his hair askew, comb-over sticking out, his safety goggles pushed up on his forehead.

"Hang up! It'll be a few minutes."

The phone rang as he adjusted himself inside his jock. He leaned his racket against the wall under the phone. The three other players continued, practicing kill shots to the corner, each time the blue rubber ball sounding like a gunshot.

"Koufax."

"Ruf, it's me," Wanda said.

"What's up? I'm in the middle of a game."

"He called again, said he'd be coming over."

"Son of a bitch… you tell him he couldn't?"

"I tried…he wouldn't listen."

"You say you were going to call me?"

"No. He said he'd be over soon and hung up."

"I'll be there in half an hour – don't open the door for anyone but me."

He'd warned Johnny Fortune that he'd had his fun, that if he bothered her again he'd be putting his job in jeopardy. The kid had promised, swore up and down that he wouldn't be a problem...so much for promises.

Now he stood a few feet from Wanda's lifeless body, trembling, in a state of near shock. He'd seen and been involved in plenty of violence, but this was different. Waves of nausea mixed with his mind spinning out of control, thoughts of all the history and emotion and relationships like tangled fishing lines – was too much. "I'm going to kill those bastards," he repeated to himself.

Chapter 6

Vernon Brito knocked at 2C, the fifth apartment he'd tried. He stepped to the side as the door opened. The huge woman had a baby in each arm, twins that looked only a few days old. She wore a thin pink cotton housecoat tied at the waist. Brito stared for a moment.

"Can I help you?"

His light brown face reddened and he made a deliberate gesture to look official, taking his memo book out, unfolding it to a blank page, his pen at the ready.

"Was some trouble upstairs a little while ago…you hear anything?"

"Yeah, heard some screams."

"What time?"

"During *Days of Our Lives*."

"It's on that early?"

"On Soapnet it is."

"What's your name, dear?"

"Cecelia Brown."

She said when she heard the screams she came to the door, opened it a couple of inches and saw a man rushing down the stairs. He made notes as she spoke. Brito didn't recognize her when she opened the door but the name rang a bell.

"What did he look like?"

"Was a white dude… not too young."

"Could you recognize him again?"

"Depends."

"On what?"

"On what he done."

"Killed two people."

"My lord! Who?"

"Woman named Wanda, and a guy was visiting."

Brito didn't reveal a police officer had been murdered, not sure why he omitted that fact. He continued to examine her face, trying to pull up where he'd met her.

"Wanda? Oh, my sweet lord…my sweet lord."

"You know what she did for a living?"

"Wanda was good people, what she did to get by was her business."

Brito was surprised when she began to cry. He paused before asking the next question. He'd worked in quite a few different assignments in thirty-two years. Patrol, detectives, vice, even a little time in the emergency services unit. He wracked his brain trying to come up with where he'd run across Cecelia. Most likely vice, he thought.

"Was he running down the stairs"?

"Wouldn't say running, was kind of hasty though."

He got some more basics: her cell number, date of birth, how long she'd lived there.

"Would you come to headquarters, look at some pictures?"

"Who gonna watch my babies?"

Falco was still on six. He'd found three people at home. The first two were elderly, lived alone, hadn't heard or seen anything.

A neat looking older Hispanic woman in a khaki dress and black heels, wearing an orange kerchief, answered the third door he knocked on. She held a red and white checkerboard dishtowel, drying her hands with it. He showed his shield.

"Detective Falco. Can I speak with you?"

"Uno momento."

She screamed something in Spanish towards the rear of the apartment. Odors of garlic and cooking meat spilled into the hallway. He heard sizzling. It all reminded him he felt hungry. A moment later a young girl appeared, the granddaughter he presumed. Grandma disappeared into the apartment. The girl said she'd thought she heard someone yelling, called 911 but hung up when the operator answered, because she hadn't heard where the yelling came from, didn't really know anything. She invited Falco inside, offered coffee.

"No thanks."

"Maybe later, or another day?"

"What's your name?"

"Nilda."

"How old are you, Nilda?"

"Old enough."

She flashed a smile. She had smooth flawless medium brown skin and almond shaped eyes, her hair plastered to her head and tied at the back, kind of J-Lo like.

"I'm nineteen," she added.

"Nineteen?"

"Want proof?"

She wore a green diaphanous blouse, skimpy white shorts, was barefoot, her toenails bright red, matching her lips. She smiled while Falco made notes.

"Did you open the door to look around?"

27

"You crazy?"

"If you or grandma remember anything else, or hear anything, call the precinct, ask for me or Detective Brito."

He handed her a business card. She took it and placed it on a table next to the door without looking at it.

"Sure."

"Thank you."

"Come back any time."

He canvassed the rest of the fifth, fourth and third floors. He felt satisfied he'd found everyone possible. They'd come back later to do it all again anyway. He liked that, enjoyed the methodical routines of an investigation, and the feeling of being thorough.

"Come up with anything?" Falco said.

"Woman on two saw the perp running down the stairs, might be able to identify him."

"That sounds good."

"How about you?" Brito said.

"Zilch. Where's the boss?"

"Talking to the brass."

Crime Scene had just about wrapped up in the apartment, and Lieutenant Bill McCoy was outside, speaking with the Chief of Detectives and Police Commissioner Lynch. More news trucks were on the block and about five radio cars. Two of the networks had cameras set up and several freelance photographers were snapping shots. Two officers kept the gathering crowd behind the yellow crime scene tape. The tape was strung from light posts to cars and back and to anything else handy, including a rusted shopping cart near the building entrance that contained a car generator, a black plastic boom box with its insides sprouting out, a rusting bicycle wheel, and a few stuffed animals that looked like they'd been fished from the sewer.

The M.E. wagon parked as close to the building as it could get. Two attendants, one thin and one heavy, both dressed in medium blue uniforms made for people that did hard and dirty labor, pulled a wheeled stretcher from the rear double doors. They rolled it to the front steps and in one motion lifted and carried it through the front door. Charlie Chan held it open.

Then the medical examiner, a tall man of about sixty dressed in a gray pinstripe suit and navy wool tie, walked up to the front of the building. The commissioner walked over and shook the famous pathologist's hand. They turned away for a hushed conversation. Brito and Falco had just walked out the front door and stayed on top of the stoop.

"Should we tell them we found a witness?" Brito said.

"Fuck no. They'll give it to the press, next thing we've got no witness."

Brito considered taking him back inside to see Cecelia Brown, but decided to wait. He could talk to her later or tomorrow. Falco looked at Brito, smiling.

"What are you grinning at?" Brito said.

He didn't answer. St. Pierre had just walked out of the building, causing several heads to turn, including Bill McCoy's. Falco walked over and began to talk to her a few feet from the entrance. He smiled widely, but St. Pierre stayed looking serious.

"Bill, are you listening?"

"Got it, chief – full court press - of course."

When McCoy got done with the chief, Falco was still next to St. Pierre. McCoy kept staring. Falco glanced his way, staring back. Brito took it all in.

Rufus had told Billy McCoy he'd break the news to Wanda's mother Sissy and bring her in to talk to Falco and Brito, even though he knew it would be a waste of time. Wanda and Sissy only spoke when the kid brought rent money once a month. They had to interview her though, and he figured, let them knock themselves out. Sissy would take it hard, but no way to avoid it. Wanda's sister Victoria was another story – Rufus avoided her like the plague. She knew the whole history of Wanda and Rufus, and hated him for it.

He walked the stairs to the top floor, slowly, noticing things he'd never looked at before, like the beige stone steps with depressions worn in by millions of footfalls over the last fifty years. Two Puerto Rican kids came rushing off the roof, looking like they'd seen a ghost. Rufus knew the neighborhood, had practically lived there for a while. Odors of Spanish cooking - plantains, garlic, rice and beans - permeated the hallways. Brown paint peeled away from the walls in large pieces, exposing white plaster. One of the kids bumped into him as he rang her bell. He cursed under his breath as the door opened.

"What's the matter with you?"

"Couple of meatballs came off the roof, almost knocked me over. You gonna invite me in?"

"Don't expect dinner or nothing. Sure you're okay?"

He breathed hard as he followed her through the kitchen, the front room of the railroad flat. The living room was in the middle, the bedroom in the rear. It had been a long time since he'd been there. Sissy flopped down onto the blue floral couch, into cushions molded to her ample figure. She actually looked better than she had in years, had her short bleached-blond hair combed and had on a little makeup. Her faded turquoise housecoat had white trim on the sleeves and collar white plastic buttons the size of half-dollars down the front, and a few holes from cigarette burns. Looking at Sissy reminded him of looking in the mirror.

Sometimes you don't see your sixty, or fifty or forty year old self. You're ageless in a certain way, even though you see gray hair, or crow's feet, or sagging skin. And in a certain way he still saw the thirty-year-old knockout with chiseled features, and long shapely legs.

He looked at his watch - ten-thirty - longer than he'd intended to stay. He wondered how she'd missed the news about Wanda. He'd left the precinct a few hours ago, then met Bill McCoy at Kennedy's, then left there planning to come right to Sissy. He didn't know what happened, what delayed him. He vaguely recalled going in the front door of a gin mill called DiGiacomo's, but nothing after that.

She motioned for him to sit next to her but he grabbed a folding chair from the telephone table on the other side of the room, pulled it close, so he could look at her creased face. Stacks of newspapers and magazines covered every surface. A coating of dust was visible on the large mirror in the ornate golden frame that hung behind the couch. The place was musty and he could tell Sissy was having a problem with digestion. He grabbed her hand, felt the broken chafed skin. Her housecoat was hiked up and twisted. Rufus looked at her varicose veins, meandering blue streams on a landscape of white bulging skin. She caught him looking, pulled the bottom of the housecoat down as far as she could. She already seemed sad and he wished he were anywhere else.

"Who cold-cocked you?" she said.

"It's nothing."

Rufus rubbed the bump over his eye, small potatoes compared to everything else.

"Sissy, I got bad news."

"Wanda?"

"Yeah, kiddo."

She began to cry, didn't stop for a long time. He moved to the couch and put his arm around her. His mind drifted back to the early 80's, Sissy crying now over her baby girl made him think of other mothers he'd met, crying over their lost babies. When's this shit gonna stop, he thought to himself.

Chapter 7

The rooms of the Newport West detective squad hadn't been painted in fifteen years. The month before a crew from Department of Public Works arrived unannounced; hauling ladders, buckets of paint, trays, rollers, brushes, and old splattered tarpaulins. They left it all helter-skelter in the corridor outside the squad's offices. After a perfunctory conversation between the sergeant on duty and the crew supervisor, furniture began to get moved, tarps spread, and scraping commenced. By June 3rd half the offices were painted, the same colors they'd been for decades – institutional green and beige - but no one knew exactly when they'd be done, because the entire crew sometimes disappeared for three or four days, so the squad room was in even more disarray than usual.

This didn't help set the mood for what had become one of the more important cases ever to be investigated by the Newport West Squad. No matter what the circumstances, the murder of a police officer merited and received an appropriate level of attention.

"You interview him," Lieutenant Bill McCoy said.

"With Brito?" Falco said.

"He'll be more at ease one on one."

"Want it recorded?"

"Not yet."

With all the false confessions and wrongful convictions in the news in recent years the New Netherland P.D. had implemented a policy requiring interrogations to be videotaped; part of a nationwide movement, particularly with big-city departments under the microscope of everyone from the A.C.L.U. to the Justice Department.

But city detectives found ways to circumvent bureaucratic policies they didn't think made sense, as with Operations Order 312/08. First interrogations often happened in the back of a squad car, or in a corner of the roll call room, or in a supervisor's office – then, after the suspect confessed, or not, the "official" interview took place.

"Use my office," McCoy said.

Rufus knew from *jump street* he'd be a suspect. He'd known McCoy for most of his life, had been with the kid plenty of times. He also felt that Billy McCoy always found him a bit mysterious. He could usually sense discomfort when they saw each other, McCoy probably thinking – why the hell do I associate with this guy?

He tried to remember the last time he'd been in his office, and why he'd been there. It was nothing official, maybe a social visit with Dave. But no, that couldn't be – Dave was gone for almost thirty years.

He'd been forgetting things recently, just part of the normal aging process, he'd told himself. Lists helped. He'd jot down things to do, made notes; things you'd do normally during an investigation anyway. Cases had to be organized, you needed to plan the steps, not just go off helter-skelter trying to figure out who done it. So how was this different? He didn't really know…and anyway, sometimes he misplaced the lists.

Earlier, at about 6:30 that morning, the sun just barely breaking, he sat at Chris's counter, ordered eggs, corned beef hash, an English muffin, and a black coffee. The waiter looked kind of familiar. He used a black felt tip pen to scribble the order onto a light green pad, ripped the top sheet off and put it onto a silver metal clip at the top of the opening between the counter and the kitchen, for the cook to grab. The waiter talked to an old guy near the register, who looked to be the owner. He took it all in, looking suspiciously at the two men.

.   "Rufus, you okay?"

"Fine, why do you ask?"

"You not dressed, my friend."

He looked down at his maroon pajamas and grey herringbone topcoat, got a slightly disgusted expression on his face, then shrugged his shoulders and commenced to finish his breakfast. Chris was still nearby when he mouthed the last of the eggs.

"How'd you know my name?"

He addressed the man named Chris in a loud voice. Why shouldn't he? The guy kept looking him over, made him feel like they were up to something. He'd seen their kind before…plenty of times…wasn't about to let them take him for a ride.

Five minutes later Jonah Koufax sat next to him, put his hand on his arm. The owner and waiter watched for a moment then got busy with other customers.

"Rufus, what's up?"

"Having breakfast…what the hell are you doing here?"

"Chris called me, said you seem a bit confused."

"Chris who?"

"Chris Koulouvardis…our friend."

Jonah's nostrils widened and twitched, from the acrid ammonia odor, then glanced down at the puddle under the stool.

He left a twenty in front of his brother's dirty dishes. At the front door, Chris held some bills in his fist, telling them they forgot the change. Jonah waved, told him to keep it. They left the diner arm in arm, like a couple.

That was three weeks after the murders. Rufus hadn't kept an appointment Jonah made for him with a neurologist at New Netherland General. Jonah said he didn't like the idea of him wandering around the city with a gun in his condition. What condition? Rufus had answered. Jonah felt impotent, probably knew there was nothing he could do about it.

At 1:30 p.m. on June 3rd Rufus stood near the door looking around the small room, just a few hours after the murders. The window faced west, light filtering through the dirty glass and cracks in the yellowed shade, dust particles dancing on the rays. The desk had "in" and "out" baskets made of black metal mesh, the "in" full, "out" empty. A black onyx and gold metal pen set, with Bill McCoy's name and rank and date of promotion to lieutenant, sat between the baskets. The wood veneer desktop was covered with a monthly calendar, neat entries in right leaning Palmer script in many of the lined boxes. Rufus stared at the writing, seemed to be admiring the look of it. The painters hadn't reached McCoy's office, one of the only instructions they'd followed, to make his room the last.

A tall houseplant in a dark red ceramic pot sat on the floor, just to the left of the window. Black and white photos of the skyline and different historic sites of the city hung in black metal frames. One, an aerial shot of a giant caisson used in the construction of the New Netherland to Providence Bay Bridge Tunnel, taken in 1969, showing several workmen about to be lowered on a platform into the claustrophobic darkness, to work on one of the uprights. Between the photos on the wall near the door, McCoy's high school and college diplomas and a certificate from the F.B.I. National Academy hung in wood frames.

Falco looked at a report, taking his time with each page, not exactly stalling. But he'd decided to take his time, this definitely not the usual run-of-the-mill interrogation he and Brito, or the other detectives in Newport West were used to. A husband or wife that stabbed or shot their spouse during a domestic, an armed robber that went too far during a stick-up, or maybe a combatant in one of the legions of drug disputes that went on in every poor city neighborhood across the country; that's what they were expert at.

He finally put the pages down, stood up and removed his navy blazer, placing it on the back of the lieutenant's chair. The jacket's gold buttons made clicking sounds when they brushed against the chair's metal frame. The noise seemed to irritate Rufus. Falco loosened his tie, grabbed the grip of his Glock nine, adjusting the position of the holster. He sat down, ran the fingers of both hands through his long, almost jet black hair. He wore a gold ring with a miniature detective's shield on his left index finger. He noticed Rufus looking at him, as if trying to read his mind or figure him out.

"Take a seat," Falco said.

"I like to stand."

Rufus rubbed his scalp, a slight grin on his face, right hand in his pocket, fingering something. A moment later he removed a piece of toast and threw it in the green metal waste can. Falco looked on with a quizzical stare.

"Sit down."

He pulled the chair closest to him away from the desk, as if to say he didn't like that Falco was in control.

"Coffee?"

"No, more coffee I'll be floating. As it is, my bladder's not so good. Get up three times a night to piss these days. When I was your age I could drink beer all freaking night and never go to the head. Now, forget it. Was a time I'd run four or five miles every morning, come back to the apartment, do some push-ups and sit-ups, some weights. Know what I do now?"

"What?"

"Get the paper in the morning, then a three-block walk to Chris's Diner, the one on Seventy- Ninth. That's my exercise…Get the same breakfast every day."

"What do you have?"

"What do I have?"

"For breakfast."

"I don't know."

Rufus hesitated, like he couldn't quite find what he wanted to say. Falco was already losing patience.

"Oh yeah, I know…same thing…corned beef hash, eggs sunny side, toast or a muffin, orange juice, two cups of coffee. Holds me the whole day, never have lunch."

The detective kept staring, with a blank expression, Rufus now thinking about what to say? He could no longer think several steps ahead, that much he knew.

"Like I said, can't do the weights no more…and can't run if my life depended on it. It's a shame I tell ya, what can happen you don't watch out. How long you on the job, Falcone?"

"It's Falco…twelve years."

"I had six when I bailed. Sometimes I think maybe I should have toughed it out, stuck around until I could at least have vested, gotten some kind of pension. But I don't dwell on it too much. Not good to stew over things you got no control over."

Falco was frustrated and Rufus knew it. He tried to frame a question in his mind, felt if he got started he could get Falcone to talk to him. Or Falco, or whatever the hell his name was. He felt the handful of change in his right hand pants pocket, cupped it, and began to shake the coins, the jingling sound calming him.

"Tell me how you knew Wanda."

"Mind if I ask you a question first?"

"Yes, I do mind. Save your questions for the end, if I can answer them I will. Meantime, just answer mine…got it? You good with that?"

"Yeah, yeah…want me to go back to the beginning, when I met her old lady?"

"Tell me about the first time you met Wanda."

"Is she here?"

"Who?"

"Wanda."

"No she's not here! She's probably at the morgue by now."

Falco's face turned red, and he took a couple of deep breaths, probably wondering what the guy's problem was, and how to pursue the questioning – hard or soft?

"Sure, the morgue…I just forgot for a minute…so she's working there, or making an I.D.?"

"Are you fucking with me?"

"Don't bust a gut my friend, won't help to get aggressive with me…just answer the questions."

"I'm asking the questions, Rufus…so again, how'd you meet Wanda?"

"Wanda, that's right…know her since she's a little baby…like the other kid…What an awful thing, and for what? She didn't deserve that…sure, she had her problems, but deep down, a decent kid, would never hurt you. So why, why? Son of a bitch…got to kill the son of a bitch that did this…ohhhhhh!"

"You all right, want a glass of water?" Falco said.

Rufus began to sob, repeating the same sound - ohhhhh, ohhhhh, ohhhh - for several

minutes. Falco appeared befuddled, looking uncertain what to do, or how to proceed.

"Can't get the image out of my head, Wanda tied to the bedposts, her head dangling,

ready to fall off, blood all around her."

He stopped abruptly, almost like a switch had been thrown. The door to McCoy's office had opened. Brito stood gazing from Rufus to Falco, not saying anything, but a look of concern on his face. He backed out, closing the door quietly.

"I met her at a party, downtown in the basement of St. Benedict's, must have been close to a hundred and fifty people. The monsignor of the parish and a couple of other priests were there, and a bunch of showgirls from the Roxy, the old emporium where they had burlesque back in the day."

Rufus looked at his feet, then raised his head and stared at Falco, a smile on his face. Like he'd left and gotten some kind of tranquilizer.

"I think you'd probably be a tough customer if it came down to it. Your nose looks like it's been busted a couple of times. Maybe you was a fighter, looks like you might have been."

"I do all right...when I have to," Falco said.

Now Rufus looked panicky again.

"Why you asking me questions? What business is it of yours to ask how I knew Sissy and Wanda? I don't have to answer...but I don't want to cause problems. Are Sissy and Wanda outside?"

He felt his chest, like checking for his heartbeat.

"Falco?" he said, more of a murmur.

"Yeah."

"Why am I here?"

He left him alone, returned in a few minutes with a cup of coffee and a couple of aspirin. Rufus tossed the pills into his mouth and took a gulp. Ten minutes later they resumed.

"Again, why don't you tell me how you met her?"

"Who?"

"Wanda's mother."

"Had a radio-run one night...on a four to twelve."

"Where?"

"The Roxy. Longshoreman with half a load on was giving Sissy a hard time. I probably shouldn't tell you this, get myself in the confessing mode, but I guess the statute of limitations has run, whose gonna give a rat's ass over something happened all those years ago?"

"Not me."

"I crushed this guy's head, give him some beating - all the way up the aisle, into the lobby, out onto the street. I asked the scumbag – what do you want to do, you want to go to court, or should I call you a cab? He motions towards a yellow Checker. So I pour him into the back seat, hand the driver a fin and said take him down to the docks...never saw the guy again."

He looked pleased, like now he felt glad to be questioned – seemed to have no problem remembering small details from thirty, forty years ago.

"When did you meet Wanda?"

"Her confirmation."

"Whose?"

"Wanda's!"

Falco pushed his chair, about to stand, but he didn't. He looked at Rufus for a long moment, as if he wanted to say something, but he didn't do that either.

"Tell me about the last time you saw her, before the murders."

"Murders?"

"Yes, the murders."

"You ever do surveillance work, ever used a camera with a telephoto lens. That's what my mind feels like lately, as if I'm focusing the lens, like the image is getting closer and farther away, blurry then sharp. The murders? That's why I'm here?"

"Yes."

"You want to cut to the chase, is that it?"

"Yes."

"Yeah, we may as well."

He paused a long time, looking at Falco, the detective staring back. Falco had a thick gold watch on his left wrist that slipped so that the dial faced his body. His fingernails looked manicured.

"You want to know if I was involved."

"That's right."

"Let me tell you something – you're wasting time. I had nothing to do with it."

"So where were you when Wanda called?"

"My office."

"Can you verify that?"

"No, I can't."

"What were you doing when she called?"

"Fuck do I know, maybe a crossword."

He found Falco really annoying. Was that why he lied to him? Why didn't he tell him he was at the Athletic Club playing racquetball? But that might make his job too easy, which Rufus had no interest of doing. In fact, he'd already decided to do whatever he could to be an obstacle.

"Listen Rufus, unless you help us establish an alibi, you stay high on the hit parade. You had the opportunity and means to kill them."

"What's my motive?"

"Could be a hundred things. If you're not involved, give us a reason to believe it, so we don't waste time. Were you on the phone with anyone before or after she called, did you take any deliveries, anyone talk to you when you entered or left the building?"

"That's your job, Falcone. You find out what happened."

"Falco."

For the rest of the interview, Rufus mostly responded with one-word answers, once in a while launching into a little speech. He told Falco that Wanda had asked him to get the cop off her back. Al Falco looked at him with a - *I'd kill you in a heartbeat if I could get away with it* - look. Rufus stared past him, over the desk, every few minutes brushing the top of his head, acting like there was something just out of reach that he needed to remember.

"Oh, yeah."

"What?" Falco said.

"Fortune."

"What about him?"

"I'm thinking maybe he done Wanda, then someone walked in and done him."

"No way. Kid was a good kid…clean as Caesar's wife…unblemished record."

Falco was lying, but that was allowed, cops lying to suspects. Rufus looked at him, then at Brito, who had just come back in.

"So what's he doing in a hooker's flat?" Rufus said.

Except for the gray, Brito hadn't changed much; a sloppy-looking black guy who looked like a small Sumo wrestler, stoic, never changed his expression. They knew each other, but were what Rufus would have called "bad friends." He looked at their belts, both with silver cell phones attached.

"I've given you enough time," he said.

"Sit down," Falco said. "There's an Assistant A.G. would like to talk to you."

He flopped back in the solid wood chair. He grimaced, turned toward the wall to his left of the hundred square-foot room, twisted back and stared at the black metallic cone that shaded the single 60-watt bulb.

Falco said they needed to move from the office. He asked why but Falco ignored him, walked out, Rufus following, Brito behind him. They marched to the interview room, stepping around paint cans, half-full trays, folded up tarps. The room looked like every other one they'd all been in, except now there were extras: a softball sized black plastic bubble in a gray metal frame mounted on the ceiling just outside the door; another one in the southeast corner of the room.

The three men sat silently. Rufus tried to clear his head, to think clearly, but thinking clearly had become his biggest challenge.

He expected to be followed when he left, to have his phone tapped, his office searched, thinking - time is not on my side, if I'm going to get the bastard that did this I need to move quickly. Then he recalled the two things that gave him an edge: the red phone book…and the message that he erased from the refrigerator. He just needed to remember to check his notes. Another siren off in the distance broke the silence. He squirmed in his seat. Falco told him he had to wait, had to talk to someone else.

At 3:25 p.m. a well-dressed attractive blond walked into the interview room, trailed by a short middle-aged guy who looked like he'd been henpecked by every woman in his life.

"Mr. Koufax, I'm Assistant Attorney General Francine Jurgenson. I'm here to question you about the murders of Wanda Kelley and John Fortune. You have a right to a lawyer if you want one."

She dropped her thick black briefcase onto the table.

"Am I a suspect?"

"Right now you're a witness, but I like to offer the advice."

She wore a navy blue business suit, jacket open, the two top buttons of a white silk blouse unbuttoned. Her gold earrings and bracelet looked more Tiffany's than Zales. She gave Rufus a cold look. The short guy had set up a steno machine on a three-legged tripod. He put on gold-rimmed reading glasses, like a sign that said - ready. Rufus wondered why the steno, when everything was recorded electronically.

"Please stop staring," she said.

Falco cracked half a smile, but not Brito.

"How can I help you?" Rufus said.

"What brought you to the apartment on West 11th Street?"

"I've been telling that to these fine gentlemen the last few days."

"What?"

"I said, I've been…"

"I heard you. You said the last few days."

"What?"

"Just go on, tell me what you were doing there."

"Be happy to, just trying to remember…some of it feels fuzzy."

"I hope you're not thinking about trying to fuck with me, Koufax."

"What happened to mister?"

"Mister Koufax."

"Why don't we start by you telling me what you know," Rufus said.

"What? Are you joking?"

"Why would I be? You think this is funny?"

Francine Jurgenson stared with disbelief. She pulled her briefcase closer, opened it and looked inside, clearly stalling, trying to compose herself.

"Again, what were you doing at West 11th?"

An hour later the stenographer packed up his machine and Miss Jurgenson stuffed her yellow legal pad into the briefcase. She asked Falco to join her outside.

"Mind if I ask you something?" Rufus said.

"What?"

"Ever live at 610 West Passage Boulevard?"

Francine Jurgenson's face, turned crimson, almost the color of her pouty
lips.

"I used to visit there as a child."

"Frank Jurgenson your grandfather?"

She paused, face still red, her blue eyes squinting a little.

"How do you know that?" Her voice cracked but still had a hard edge.

"Just a guess…we met in the old days. Nice man, Frank Jurgenson."

Brito and Falco stared at each other, then at Rufus, then shook their heads.
Francine Jurgenson turned and looked at them. She gathered herself, shaking
her briefcase once or twice.

"Please see me in the lieutenant's office," she said.

The stenographer followed her out the door, almost in a little trot.

Rufus sat on the wood bench outside the squad office, staring at the bulletin
board with wanted posters and memos, hanging on the opposite wall. He thought
about Wanda. They'd had a thing for a year or so. He remembered that pretty well,
great times in some ways, but he knew he'd crossed a line – and not just because of
the age difference. The prospect of explaining it to Sissy worried him. The
romance ended a long while ago but the relationship survived. After all, he'd been
there almost since she'd been born and knew Sissy a while before that. If she got in
trouble, needed something, Rufus could never say no to Wanda. And they really
liked each other, which probably seemed crazy to anyone else on the planet.

He looked around the squad. Most of the detectives were too young to know
him. The light- duty officer who was the receptionist was the exception. His name
was Callaghan and they had crossed paths somewhere in the old days.

"Callaghan, do me a favor, ask the lieutenant if I can go."

He nodded, his thick gray hair falling over his forehead. He picked up the
phone, mumbled something then hung up, shaking his head no. A few minutes
later Miss Jurgenson and the steno came out, walked by without a word. McCoy
walked to the entrance of his office, motioned Rufus to come in.

"She didn't much appreciate your square-rooting who her grandfather was.
Thinks you've got a dossier on her," McCoy said.

"Nice looking woman…too bad she's forty years younger than me."

"More like twenty-five, not that it'll do you any good. You didn't exactly
score points with her. What's all that about her grandfather?"

"Frank Jurgenson? Biggest layoff-man ever - bookmaker's bookmaker.
Close with the old man, Patriarca; and Frank Costello, Meyer Lansky, guys like

that. Jurgenson got called to testify before the Kefauver Committee on organized crime back in the fifties."

"How'd you know she's related?"

"I know what I know, Billy. What do you know about Fortune and Wanda?"

The murders would have been front page news, except Barack Obama just became the country's first serious black presidential candidate, and the media couldn't get enough. Wanda might soon be yesterday's news, but the murder of a cop wasn't going away.

"What the hell were you doing there?" McCoy said, ignoring Rufus's question.

He told the same story he'd told Falco and Brito, and Miss Jurgenson. Lying to Bill McCoy weighed on him, but he didn't see what choice he had. He'd made his decision in Wanda's apartment, had tampered with the crime scene. He knew that he'd need an edge to catch the killer, before the detectives got to him. He'd done a lot of things that could or would be considered off-color, perhaps even illegal, but he'd never tampered with evidence before. But he also never had the close to primal rage that overtook him when he saw Wanda's body.

"You willing to take a polygraph, give a DNA sample?"

"Anything you want, lieutenant."

"And you're going to have to stand a line-up."

"You're shitting me."

"No, I'm not."

They met later at Kennedy's on Moses Brown Boulevard. June was usually warm but tonight was steamy. Rufus carried his hound's-tooth jacket over his shoulder, covering his Walther PPK. He'd walked west from Fifth Avenue and Moses Brown, worked up a good sweat. He looked around the front of the place, then along the curb and at the parked cars facing westbound. The NO PARKING – NO STANDING rules expired at 7 p.m. and the spots had filled up quickly. He stood staring at the signs for ten minutes, reading them over and over.

He searched his pockets for his car keys, a little frantically. Then he remembered he didn't have his car. Maybe he left the keys on his dresser.

He put his jacket on, walked inside, maneuvering past several groups, stroking the top of his head a couple of times. Halfway up the crowded bar three young broker types, laughing hysterically and jostling each other, blocked his way. After his second "excuse me" he just shoved the biggest one with his right shoulder and walked past, ignoring their whiney threats.

McCoy was half-draped over the bar, a cocktail in one hand, talking to the bartender, Jimmy Lane. Lane, tall with black frame glasses, a white shirt and tie, was what a bartender should be - a good listener. McCoy, on a roll, was animated,

Rufus wondering how he kept from spilling his drink. A pile of money sat on the bar in front of him, so he figured he'd been there since at least six when his shift ended. For a Wednesday night the place was packed, everyone watching the reports on the primary, as if the World Series was on.

Rufus, for a second, wondered why Billy McCoy was there. Then he remembered he'd agreed to meet him. Then he thought, a double homicide didn't happen every day, especially with one of the victims a city cop, so he should have been working the case with his men, going twenty-four, thirty-six hours straight if he had to; until they broke it.

"Rufus, what'll you have?" Jimmy Lane said.

"Makers, neat."

"Makers? Must have made a score," McCoy said.

Rufus smiled, threw a few twenties on the bar.

 "Want a table, where we can talk better?"

"Nah, this is good."

Sober, McCoy was a real gentleman, quiet and reserved. Rufus thought, the kid's *three-sheets-to-the-wind*.

"Who's the spook?"

"That "spook" could be your next president…where the fuck you been hiding, Rufus?"

"Don't get so touchy?"

"I've got to ask you something."

"So ask."

"You fuck around with anything at the crime scene?"

"Absolutely not."

"You're sure of that?"

"Course I'm sure…what are you talking about?"

"Dove thought he saw something written on the refrigerator, on the note pad…then it disappeared."

"News to me, Billy…go back and ask him what was there."

Rufus stayed another hour. McCoy told him they didn't have much yet, said they'd dump her cell, find out who she called and who called her. Rufus knew his number would show up in the dump, but that was consistent with his story. He wondered how he'd missed the phone.

He was feeling something he hadn't experienced in a long time. Like he had a purpose, something important he had to do, instead of following around a deadbeat husband, or putting a tap on some guy's phone, though in reality, it'd been over ten years since he'd done that. He didn't have a clue how to tap a cell and most people now weren't using landlines.

Rufus wanted Wanda's killer. He'd felt angry plenty of times, but this was different. He'd never felt such a need for revenge - not only for the murder, but also for the way he debased and mutilated her. But time was his enemy, even more than usual in a murder case. By now every crime buff that watched television knew that chances of solving a case lessened rapidly after the first forty-eight or seventy-two hours. But that was the least of his problems. Much greater concern was how he'd been feeling and behaving lately.

He began to feel nauseous again, like at the crime scene. He asked Jimmy Lane for a club soda. After a couple of gulps he felt a little better, his head cleared.

It could have been Fortune, but that didn't compute for him. Why would he kill her? He still was getting free pussy, and anyway, he'd sized the kid up when they spoke the week before, and he didn't act like a killer. He remembered thinking that.

Rufus was pretty confident Bill McCoy's main suspect was himself, Rufus. And he was definitely Falco's suspect. Brito? Who knows what Brito thought? Not much he could do about any of it. He couldn't help wondering though, what Dave would be thinking of all of it.

Meantime, he tried acting casual, while he racked his brain trying to remember this kid's name. He knew he knew him, it just became like vapor for a few seconds.

He asked about Grunge, thought - the condition the kid's in he probably won't remember their conversation tomorrow. McCoy! That's right, he said to himself. McCoy said Grunge had a reputation in the job and on the street as someone you definitely did not want to mess with.

"I got a feeling you need to look at him," Rufus said.

"Why?"

"He'd been to Wanda's before."

"How do you know that?"

"She told me, and so did Fortune."

"Why didn't you tell me that?"

"I forgot. But I'm telling you now."

He could sense McCoy's annoyance. He'd asked a legitimate question – how did he forget? Or did he? He couldn't be sure himself if he'd intentionally held back, or not. His brother wanted him to see a neurologist…"fuck that," he'd told him.

He shoved a bunch of bills and coins, his change, toward the lip of the bar. Jimmy Lane thanked him. Rufus excused himself to go to the head.

He stood at the urinal looking at a few sports articles hung on a cork bulletin board on the side wall, with yesterday's baseball box scores and a couple of articles on the New Netherland Traders. One article reported that the Traders had offered almost their entire roster to the Yankees for Jeter.

It took almost a minute before he could go, then he felt and heard his feeble yellow stream, looked down and shook his head. The kid next to him who had just got done sounded like a god-damned race horse, what he'd been thinking when he felt a hand cover the back of his skull and bang his forehead against the white ceramic tiles. McCoy found him with one knee on the floor, a bloody golf ball over his left eye.

"What the fuck happened?"

"I don't know."

"Want an ambulance?"

"Let me sit a few minutes."

"I'll get some ice."

McCoy returned with a white towel full of cubes, putting it gently against Rufus's multi-colored golf ball. Water from the cubes dripped into his eye, which had swelled and was quickly closing. He groaned then put his hands on the tile floor, trying to get up.

"Don't rush, sit a while longer."

"You call my kid?"

"Who?"

"Sabrina…calls her. Let her know I'm okay."

McCoy had a quizzical look on his face, as if he never knew Rufus had a child. But there were a lot of things he didn't know about him.

Civil unrest plagued other cities in the mid-sixties but it hadn't quite erupted in New Netherland. Still, there was little question that a racial divide existed and all the disparate treatment that took place elsewhere was present there, as well. It wouldn't have taken much to set things off but the city had been lucky.

Still, roaming gangs sometimes looked for trouble, and a black person walking in the wrong neighborhood could be in peril. Rufus was already on the list for the police department when he spotted a few black kids being chased into the projects. He stepped right into the path of about twenty north-side punks carrying chains, two-by-fours, garbage can covers, anything they could use as a weapon. He knew most of them, and they knew him.

"Get the fuck out of here, Rufus…What are you – a nigger lover all of a sudden?"

"Don't worry about what I am, just turn around and walk away."

The kid who confronted him was a muscle-bound Italian from the adjoining neighborhood. The crowd behind him wanted blood from someone. If not the three black kids, who'd already disappeared into one of the red brick buildings, it might as well be Rufus. He stood toe to toe with the leader, kid named Gaetano, for what seemed like a long time. Finally, they all began to mill around, then a few moments later turned and left.

"I'll see you another time," Gaetano said.

"You know where to find me."

Chapter 8

"Mis" Fortune

It took only a month before one of the older cops in the command pinned the nickname on Fortune, and every time he screwed up, which was often, the moniker was reinforced.

They stood outside the precinct. A hook-and-ladder trying to negotiate the double-parked cars had its lights and siren going full blast. Grunge leaned in to Fortune who was nervous to begin with. He hadn't shaved that morning and though still considered a rookie, with barely a year on the job - his uniform looked like he'd slept in it.

Patrolman Fortune nervously told Sergeant Grunge about Wanda. The sergeant tried to act blasé.

"Sarge, can I talk to you privately?"

"Sure, Mis."

"I met this girl on post last month. She got hassled by an asshole and I locked him up. So after court she told me she'd like to show her appreciation."

"Very nice."

Grunge rubbed his right thumb and forefinger against his chin, a knowing smile on his face. He had a habit of spitting when he talked, excess saliva collecting under his lower lip, mostly obvious when he smiled. His curly gray hair, still tinged with red, needed trimming. He waited until two black boys, one dressed in faded blue jeans and a Boston Celtic tee and the other in a navy blue sweatshirt with the arms cut off above the elbows, passed by them, pushing a shopping cart, obviously taken from a local supermarket. The metal cart contained several car batteries that one might have easily inferred were stolen, but Grunge and Fortune paid no attention to them.

"But what exactly are you talking about?"

Fortune hesitated, wondering if he'd made a mistake.

"She took care of me...has her own place not far from here."

"I knew I liked something about you, Mis. When are you gonna introduce me?"

Grunge was no ladies' man, meaning he never had too much success dating women. But he did have his needs, and he'd found the perfect job to satisfy them. A cop who wasn't very concerned about rules, mores, legalities, and such could easily exploit women who had little going for themselves besides their bodies and some sex appeal. And lack of self-esteem made them easy targets for brutal Johns, pimps, or unscrupulous cops.

Fortune on the other hand, was nothing like Grunge. The only trait they shared was a weakness for free and uncomplicated sex. No need to worry about rejection, courting, demanding girlfriends or wives. But the similarity stopped there, Fortune wanted nothing to do with illegal payoffs, schemes to defraud, exacting street justice or any other form of misconduct. Basically, he was a lonely young man, which in the end killed him.

Chapter 9

"**This** is Tom Crewing."

"Mr. Cerwin, Al Falco, Newport West Squad, my boss asked me to call."

"He beat you to it, just hung up with him."

"Oh."

"Tell me what you need."

Falco looked at his watch, annoyed at himself for not calling at 9:00. He gave Tom Cerwin, the Director of Security for Rhode Island Bell, the numbers they'd retrieved from Wanda's cell. There were eight 401 numbers and two others with out of town area codes, one 508 - Massachusetts, one 203 – in Connecticut. Falco had already listed them on the left side of a page, lined it off and made captions at the top with the dates and times that the numbers were called, left space for the subscriber's names and addresses. He wasn't sure how to make a note of text messages, maybe just put a little t next to those.

"How long till we get these?"

"Should have most of them late today, the out of town numbers another day or so."

"Thanks very much."

"Happy to help – but make sure you get a subpoena to me from the A.G.'s Office."

In everyday drug related ghetto murders nobody paid too much attention. The fact that half of them went unsolved got little notice from the media or the public. Multiple homicides, or the killing of a cop, or a child, or even an average solid citizen, were treated very differently.

Four hours later Brito had contacted all the other subscribers. He'd merely dialed each number, identified himself to the person who answered. If it sounded like the man of the house he got right to it, otherwise he waited until he reached him. When he told them the purpose of the call, half hung up immediately, but the others actually listened and agreed to come in and talk. McCoy seemed non-plussed about Brito independently taking that step and not waiting for the subscriber information from the phone company; and not discussing it with him first. McCoy considered having a talk with him about the lack of communication, but he felt a bit conflicted – he actually admired Brito's initiative, the way he got right to the task. And the reality was he didn't care so much about those numbers anyway. Falco on the other hand, steamed when he found out what Brito had done…but he didn't say anything either.

But in reality, a consensus was building, a sort of groupthink, all too common in big murder cases. Rufus was the primary suspect; and McCoy, Falco, and Francine Jurgenson and her superiors, quickly got into lockstep. Only Brito wavered, seriously considered other possible suspects and theories.

Late that afternoon McCoy, Falco and Brito sat in the interview room. Falco hammered away at all the reasons Rufus was more than likely the killer: last known person to see her alive, showed up at the crime scene less than a half hour after the murders, owned up to his relationship with Wanda, admitted having had a confrontation with Fortune.

"There's an awful lot that points to him."

"Maybe, but we can't just focus on him. A hooker could have lots of people who want her dead. Maybe she shook down one of her johns," Brito said.

He ticked off the names on the list of Wanda's clients, which had grown to twenty-three. He told McCoy and Falco which he'd already spoken to. Brito said the phones might be the key to breaking the case, that eventually a careful analysis of the call history combined with interviews of the most likely suspects, might lead to them figuring out who had a motive to kill Wanda. And he added, maybe they'd get a break from the lab. Crime Scene had lifted quite a few latent prints. Maybe one might turn out to be the killer's. Or some trace evidence or the fingernail scraping might come back with the killer's DNA.

"So how do you explain Fortune?" Falco said, a sour look on his face.

He seemed like he could no longer contain his annoyance. McCoy didn't interfere. He waited for Brito's response.

"Collateral damage," Brito said.

A few minutes later they began re-dialing the subscribers. Five more men were stupid enough to talk. The other customers, the ones who'd seen enough 60 Minutes and 20-20 segments on false confessions and wrongful convictions, wouldn't talk until they had a chance to speak to their attorneys. Most of Wanda's customers had a similar profile: married, children, several with grandchildren, most successful businessmen. Two were dentists.

"We're wasting our time with these meatballs." Falco said.

"It's not a waste. Anyway, what are you doing? You expect some kind of inspiration to strike?"

"Facebook."

"What?"

"Facebook and MySpace – we have to check them out, see who was on her "friends" list, what kind of shit she might have been posting; see who she'd been texting."

Bill McCoy looked distractedly out the window. He spun his chair. He and Brito stared at Falco. Social networking wasn't something most detectives in the NNPD thought about yet.

"What are you talking about?" Brito said.

"About how young people communicate today. We don't keep up they'll be way ahead of us – you ever see how dealers operate lately? They don't even keep the same cells any more, buy the disposables at least every thirty days, figure there's no way we can keep up, and they're right."

"Good points, Al. So let's make sure we do that for all her customers," Bill McCoy said.

Falco agreed to follow up on all the names they'd accumulated, but also kept saying he didn't believe it would be productive, that they ought to be concentrating on Rufus, recover any communications they could between him and Wanda, and between her and Fortune; develop a timeline that focused on them.

"What about Grunge?" Brito said.

"There's an Internal Affairs team on him," McCoy said. "And the F.B.I. has offered whatever help we need."

"I think Rufus is trying to get us off of him, maybe offered Grunge as a red herring," Falco said.

"We get a DNA sample on Grunge yet?" Brito said.

"Not yet. Rather than ask him I.A. is trying to get it some other way – waiting to see him use a cup or a glass, or toss a cigarette butt," McCoy said.

"We should take over the Grunge surveillance, get it settled?" Falco said.

"Thought you didn't like him for this," Brito said.

"I don't, but it's a fucking distraction. Let's watch him a while, then get him in and question him, get it out of the way."

"Let I.A. stay on him – wouldn't look too politically correct for us to try and push them out right now," McCoy said. "Don't forget, this is the murder of a cop, one of our own…doesn't matter what you might have felt about him, or what you'd heard."

After Rufus gave him Grunge, said they ought to look at him, it hadn't taken Bill McCoy long to check him out in the Internal Affairs files. Unbeknownst to him or any other supervisor in the command, including the precinct captain, Grunge had four allegations against him for sexual misconduct or moral turpitude. Each complaint had been investigated but the results were all the same – insufficient evidence to file criminal or even departmental charges. If they'd compared notes, the I.A. investigators would have probably been able to make a case for witness intimidation.

The night before, Jonah Koufax, in bed, gripped an *Advanced Reader's Copy* of Dutch Leonard's *Road Dogs*. Each time he got to page ten the book fell from his hands. After the fifth or sixth time, he put it on the nightstand and pulled the blue cotton blanket up to his chin. Suddenly he felt awake, knowing he'd missed the moment. He got out of bed, put on his white terrycloth robe, went into the living room and put a Ravel CD on the Bang and Olufsen. He poured an Irish whiskey, walked over to look out the terrace slider at the black night, listening to the classical guitarist. His mind drifted. He thought about his brother, the private detective whose mind seemed to be incrementally unraveling. Then he thought about Rufus's early days in the N.N.P.D.

Back then, cops so inclined made all sorts of arrangements or accommodations. If they made a few bucks on the side, well, that's half of what made cops effective. Community policing, they call it today. The cop knew most of the people on his beat – and they knew him. Jonah recalled hearing the phrase *police discretion*, intended to mean that cops could use common sense enforcing minor laws and infractions. They didn't have to be Javerts - not necessary to make an arrest for every minor offense. Somehow, the original meaning got lost, and discretion mostly got used after cash or some other benefit was passed on.

His brother survived just six years in the department. They used to talk over cocktails into the early morning, about all the corruption in Rhode Island. Rufus didn't like it, but he learned to live and let live. If cops made money on the side he really didn't care, as long as it didn't happen in front of him. But he hated the real shakedown artists who abused their authority like schoolyard bullies.

And he'd told him that's how he felt about Fortune. Though he felt sorry the kid got killed, he said he only had himself to blame, getting himself into a bad situation, extorting sex from Wanda. Rufus seemed especially obsessed with finding out what other cops visited Wanda with Fortune, felt sure that was what led to their deaths.

But Jonah wondered whether Rufus might have been responsible for the deaths of Wanda or Fortune. He'd pondered it a while, then felt very guilty over his suspicions.

At a recent dinner, he'd almost gagged from the combination of Rufus's breath and the odor of his clothes. He couldn't help thinking - *who knows what else may be going haywire?*

At six-thirty the next morning Jonah walked out the entrance of his building on East Eighty Third, or Newport Terrace as the snobs called it. He walked fifty feet, over to the Strand, the promenade along the waterfront, and began a very slow jog north to Redwood Island. If he timed it right, the footbridge would be lowered and the gate opened so he could cross the black water of the Sakonnet River to the manmade Island. A lift bridge that used counterweights to raise and lower the deck allowed boats to pass under it. He loped across the bridge wearing a pair of navy running shorts, a dark orange tank top, and white New Balance running shoes. His black sweatband made his brown hair stand up in a bird-like pompadour.

The sun was still low in the sky and even on another humid day, the blazing orange ball couldn't do much damage. He'd just read an article on global warming in *Atlantic Monthly*, wondered when or if the world would wake up. He circled the soccer field, the New Netherland skyline only a half mile to the west, windows beginning to glitter with the reflection of the rising sun, traffic rolling silently, slowly along Chafee Highway, too far for the cacophony of horns to be heard. He stopped for a couple of minutes, to get a good look, and to take time to think. It felt like watching an old silent film, alone in a theater pondering his life, wondering what would be recorded in *the great ledger*.

He passed the daytime doorman who liked to wear his hat cocked over his left eye. Juan was preoccupied with Mrs. Minifee's two black toy poodles. Jonah got off on twelve, wondering if he should get a paper towel to sop up the sweat he'd left on the elevator floor. He opened the door to 12A; 12B was Mrs. Minifee, the only two apartments on their floor. Her balcony looked out on the river and Little Compton, his at the river and bridges to the north.

He grabbed the towel off the warmer outside the glass enclosure of the light-brown marble shower. Still dripping when he reached for the ringing phone, he almost slipped on the matching marble floor. He frowned in the mirror. Dressed, he looked like an aging, slightly overweight middleweight, but in the buff – not a pretty sight.

"Hello."

"You dressed?"

"Not quite."

"Get dressed. I'll pick you up in about twenty minutes."

"What's up?"

"Tell you later."

He finished drying, walked into the kitchen and switched on the Braun coffee maker. It sat on a gray granite countertop along with a stainless convection oven. Next to that sat an etched frosted glass bowl full of oranges, apples, and pears. And three ten-inch high white ceramic canisters; each with brown script labels - cereal, coffee, and tea - sat next to the bowl.

He listened to Meredith Vieira interviewing a husband and wife whose fourteen-year old daughter was missing. A couple of minutes later he switched to CNN, to Anderson Cooper talking about the latest "person of interest."

Person of interest - Rufus hated the expression, would say – "you're a suspect or you're not! What jackass came up with that phrase?" Rufus - the private detective with the steel-trap mind who lately could barely remember the day of the week, or whether he'd showered or not. Jonah couldn't convince him to see a specialist. He felt hopeless.

He grabbed the little atomizer on the side of the sink, unscrewed the top and filled it. In the living room he misted the five orchids on the long thin table in front of the windows. One of them was failing. Why do the others thrive and one look like a convicted murderer about to get the chair?

Fifteen minutes later he stood in front of his building, dressed in a tan summer suit, buried in the *Tribune*, looking like a successful businessman. He wondered if his brother was going to stand him up – he'd done that several times recently, called and said he'd see him a certain time, then not show. When he'd call to ask what happened he always gave a different excuse, none of them making much sense. And he wondered what kind of condition he'd be in. Some days were better than others.

He heard the horn, looked up, folded the paper and got in.

"What the fuck happened to your head?"

"Fight with a wall."

The lump over Rufus's left eye was half a dozen different shades of purple and blue. Jonah thought – just what he needed, a shot to the head.

They drove down to Pell Justice. On the way he showed him the subpoena to appear at the A.G.'s Office. Being summoned to the Attorney General's Office was serious, even to him. Rufus had never gotten over the fact that the A.G.'s Office had considered arresting him in the early eighties, for facilitating major drug operations in New Netherland.

Back then Rufus had given rambling answers, confusing the Assistant A.G. that questioned him. He had told his brother that he had an informant who was getting squeezed by Internal Affairs and the Garabedian Commission, the latest commission formed to investigate police corruption. What had been an outstanding piece of investigative work by Rufus and Dave McCoy got twisted into nefarious motives and deeds, allegedly to help a big time drug dealer. In the end, the case on them disappeared. But the damage done, and the real story, as often happened, never got told.

Almost thirty years later, Rufus was not quite as sure of himself, not as quick on his feet. And lately, he'd been giving Jonah bigger cause for concern.

They waited outside Francine Jurgenson's office, sitting on a long blond wood bench. Jonah felt a sort of palpable relief when he first saw Rufus dressed nicely and smelling fresh.

About twelve other offices off the corridor had people occasionally walking in and out, including a few uniformed cops. He enjoyed watching the cops, and witnesses, and lawyers, all with serious looks on their faces. Rufus was reading the *Tribune,* looking totally bored. He liked to refer to Jonas's paper as a liberal rag, compared it to the *New York Times,* but he read both papers almost every day. Falco walked out of Jurgenson's office and told him to come in. Jonah made a motion to get up but Rufus grabbed his shoulder, shaking his head no.

Chapter 10

Wednesday June 4, 2008, 2:00 p.m.

She looked smaller seated behind the large oak desk. Her hair was gathered in a ponytail and she wore no makeup. Two sweaters, one gray and one burnt orange, hung from a clothes tree to her right. She remained seated, made no pretense of friendliness.

"What's your address, Mr. Koufax?" Francine Jurgenson said.

"Ten East 83rd Street, New Netherland."

Rufus had long used his brother's address for his own, for any official purposes; a pain in the ass to him at times, but Jonah Koufax always told him - your my brother, what can I do?

"What's your occupation?"

"Private detective."

"And how long have you been so employed?"

"So employed about twenty-five years."

Closer to twenty-seven but he deducted the eighteen months he'd had his license suspended, years earlier. If Miss Jurgenson had done her homework she knew his background. Rufus was pretty Googleable and of course she had access to all the databases her office routinely used, not to mention all the P.D. files and her own office's archives. She could find out plenty on Rufus in official records. But as always, if she had someone like him do some digging around the underbelly of the city there'd be a lot more. She stood up, walked past him and Falco, who was sitting next to him in an identical grainy wood chair, and shut the door. A large white-faced clock hung on the back wall, with black metal arrows for hands. Her skirt was from a gray business suit. The top button of her white filmy blouse was open. He wondered where the jacket was.

All of a sudden he felt uneasy. The crimson blue knot over his eye throbbed. He touched it gingerly, like it might burst if he pressed too hard, wondering how he'd gotten injured. He turned to look at Falco. Maybe he worked me over, Rufus thought. But he couldn't recall anything, wasn't going to make accusations. Anyway, if he did cold-cock him, he had to have been half-in-the-bag, or in some other way incapacitated. Rufus didn't consider himself a great fighter, but somehow, in the fights he did have, he'd always been just tough enough.

She sat back down and looked at him. He felt Jurgenson staring at his eye, then for a moment or two, he felt uncertain about where he was.

"Why were you at three ten west eleventh yesterday?"

That reminded him. He paused a few seconds deciding how much to volunteer. The murder scene was easy, but his history with Wanda and what brought him there was dicier.

He'd been watching an errant husband when his cell went off - Wanda, sounding breathless, saying to get there as soon as he could.

Two years ago she'd been living large in a condo on upper Thames Street and east seventy-ninth, till sugar daddy and her parted ways. That was the last time he'd seen her until about a month earlier. The Westside dump she'd moved to was a far cry from the Upper East Side.

"Mr. Koufax, please answer my question."

"I'm thinking about it…want to make sure I get it right. Sometime between nine and nine-thirty in the morning she called, asked me to come over, said to hurry."

"Had you been there before?"

"No, I never was."

When he told Jonah about it later he called him an idiot, said he shouldn't have lied. Rufus said he had his reasons. He couldn't recall the reasons, but he must…or did he just not remember.

"Then what happened?"

"I dropped what I was doing. Made it over there as fast as I could."

With a sarcastic smile, Miss Jurgenson said, "So you knew Miss Kelley?"

"Sure, knew her since she's a little kid. Know her mother, too."

"What happened when you got to her apartment?"

"The cops were already on the scene when I got there. I went inside and saw the bodies, Wanda and a cop named Fortune. Both dead…her sliced up pretty good."

"What did you do then?"

"Called Lieutenant McCoy - he got there in less than ten minutes. A little while later it looked like half the N.N.P.D. showed up."

"Why did Wanda call you?" Falco said.

Francine Jurgenson glanced at Falco, with an annoyed look. Rufus understood the look. Like a hundred prosecutors he'd met before, she treated detectives like hired help. He felt a little sorry for Falco at that moment.

"Ask her."

Jurgenson and Falco both stared at Rufus, with the same incredulous look.

"Well, what was the nature of your relationship?" Jurgenson said.

Here we go, he thought. Where to begin and where to end? Truth be told, if she hadn't been a working girl, and fucked up on junk half the time, he might have married her. Even though it would have driven Sissy up the wall. Wanda was a real looker, tall redhead, with that sway that make men salivate.

"What was your relationship with her?" she repeated.

"I knew her twenty, twenty-five years, but we'd lost touch for a long time, until recently. So I'm as shocked as anyone."

That seemed to slow Jurgenson up. Her cheeks reddened. She picked up a yellow legal pad from the desk, thumbed through some pages then looked at Falco. She held a pen in her right hand.

"When you entered the apartment were both victims dead?"

"Yes."

"You're sure of that?"

"Well, I'm no medical examiner, but I believe so."

"Did you have your gun with you?"

"No," he said.

She glared at him with another incredulous look. Both victims were cut up, their heads almost severed, what difference would it make if he had a gun. He looked blankly at her, thinking - who is she to ask me that, and who is this good-looking fella? He looks like a cop, as a matter of fact, I think I've met him - but where, and why – can't really say. She looks very unhappy…did we have lunch together? I know her, too.

"Any more questions?" Jurgenson said.

"Not right now," Falco said.

Rufus grinned, thinking: okay, okay, now it's coming clear, I know what's what…But what the hell just happened? Did I doze off in front of them? That wouldn't be good – always the guilty ones that fall asleep in the cell. Smart bastard this kid - just like I would have played it. Why question me here, in front of her? There'll be plenty of opportunities.

Then he wondered why she asked about the gun, what was her point? Of course he had guns, including a couple of specials, untraceable - but not even Jonah knew that. A good thing, too, since he had plans for them.

"Okay Mr. Koufax, we're done."

He got out of the chair and stepped toward the door, looking at Jurgenson, smiling, as if he might be able to charm her.

She asked him to wait outside for a few minutes. He agreed but wasn't happy about it. He sat silently on the bench. Jonah asked how it went but he ignored him, stared at the ceiling then let out a laugh.

He had a funeral to arrange and a lot of thinking to do. Sissy wouldn't be able to handle the arrangements. He'd always done things like that for her, handle some of life's unpleasant complexities - a letter to the landlord asking for a new appliance, or a parking ticket, or a request from Wanda's school for records of her inoculations - shit like that.

He and Jonah had talked on the way to the A.G.'s Office. It seemed to Rufus that McCoy and his men had no leads or suspects other than him. He told Jonah that, and that he felt McCoy's concern wasn't just the double murder. Rufus knew McCoy a long time and he could sense his discomfort. If Billy McCoy's uncle Dave were still around he might have run interference for Rufus. But McCoy had to be under enormous pressure from his chief and everyone above him, including the mayor, to clear the case. A double murder and the murder of a cop in the new New Netherland didn't sit well with City Hall.

The day following the story of the murders, appeared on page two of *The Tribune*:

DOUBLE MURDER IN THE DUTCH CITY

Two people were found brutally murdered yesterday morning at 310 West 11th Street. Right now, the police claim they have no suspects in the savage crime.

A few years ago, after almost forty years of rising crime rates, rising unemployment and underemployment, failing schools, white flight, municipal corruption, the crack epidemic, and periodic police scandals; and since the civil rights protests and anti-war demonstrations of the late sixties and early seventies - the city finally seemed to be turning around. Now, the sensational double murder - one of the victims a supposed hero cop who'd been fatally shot, and found alongside a beautiful call girl who was savagely stabbed to death - brings into question the actual state of the city of New Netherland... and so forth.

Francine Jurgenson came out of her office after ten minutes, spitting fire. She walked by them, went about ten paces down the hallway, her stiletto heels making cracking sounds on the speckled gray marble floor. He wondered why Falco was still inside, and what they'd talked about. She stopped, stood still for a few seconds, then spun around and walked back.

"Mr. Koufax, please come back in for a minute."

"Sure," he said.

The corridor had become crowded with lawyers and their clients, and uniformed and plainclothes cops - part of what Rufus liked to call "the greatest show on earth." But the real show was out on the streets. And Rufus and every other cop or investigator had front row seats.

She shut the door behind them, returned to her desk, waving her arm for him to take his seat next to Falco. The detective's expression hadn't changed. He sat with one leg crossed over the other, looked like a guy waiting for a train. Rufus sat down.

"Tell me about Grunge," she said.

"What about him?"

"Why did you mention him to the lieutenant?"

"Mention who? Who the hell is Grunge? This is starting to get exhausting, all the questions, throwing names at me, like I'm supposed to know them."

Rufus thought - Grunge, that's what she said. Yes, I know him, just will take me a while to figure out how, what our relationship is – are we related? Do I work with him? Is he one of my teachers…no not teacher, I'm not in school anymore, not for a long time…police…

This was Rufus, off in an orbit nobody understood, least of all, him.

Mentioned to the lieutenant? So that's what she's so bothered about. Falco must have just dropped the name on her. She must wonder why it took a whole day for him to do so, he thought.

Now it came back. Of course, he'd told Billy McCoy to look at Grunge. It bothered him. Bad enough Billy hadn't kept it to himself, but why did he tell Falco and Brito that it came from him? Wouldn't have happened with his uncle. Dave McCoy, sharp as anyone he'd ever met, never missed a signal, great partner.

And to make matters worse Falco told Jurgenson. Then he thought - maybe it will take some focus off of him, which at this point was more important than anything else. It will be hard to operate with Falco and Brito or other detectives from the quickly formed task force, breathing down his neck. Hard enough to do anything these days, to keep his mind straight. On a downward spiral – memory escaping like a vague dream.

"Just a hunch," Rufus said.

"Just a hunch?" she said.

"That's right."

On the elevator ride he thought of the red phone book…and the erased note. It could turn out to be his ace, if Grunge was in fact the killer. But who else could it be? There were other possibilities. But he felt Grunge probably knew what happened, if he didn't in fact kill Wanda.

Outside the A.G.'s Office, (a separate building within the Pell Justice Center complex,) a few dozen people were loitering or having lunch on the plaza. Dozens of granite benches surrounded a fountain with a green copper statue of Atlas in the center, water spouting from the globe over his head. He looked around for his brother, finally spotted him speaking with a blond young man dressed in a tan poplin suit. He waited until the conversation ended then waved. Jonah walked over. They stood looking at the water, talking secretively.

"It's time you got a lawyer."

"To make myself look guilty?"

"You're entitled to one."

"Doesn't mean it's smart… don't worry, I'll be okay."

Jonah dropped him at Newport West, told him to call when he got done. Rufus could read the look, could tell his brother was worried. He grabbed his left knee and shook it.

"I'll be fine."

"Rufus?"

"Yeah?"

"Next time wear socks."

McCoy and his detectives cut him loose after an hour. He went back to the broom closet he called an office, on Old Broadway in midtown. He made some notes, read them over, then put them into a manila folder and slid it into the center desk drawer. He'd start his investigation in earnest soon, knew what he had to do. He had a big advantage over Billy McCoy and his team – they had rules to follow.

In addition to the mahogany desk that looked like it'd been dropped out a window, the office had a gray metal file cabinet, and a worn dark green leather couch with cracked misshapen cushions. He turned on the pole lamp next to it, removed a dark orange and brown wool blanket with a Navaho design from the closet and spread it on top, sat down with the Tribune and half a water glass of Makers. In a few minutes his legs were stretched out and he began to fade from consciousness.

A couple of days later, on Saturday June 6th at 2:30 P.M. he sat on the white plastic milk-crate he'd carried into the dank dimly lit basement. He'd also brought an empty gallon water jug with the top half cut off, a pint bottle of Poland Spring, and all the equipment he'd need in a small brown canvas gym bag. He looked at the panel of terminals and wires as if he could will the man to make or receive a call. He didn't have to wait very long.

In   *You have anyone new?*

Out   *Same four.*

In   *When you going to get a new one?*

Out   *When I get one.*

In   *Maybe I'll be over anyway.*

Out   *Up to you.*

The first conversation he listened to lasted thirteen seconds. He made notes on a yellow pad that he'd filled with captions at the top: the date and time, a column to note whether the call was incoming or outgoing, another for the phone number if the call was outgoing, and a wide space to allow for a summary of the call. In this particular case he noted the number: a local call to 847- 2100. In the comments column he wrote *anyone new*. An objective observer might have asked Rufus why he was going to the trouble of meticulous record keeping. Everything he had would be of no use to the police or a prosecutor, would be inadmissible in court, as would anything derived from it. In reality, it could only be used to convict him of illegal wiretapping.

At 2:40 P.M. the handset came to life again, made a muffled ratchety sound with each impulse created by the dialing of the phone. He put the device to his ear.

Out *Newport West, Officer Egan.*

In *Sergeant Grunge here. Give me the desk.*

Out *Hang on, Sarge.*

In *Lieutenant Monahan*

Out *Grunge here. I need a couple of hours, lieu. I'll be in by six…that okay?*

In *No problem.*

He scribbled a few notes, quickly dismantled the equipment, including the micro cassette recorder he'd wired to the handset. It took less than two minutes. While he climbed the stairs to the rear alley of the building he heard a car door slam. He paused until the engine started then counted to thirty. He stepped through the passageway onto the sidewalk, noticing that the space where Grunge had parked was empty. He got a self-satisfied feeling. Even though his instinct was to follow him, he thought - better off letting him go. A magnet glued to a GPS tracking device was attached to Grunge's gas tank, which obviated the need to do a moving surveillance.

It had been years since he'd tapped a phone. He already felt better about himself, more confident - something therapeutic in some way, going back to his old ways. He'd been hearing for years that wiremen no longer needed to sit in dark moldy spaces to intercept calls. They had more modern techniques that required much less work. Rufus liked the old ways.

Keeping a log and making notes of everything coincided with his need to make lists for everyday things, post-it notes hung all over the apartment to remind him to do things. The last item he'd been writing on the lists lately was to look in the mirror, to make sure he looked reasonably normal.

He bought a shaved ice from a vendor at the curb, about twenty feet past the building entrance, at an aluminum cart with two compartments, each with a circular lid with a u-shaped handle. He fished a five from his right pants pocket and asked for lemon. The Hispanic man dressed in cut off blue jeans and a white tee, had a gray and white fu-man-chu. He opened the left compartment and reached in with a scoop in his other hand. A paper cup appeared and he stuffed the sugary ice into it.

Rufus got to his car a block north of the building a few minutes later, trying to plan his next steps. He shrugged his shoulders and pulled his cell out of the center console and dialed *847-2100.*

"Rio Hotel."

"What?"

"Rio, what can I do for ya?"

Rufus hung up, feeling panicky. He looked around expecting someone to be watching him. Some kids across the street were laughing. He thought they might be making fun of him. They stood in front of a white and blue Mr. Softee truck, the incredibly loud bells and music causing him to become more upset. He looked at his cell, wondering - why'd I call there…I know the Rio, it's a dump…must be a reason.

He tossed the yellow pad with his notes and the recorder, next to him on the front seat. He looked at his keys, trying to decide which one fit the ignition. In the back was his laptop, programmed to receive the signal from the GPS tracker. If he'd only remembered to look at it he would have seen an image of Grunge's car weaving its way towards the Rio. When he realized it later he felt totally frustrated and furious with himself, but that didn't last, because in a short time he forgot all about it.

Later that night, Sergeant Herman Grunge circled the same three or four blocks for half an hour. Every so often he'd pull into a parking spot, sit there for a few minutes. Rufus saw him hold his cell to his ear a couple of times, thought he might be trying to spot a tail. He'd picked him up when he left Newport West at about 12:30 a.m., when he had just gotten off duty. He wore a pale red polo outside his faded jeans, his pistol bulging through the right side of his shirt.

Grunge was sharper than he'd given him credit for. Under normal conditions, Rufus was an expert surveillance man. He'd learned from Dave McCoy thirty years earlier and on his own as a private eye. But he noticed that he'd slipped up - the gas gauge indicated he had less than a quarter of a tank - one of the basics, make sure you have plenty of gas when you begin surveillance. Luckily, Grunge didn't go far, and his car was easy to spot – a '92 burgundy Cadillac Eldorado that resembled a small boat.

The night before, late Thursday, he'd crawled underneath the car while it was in the precinct supervisor's parking lot. The whole installation took less than thirty seconds. Rufus had walked the entire length of the block and turned into the lot without one person noticing him. On his back, with half his body under the car, he reached into his pocket and removed a black plastic box about the size of a cell phone, slid it alongside the gas tank and jumped a little, startled when the strong magnet glued to the GPS tracking device attached itself to the tank with a loud click.

He'd spent most of Thursday preparing the device, writing down everything he knew about Grunge, which wasn't much. But Rufus had become reasonably proficient at using Google, had done the routine White Pages, Zaba, Intellius searches. And luckily, Herman Grunge was a rather uncommon name, only two in the entire country.

Grunge must have been satisfied that no one was on him because moments after he stopped his evasive maneuvers he drove to the edge of his precinct and parked on Fulton Place, a street with nothing but a taxi garage, two body shops, a tire shop, a wholesale fruit dealer, and vacant lots filled with the rubble of long ago demolished buildings and the detritus of people too lazy to use conventional disposal methods. The only activity was from yellow cabs pulling in and out of Lucky's Taxi Service. The other businesses had large dumpsters in front of them and gray accordion steel gates covering their windows. A green and white delivery van was parked in front of the fruit dealer with the name stenciled in black italic letters on the rear doors and side panels: Menis Wholesale Fruits. The truck had seen better days.

Rufus sat a block back on the opposite side. He cracked the windows an inch then climbed into the rear seat and took out his laptop, put the cursor on the GPS icon, allowing him to see in real time where the car was. Of course, this made little sense at the time, since the car was less than a block away, quite visible.

At 1:30 a.m. a brand new 2008 white Lexus with Pennsylvania plates, pulled alongside Grunge for a few seconds, then rolled a car length ahead. He got out of his car, walked to the Lexus and leaned in the passenger door for about a minute, then returned to his Caddy and drove away. Rufus decided not to follow. Then he thought, even though the tracking device he'd installed seemed like a great tool, it couldn't make an observation for you. But still, he had a feeling he'd been following Grunge a little too long and too closely.

For a little while he looked at the green screen, at the icon that was Grunge's car moving across the black grid of New Netherland's streets.

A moment later a uniformed cop tapped on the window, shining his light into the car.

"Old lady kicked me out tonight, so I looked for a quiet block to get some z's."

"Your name's familiar, do I know you?" the cop said.

The cop was a heavyset Italian guy with a dyed black comb-over. Rufus wanted to tell him to keep his hat on, that he'd look better. Rufus thought the other cop must be a rookie. He looked Vietnamese or Cambodian, and was doing most of the work.

"I don't think we ever met," Rufus said.

"Were you on the job?"

"Long time ago, just did a few years."

"Yeah, now I remember you," the older cop said. "Catching some z's, huh? Let me give you some advice – stay the fuck out of this neighborhood…it could be dangerous."

Ordinarily, Rufus wouldn't let something like that go without a response, but told himself, I've got enough shit to worry about. He looked around, as if Grunge's car might suddenly reappear.

Chapter 11

Brito drove to Massachusetts to visit a man named Robert Gilbride who had spoken to Wanda ten days earlier, according to her cell phone history. He had been evasive for several days. During one brief conversation he'd said he had a call coming in that he had to take. Then he'd failed to return several more calls, so Brito figured he'd pay him a visit. He didn't tell Falco or the lieutenant, decided it'd be easier to just knock it off the list rather than make it a subject of discussion.

The house was in North Andover, on Sable Court, a cul-de-sac with six homes on wooded one-acre plots. He pulled up just before nine in the morning on a warm sunny day, with no sign of life in the semi-circle. The cars in the driveways were newish BMW's, Audis, or Infinitys. Brito drove a faded dark green '98 Chevy Malibu. He parked it at the foot of #10 and walked up the eighty-foot driveway.

The chimes reminded him of a classical composer but he couldn't say which one. A tall woman in blue jeans and a lavender tank top opened the door, her mouth slightly agape, as if she'd never seen a black man.

"I'm Detective Brito from the New Netherland P.D. Is Mr. Gilbride here?"

Brito had his credentials in his left hand held at shoulder height so the woman could easily see them. She motioned, as if she were going to grab his badge and I.D. card, so he let her. She looked at them a moment, handed them back and looked at him with half a grin.

"Hold on a second, I'll get my husband. Please come in."

The entrance hall had an oak parquet floor and a few pieces of dark walnut furniture that he thought might cost more than everything in his entire apartment. The living room had two couches and several large wing chairs. The husband, Robert Gilbride, looked quite a bit older than his wife, and a little taller. He had gray hair, looked out of shape, but wore dark gray running shorts, a matching sleeveless tee, and light gray New Balance running shoes.

"What are you doing here?"

Gilbride said it in a loud whisper, with an edge of outrage. His look of ire was just right, Brito thought, exactly the reaction he'd expected.

"I left several messages, Mr. Gilbride, but you never returned my calls. Is there somewhere we can talk?"

He turned toward the entrance to a patio just off the living room. His wife stood just inside the glass slider, a puzzled look on her face. She held a black coffee mug at waist level that looked like it might spill. Brito stared at her for a moment, thinking she's better looking than I first thought. She stared back; the puzzled look gone, replaced by a smile.

"There's a coffee shop in town, about six blocks from here. I'll meet you in half an hour?"

"You know why I'm here?"

"I think so."

"We're talking to everyone that knew Wanda Kelley."

"Please, just give me half an hour."

The North Andover Coffee Shop had fourteen tables and booths, and ten counter stools covered in red plastic that looked like covered tire rims mounted on silver metal posts. The restaurant was decorated in mostly yellow, with two skylights in addition to large plate glass windows in front, and three casements on one side. The grill and kitchen were behind the counter. A pile of sizzling hash browns took up a third of the grill, next to a pile of well-done bacon, the smoke and aromas pulled into a vent over the stove, but enough left to be the diner's best advertisement.

Brito sat at the counter, between two elderly men, both looking at folded Wall Street Journals. A round bald heavyweight flipping fried eggs, moved potatoes and bacon around the grill, covering some with plates. Brito asked for three over easy, potatoes and bacon, and a toasted English.

"The waitress will take your order."

A few minute later a blond trying to hang on to her youth, asked what he'd like. Brito repeated the order.

"Coffee?"

"Please."

 Just as he sopped up the last of the yellow from the plate Gilbride tapped on the shoulder. He'd changed into a gray Glen-Plaid suit. He introduced his lawyer, an overweight balding man in a wrinkled brown suit, and white dress shirt open at the collar. Gilbride and his lawyer were about the same age. Brito found out later they were also neighbors and friends.

"My name is Howard Felder. I'm an attorney and I represent Bob Gilbride. How can I help you, detective?"

"You can't help me at all, but your client might be able to."

"I'm afraid any questions need to be relayed through me."

"No problem, counselor, I'll just call his wife next time I'm in the area, see what she knows about the dead prostitute that your client was banging."

Gilbride looked ready to faint. The questioning didn't take long. Brito decided after about twenty minutes that Wanda's suburban client would be offering no information of value, and was almost certainly not involved in the deaths – at least it seemed that way.

Later that afternoon Brito met Falco for their scheduled tour. He'd decided not to mention his Massachusetts visit yet. Falco and the lieutenant were totally stuck on Koufax, to the point where they ignored other possible suspects. Brito was ten years older than McCoy, had close to twenty on Falco, and though the lieutenant often deferred to his opinions on cases, he seemed to have put a lot of stock in Falco recently. Vernon Brito didn't like his partner but he allowed him wide berth, let him take the lead on most cases. Still, he had his own professional pride and ego, wouldn't follow blindly when he saw them going off track. In this case, he'd decided he'd just quietly go down the list of Wanda's customers, slowly eliminate them – or not.

"You think it's him?" Falco asked.

"We'll see," Brito said.

"That all you can say?"

Brito told him several times that they had plenty of steps to take, before they got close to an answer. But after a while he stopped – didn't like to waste much breath on things like that.

At 8:30 that evening, back at 310 West 11th, they knocked on Cecelia Brown's door. They had more questions. Brito and Falco agreed, in fact were certain that she'd acted scared at the line-up and was holding something back. They heard the television before she opened up and ushered them in.

The apartment was clean, with thick beige carpeting, medium shade walnut tables and chairs on either side of a light green couch. On the opposite wall, fourteen feet away, a large flat screen was showing "Days of Our Lives," the same soap she'd said she watched the day and time of the murders. Brito and Falco looked at the screen then at each other. Cecelia Brown sat on the couch and crossed her legs. Her silk green and tan robe with a Japanese Zen garden design was loosely tied, not concealing much.

"TiVo," she said.

"TiVo?" Falco said.

"My shows. If I got to work in the daytime, I tape them."

"We have a few more questions about last week," Brito said, "if you don't mind."

"You boys fooled me. I thought you all was here to keep me company."

"Let me get to the point, Cecelia. Mind if I call you that?"

"That's my name."

"By the way, - where's your babies?"

"With my moms."

Falco asked if she felt afraid to identify someone in the lineup. She protested, said she'd thought about it, and didn't recognize anyone. After a while

Falco excused himself, saying he had to make a phone call. He took out his cell and she directed him to the bedroom, waved her arm at the royal blue comforter covering the bed, which had gold Japanese lettering. She smiled broadly before she walked back out to the living room.

"Go ahead Brito, ask anything you want."

"I don't have to tell you how important this is. I remember you told me how much you liked Wanda."

Her demeanor changed. Brito thought he'd touched a nerve. Either way, she no longer had a bright toothy smile. He and Falco discussed later whether she wore dentures. Falco said they reminded him of piano keys.

"So Cecelia, let me not fuck around with you here. I'll tell you straight up we know you're lying."

She walked over to the bar, folded in the middle, and pulled the two halves apart. The gold casters of the four and a half-foot high black bar had worn an arced rut in the carpet. She reached down, grabbed a crystal cocktail glass and poured amber liquid from a bottle on top of the bar.

"Want some?"

"No thanks."

"Didn't think so - you two is real straight arrows, huh?"

"Not all the time."

"You is with me."

"Tell me why you lied."

"Who says I lied?"

Falco had walked back in. Brito's face said he'd returned too soon, that he needed more time alone with her.

"Was he here that day, Cecelia? Is that who you saw running down the stairs?"

"They wasn't running, was more like fast walking down, cool as could be."

"They?"

"Didn't mean that, meant he."

"Who?"

Falco shoved a photo of Rufus under her nose. Brito felt like grabbing the picture…but wouldn't do that in front of the witness.

"Could have been him. I'm not sure, but could have been. I got to think on it some more."

"Think on what? Was it or wasn't it?" Falco said.

A few seconds passed. Falco removed a second photo from his inside jacket pocket, pushed a picture of Herman Grunge in front of her – his recruit photo.

"How bout him?"

She got a disgusted look on her face, stood up and walked to the door and pulled it open, said to please call if they intended to come back. She flashed a big smile, one full of contempt.

Outside, in front of her building, they spoke heatedly for a few minutes, Brito telling Falco that that was no way to try and get an identification, that he should have prepared photo arrays.

"Hey, Vern, let's not worry about the small shit now, okay? She makes an I.D. I'll put together a folder after."

"No fucking way to do business."

Falco had run Cecelia through B.C.I. and came up with her arrest record. Herman Grunge had locked up Cecelia Brown twice for loitering for prostitution. He told Brito about it - both surprised that she'd once been in the business. Neither of them knew her, though she continued to be familiar to Brito, he just couldn't say from where.

He could tell Falco was bothered. If Cecelia had made a positive I.D. of Grunge then he'd have to shift his theory, away from Rufus. Falco had locked onto Rufus from day one, couldn't get himself to look much past him, so Brito wondered if he should give him credit, because he did show Cecelia Brown Grunge's photo, too, even though he might have to eat some crow. Not like some detectives they'd both known, who went to the wall with a suspect, even in the face of incontrovertible evidence that pointed to another suspect. So maybe he'd just been too hard on Falco, he thought. But then again, even though Vernon Brito might not have had the highest batting average in his cases, he never lost one due to sloppy detective work.

The same bongo player and dancers were on the stoop of 310. Three of them were looking down, thumbs in constant motion on their little black devices, almost as if they were keeping beat with the drummer. Falco and Brito began to walk away, got half way toward Moses Brown when Falco stopped. He grabbed Brito's elbow.

"You question those kids the other day?" Falco asked.

"No, you?"

"Dove and Charlie Chan did, there's a report in the file – called them uncooperative."

"Let's try again."

The six Dominican kids balked and began to walk away. They all laughed when Falco screamed for them to halt. One of them, a tall black haired girl in tight cut off jeans, a black halter and black stilettos, turned, a derisive look on her face.

"Fuck off, five-oh!"

Brito told Falco to grab the guy with dreds and red do-rag, while he, Brito, was already grabbing the power-forward of the bunch, putting him into an arm lock.

Sirens wailed, drowning out the crying and complaining of the handcuffed kids. Falco and Brito looked at each other and shrugged. Someone from the building must have seen the struggle and called in an "assist patrolman."

Falco was still gasping for air after chasing the kid with the dreadlocks for two blocks, subduing him and dragging him back. His suit jacket was slung over his shoulder, his Glock looking half floppy on his waist, and the armpits of his yellow dress-shirt stained with sweat. Six radio-cars responded. Brito began talking to a woman sergeant who'd just gotten assigned to the precinct. Charlie Chan was shoving the kid with the dreds and do-rag into the backseat of a green and white.

"This is Detective Falco, my partner," Brito said.

The sergeant looked Navaho, long black hair in a ponytail, angular features and high cheekbones, and wore no makeup.

"Nice to meet you," she said.

"Better put that hair up before someone hangs off of it – takes you to the ground," Falco said.

She gave him a dirty look and walked away. Dove and Chan were driving away with the potential witness.

"What's the matter with you?"

"You sure know how to make friends," Brito said.

"Fuck her - it's for her own good. Other kids give anything?"

"Not yet. Let's go in, see what we get from your guy."

Inside the precinct about fifteen people were shouting and generally behaving badly. The lieutenant behind the raised front desk seemed to be trying to decipher what the complaining was about, but anyone within earshot could hear the words "police brutality" repeated often.

Falco and Brito, on either side of the kid Dove and Chan had brought in, looked confused. He turned to look at them. If nothing else it caused a temporary halt to their rant.

They put him in a wooden chair inside one of the two interview rooms. Falco cuffed his right wrist to the arm of the chair.

"I'm under arrest?"

"It's for your own protection…tell me your name," Falco said.

"What's your fucking name?"

The sound of Falco's open hand slapping the kid's face startled Brito. The kid fell back in the wooden chair cracking the back of his head against the floor. He lay silent for a moment before he sprung to his feet, attempting to leap across the table toward Falco. He dragged the chair with him but didn't get far. Brito got him in a bear hug.

"Calm down," Brito said, more of a scream.

"He got no call to do that. That's fucking brutality man. I got a good mind to make a complaint man, fucking police brutality man… motherfucker!"

Brito motioned with his head for Falco to leave the room. He hesitated a moment until Brito made the same motion again, but more emphatically. Before he closed the door he told Falco to bring him back some wet paper towels.

Half a stack of brown paper towels sat on the table between the kid and Brito. The rest of were in the green metal wastebasket by the door, saturated in blood. Brito had taken the cuffs off of Felix Melendez and gotten him a Coke and a Mr. Goodbar. The red can matched the color of his do-rag, which luckily had absorbed some of the impact went he fell backwards. Felix was seventeen years old and aside from the rag and being all tatted up, he had an average look to him. In two weeks he'd be graduating from Cardinal O' Connor High School, one of the better parochial schools in the city. He also had an outstanding warrant for a "farebeat."

"Listen Felix, I don't want to see you get fucked up. You've got a future, going to graduate soon. We drop this warrant on you it could mean you go to the Dungeon, at least for enough time to miss the big day. I don't want to see that happen to you."

Brito had slid his chair close to Felix and placed his hand on his shoulder. He wore a Kelly green and white Celtic's jersey with the number 20 on the back. Brito shook him a little then stroked his back.

"Come on man, talk to me."

"Why he got to be like that man… like my old man, slapping me for nothing."

"What happened to your father, Felix?"

"Dead."

"O.D.?"

"Yeah… how'd you know?"

"Don't matter. Come on Felix, let's start again. Talk to me, tell me what you saw, maybe we can make this warrant disappear."

"You would do that?"

"Of course man - I want to see you have a future. What you gonna do after high school?"

"Thought about culinary school."

"Used to think I wanted to be a chef myself. Sometimes wonder if I should have."

"Why'd you become a cop?"

"Thought I might get to help people…and the pay and benefits are pretty good."

Felix sat quietly looking at the floor. Brito noticed tears forming.

""Yeah, I seen something, but I can't be known for helping five-oh, man. I got a reputation… don't want to be tagged a rat."

"We're not asking you to dime one of your boys."

"Might be worse, I dime one of you all."

Chapter 12

July 17, 2008, 11:50 a.m.

Jonah Koufax hesitated for a couple of minutes before getting out of his car and approaching the house. He felt nervous, which wasn't unusual, even after all the years of knocking on doors, conducting interviews. He removed the white handkerchief from his left breast pocket, used it to wipe his brow, left it on the car seat. It was a hot July day, the temperature predicted to hit one hundred.

The faded yellow aluminum siding had rusted dents. The windows of the little cape had no shutters and the house had the look of prefab construction. Some patches of grass had managed to survive but the property looked barren, devoid of landscaping. He walked up three concrete steps and pushed the black button to the left of the door. The loud chimes inside echoed the first bars of the Marine Corps hymn.

The retired detective opened the door, stood staring at him with a "what the fuck do you want" look. Despite gray hair and some wrinkles he still looked like he could handle trouble. He'd retired on a disability pension fifteen years earlier, from a head injury sustained while trying to climb a fire-escape ladder to reach a junction box in the rear yard of a tenement.

"I'm Rufus Koufax's brother."

It took a little convincing to get past the threshold. For a moment he wished he'd brought someone with him.

"Why should I talk to you?"

"It might help Rufus."

"Him and Hawkes were close, I didn't know him that well."

"Still…"

"Piece of work your brother."

He ushered him in to a couch covered in something that looked like animal skin. The room smelled of cigarettes and stale beer. The pine paneling looked real. Several mounted deer heads decorated the walls. He wore dungarees, a gray sweatshirt with the NNPD logo over his heart, and brown work boots that looked like they'd never seen polish.

"What do you want to know?" Gunshannon said.

"Tell me how you met him."

"I only met him two or three times."

Gunshannon paused, took a drag on his cigarette, squinting from the smoke. Sad looking eyes, maybe because they drooped, but then Jonah looked around the bachelor's home, decided the place matched his eyes.

"Want a beer?"

"No thanks."

"Come on downstairs."

Gunshannon got out of the recliner with some obvious effort, walked to a door between the living room and eat-in kitchen. Pizza boxes were stacked on top of the stove. The small rectangular table had an open newspaper, a dirty plate and a tall yellow plastic tumbler next to it. The old detective pulled the door open, flipped a switch and went down carpeted stairs. Jonah Koufax followed. The two rooms surprised him: a den with a forty-inch plasma TV atop an expensive looking oak colored credenza with glass doors; several amplifiers or receivers inside and two large black speakers at either end; the next room separated by two paneled half-walls. Gunshannon walked in and turned on another switch.

They sat on a worn tan corduroy couch opposite two brown upholstered chairs, a bamboo coffee table with a glass top, in between. A dozen or so awards and certificates hung from the wood paneling. A highly polished blond wood case had an array of rifles or shotguns behind glass doors.

"I don't know how I can help you. Sorry to hear about Rufus's troubles. Poor guy never caught a break."

"How so?"

"Back in eighty, or eighty-one, when the Commission tried to set him and Dave up."

Jonah Koufax asked a question that had bothered him since the first time he visited his brother in jail.

"Why didn't Rufus and Dave put their own wires in?"

"You shitting me? Those two?"

Jonah wasn't so sure that Gunshannon was right. Around New Netherland the word was, a lawyer or client willing to pay could get Rufus to install a bug or a wire. Usually the case involved marital discord but rumor had it that some of the dirtier politicians around the state weren't above trying to get something on their adversaries.

Jonah Koufax thanked him. Gunshannon said come back any time. Jonah didn't ask if he'd ever married, was a widower, or what his situation was. Something made him feel sad for the old wireman.

Chapter 13

November 19, 1980, 10:45 p.m.

On the evening of November 19, 1980 a call came in to the S.O.D. Most of the calls to the Special Operations Desk were from anonymous citizens, who sometimes merely had an ax to grind with a neighbor. The system was mostly a charade, with the public getting little attention paid to their complaints, unless the citizen was lucky enough to get the right detective.

"You and Koufax want to handle this?"

"What is it?" McCoy said.

"Call from a citizen - want it or not?"

Patrolman Raskol a light-duty man who'd been manning the S.O.D. while his phony line-of-duty claim wound its way through the labyrinth bureaucracy of N.N.P.D. had taken the call. If he got approved, the stooping six and half foot man who'd never used an iron and rarely visited a barber, would get a tax-free three-quarters pension for the rest of his life. He had four years on the job, half of those spent inside.

McCoy rewrapped a half-eaten hero in white waxed paper, shoved it to the side and took a long swallow of Dr. Pepper. The sleeves of his light blue shirt were rolled halfway up his forearms, faded tattoos on his thin arms visible through wispy brownish red hair. One on his right arm showed the letters USN over an anchor.

"Transfer it to eight-seven," McCoy said.

At 10:45 in the evening their shift was almost done. That didn't matter to Dave McCoy or Rufus, if it meant a chance to find a new informant. The woman said her name was Pam Stith.

A half hour later they sat in a ten by fourteen-foot room, opposite a six-foot tall black girl that if luck had shined on her she would have been walking runways in Paris. The Martinique Hotel was another run-down dump in the Newport West District, well known to them. Dave interviewed her for about ten minutes.

Pam Stith did nothing to hide the track marks on the inside of her elbows; deep purplish scars a quarter inch to an inch long. Her speech had the slow cadence of a heroin addict. They tried to make sense of what she said. The television blasted – Letterman interviewing Julia Roberts, who was laughing hysterically.

"Can we turn that down?" McCoy said.

"Go head."

She wore a silver colored skirt, a red silk diaphanous blouse with a black bra, and three-inch black heels. Her clothes looked like she'd slept in them. Her hair dark brown hair was worn in a short Afro. She smelled like a dancer in a strip club.

"Take this shit to the bank."

"How do we verify it?" Dave McCoy said.

"You five-oh, that's your fucking job."

Dave lit another cigarette, offering her one. She leaned across the glass coffee table that was one big stain; waiting for a light, long slim brown fingers cupped over his hand. She sat on the double bed on top of a worn light-green cotton blanket, Dave in a straight-backed chair with wooden arms and frayed tan fabric with cigarette burns in the seat. Rufus stood close to the door. She held the cigarette at shoulder height, a red smudge visible on the tip. The smoke made an irregular spiral toward the ceiling.

"What are you looking for?" Dave said.

"You take care of me...I take care of you all."

"We make a seizure you'll here from us," Rufus said.

"You gonna turn me on, Rufus?" Pam said, a slight smile, teeth barley showing.

"How'd you meet this guy?"

Pam was a stone junkie and a hooker, and unbeknownst to them she worked as a snitch for other people. Had Rufus and Dave known that, they might have avoided a boatload of trouble.

Chapter 14

Monday June 9, 2008, 8:30 a.m.

He called Jonah and told him to meet him downtown, at the Dungeon, at the Pell Justice Center. Anyone who'd lived in the city knew the Dungeon, New Netherland's infamous lockup holding prisoners awaiting arraignments, hearings or trials. Plenty of young men who went in overnight on some minor charge didn't come out whole. Jonah heard shouting in the background, just before Rufus hung up.

He got there at 9:30 a.m. and stood near the entrance, looking at the combination of thick glass blocks, dull gray steel, and revolving door that led into the lobby. Over the door was an eighteen-inch high black Plexiglas sign – **New Netherland Department of Corrections,** underneath that - **Raymond J. Vassal, Commissioner,** in slightly smaller letters.

He got tired of standing in one place, so he walked around the gray granite plaza for fifteen or twenty minutes before approaching the entrance. He waited for an opening and stepped in to the revolving door, taking baby steps for one hundred eighty degrees. The rubber at the bottom of the door scraped the granite making a shhhhhhh sound. His light brown brogues needed a shine, at least by Jonah's standards. Inside, he buttoned his tan suit jacket, tightened the pink tie he favored.

Ten rows of pale red plastic bucket seats, twelve across, took up most of the space in the lobby. Most of the people sitting in them were black or Hispanic. A black haired little boy sat dangling his legs like pendulums, eating a white bread sandwich with some type of coldcut and yellow American cheese, half of a half gone. The child chewed slowly, looking at it as if it were a delicacy. A few people stood at the glass counter in the rear, leaning, filling out visitor forms. An elderly black man stared at the ceiling, apparently uncertain how to answer a question.

He stood behind a tall wide black woman in a royal blue dress and high heels, with a large Afro. He couldn't quite make out what she'd said, with the din of dozens of conversations filling the room. The C.O. behind the glass, a large light-skinned black man, looked bored. She pleaded with him for something. After a few minutes she turned to walk away, using a crushed tissue to dab at her eyes. Jonah stepped forward.

"How you doing, Koufax?"

Jonah had been there a number of times to interview prisoners, so he knew the drill, had grabbed a form and gotten on line.

"Good, Johnson. You?"

"Everything's everything. Here for your brother?"

Johnson answered his question before he had a chance to ask it. He gave him a blank form, Jonah exchanging it with the one he'd already filled out. He held the blank in his right hand, unsure what to do with it.

"Shove it through," Johnson said, motioning to the opening at the bottom of the glass.

He told him to stand by the green steel door that was the entrance to the holding area. There were four stories of cells in the Dungeon, eighty on each floor, each with three bunks. Jonah stared at the tiers of cells, sad that his brother was now in the system. Many years he'd worked at catching bad men who deserved to be there, Jonah feeling certain Rufus never expected to end up there himself.

"Koufax!"

Simultaneously, the green door groaned open. Close to a hundred people were ahead of him but no one said anything. Neither did he, but he felt funny. He turned toward Johnson, intending to say thanks, but the he never looked up from his desk.

Up on the cellblock the screw unlocked the cell door, growling some unintelligible words, like he and Rufus already had bad blood. Rufus turned his head, didn't say anything. The door closed, making a crashing metallic sound. He motioned for Jonah to sit beside him, so he sat. They stayed like that for a couple of minutes. He felt like crying, seeing Rufus like that. He looked like he'd just lost a four-rounder. The orange jumpsuit and matching sneakers didn't help. But his grayish skin, three-day growth, and eyes that looked like they'd burst every blood vessel, made him look like an old man. It'd been about six days since he'd gotten whacked in the men's room – the golf ball over his eye almost gone, but the discoloration was still visible.

"What the hell are you in here for?"

"A little R&R."

"Really Rufus, what the fuck's going on? And why didn't you tell me you were inside when you called? You made it sound like I should meet you outside – I wandered around for half an hour, like a fool!"

"Sorry about that."

"So why are you here?"

"Why am I here?...I'm not sure."

"Damn it Rufus…"

Jonah had shrieked, his voice up a few octaves, causing a few prisoners to begin to hoot. A C.O. came by to ask if he was all right.

"Calm down – I'm just fucking with you. They picked me up on a material witness order. Freaking bogus move…very inconvenient."

Before Rufus's career was cut short he'd loved the job. In fact, he still enjoyed being around cops. He'd considered trying to get back in the department a few years after he'd left, but was talked out of it by Herb Reitman - "Let sleeping dogs sleep, boichik. Stick with the P.I. stuff, I'll get you plenty of work."

But the cases Herb had were criminal defense work, and Rufus couldn't make that leap - from spending the best years of his life putting bad guys away - to helping to get them off.

"You know what it's like, when I look back all those years? That first day in uniform I remember looking in the mirror, feeling so proud. Same time I was very scared. Embarrassed walking into roll call with the sergeant and all those older cops. Then walking out to post, the first day on the street. Trying to remember it now? It's kind of like trying to remember how it felt the first time you jerked off, wonderful sensation – but you can't really remember it, only the idea of it."

They sat staring at each other, not talking, which gave Rufus time to think, and though he couldn't remember much about the last twenty-four hours, he seemed able to recall clearly, the day in 1980 when he and his old partner first met Pam at the Martinique. He talked to Jonas about that for a while.

"Things got fucked up to a fare-thee-well?"

Rufus sat for a few minutes with his head bent toward the cell floor. Then he looked up, staring at the ceiling, scanning the small cell, as if he were expecting to find some sort of hieroglyphic that might help him tell the story. Then he continued and Jonah listened, occasionally making some notes.

Pam Stith had crossed and uncrossed her legs about a dozen times. She had the looks of a model, or an actress, or an R&B singer, but unfortunately the mannerisms of a junkie.

"How did you meet this guy?" Rufus said.

He doodled in his memo book - circles and triangles, and parallelograms; inside each shape smaller doodles, resembling animals of some sort. He looked at her periodically, until they made eye contact; then held it until she looked away. He noticed a slight shadow on her upper lip, as if she might occasionally shave. Aside from her track marks that was her only imperfection.

"Told you before - through an old boyfriend. An Italian gentleman."

Italian was pronounced "eye-talian." She looked from Rufus to Dave and back - the kind of look husbands wished their wives gave them.

"What's his name?" Dave said.

"Not ever telling you that… he been good to me - except for introducing me to the fucking Frenchman."

"And all you have is his first name?" Dave said.

"Yeah, Mar-fucking-cel. Like I say, he at the Netherland Plaza."

"Room 3101?" Rufus said.

"Right - I'm telling you, he the man supplying all the Italians."

"How do you know this?" Dave asked.

"Been fucking the man since he's here, three or four times. Don't you think I'm gonna know what's going on?"

"He paying you?" Rufus asked.

"Paid me jack shit- done this as a favor - then he got to go and get rough with me."

They offered her a twenty. She didn't refuse. Before they left she maneuvered herself around the tiny room, giving each of them a kiss on the cheek. They hesitated at the door, speaking in low voices.

"You sure you're not working with anyone else?" Dave said.

"Fuck no."

"Never did?"

"No sir."

They stopped for hotdogs at Goldberg's, took a table in the back of the cavernous cafeteria-style delicatessen. Rufus sat facing the entrance. Over a hundred white Formica tables were crammed into the store. The counter, almost half a football field long, lined one wall, huge frosted white chandeliers lighting the place up like daytime. Behind the counter long mirrored signs written in white, showed the prices - pastrami, corned beef, turkey, tongue, salami, listed by the pound or per sandwich. Steam seeped from the metal drawers that held the garlicky smelling warm deli meats.

Ben Goldberg, a bald seventy-year-old Goliath in a stained white apron, waddled over with a crowded red plastic tray - with two plates of hot dogs smothered in mustard and sauerkraut, a serving of thick-cut French fries, and a couple of Dr. Brown's Black Cherrys.

"To what do I owe the pleasure, gentlemen?"

"In the mood for good home cooking," Dave McCoy said.

"Maybe you'd know about that, David, but not your goniff partner."

"Nice to see you, too," Rufus said.

"Ha!"

"Where's the check?" Rufus said.

"Some komiker! A real comedian, this one."

He lumbered away with a wave of his huge hand, his black rubber-soled shoes making squeaking noises. They dug into the Hebrew Nationals, only interrupting their chewing several times to whisper.

"She's no cherry, Ruf. Guaranteed, she's been a C.I. before, could be working for someone right now."

"We'll check the wheel, see if she's registered."

"Don't bother, not worth the risk of tipping someone off… and it won't prove anything. How many times have we worked unregistered snitches?"

An hour later, at their desks in the Division, well after hours, them the only ones there, they began to work the phones. Even at that time of night, it didn't take long to get Marcel's last name. Dave McCoy had contacts in the Hotel Workers Union. Marcel Petit had been in Room 3101 at the Netherland Plaza for two weeks. He'd given his home address as 13 Rue DeGaulle, Marseille, France, was paying with an American Express card.

Rufus called Joe Grunewald at AMEX security, a retired dick that once worked in Narcotics. The next day they had copies of Petit's billing since he'd arrived. He'd been eating at the same place every other night – La Casa Sofia in Little Italy. They called Pam, told her to meet them a block north of the Martinique.

She jumped into the back seat, slid behind Rufus, lifting her legs up onto the seat, stretching them to the other side. They drove to State and Broadway, a block from the restaurant. The rear windows of the department car were tinted so no one could see her, especially at night. She pulled her legs into a sitting position, leaned forward, rubbing her red nails along the back of Rufus's neck. In the rear view mirror, he could see her white teeth and full red lips. He didn't tell her to stop. Dave grinned, shook his head and looked out the passenger window.

At nine-thirty a dark skinned man, about forty, exited La Casa Sofia, stood under the dark green awning looking around. He wore a long brown leather jacket draped over his shoulders, dark brown trousers and a white turtleneck. He removed a cigarette from a metal case and placed it in his mouth, used a gold lighter to light up, the flame shooting several inches higher than needed.

"That's him!" Pam said.

"Guy looks good," Dave, said, "definitely Southern Mediterranean."

"Could you get back into him?" Rufus said.

"I don't want to baby. That's a bad-ass French mother-fucker."

He chain-smoked for half an hour. At nine-thirty a Checker cab pulled up. Marcel Petit dropped his cigarette, ground it with his right toe, and got in. Dave jotted down the plate and medallion numbers. The cab pulled away and they began to follow, letting Pam Stith out at the next traffic light. They gave her another twenty, said they'd call.

An hour later, in a rural part of northeastern Connecticut, there were only two cars on the road. It was the kind of darkness with different shades of black, with nothing for contrast.

"We stay on this guy we're gonna get made," Dave said.

"Let him go then."

Dave turned the car around, drove to an intersection, stopped and lit another Camel. Trees lined both sides of the road. There were no signs and they had no idea where they were. Large homes set far back off the road now provided some dim light. The last car they'd seen was five minutes earlier – the taxicab with the Frenchman.

"Which way?" Dave said.

"How the fuck do I know."

"This place gives me the willies. How do people live here?"

"Go straight till we come to a bigger road."

A half hour later they found a strip-mall with a Seven-Eleven a few hundred feet from the highway entrance.

"Head in there, I gotta piss."

On 95, heading back to Rhode Island, Dave lit another Camel, careful to blow the smoke out the window. Rufus hated smoking. He turned on the radio, to a Country station, Hank Williams singing *"Hey good looking, what you got cooking, how bout cooking something up with me?"* Rufus had fallen asleep. Before they exited onto 138, Dave woke him.

"I gotta piss now."

"What are you telling me for?"

"I'm gonna stop at that diner up the road. Want something?"

"Coffee."

A few minutes later, they sat in the converted aluminum trailer, eating bacon and runny eggs, home fries. Cardboard signs filled every window and any wall space, advertising daily specials, appetizers, one saying *our coffee mugs are bottomless.*

"What do you think?"

"About what?" Rufus said.

He sounded annoyed. He dipped toast into the soft yellow yolks. Rufus had a dilemma. He didn't tell Dave, but practically every waking moment he'd thought of the fetching junkie. He knew she'd be nothing but trouble, but one of Rufus's weaknesses was, sexy black women. And he didn't care much whether they had problems, or bad habits, or husbands.

"About the whole thing - about Pam and Marcel." Dave said.

"He looks good…we'll see."

"Something's wrong."

"What?"

"What's her motivation? Why'd she call in on this Marcel?" Dave said

"She told us, he got rough, abused her."

"Not enough. She didn't even sound too excited about getting taken care of if we make a seizure. I don't like it."

"Let it play out, it don't smell right, we shut it down."

"She's a piece of work."

"Beautiful girl, too bad she's fucked up on junk."

"Gonna give her a whirl?" Dave said.

"You nuts? She's a C.I., no fucking way."

They returned to their office half an hour later. The cop on the desk gave them two messages, both from Pam. She wanted to meet.

"You go home, I'll swing by, see what she wants," Rufus said.

That was a decision he'd often regret, but now, over thirty years later, he seldom thought about it. In fact, he'd stopped thinking about much in recent days, other than Wanda.

He looked at Jonah, eyes burning a hole. Jonah trying to look sympathetic, but sympathy wasn't an emotion Rufus was ever interested in. He had a little grin on his face, the most Jonah got out of him recently. In fact, he'd never laughed or smiled much, even as a kid. The lighting was bad. He looked for the boy he'd known with close to movie actor good looks and an athlete's physique, who could play any sport. But overnight it seemed, he'd morphed into a flabby, jowly, middle-aged man. Jonah thought, is this a dream? Did I blink and fifty years passed?

They talked quietly for a little while. He'd wanted to ask something for a very long time, but never had the nerve or the heart. Now, with Rufus's in and out mental state, he thought he'd better. The last hour gave him some confidence in Rufus's ability for recall of the distant past.

"Ruf, what else happened back in eighty, with the Garabedian Commission?"

He looked up from his cot, with eyes that looked dead, like all the enthusiasm or passion had been sucked out of him.

"I was just thinking about that...you certainly waited a long time to ask."

"I've read a lot about it, and used to speak to the guys covering it for the paper, but I'd like to know the real story. Lots of rumors but I'd like to hear from you."

He stood up, trying to pace the cell, but it hardly had room for two people. Jonah slid his legs under the cot so he'd have a couple of more inches. A few seconds of that and Rufus sat back down. Then he stood again, walked to the metal toilet at the rear of the cell and urinated. Jonah turned his head. The weak dribble smelled like ammonia. He came back, several dark stains visible on the crotch of his jumpsuit. He sat down.

"Dave and I were the best team they had in the Division. You know what I mean when I call it that? Everyone in Narcotics called it that – the Division. We'd made some great cases, multi-kilo seizures, took lots of guns off the street, locked up some of the city's worst. Remember when selling dope was supposedly verboten in Providence and New Netherland? When the "old man" spread the word that there'd be no drug dealing?"

"Patriarca? Yes, I'd heard that."

"That was true at first, but then he gave in like every other greedy mob guy, too much money in it. A whole division of narcotics dicks managed to keep busy. But Dave and I were pretty much the only guys doing high-level stuff. We'd run into the D.E.A. all the time. Either we'd be working on one of their snitches or they'd be on one of ours - crazy, I tell ya."

Rufus's voice got low, close to a whisper. Jonah leaned forward also, straining to hear.

"Know how we got jammed up?"

"How?"

"Wires."

He paused a while, got up, stretched, turned and grabbed two of the bars on the cell door and rattled it. He started to scream like a maniac – "Let me out of here, let me the fuck out of here!" He turned back, a big grin on his face, the most Jonah had seen him smile in a long time.

"We were pretty good at wires, Dave better than me though. Sometimes we'd need a real wireman to do the work, but an easy job we'd do ourselves."

"Who did the tough ones?"

"Vinnie Hawkes."

"He still around?"

"Dead... otherwise I'd never mention his name."

"Why?"

"I'm talking illegal wires birdbrain – no court orders - it's a felony."

A corrections officer passed, pushing a gigantic inmate ahead of him. The guy was at least six-five and two-fifty, shaved gleaming black scalp and a white goatee. He looked at the Koufax brothers, his rheumy eyes widening.

"Put me in there...I'm gonna kill that motherfucker!"

He lunged toward Rufus, making Jonah feel terrified. The C.O., a wiry young Hispanic man with bad skin, looked uncertain. He pulled on the guy's orange jumpsuit dragging him back. Rufus laughed the whole time.

"Who was that?"

"Phillip Morris, penny-ante bookmaker from uptown. His wife's a pretty good jazz singer. Sings at clubs here and in New York, even had a few Vegas gigs. She once hired me to catch him cheating...didn't take long."

"You don't seem too upset."

"Fuck him! He's all talk, big blowhard."

"So how'd you get jammed up?"

"For an educated man you really are a nitwit. Ma would have figured it out by now."

"Ruf, I'm not here to be tortured."

"My apologies. Let's hope this joint ain't bugged. But what's the difference now, right?"

Jonah didn't answer. He felt the legs of his pants sticking to his skin. He'd removed his jacket, held it across his knees, trying not to let it touch anything in the cell.

'We'd watch a guy a while, get his pattern, then if we both agreed he looked good, we'd put his phone up."

He went on some more. He'd given Jonah a lot to process. He needed fresh air, to clear his head. He'd be talking to Rufus plenty in the coming days and weeks. Of course, he didn't know from day to day which Rufus he'd be talking to.

"I'd better be going."

"Let me get my stuff."

He began to look around the cell, saw nothing except a towel, toothpaste and a toothbrush, a bar of brown soap, and a worn copy of Tale of Two Cities. Still, he gathered the few items into the middle of the cot and continued looking underneath it and in the corners of the cell.

"Suitcase, can't find the freaking thing...maybe the bellman's got it."

"Rufus, this isn't a fucking hotel."

Rufus's face had changed. He looked worried, even scared. He'd never seemed scared of anything. Jonah, on the other hand, was sometimes afraid of his own shadow. He began to tear up a little, rubbing his eyes with the handkerchief from his left breast pocket.

"What's the matter, can't take a joke? I'm just breaking your balls - I know just where I am."

"Don't do this to me."

"Listen...I might have another problem."

"What?"

"They'll find my DNA"

"So? You were at the murder scene."

"Not just there."

"Where?"

"Inside Wanda."

"Shit!"

"I never should have gone there," he said.

"Why did you?"

"She needed help. She only called when there was serious trouble."

He kept talking. Jonah took more notes, like it were any interview in any old story. He'd been waiting many years to get him to open up, so he knew this was very far from ordinary.

In a certain way he'd always thought of him and his brother as obverse sides of the same coin. Curious, information gatherers, noticers, analysts, reporters of facts, but then he'd always say – who am I kidding?

Rufus sometimes said he wished he'd made different decisions. Other times he'd say he had no regrets - "what's meant to be is meant to be." But now, in his jail cell, in the stinking orange jumpsuit, with a three-day growth, he looked like a beaten man. Jonah sat trying to think of things to say. He couldn't. He'd always looked up to him, even though he knew he had plenty of flaws. Now, he thought Rufus could be on the verge of some sort of total break with reality.

Jonah wasn't quite ready to leave, but also couldn't wait to breathe some fresh air. Rufus was in as a material witness, but Jonah felt he might be on the verge of becoming one of the falsely accused. He sat on the cot for a long time.

"What's funny?"

"In the middle of all that, I was waiting for the rest of the cops to barge in… and I took a minute to look in the mirror - wondering if I should get plugs, or try that Rogaine. Imagine? At a time like that I'm thinking of that shit. Sometimes I wonder what the fuck is wrong with me."

He tried convincing Jonah that Sergeant Red Grunge killed Fortune. Rufus's theory was similar to a lot of what he'd heard from him through the years. Full of "facts" that he might as well have learned from a crystal ball or Ouija board - little more than supposition and innuendo. Trouble was, he often turned out to be right.

"That's enough for now. Come back for the rest. This one might get you a Pulitzer."

"I can't wait."

"You're a sarcastic prick."

"I've been told that before."

"Jonah?"

"What?"

"Say hello to my brother if you see him."

His eyes filled again, stunned by the gaffe. He turned to yell for the guard, hesitated, turned back and looked pleadingly at Rufus.

"Calm down! I'm just fucking with you."

Chapter 15

Badway

There was no question about who had primacy in a prosecutor's office, or in an organization like the Garabedian Commission. But savvy lawyers like Romandella, Furillo and Wilson knew that they'd need good investigators to accomplish their goals. They'd told Badway that when they interviewed him, so he was clear that his first mission was to find men like Amoroso, who knew the city and knew the department. The initial interview set the tone. The Commission should have become a first-rate investigative body. After all, they hired Badway on the recommendation of several department chiefs, all of whom had expressed their earnest desire to help clean up the corruption that plagued the department.

"Why do you want to work here, Detective Amoroso?"

"It's a good opportunity. I could read the handwriting on the wall. The Mayor and P.C. Lynch was on the news about cleaning up the department, said they support the commission."

"That's it - you think it's a good opportunity?" Badway said.

"It's more than that…you been around, seen the same shit I seen. I'm tired of it."

Pedro Amoroso emigrated to the U.S. from Cuba at the age of fourteen. He would soon be fifty, older than Badway, but showed the proper respect to the sergeant. He came dressed in a gray suit and white shirt and tie, shined shoes. His salt and pepper hair was short and kinky. He'd retained a heavy Cuban accent, which came in handy, especially in undercover assignments.

"You only spent three years on patrol then went directly into detectives."

"Yes, sir. I always wanted to be a detective so when they offered me the opportunity I went to Narcotics, did undercover for five years, then to Major Crimes."

"Ever work with the Special Investigations Squad?"

"S.I.S.? I wasn't assigned there, but I worked for a few of those guys, used to do some of the U.C. work."

"What was that like?"

"Like any undercover job I'd get introduced to an informant by the case detective, then the C.I. would introduce me to his connection as his cousin or friend or whatever. We'd make a buy, then soon as I could I'd cut the informant out, deal with the connection myself."

"After that?"

"After that the case detective or the sergeant would tell me when the operation was gonna end, when they was going to lock the guy up. Then they'd lock him up. After that I'd testify in a preliminary hearing, and usually the guys took a plea. Once in a while I'd have to testify at trial."

"Did you ever take money?" Badway said.

"What?"

"Did you ever take money?"

He spoke in a monotone, looking at Amoroso, thinking if his skin weren't so dark he'd probably be beet red. Amoroso shifted in his seat. Badway had reserved the Commission conference room for the interview. He'd made sure there were no distractions: told Sandy, the secretary, to hold all his calls; cleared off the conference table, made sure the room looked uncluttered.

"Sergeant, I been in the job a lot longer than you. Back when I started you had to do certain things to get along. But I tell you this for a fact, I never shook no one down, never took drug money or money from a hooker or pimp, nothing like that. Never threw a case."

"Ever get approached to throw a case, alter your testimony?"

Amoroso squirmed again, looked around the room for a few seconds, as if searching for a camera or a microphone.

"Yeah, been approached a few times. Never once considered it, boss, never took nothing."

"Did you report it?"

"…To who, sergeant? Especially ten, twenty years ago. Ain't that why we're here, why the commission was formed, so an honest cop could report it somewhere?"

"How about gambling money? Were you ever part of an organized pad, or ever make a score off a bookmaker?"

Amoroso exhaled, like blowing out the candles on a cake, stared at Badway for a moment and then stood up. Badway frowned, wondered if he'd gone too far. He felt good, like he'd been thorough, what he thought a tough interviewer ought to be. But now he felt uncertain.

"Listen sergeant, I mean no disrespect, but maybe I make a mistake. Maybe I better just go back to my command."

"Sit down, Pete. Isn't that what they call you?"

"You done your homework."

Amoroso sat down, began to play with the knot of his tie. After a long minute Badway smiled and extended his hand.

"You've got the job if you want it. I had to ask some of those questions, see if you'd be straight with me. You never lied, and you told me what I wanted to hear. I'm not looking for choirboys, I need guys who've been around, who'll know what to look for."

Sometimes it takes a thief to catch a thief. Amoroso impressed him as one of the masses who went along with the system. If that meant taking a few dollars off gamblers, or skimming some junk from seizures to help out informants, or perjuring yourself to put a bad actor away to keep him from victimizing more citizens, Amoroso and most cops like him did what they had to do. And that went for the other five detectives Badway interviewed later on.

Bob Badway left the conference room and walked to the reception area of the Commission offices. Seated behind a frosted glass partition was Sandra Cruz, the twenty-year-old secretary hired by Vin Romandella. It had taken Badway less than a day to become friendly with the tall Puerto Rican girl.

"Sandy, give Detective Amoroso a personnel packet. When he returns it bring it in to me."

"Okay, Bob."

Badway shook Amoroso's hand once more before pointing him to the elevators.

Sergeant Bob Badway had ambitions. He went to Jesuit schools and was a good writer, had read his share of the classics. He considered himself a student of Machiavelli, and enjoyed watching the machinations of the hierarchy in the police department. He sized people up, especially the commanders he worked for, watched them vie for face-time with the higher ups, and make decisions that put themselves in a favorable light. He harbored little doubt that he could play their games better than they could, and he spent a lot of time thinking of strategies and opportunities to further his career.

The Commission was exactly that kind of opportunity. A lot of department supervisors didn't even consider applying for a job there - too concerned with how it would make them look in the eyes of other cops. Badway didn't share those concerns. As sometimes happens with strivers, their egos manage to cloud good analysis and judgment.

When he started with the Commission Badway began to obsess about Rufus Koufax. Rufus, who was called at different times a lone wolf, a boss fighter, a cop who wouldn't go along with the system, who liked to rock the boat, and refused to take payoffs. When the rumors and the scandal began to emerge his brother Jonah once said, "if Rufus is corrupt I'm a Pulitzer winner." Badway could have chosen a thousand other cops who'd been playing the system for their entire careers, and who would have been more viable targets for the commission. Instead he set his sights on Rufus and Dave. In his mind Rufus's reputation was undeserved. As far as he was concerned Rufus was just slicker than all the rest. After all, he'd been practically raised by Patriarca – at least that's what Badway had convinced himself of.

Chapter 16

Wanda had called Rufus a few weeks earlier and told him a cop named Johnny Fortune had been coming around for freebies, adding that she didn't mind it so much, until he brought along two of his bosses.

She'd met Fortune about a month earlier on Narragansett Boulevard, between Twenty-Third and Twenty-Fourth Streets where mostly prostitutes, pimps and johns are found after dark. At night, the stores all shut down, plate glass covered by black iron accordion gates or gray corrugated ones that look like pieces of Quonset huts. A few lampposts were spread between corners, one directly in front of George's twenty-four hour coffee shop. In good weather the crowd spread up and down the block, with people in secretive conversations. Some of the prostitutes were trannies, good enough, maybe too good for half-in-the-bag Rubes.

A drunken truck driver, a large blond haired man with tattoos up and down his arms, had Wanda pinned against the iron gates of a darkened storefront. Fortune walked over, told the guy to take off. The driver laughed. Then he laughed louder when Fortune told him that he was under arrest. So the young cop reached up and smashed the center of his crown with his blackjack. Blood gushed like a geyser, making a wet tangled mess of his hair, before he collapsed in a slow twist to the concrete sidewalk.

Leaving court Wanda gave Fortune a piece of paper with her phone number, told him to call anytime, said she'd show her appreciation.

A few days before the murders he'd approached the tenement on West 11th for about the dozenth time. Last time she'd said to him - "we're not going steady, Johnny, you better slow down."

Rufus watched from upstairs, thinking about Wanda. She'd turned into a gimcrack of a broad, not the willowy beauty that had captured him years earlier. But a friend's a friend, what can I do, he said to himself.

The kid had buried his blotchy red face in his raincoat, as if he knew someone was watching. The vestibule floor was covered with filthy one-inch black and white tiles, and the walls hadn't seen paint in decades. Fortune pushed the button to 3C. A few seconds later a loud buzz from the intercom's built-in speaker signaled him to push the door. He plodded up the worn oatmeal colored stone steps.

He wore old-fashioned clothes, as if he were trying to look older. Rufus waited, listening to him climb, Fortune sounding like he kicked every third or fourth step. He knocked, glancing left and right. The oil-starved hinges cried as the door opened. He stepped past the threshold, head down. He gasped when he got dragged to the floor. Rufus spun him onto his keister. He looked up, squinting, the right arm of his olive raincoat in front of his face, waiting to be struck. Rufus yanked him to his feet. The kid's head twisted violently from side to side from the force of slaps, like you see in movies. Fortune was bigger, younger, a cop, and he could throw a punch.

He must have wondered why he seemed unable to do anything. Rufus could do that to a man. And a lot of power is lost when you're someplace you shouldn't be. Fortune had been rendered weak from his own guilty state of mind.

Moments later he sat looking morose, on an old kitchen chair with a torn red plastic seat in a frame of silver metal tubing. Disheveled, confused, his skin looking like he'd leaned into a hot oven. The small round kitchen table had a flowered ceramic bowl containing two bananas, more black than yellow. A green and white houseplant in a dark green plastic container, sat on the windowsill, pleading for water. The dusty white vertical blinds hung askew, as if someone had tried to open them by pulling the slats.

"You're Johnny Fortune?"

"Yes," he said, sounding like half a question.

"My name is Rufus Koufax."

Rufus held a blue and white coffee container, from the Greeks around the corner. He remained standing a few minutes, to further establish a position of power over Fortune.

Fortune didn't hold back. He told Rufus he'd gotten upset when he heard Sergeant Grunge brought Captain Benny Fields to Wanda's. Wanda took care of them, but, according to him, she gave Fortune a tongue lashing afterwards. He said he'd make it up to her. When Rufus asked how he intended to do that, he had no answer. He just stared at the floor shaking his head.

"That's the whole story," Fortune said.

"Let me be clear with you, this shit is over. Tell me now if there's anything you don't understand."

After he became a cop Rufus quickly developed a voice that combined authority with earnestness, a kind of nasally deep baritone; sometimes caused suspects or prisoners to say to another cop: *this guy means business, huh?*

"I understand."

Fortune continued looking at the linoleum, still shaking his head. The kid had convinced Rufus he'd never show up again. He said he felt very sorry. Rufus didn't care much about the apology. Then Wanda walked in.

"What the fuck is wrong with you, Johnny? Not enough I take care of you whenever you want, you had to give my number out?"

"Sorry."

Her robe, tied at the waist, didn't do much covering up. A lighted cigarette dangled from her lower lip as if glued there, her hip thrust against the right doorjamb of the kitchen entrance.

"Sorry my ass - what fucking good is sorry?" The cigarette bounced up and down in her lips. "Now I gotta worry about these assholes getting Public Morals after me if I don't put out for them. What fucking good is sorry gonna do me?"

"Let me finish this," Rufus said.

"Am I gonna have to lay down for half the fucking P.D.?"

"Wanda, get the fuck inside!"

He stared at the young cop, whose hands shook as he sipped coffee from a yellow mug. He'd spilled some on the table, grabbed a bunch of napkins to sop it up, leaving them in a crushed brown and white ball. A few minutes passed without a sound.

Rufus and Fortune shook hands. The cop waved feebly at Wanda as he left. She sat on a kitchen chair, her arms crossed, smoking another Parliament, the filter stained red. Her short forest green cotton robe had nothing underneath. One light blue slipper with lavender flowers over the instep hung off her left foot, teetering as she flexed her ankle, like one of those toy birds that bob up and down above a bowl of water. She had a sad smile on her face. Rufus closed the apartment door.

"What's the matter with you?"

"I'm sorry I went off on him."

"Forget that - he's an asshole! For God's sakes Sabrina! You give blow jobs like other girls give a kiss… let yourself get used and abused."

"Who the fuck is Sabrina? That's the second time you've called me that?"

Rufus stared blankly…then smiled…but all of a sudden he couldn't think…she's his kid…no, a friend of his…

He'd told Fortune that if he showed up again it would cost him his job. He should have been so lucky. A few weeks later Rufus looked at Fortune's body and said to himself - worst thing you ever did, kid, take that number. Second, was not keeping your word.

Chapter 17

Monday June 9, 2008, 12:50 p.m.

He left the jail in tears, not sure if Rufus was playing with his head or not. They'd had several arguments over the past couple of months, Jonah pushing him to get evaluated. It's conceivable, he thought, that his warped sense of humor might have been responsible – but who could know for certain?

He tried calling Reitman three times, left as many messages over the half hour he sat outside the Dungeon. Then he stood and looked around. For June, it was a cool afternoon, a breeze blowing from the southeast carrying ocean air. He saw a small piece of the Newport, New Netherland harbor; the dark green water choppy, covered with small white caps set against a cloudless baby-blue sky. He needed a drink, was deciding between his two favorite watering holes - the bar at the Ida Lewis, or the lounge at the Dutch Island Hilton, in the western passage of the bay.

His mind wandered, thinking what if Peter Stuyvesant hadn't sailed up the coast after the British kicked him out of New Amsterdam? New York was the center of everything financial in the country, but New Netherland had for a long time held the edge in factories and industry. During the eighteenth and nineteenth centuries the Dutch had cornered the markets on the production of fabrics and clothing. Then the food processing industry got a foothold in the New Netherland. But both cities were now like the rest of the country - so many of the jobs that used to support families struggling for their piece of the American dream; in China, India, Pakistan, or Latin America.

Jonah shrugged, reached for a cigarette, then he remembered he'd quit two years ago. After a couple of hours in the Dungeon he felt like he needed a shower.

He wandered from the plaza out onto the boulevard, passing about a dozen conversations between lawyers, bail bondsmen, cops, and scumbags. Deals being made every place he turned. He stopped to watch a cop who looked familiar bending down into the face of man in a light gray summer suit. He looked like a lawyer and he had a worried look on his round face. Jonah thought he might have heard the lumbering policeman use the word kill. He turned and walked on.

Downtown, at the Ida Lewis Yacht Club, on the little spit of land called Lime Rock, close to a quarter mile out in the bay, he gazed at the sail boats moored off the dock, and at the handful lucky and rich enough to have slips, as he walked the thousand foot pier toward the clubhouse. Once the home of the famous nineteenth century lighthouse keeper who saved a couple of dozen sailor's lives, it had become a haven for the *well to do* and those pretending to be.

He knew he could expect a nice reception from Mary, the daytime bartender. She had a martini shaken before he walked through the door. Four sailors in matching red shorts and white shirts, all blonds, two boys and two girls, were talking about the twelve-meter race coming up on the weekend. Four or five people made the tiny bar seem busy. Part of the Newport crowd that may as well have been on another planet, the sailors probably from families that lived in mansions on Bellevue Avenue or Ocean Drive – or from one of the other of the nine cities of Newport - as Thornton Wilder had aptly put it in his novel *Theopholis North.* Newport was the biggest borough of New Netherland and the most densely populated.

The bar was noisy, so he moved to the patio, took a seat at a table looking out toward Fort Adams, at a cluster of sea birds following a light-green and white trawler, nets waving from the rigging. They hovered near the stern looking for early dinner from scraps two fishermen kept tossing overboard as they cleaned their catch.

"Rough day?"

"You might say that."

"This will help."

She set down a perfect vodka martini, in a frosty glass with a floating lemon peel. He took a healthy sip, began to think about Rufus and the story he'd just heard. It had the makings of a great book, but could he do it justice? His pieces were ordinarily about a thousand words. Then as he thought about it – despite what mother might have thought, no one else could tell it better. Not only because this was Rufus's story, but also because it was a New Netherland story…and a Rhode Island story.

About two-dozen twelve-meter yachts, gleaming white hulls and gray and brown Dacron sails, moved out of the harbor and into the bay. He wondered why his blond friends at the bar weren't with them. A lot of pleasure boats moved around, turning often to avoid each other. A huge cruise boat was anchored on the west side of Goat Island, a quarter mile away. The arcing gray Newport Bridge, lights strung along the cables, at night lit like huge pearls, loomed in the background. The stiff breeze had shifted to the south, plenty for the sailing enthusiasts and a bit too much for the recreational motorboats.

Half an hour later he lifted his glass and motioned. In a few minutes the tall fetching brunette in khaki shorts and navy blue polo delivered his second - no extra charge for the smile - which made him wish he had some interest.

Halfway into his second, he put the glass down and walked to the end of the patio. He thought about what Rufus had said, about keeping their conversation between the two of them. So much of what he'd told him seemed to make sense, but he couldn't make that jibe with the fact that recently Rufus's memory had become as unreliable as a junkie on the make. He took out his cell and called Bill McCoy.

Chapter 18

Wednesday June 11, 2008, 8:25 a.m.

Billy McCoy got a call to respond to the Puzzle Palace (what a lot of the dicks called headquarters,) *report to the Office of the Chief of Detectives, forthwith. The call was difficult enough without the forthwith.* Forthwith! (Totally unnecessary - like jacking a handcuffed prisoner.) But McCoy knew department protocol. A lowly lieutenant was not about to question the inhabitants of One Police Place, the gothic looking monstrosity that was headquarters.

Falco and Brito were driving downtown anyway, to the Crime Stoppers office to see if they could get the double murder onto the queue for a reenactment. The murders had gone viral, were all over the Internet, sometimes even preempting coverage of Obama. A reenactment aired on *primetime* might prompt someone to drop a dime. Seven days was a long time to come up empty on a cop murder. They now had more help around than they knew what to do with - primarily from the Major Case Squad; but also from the F.B.I. Task Force, the A.T.F., and D.E.A. - a classic case of overkill.

Despite too many players, the investigation moved ahead, McCoy satisfied that they were covering the bases. Falco concentrated on Rufus Koufax, and Brito slowly but steadily eliminated Wanda's customers, checking alibis, making sure they didn't miss someone or something obvious. McCoy had asked Mike Harnett, the lieutenant in Major Case, to put a team on Grunge, to see if he had any unusual habits. Aside from analyzing his phones McCoy wasn't really sure what more to do. They'd considered getting the sergeant into "the room" for an interview, but McCoy didn't want to do that until he felt confident they knew everything possible about him. "The room" was what the dicks called the interrogation room, called "the box" in some other departments. But it had been "the room" for about five generations of cops and detectives in New Netherland and wasn't likely to change.

Another possible avenue of investigation that Brito had brought up was the possibility that Fortune may have made a bad enemy, maybe someone he'd arrested or had some conflict with. But they quickly eliminated that, through interviews of some of his co-workers and supervisors. "Mis" Fortune, for all his faults and quirks, didn't make enemies, in fact, was pretty non-confrontational and had to be really pushed to react. Like what happened with the truck driver who'd threatened Wanda.

As they got closer to headquarters McCoy thought - the only suspect the chief seems interested in is Rufus. Falco liked him for the murders as well, but McCoy wasn't sure. He knew a lot about him, mostly from stories from his Uncle

Dave. And he'd heard some from Rufus himself, who loved telling war stories, never seemed embarrassed to talk about some of the antics he pulled in the old days. But murder, McCoy thought, was an entirely different matter. And anyway, he'd seen enough of him in the days since the murders to realize Rufus was going off the deep end, that something was seriously wrong with the guy. McCoy also knew that Chief Badway had it in for his uncle and Rufus, but was never sure why. Ancient history, thirty years in the past, but he kept it in back of his mind.

He gazed out the window as they drove south on West River Drive, looking at the skyline. A large red and black-hulled sea-going tug pushed a huge barge upriver towards Providence forming a big white rush of water at its bow. Two gleaming white motor yachts cruised south towards the mouth of the harbor. Both shores were lined with marinas and hotels. The tug and barge passed under a giant jumble of gray steel girders and cables that was the towering Verrazano Bridge, the upper half part orange, where bridge painters had hung scaffolding.

"What do you think Chief of D. wants?" Falco said.

"I'll know in a few minutes."

"It's not like we haven't pulled out all the stops," he said. "We've spoken to every C.I. we know, got Anti-Crime and Narcotics talking to their informants, done three canvasses, we're staying on top of the crime lab for prints or DNA, doing the phone analysis, Major Case assisting. I don't know what they expect."

McCoy didn't respond. He kept thinking about Rufus, thinking he's bad news, then shifting, wondering why he enjoyed his company, loved hearing his stories. Since the murders, actually from the first minutes at the crime scene on West 11th, he noticed something not quite right with him. But maybe the guy was just thinking ahead, planning an insanity defense. Even though part of him liked him, another part didn't trust him and often made him uneasy.

He was always wary or him, never wanted Rufus as an enemy – always recalled Uncle Dave telling him -"tough piece of work, Rufus Koufax." He'd also heard stories about Staff Sergeant Koufax, Recon Marine. The kind they dropped behind the lines with just a rifle, a sidearm, a bayonet, a compass and a canteen. Rufus left a lot of dead gooks behind in Nam…at least that's what he'd heard. But he'd pressed him about that a few times, and it seemed to be the one thing he wouldn't talk about.

Brito sat sphinx like, not moving, not saying anything the entire trip. Falco steered off the Drive, drove two blocks east to the headquarters garage on lower Thames.

Behind the building a group of about thirty demonstrators, some holding signs about police brutality, were making a lot of noise. Most of the signs were crude, cardboard with scribbled slogans, but McCoy noticed one that was professional looking, had block lettering that seemed like it'd been done on a giant printer, carried by a young woman with black hair streaked with pink: *THE POLICE DON'T PROTECT AND SERVE – THE POLICE VICTIMIZE, LIE AND STEAL!* She screamed something that he couldn't understand. The demonstrators were herded behind gray wooden police barricades by four burly headquarters' cops. One of the cops had a black canister in his hand, raised over his head, in a threatening way. A sergeant appeared out of nowhere, grabbed the cop's arm, jawing at him.

"See that?" Falco said.

"Smart sergeant…probably prevented a heap of trouble," McCoy said.

"Those dirt bags deserve to get sprayed."

"Still the United States. Not the independent republic of New Netherland," Brito said.

The car got silent for a minute. McCoy agreed with Brito. Conversely, he'd had problems with a few of the prisoners Falco had brought in - the ones needing hospital visits. Falco charged all of them with resisting. It didn't go unnoticed by McCoy that Brito wasn't working on those occasions.

"What about the line-up?" McCoy asked.

"The witness is reluctant. I'm working on her - maybe in a day or two," Falco said.

"How bout the other kid…from the stoop?"

"Same thing. He isn't there yet. We have to keep working on him."

Falco drove past the glass enclosed security booth in the basement, slowed to a crawl, gave a friendly wave and smile to the officer on duty. He seemed to know someone wherever he went - restaurants, bars, theaters, police garage, like he had a contract for everything. But getting permission to park in the garage since September 11th was especially difficult.

Falco slammed the car door, looking like he'd just showered and dressed. Vernon Brito groaned when he got out, beads of sweat on his brown scalp. McCoy got out looking at his cell, then holding it to his ear.

"Bad reception down here," Falco said.

They walked toward the bank of eight elevators, their shoes making noise on the wet concrete floor. A pasty skinned maintenance man dressed in dark green work clothes pulled a black hose with a brass nozzle, spraying the garage floor as he went. Someone shouted at him from the other side of the garage but the wan looking man either didn't hear or just ignored it.

Falco stopped talking when a couple of headquarters types got on the elevator, middle-aged lieutenants, with the gray pallor of men who worked indoors, whose uniforms looked almost new, like they'd never seen the street. There were stares all around but no one greeted each other or even nodded. The elevator doors to the eighth floor opened, McCoy and his men stepped into the brown marble hallway.

"I don't buy his explanation of why the hell he was there," Falco said. "And he's got quite a history. I wasn't around but you know the story, about the witness in the early eighties about to testify on the Corsican connection case and the Special Investigations Squad."

"Yes," McCoy said.

"Witness disappeared."

"I know the story." McCoy hesitated in front of the door to the Chief's office. "But Rufus was never charged with anything."

"Yeah, but half the unit was, and three guys ate their guns…did the Dutch Act. Most of the rest did state or federal time. French Connection redux. Same shit happened in New York ten years earlier. But Koufax gets away scot-free. What does that tell you?"

"What does it tell you?" McCoy said.

"No secret he testified…was a rat for the commission."

"Rufus is a lot of things, Al…rat isn't one of them."

"Depends on the prism you look through, I guess."

"…Anyway, it doesn't jibe – he and the chief hate each other, and Badway was chief investigator for the commission."

"Still, you see how he lives, up on the East side? He ain't doing that on a P.I.'s income, I'll tell you that."

Falco had the impression that he actually lived at his brother's address. Rufus never gave out his own address - never even had a phone – before cell phones, email, had always used mail drops, answering services.

McCoy's uncle Dave told him more than a few times, always in his cups, about the Corsican Connection, S.I.S., and the bad old days, about the supposed secret agreement between the mob bosses and the P.D. hierarchy. Akin to the hand-in-glove relationship that the Corsican mob - Union Corse - had with the Allied forces during the European invasions, August of forty- four. The crime group helped the Allies, defeat the Nazi's and oust them from France. The quid-pro-quo was understood - surveillance and enforcement of the Corsican mob was relaxed for at least a generation. Not too much later junk, most of it coming through Marseilles, began to flood American cities.

McCoy's meeting didn't amount to much more than the chief telling him his version of what happened in 1980, what he knew about Rufus Koufax. It felt awkward for Bill McCoy to listen to, because everything Badway told him about Rufus applied to uncle Dave, and of course, Badway knew that.

"We got them using an illegal wire on a narcotics target; they'd put up another one on a call-girl who was servicing a deputy mayor. That became an important bargaining chip for them. When we grabbed them we had no idea about that one."

McCoy didn't really want to engage in a conversation with the chief, he wanted to answer whatever questions he had about the murder investigation, and get the hell out of there. But he couldn't very well sit there mute. When Badway paused and looked at him he had no choice, he had to say something. Then he noticed something peculiar. The chief was known around the department for his beautifully coiffed silver hair. It was now black, and a bad die job at that.

"All this in '80?"

"'80 and '81."

"When we grabbed them I told them they had no choice but to cooperate. But we weren't really ready to lock them up, didn't quite have enough…then that prick Reitman shows up."

"What happened then?"

"You know what happened."

"Rufus resigned. But how come, what were the circumstances?"

"We were in a stalemate. They had incriminating tapes on the deputy mayor, and Mr. Cutie, Koufax, sends the Mayor a copy. And that was that. I was happy to get that crook off the job…Billy, don't dismiss the possibility that Koufax is your killer…he's a bad actor…you need to look seriously at him."

"He resigned."

"Right, he resigned…you hear what I just said?"

"Heard you, boss."

Badway wandered over to his window, looked out on the water; while Bill McCoy looked at him wondering how in heaven's name, he'd ever risen this far. Neither one of them mentioned Dave McCoy. Badway had referred to "them" or "they" but avoided using his uncle's name. McCoy thought about putting him on the spot – asking him what he knew about his uncle's disappearance.

At the precinct McCoy got in his car and drove to where he'd been going too often lately, when he didn't feel like going home. To the upper west side, to the rear of a modern glass and brushed steel high-rise overlooking the West Passage. At sunset tenants with windows facing west were treated to spectacular views. The night doorman was a large Polish kid with a shock of blond hair and a pock marked face, who hadn't learned how to tie a tie. Apartments in the building were too expensive to maintain on a cop or detective's salary, which made McCoy wonder, but he never asked.

"Can I help you?"

"Miss St. Pierre."

"Who's calling?"

"Joe Biden."

"Have a seat, I'll see if she's in."

"I'll stand, thank you."

The hulking kid shrugged, picked up the phone from the brass wall panel and pressed Marie St. Pierre's intercom number. McCoy watched with an annoyed look on his face. The kid knew exactly who he was. He overheard Marie's voice.

"A man named Biden." He held the phone to his ear for a moment or two, nodding up and down. "Okay, Marie, no problem."

Riding up in the mirrored elevator McCoy thought of Marie and Timmy - on a first name basis - wondered if he should say anything. He didn't like it, but decided he'd be better off not bringing it up. He had more guys to be worried about than Timmy. Half of the twenty thousand cops in the department would give their next few paychecks to be riding this mirrored box up to Marie's apartment.

They made love twice and unbelievably to him, he felt himself getting hard again. He looked at the black-faced glass circle on top of her dresser. The clock had no numbers but the two gold hands seemed to indicate almost three a.m. The light purple curtains on the floor to ceiling windows on the west wall were pulled back. The mainland's apartment towers were dark, except for an occasional rectangle of light.

She rolled over and kissed him, her tongue softly probing inside his mouth. Her breast rubbed against him and he felt between her legs, became more aroused from her wetness. She groped him gently, then a little harder. She tugged his hip and rolled onto her back. After eighteen months they knew each other quite well. He shuddered and came while she quietly, repeatedly screamed - "yes, yes, yes!"

At home they did it maybe three times in a good month. He didn't blame his wife, that's just the way it is, he'd often said to himself. He often wondered if she suspected anything. He tried to cover his tracks, in fact had become a much too proficient liar, led to too much self-loathing. And he also knew Ann was no dope. When they went to Mass he had a lot of trouble containing his guilt. So he stopped going about a year ago, and she never asked why.

"Why don't you call her?"

"I better go."

"Come on McCoy, it's too late. Say you got stuck on a case, you're staying in the precinct dorm."

He sat on the edge of the bed. He liked when she called him McCoy. And he could still smell her; on his fingers, on the sheets, could feel her moistness, the incredible flow of her that seemed irrepressible. But other times he wondered if he were really satisfying her, if the moans and muted screams were real. He knew women often faked it, but Marie didn't seem that good an actress. He could call and say he's stuck. But the kids would be up in a few hours and he liked seeing them before school. If he timed it right he'd get home, get a few hours sleep, be there to walk them the half block to the bus, and watch them get on.

Her soft yellow top sheet was pulled up, wrapped around her. He bent over and kissed Marie, then got dressed and came back, bending to kiss her again. Her back was to him and she didn't turn, so he moved her black hair from her right shoulder and kissed her there.

"Going to walk me to the door?"

On the drive home he thought about Rufus again and about Johnny Fortune and Wanda, hoping that this time Falco was wrong. But Billy McCoy had to admit - he seldom was.

Chapter 19

Thursday June 12, 2008, 8:15 a.m.

Rufus hated prosecutors. Totally understandable given that they tried to have him indicted and arrested in the Corsican case. Despite a secret and tacit agreement between the mayor and the P.D., the A.G.'s Office wasn't on board with it. If not for the disappearance of the evidence seized in the drug case, and the sudden unwillingness of witnesses, there's a good chance Rufus would have done time.

Fast forward to 2008, close to thirty years later, and he was getting a taste of what he narrowly missed. His orange jumpsuit and matching slip-on sneakers looked dirty. His skin had become the color of putty, and his comb-over spilled onto his left shoulder, going the wrong way. Three days in the Dungeon wasn't much of a strain for most criminals, but Rufus was pushing sixty-five.

Two C.O.'s walked by the cell holding the arms of a small wiry light-skinned black kid whose shaved skull was covered with tattoos. They remained in sight only a couple of seconds, the kid squirming, raising hell, the guards having all they could do to hang on to him. He screamed the entire length of the hundred and fifty foot corridor, and like a virus let loose, half the inmates began letting out yelps. When the big iron-gate clanged shut the place quieted down.

"Want me to talk to Reitman?"

"Nah, I called him. He's working on getting me out."

"So what's causing all this?"

"Pressure from downtown, I guess. But I'll be out soon...then whoever did that to Wanda and Fortune..."

"Leave it to the dicks."

"Leave it to them it'll get fucked up. Anyway, this is personal, same as if someone fucked with you."

Jonah looked at the pitted cement floor. He wondered how much trouble never came his way just because people knew Rufus Koufax was his brother.

A cockroach crawled past his foot, took about fifteen seconds to travel a zigzag path to Rufus's side of the cell. He lifted his left foot and brought it down, making a barely audible crack and squish. He crossed his leg, looked at the remains on the white rubber bottom of his sneaker. Jonah handed him a tissue - he wiped it off and tossed the crumbled ball to the back of the cell.

"I know what I gotta do."

Jonah felt uncomfortable. The steel bunk he sat on hung from heavy metal chains attached to the cinderblocks, all painted green. What was it about prisons and green? A couple of more roaches ran under the door and into the cell. He stood up.

"You fucking pansy! Think they're gonna bite?"

"Fuck you. Go ahead, continue the story."

Jonah thought of his brother's increasing forgetfulness, astonished at how his long-term memory seemed unaffected. But his recall of the scene and the events leading up to the double murder also seemed pretty clear. Or mostly clear, Jonah couldn't quite decide. He'd spoken with a friend of his, a geriatric psychiatrist named Rosenblatt, who'd said this was typical of the early stages of the disease. He'd encouraged him to get Rufus in for an evaluation. Jonah told him he had a better chance of cleaning up the corruption in the statehouse.

"Well, that's up to him…as long as he's still making his own decisions."

"What can I expect, in terms of progress, or should I say deterioration?"

"Probably the latter. You know, it depends, there are no set rules or schedules, but one thing is certain, if it is Alzheimer's there's no cure…and the prognosis is never good. Keep in mind, Jonah, this disease is much harder on the families than it is on the patients."

"Cheery thought."

"You've probably already encountered his forgetfulness, disorientation, things like that. There are some exceptions: Alzheimer's patients do have an ability to remember significant emotional events, especially anything traumatic."

"That's interesting."

Jonah thought about the murders, thinking too bad Rufus couldn't simply have that erased from his hippocampus. Dr. Rosenblatt had given him a brief lesson in the physiology of the brain and of the disease - the hippocampus, the region where the synapses and cells are devoured by plaque and tangles, eventually rendering the victims of the disease unable to lead normal lives. The worst devastation takes place when the tangles attack the brain stem, just above the spinal column. That's when patients quickly lose their most basic functions: continence, blinking, blood pressure, heart rate, eventually the ability to breathe.

"Thanks for seeing me Doc. Let's have dinner soon."

"I'd like that…and don't forget Jonah, it's important that he get diagnosed. There's nothing to say there isn't something else going on – it doesn't necessarily have to be Alzheimer's."

Jonah left more depressed than ever. He had serious doubts about Rufus, both about his involvement in or knowledge of the murders; but also about what he might be planning, assuming he still had the ability to plan. He thought about going back to Bill McCoy, wondered if it would be wise to share all his concerns, not the least, that his brother may be a murderer.

He'd visited the lieutenant after his first visit to Rufus, to see if he could feel him out, find out if his brother was a serious suspect. He didn't learn much. They'd known each other for years, and if you asked either of them, you might have gotten them both saying the same thing – he's a good source, helps me out from time to time. But the truth was, neither McCoy nor Jonah ever gave up much.

Rufus stared at the floor for a long time – stains of a hundred years of sweat, urine, feces, and who knows what else. It smelled putrid, an odiferous history of un-bathed prisoners who left their scents in the pores of the walls and floor. The cinder blocks looked like they'd never been cleaned. A dim bulb covered a bowl shaped grid of black iron mesh.

He talked for two hours. Jonah knew a lot of the people he mentioned. He struggled not to interrupt; had so many questions. But he just listened and took notes.

Chapter 20

November 20th, 1980, 9:30 a.m.

Rufus and Dave sat in Captain Marvin Mazur's office, the commanding officer of the Special Investigations Section. He'd been their C.O. for less than three months and they both liked him, and more importantly, they trusted him. Around the city of New Netherland and in the N.N.P.D., Mazur had a reputation for incorruptibility. They also wondered how the hell he ended up getting S.I.S.

A tall scholarly looking man, Mazur wore thick glasses, the result of steadily deteriorating vision since he'd joined the department twenty-five years earlier. His suits were always pressed and he wore white shirts and conservative striped ties. Behind him, on either side of the large casement window, were an American flag and a state flag.

"What can I do for you fellows?"

"We don't want to put you in an awkward position Captain, but we got some information a couple of days ago and think it could turn into a terrific case," Rufus said.

"Great...so what's the problem?"

They glanced at each other. Both wore khakis with navy blue turtlenecks, and almost identical tan tanker- jackets. They normally avoided hats but since New Netherland had gotten its first significant snow of the season each held gray Irish-tweed hats on their laps. They'd been the brunt of a few jokes because they sometimes dressed alike.

"The thing is, boss, we'd like to report directly to you, and not have to report to the office for a while," Rufus said.

Even though Rufus and Dave never told anyone much about their investigations, they still had to appear at the office at the beginning and end of tours. On this case though, they'd decided to try to get the captain to agree for them to call on and off-duty, directly to him.

Mazur looked down at his desk for a moment, at the mountain of paperwork. Then he looked up and turned his head between Rufus and Dave, a couple of times. He took a mahogany pipe out of his middle drawer and a pouch of tobacco. He went through the process of filling and lighting the pipe. Some tobacco spilled on top of the desk during the process. He finally inhaled deeply, before blowing a cloud of smoke toward the window. He put the pipe down in a round glass ashtray, brushed the excess tobacco that had dropped onto his desk into his hand. He reached underneath to discard it.

"This suggests we have a problem."

"We do, boss," Rufus said.

"Dave? You haven't said anything."

"Like he said, skipper, probably be good if we could report direct to you."

Dave had spent the last two years of World War Two aboard a Navy destroyer in the Pacific, referred to all his police commanders as skipper.

"But do we have a problem?"

Dave turned red, puffing his cheeks slightly. Rufus was known around the squad, and throughout the division as a confrontational and difficult man, who wasn't the least bit interested in being liked by other detectives. Dave McCoy was his opposite, went out of his way to get along with people.

"I don't want to say that exactly, but it could be. You know how the job can be, skipper."

"What do you think you're on to?"

They told him about the phone call to the operations desk, and of their interview of Pam Stith. And of their observations and tail of "Chevalier," the code name they used. Rufus had checked out Marcel Petit through a contact in Interpol. He may have been the only detective in the department with his own connection to the European based agency that tracked criminals worldwide. He didn't trust many people and he certainly wasn't going to rely on normal channels on this case, and go through the department's Intelligence Division.

Petit was a known international drug dealer, born in Corsica and in possession of three different passports. He'd been mentioned in the French Connection case and though suspected to be involved, he never was charged. He'd been the subject of several major drug investigations by the Surete' in France, but none came to fruition. There were no outstanding warrants but the French authorities and the D.E.A. wanted Interpol to notify them of any information or inquiries on him. In this inquiry, no such notification occurred.

"How do you want to proceed?"

"We'll stay on him a while, see if he meets with anyone," Rufus said.

"All right, but keep me informed… I'll tell your bosses you're on special assignment, not to ask questions."

"Should make us more popular than ever," Dave said.

"What else?" Mazur said.

"We're going to subpoena the telephone records of the Netherland Plaza."

"The entire hotel?"

"No choice. If we made an inquiry specific to him and his room he's more likely to get tipped off. We'll sift through it quickly. Rhode Island Bell will have it for us in a couple of days."

"Don't forget to make memo book entries, cover yourselves."

They sat looking at each other for a few moments. Rufus and Dave hadn't kept memo books in years, even though department rules required it. They believed it could only get you in trouble on a case, too much room for discrepancies with the investigative reports in a case file. And if you had a particularly savvy defense lawyer, Herb Reitman for instance, he'd tear the detectives apart on what they didn't put into their official memo books.

But Dave McCoy had a major shortcoming - he couldn't lie with a straight face. Rufus, on the other hand, could bullshit the Sunday collection out of the hands of a parish priest.

"No problem, boss," Rufus said.

Outside the building they stopped by Louie, the Sabrett's vendor, a small wiry man with a white handlebar moustache. They crowded under the blue and yellow umbrella to get out of a sudden wet snowfall.

"Two dogs, Louie, with the works," Dave said.

"Sodas?"

Louie wore a red plaid wool coat, a black wool scarf, and a fur hat that was a mixture of grays and browns. He used tongs to remove the hot dogs from the hot steaming water. The rolls were kept warm in the adjoining compartment.

"Cokes," Rufus said.

"What do you think?" Dave said.

"We'll find out when we find out."

"I guess so."

"Yep."

"You two act like you're in the C.I.A.," Louie said.

Rufus and Dave looked at each other and smiled.

The telephone records of the Netherland Plaza were more than they'd bargained for - over three hundred pages of single-spaced data indicating dates, room numbers, time each call was started, the time ended, all scrunched together so that it took painstaking examination to extract the significant data. And these pages covered only the fifteen days requested.

Dave McCoy used a wooden ruler to scan down the page, looking for Petit's room number. His horn-rimmed reading glasses rested on the tip of his nose. He wore a tweed sport jacket with tan suede patches at the elbows. He could have been mistaken for a college professor or researcher. That was one of the things that made him effective as an investigator – his chameleon quality. Sometimes he'd show up for work dressed in matching dark green work shirt and pants with a toolbox in his hand, which allowed him to easily walk in and out of most any building.

It worked well in another way, because suspects or just the average scumbag on the street sometimes made the mistake of thinking the mild mannered middle-aged man was an easy mark. On a few occasions, Dave revealed his actual nature. Sometimes he'd be likened to a cornered badger or wolverine. His blackjack and revolver were never far from reach, and when forced to, he'd use them.

He found Petit's room on page twelve of the records, which were printed on large sheets of paper in green ink, with perforations lining the sides of each sheet. They transposed the numbers called, noting the times and dates on three-by-five index cards. Dave did the scanning and Rufus wrote. After Rufus finished the first card, for November 12th, over one week earlier, they both realized that was just the first day that Petit checked in and that they had several hundred more pages to examine.

They'd picked an office in headquarters, one where nobody from Narcotics would wander in to - in the Internal Affairs Bureau. The rear room would usually occupied by a friend of Rufus's named Harry Solomon. The police administrative-aide was in charge of monitoring the department's overtime abusers and he worked alone, from six in the morning until two in the afternoon.

"More coffee?" Rufus said.

"We better," Dave said.

They sat at a four by six foot table. The floor had stacks of papers, from two to three feet high, lining the walls and file cabinets. When they came in or out they stepped over and around the piles. Over Harry's desk was an almost life-sized poster of Thurman Munson, the Yankee catcher.

"Wonder what's in the cabinets?" Dave said.

"We don't want to know."

They worked until they felt satisfied they had the information they needed. At 7:30 p.m. Louie might still be open. Rush hour had subsided and there weren't many pedestrians. A few minutes later they ate more hot dogs and Cokes then walked back through the snow to headquarters. Their shoes were saturated and snow covered their caps.

When Rufus knocked the next afternoon, Captain Mazur was reading reports, puffing on his pipe. Dave stood behind Rufus.

"Come in fellas, close the door."

"We got the records for Petit and I sent the international numbers to my friend at Interpol."

"And?"

"We're on to something big, skipper."

"What's next?"

"We need a subpoena for pair-and-cable information - for a pen register. The two main numbers Petit called are in Argentina. One to his uncle in an area called

Cordoba, and the other to a nearby restaurant, a place called La Toque Blanche. My source tells me that's where Chiappe spends a lot of time. You know the name boss? He's a Corsican, major exporter of heroin."

"Yes…I know the name."

Mazur stood, walked to the window and raised the Venetian blinds. The rooftops on the opposite side of the street were blanketed with several inches of white powder. Rufus and Dave looked at Mazur, then at each other. Dave raised his chin telling Rufus to keep going.

"If we monitor the pen and a call goes to the uncle… it might indicate a meet or a deal is gonna happen."

Captain Mazur nodded and sat back in his chair.

"Okay, go for it… by the way, what have you two been eating? You reek of garlic!"

"Franks," Rufus said.

"You'd better watch it. I don't want to lose good men to gastritis."

"Thanks, boss."

"One more thing - don't come in here anymore. Your bosses are suspicious enough. Anything we need to discuss we'll do over the phone, or we'll meet outside. The less they see you the better."

On their way to the Attorney General's Office, Rufus turned on the radio and raised the volume. A Chicago song, Twenty-Five or Six to Four, was blasting, making it difficult to hear. Dave went to turn it down.

"Leave it," Rufus said.

"Can't hear myself think."

"That's the idea."

"Think the car's bugged?"

"You never know. What'd you think of the meeting?"

Rufus asked the question in close to a whisper.

"The skipper's smart, about us not coming to the office."

There were a few minutes of silence, as they both did their own private calculus. Like most long police partnerships there were common bedrock beliefs that both shared – about the limits of police authority, about the efficacy of the criminal justice system, about the Supreme Court and constitutional issues, but more simply, about right and wrong. Sometimes disagreements surfaced, too, but street cops and detectives don't often enjoy the luxury of debate, like lawyers and judges. On the street, ponder things like reasonable suspicion for too long, it could mean letting a predator escape – or in the extreme - it could cost you your life.

Life or death wasn't what they mused about now. They contemplated doing an end run around the law that said cops need a warrant to listen in on a private conversation. It didn't matter whether the target was a corrupt politician, or a dishonest corporate swindler, or in this case a major drug importer and dealer.

"Davey, you getting cold feet?"

"Just wondering if it's worth it."

"The Frenchman's a bad actor."

"Of course he is, but every time we've done something like this the targets weren't so sophisticated."

"You're losing your balls."

"Don't laugh, Rufus. This guy's big...a Corsican for God's sake. When the hell did we ever get near someone like that? And we have that freaking Commission to worry about, that prick Badway - who has a hard-on for you."

"He'd piss his pants if he saw us waltzing in and out of his old office," Rufus said.

Rufus didn't answer Dave's concerns, but he was thinking hard about them.

A month earlier the Tribune had run a series of articles for a week focusing on endemic (their word) corruption in the New Netherland Police Department. The entire department was on edge, especially the bosses at headquarters, who after all, had the most to lose. Internal Affairs had been put in a backseat role. The Garabedian Commission was leading the broad reaching inquiry. They'd made a big show of it from the outset, by issuing a press release spelling out the different types of corruption they intended to investigate: payoffs from gamblers, thefts from drug dealers, shakedowns of motorists, receiving gratuities from storekeepers and peddlers, payments to alter testimony in court to insure cases got dismissed (this was an especially insidious type of misconduct – a direct attack on the entire criminal justice system,) and maybe worse still – payoffs to high ranking members of the department by cops and detectives looking to get promoted.

Sergeant Bob Badway perspired and his mouth was dry. He sat at a conference table with several lawyers, all prosecutors on special assignment to the Garabedian Commission. Badway wore a gold-buttoned navy blazer with charcoal gray slacks and black brogues. His necktie was a yellow knit, square at the bottom. His hands were on top of the table folded into each other, his silver Rolex Explorer hanging loose on his left wrist. His right index finger had a gold and blue enamel ring, a replica of a sergeant's badge on top. The brown holster that held his thirty-eight Smith and Wesson revolver, M&P model with the four inch barrel was slid forward on his belt, conspicuously visible.

The Chief of Internal Affairs had recommended him for the job of Chief Investigator for the commission. Sitting, he looked taller than the four other men at the table. Badway was taller, and also carried an extra fifty pounds on his large frame. He had the look of someone who spent time outdoors, a florid complexion (actually the result of a love for vodka martinis.) He could tell that these were serious men, ambitious men, who wouldn't be timorous about going after corrupt cops.

"If you came on board what would you do first, sergeant?"

"Assemble a staff I could trust."

"After that?"

"Find an informant."

"How would you do that?"

"Target someone we thought was vulnerable, someone we could flip."

Vincent Romandella, the newly appointed number-two man on the commission, former chief of the Attorney General's Racket's Bureau, was the questioner. He wore a three-piece suit, dark brown tweed with a muted herringbone design, and light brown brogues. Romandella had a reputation as a bulldog, with a string of convictions for major crimes.

"There are a few cops I'd look at. Eventually we'd catch one dirty. Then we'd pick him up and explain the facts of life - explain his options. Internal Affairs gave me a good handle on the department's movers and shakers. We'd need to develop a source…someone we could wire up to go after other dirty cops."

"What about the blue wall of silence?"

Romandella's deputy, a short, balding, portly man named Wilson, asked the last question. He also wore a three-piece suit, navy blue, with the vest unbuttoned and his yellow tie loosened. Harris Wilson had handled several indictments and trials of New Netherland cops, as a result was hated and feared in the department, known as cold and ruthless and not afraid to cut corners, if it meant catching a cop dirty.

"That's a crock, Harris. Cops will roll faster than anyone. Dangle a carrot, make them believe they could avoid jail, maybe keep their pension, they'll roll," Badway said.

Wilson wasn't used to a policeman firing back at him. He believed in maintaining a professional distance, and didn't especially like being called by his first name by a cop.

"Give us some names," Romandella said.

"I'll be happy to," Badway said.

He paused for a few seconds, looked at Romandella then at the other men. The old worn wooden furniture was stacked with cardboard bankers boxes, all filled with case files. He wondered what was in the files, since the commission was brand new. Boxes lined the edges of the room, as well. Four big caramel colored glass ashtrays sat on the table but no one was smoking, so Badway refrained, as well. He wondered if these men understood the depth of corruption in the N.N.P.D.

He'd been in the job twelve years and had seen it all. At least that's what he thought.

"Soon as you tell me I've got the job."

Chapter 21

June 13, 2008, 9:20 a.m.

Rufus answered the door in pale blue pajamas, the shirt stained, as if he'd just gotten out of the shower, forgetting to dry himself. The well shined heavy brown brogues shoes on his feet looked incongruous. Jonah's face twisted into creases and lines of concern. Rufus, on the other hand, smiled, reached out and touched his brother's cheek affectionately. The apartment smelled of burning coffee.

"I thought you said you were ready?"

"For what?"

"We've got to go see some people…who want to question you."

"About what?"

"You feel alright?"

"Fine, why do you ask?"

Jonah had called an hour and a half ago, said to get ready. Rufus said he just had to brush his shoes, would meet him outside the building in an hour.

"You look like you've lost weight. Have you been eating?"

"Course I been eating."

"What'd you have for breakfast?"

"How do I know?"

"Don't get all pissy."

Jonah walked past him into the tiny kitchen. The six feet of beige marble counter was stained, full of crumbs, and a half-eaten deli sandwich in yellow Subway paper had obviously been there awhile. A toaster oven sat on one end of the counter, a microwave next to that. The stainless-steel sink in the center of the counter had a ten-cup coffee maker next to it, the bottom of the glass carafe blackened at the bottom with irregular edges of burned remnants of coffee. He looked at the lit red light, pulled the plug out of the wall, removed the carafe from the burner and set it onto a round black iron trivet. He saw another roach crawling on one of the dirty dishes in the sink.

Rufus sat on the couch, eyes closed, dark red wool blanket pulled up to his chin. Jonah was uncertain if he were asleep or not. He looked at the black face of his gold Movado. Nine thirty. They had half an hour to get downtown.

"You got to get ready, Ruf."

His eyes popped open, as if he'd been doused with cold water. He smiled and tried to mouth some words but no sound came out. He pulled the blanket off, letting it fall to the floor, began to push his hands down on the cushions to try and get up, got halfway and collapsed, smiling the whole time. Jonah's physician friend had warmed him to be alert for signs of aphasia.

"Yeah, but I've gotta wait for Jonah."

"I'm Jonah, Ruf."

Sometimes he'd think that Rufus was just putting him on, seeing how far he could go before he'd react. He had a history of doing those kinds of things anyway. It wouldn't be unusual for him to speak in meandering and circular ways. Jonah often felt Rufus was testing him, that if he wanted to he could speak as clearly as anyone…but he didn't feel that now.

"I'm calling an ambulance."

The diagnosis was sketchy. The E.R. doctor put Rufus through the usual battery of tests for a confused patient: stick out your tongue, count backwards from a hundred by sevens, who's the president, what day is it, what's your name, do you know where you are? She examined his eyes several times, used the tiny hammer on his knee to test his response, same with the needle she drew along the sole of his feet.

"Hey, that tickles!"

"It's supposed to."

"You married?"

The tall Indian woman with raven black hair, laughed. She had a red dot in the center of her forehead, brilliant white teeth, slightly Asian features, and wore pale green scrubs with a stethoscope hung from her neck.

"No, why do you ask?"

"Why do I ask...think I'm too old for you?"

She ignored the remark, explained that it was a good sign that his toes turned outward. If they'd turned inward, what they called the Bibinski effect; it could indicate a more serious problem.

"Still, you need to follow your brother's advice, go see a neurologist for a full work-up."

On the cab ride home Jonah urged Rufus to go for the follow-up consultation, if not with a neurologist, then at least see a G.P. He didn't get anywhere. Even though Rufus was a bit of a hypochondriac, he almost never went to doctors.

Jonah tried to convince him to pack some things and stay a few days with him. He did that often enough anyway, and if he wouldn't go for further evaluation, at least stay at his place.

"You gotta be shitting me."

"Why do you say that?"

"Since when do you think you need to keep an eye on me?"

"Something's not right, Ruf. Please, for my sake - promise you'll go see someone."

"Okay, I promise...soon as I do what I gotta do."

He left him out at his apartment and kept the cab, told the driver to continue downtown to the Ida Lewis Yacht Club. On the way, he called Dr. Rosenblatt, explained why they didn't keep the appointment.

Later the same day he called and asked Rufus to come over for dinner, said they'd order in. He said he would, as long as they ordered Chinese. Jonah began to worry when Law and Order ended. He turned off the television. Rufus was two hours late and hadn't answered his cell. Then the intercom buzzed from downstairs.

Two things caught him by surprise: Rufus looked good, better than he had in a long time. But more importantly, he seemed totally lucid, didn't drift in and out or grope for facts or memories...at least when he first got there.

By the time Rufus stopped, Jonah's second steno book was almost full. He didn't know if Rufus sensed his disappointment - his brother, the great policeman and detective, confessing that his best cases were the result of cheating. Was he being naive? The story he'd told, or that portion of it, had him on the edge of the couch.

"The wire on our narcotics target was the one they discovered. The other one was on a call girl who'd been servicing a deputy mayor. That became an important bargaining chip when we got grabbed by Badway and his investigators."

"All in '80?"

"'80 and '81. Remember the Algiers Accord?"

Sometimes he stunned Jonah. He'd spent most of his adult life drinking and carousing, often in the company of criminals, prostitutes, and other unsavory types. But despite occasional protestations, often accompanied by some bon mot like – what do I know, I'm just a dumb cop – Rufus was extremely well-read, often recalling arcane facts.

"Yes, before the hostages were released."

"In '81, day or two before Reagan was inaugurated. Anyway, that's when we get grabbed and Dave pretty much went to pieces. I told him they wouldn't be able to use what they had, not with what we found out about the Mayor's number two...and add to that my inspiration, and I don't use the word lightly."

"Your inspiration?"

"Yeah...for us to be witnesses for the Commission."

"I was there for some of your testimony, always wondered how much was true."

"Every word of it! What'd we have to lose, especially me…I wasn't that popular to begin with. And me and Dave never liked all the shit that was going on…Yeah, I know, you're probably saying what about the shit you were doing."

"I didn't say anything."

"You don't have to…I can read your face. Lucky you never played poker. But I'll tell you what, we never stole from anyone, never shook anyone down. You know what I'm saying?"

"Then Dave killed himself."

"Who the fuck said that? That's bullshit, it's never been confirmed…maybe he's an ex-pat on some island…the Bahamas or Caribbean…maybe. They never found his body, nothing to prove he's dead."

"I thought his wife got the life insurance."

"Seven years later. The company's investigators jumped through hoops to find him, wrote reports saying that he's just as likely alive as dead. I think the insurance dicks were on to something."

"What happened with you?"

"You know what happened."

"You resigned"

"We were in a stalemate… me and the Commission, and the Department. I could have fought to keep the job but why take the risk – I figured they had too much on me."

"Like what?"

"Tapes, wiretap equipment."

"Yours?"

"Mine and Dave's. The whole thing was a debacle, should have been the case of a lifetime, but I let my little head control my big one."

"Meaning?"

"Pam. We should have gone wide of her…you ever meet Bobby Levinson?"

"Who's that?"

"F.B.I. agent friend of mine…but one of the greatest cops ever lived…taught me most of what I know, like with snitches, he had this saying – if they'll inform for you, they'll inform on you…must have forgotten that one. And you've always got to know their motivation, but with Pam? I thought I knew, but then in the end I wondered. And it was all obfuscated by my libido…you'd think I'd of been savvy enough to avoid her like the plague. Dave was very wary of her…I should have listened to him…but the thing with Pam? Great looking – and for a black junkie, she had a great line of shit."

"Pussy was always your downfall, Ruf. That and your so called second-sight – you see shadows every place you turn."

"Should I keep going or you want to keep spouting?"

"Go ahead."

"It sounded good in the beginning. She tells us about the Frenchman, that he deals in weight. Says she could introduce an undercover. We decide we got the perfect guy, a detective named "Frenchy" who looked more Corsican than the subject."

"Then what?"

"We got as much as we could from her, then did surveillance on the Frenchman. No one could do a tail like us. Especially Dave - very good at blending in. He could walk into a joint and no one would notice him.

"Where'd it go wrong?"

"In the end the illegal wire was nothing… I got accused of making a big score, but you probably heard that."

Rufus was a lot of things but thief wasn't one of them. But getting him to tell the whole story was like trying to get a dog to give up a bone. He had to be convinced that it did no good to hold back now. But Jonah felt very uncertain about what his brother remembered and what he imagined.

"See how fucked up it is? Wanda ends up leading the same kind of fucked up life thirty years later, leads to her getting murdered, now me looking to find out who killed her. And Billy McCoy and his guys are trying to pin it on me. Do you see the freaking irony here?"

"You might even label it tragic irony."

"Don't go all academic on me."

"Keep going, Ruf."

He did, went on at some length, Jonah scribbling, trying to keep up and also trying to gauge how much to believe.

"Let me give you a little history here, about our beautiful city, and about my beloved department. What was happening to the P.D. was more than benign neglect – a malignancy had formed – and the patient, the people of the city, didn't even know they had cancer. So when the latest news of corruption broke in 1980 and the Mayor formed his commission to investigate the department, the public was in a state of shock. Remember?"

"Of course I remember."

"Well, it didn't help that the rag you work for, and all the broadcast media, couldn't wait to smear every cop in the city with the same dirty brush."

"I don't think that's exactly true."

"In a pig's ass it ain't…but all of you were missing the big picture. Like always, you went after the easy stories, picked the fish floating near the surface, never bothered to go deeper."

They had divergent views of that part of New Netherland history, but Jonah convinced him to go on about the case.

"We were a little too late when we found out Badway had Petit working as a snitch for the Garabedian Commission."

"How'd you find that out?"

"Never mind that…I had my ways."

"So what'd you do, I mean once you knew that why didn't you stop the investigation?"

"You gotta understand…me and Dave took this shit seriously. To us, a prick like Petit is bad as they come - bringing that shit into the country that's putting a whole generation of kids at risk. So we figured - fuck him, and Badway, and the Commission – we'll work the case and lock the bastard up anyway."

"Would you do it again?"

"What do you think?"

"Knowing you…yeah, of course you would."

"I got to get the fuck out of here."

"Keep going a while."

"So we thought we'd found the greatest informant ever in Pam Stith."

"What about all the complications…with you and her?"

"Yeah, yeah, yeah…well anyway, before she disappeared she finally agreed to go back into the Frenchman, wear a wire, the whole nine yards."

"And the whole time you knew Badway's after the two of you?"

"Maybe it sounds stupid given all that happened, but we were on the level…or as on the level as anyone in the whole department. Yeah, we did some shit to cut corners, but never for bad reasons, never to make a score or anything like that – always to get the bad guy!"

"So the ends justified the means."

"Hey, fuck you brother, don't tell me in your morally reprehensible world there's not a bunch of scumbags have done much worse just to get a scoop."

At the door they looked at each other for a moment then embraced.

"I digressed a bit, next time I'll tell you the rest."

Chapter 22

Saturday June 14, 2008, 10:30 a.m.

A few days earlier, Reitman got the A.G.'s Office to agree to bail, after insisting that they either charge Rufus or release him. He threatened a federal habeas corpus petition if they kept holding him as a material witness. Relief from illegal detention was ordinarily used after conviction and sentencing, but Herb Reitman made so much noise about his client being unlawfully detained that Francine Jurgenson blinked and agreed to Rufus's release on $50,000 bond. Reitman forked over the $5,000 to the bail bondsman himself, a shady operator named Alan Hopkins, who in turn posted the surety bond.

The benches by the public docks in Melville, in Portsmouth, just north of the city, give a great view of Narragansett Bay. Hundreds of boats were attached to moorings, and behind them as many stood on poppets over crushed shells covering the ground of the shipyard. Brass hooks on halyards banged against aluminum masts, sounding like a chorus of wind chimes. The sight and smell of the bay could be soothing after spending most of your life in the city. The bench they sat on was gray faded teak. At the beginning of the dock nearest them were three coils of bright green hose; a black rusting 55 gallon drum overflowing with cardboard, cans and bottles; and several insulated yellow electrical cords plugged in and running down to boats. Four seagulls sat atop the railing of the dock leading out to the boats. About thirty feet away was a ramp that led to the marina's dinghy dock, where a couple of dozen gray inflatables bobbed and bumped against each other and against the dock.

"Jimmy Pabon was a great C.I., told me everything about Buster Alito…at least he said he did. He'd worked for him since he was a kid. But I knew him even longer, knew his mother good. But you know, with informants, you're never really sure it's the whole story…so what else you want to know?"

"Buster Alito – the boss?"

"Yeah, the boss…who else?"

"Okay, go on."

"We tried to follow the Frenchman…I told you that… I always thought Dave knew about me and Pam…wasn't much I could hide from him. But I never told him. That was wrong you know, you're not supposed to keep anything from your partner…but I knew what he'd think.

"Later, I found her at the address she gave us. It was close to midnight when I rang the bell. She came to the door all bright-eyed, like her day was just starting.

I knew from *jump street* she was on junk, heroin. But took me a while to figure out she'd also been free-basing. She was really fucked up."

"I expected it to be a shithole, but I was wrong. The apartment was on Marcus Wheatland, a block off of Marlborough."

"Near the projects?"

"Right... Anyway, there was three other people there - two little spooks that looked hard as nails, and a blond, even taller than Pam. She tells the guys to take a powder and they get up and leave, not a peep out of them. Then she surprises the shit out of me, introduces her roommate Colleen. She had this beautiful smooth white skin and thin tapered fingers with inch long red nails, and a busty figure. She got up, walked over to the bar and mixed us all a drink. Few minutes later, Pam gets up from the couch, walks over, bends down and gives her a long passionate kiss...then asks me if I wanted to come inside with them."

He paused for a long few moments and stared at Jonah, who looked away, like he didn't want to look him in the face.

"Have you talked to Billy McCoy?" Rufus said.

"No. Why?"

"Just wondering."

"So what happened to her?"

"Who?"

"Pam?"

"Wish I could tell you. We became very friendly after the case was done, maybe for a few months, then she disappeared...I was nuts about her."

He wondered if Rufus sensed his discomfort. He didn't care much about his sexual peccadilloes, or even about the secrets he kept from his partner, Dave. It more had to do with his casual use of the word spook in describing the two black guys, which to Jonah was as bad as calling them niggers. It bothered him, and even more, it confused him, because growing up Rufus was always the first one to step into a fray to protect someone being picked on because of skin color, or accent. He sat quietly, not sure what to say or ask next.

"I think she ruined me forever. I mean for other broads...know what I'm sayin? Set the bar too damned high...never did meet anyone else could compare...even Wanda."

Rufus stood and watched a thirty-foot Cape Dory maneuvering into the dock under sail. The main was reefed and the skipper was shouting orders at his wife or girlfriend to pull in the jib; she looked confused, was dressed more for a lunch downtown than for sailing. The skipper looked like he'd make a great Santa.

"Good looking broad, no?"

"But not much of a sailor," Jonah said, finally breaking his silence.

"So, what else you want to know?"

They walked out on the finger dock closest to the bench, Jonah dressed in a light blue summer suit, Rufus wearing a pair of navy blue pants and a gray v-neck wool sweater over a white tee. They looked very out of place, everyone else at the docks or on the boats, in shorts or khakis, some in blue work shirts spattered in paint or oil…except for Santa's mate, her one leg now over the top rail of their vessel, her shoe dangling perilously, about to slip between the boat and the dock.

"Tell me more about the Frenchman."

"Could have been some case I tell ya…if wasn't for two things."

"What's that?"

"If I could have kept it in my pants - that's the first thing. But I thought about it a lot over the years and the way I look at it is that no way I could have done it differently. I just wasn't wired that way… and what do I have to be ashamed of? It's not like I'm one of those freaking pedophile priests, or a rapist, or some sort of degenerate, know what I mean?"

"What's the second thing?"

"That freaking Badway got it in his head that we were dirty, then convinces those other assholes at the Commission. Luckily, I'd found out about the deputy mayor screwing around. I'm not sure what made me do it, but I figured it wouldn't hurt to have some ammunition in case things went bad, know what I'm sayin? If not for that, we wouldn't have stood a chance."

Rufus said he felt like he'd lost a lot of time, and not just the few days in the Dungeon. He actually felt, in some perverse way, good about being inside. He'd often heard bad guys refer to it that way, of being in, or doing a bit. He felt like he'd passed some sort of test, especially given his age…and his condition. Not that he knew exactly what "his condition" was, or how much time he had. He did realize that sometimes he acted inappropriately, for instance would show up somewhere dressed inappropriately. Then when his mind cleared, he'd feel embarrassed and uncertain whether to say anything or to just ignore it.

Within an hour of leaving Jonah, Rufus was back at Newport West, looking for Herman Grunge. In his mind, Grunge was the killer. Locking him up, even in his mental state, didn't make much sense to Rufus. It had been a long time since he'd been a cop. He'd simply have to kill him.

139

Chapter 23

December 24, 1980

There were rumors that Jimmy Pabon took off, that he might be alive somewhere, but Rufus placed little stock in those. He felt the kid had probably played too many angles, and when Buster Alito finally got wise to him he probably did him the way he did a couple dozen other suspected rats. He thought of him at the oddest times, wondered, did he die because he thought he could get over on everyone? That's the downfall of many a snitch, believing their sociopathic line of shit would work forever. These were the kinds of things Rufus spent too much time pondering.

It all began to go wrong a few years after he met the kid. He rode a sector car in Newport North, when Jimmy and his five younger brothers were the scourges of the neighborhood. Not bad kids really, just wild, with no father to keep a rein on them. Jimmy took a liking to Rufus and the feeling was mutual. Once in a while he'd throw a few bucks his way, tell him to buy dinner for his mother and brothers.

Selma Pabon had curly black hair she kept long, shiny red lips, and favored tight skirts or shorts. Half the cops in the precinct would have loved to get into her drawers, but Selma was dangerous and everyone knew that. She'd killed one of her common-law husbands and beat the murder charge, using a domestic violence defense. After that, not even Rufus would take a chance of sleeping with her.

Jimmy, barely five feet tall, used to rush up to the car, tell Rufus everything going on in the street. The information was useful, but most of the time he'd shoo him away, tell him talking to cops could be unhealthy. But the kid was hard to discourage.

Jimmy Pabon knew the underbelly of New Netherland as well as anybody. Rufus had kept track of him from a distance, knew he'd thrown in with Buster Alito and his crew. That always mystified him, because when he knew Jimmy he didn't have much of a violent streak, but people change.

They met out by the Sachuest bird sanctuary, a measly thirty acres the government protected when New Netherland began to boom. Most people didn't even know about it. He and Jimmy used to go for hikes, did some fishing off the rocks. He drove into the crushed shell parking lot, to the one-story pale green building that housed a U.S. Park Ranger in the season, and provided rest rooms for the public. Jimmy was bent over a vending machine. Rufus watched him retrieve a Mounds Bar. He stood and turned, his face breaking into a familiar wide smile. He looked almost the same to Rufus, except for three new gold teeth on the right side; and white bell-bottoms and a black muscle shirt. He looked like he'd been lifting weights.

"How you doing, man?"

"I'm doing, Jimmy. How you doing? "

Jimmy shook his head from side to side, grinning. To Rufus it felt bittersweet seeing him again. He always felt the kid had potential, could have amounted to something, if he'd only had the right influence. But that wasn't something Rufus could undertake, which he hated admitting to himself.

"Still with that asshole?"

"What asshole?"

His smile quickly faded and his brown face got darker. Rufus thought - Jimmy would intimidate most people with that look.

"Buster," he said. "I expected more of you, kid."

"Fuck you, Rufus. Where the fuck was you man, the years I needed you? I ain't seen you for what, six, eight years? Who gonna look out for me, man, who gonna watch my back?"

"Alito looks out for Alito. Only reason he'll look out for anyone else is if he helps him earn."

"Listen, what'd you bring me out here for? You know what happens I get spotted with you."

"Whose gonna spot us, some squirrels? Come on, let's take a walk."

"Someone spotted me already, few minutes before you got here."

He said he had seen four men sitting in two nondescript dark colored cars in the lot of Sachuest. He got stuck for a minute or two on the snow-covered hill leading into the park, and by the time he got traction the two cars passed him exiting the sanctuary.

"You don't sound too bothered, Rufus, but I'm fucking worried."

"You get a plate number?"

"No."

"Next time get the number, I'll take care of it."

"Yeah, you take care of squat - you know Buster got half you guys in his pocket."

"I ever get you in a jam?"

"Only takes one time, Ru."

An hour later he had Jimmy laughing, Rufus with his arm around his shoulder, the way he wished his own father had done.

They stood looking out on the Sakonnet River, at a dozen sail boats going south on a starboard tack, strung out over half a mile, all with colorful genoas bulging. The disappearing sun reflected off the choppy surface and off the shiny white hulls and windows of the public housing of Little Compton, across the river. The boats rose up and rushed down a few seconds later, in an almost choreographed dance, huge spray flowing over the bows. Jimmy shook his head, sucking hard on the tip of a Camel.

Rufus reached over and tousled his hair – like he was still twelve. Pabon smiled and shook his head, letting the tough guy float away.

"You come up with something?" Rufus said.

"I'm waiting for my boy to come back."

"Shorty?"

"Yeah, no one's wired in like Wilfredo. "

"Never gave him much credit for smarts."

"He the man now, Ru…Everybody afraid of Wilfredo."

Buster Alito groomed both boys. He had been the closest thing to a father figure they had. And Alito was good at putting square pegs in square holes. Jimmy Pabon worked in his gambling racket. Within two years Jimmy knew the entire operation. He also knew how to get along with everyone - including handling payoffs to cops. He never told Rufus about that.

Everyone knew that gambling enforcement was a big sham: the numbers runners and collectors, the cops themselves, even the judges and lawyers on both sides of the bar. Arrests were almost always by accommodation. Plainclothesmen would approach one of the runners or collectors, or sometimes Jimmy, tell them they needed to make a pinch the next day, say where and what time the defendant should show up, and how much work to have on them. After the arrest they appeared in court and if the Assistant A.G. and Judge were amenable the defendant would plead guilty on the spot, pay a two or three hundred-dollar fine. Everyone was happy: the department got an arrest number, the A.G.'s Office showed they wouldn't tolerate illegal gambling, the judge got another case off the calendar, the lawyer made five hundred or so just for the appearance, and Buster Alito's biggest moneymaker kept working like a well-oiled machine.

Jimmy Pabon once made the mistake of asking Buster why he risked fucking around with junk, when he made so much with gambling. Everyone knew what would have happened if Patriarca found out. The old man didn't care much about junk one way or the other, but he didn't want to go to war with the New York Mafia bosses unnecessarily, and he didn't want the Feds on his ass.

They were sitting in Buster's red Eldorado, Buster behind the wheel, Wilfredo next to him. Wilfredo had taken to wearing his hair in Gerri-curls. He'd recently bought a lot of gold - three chains around his neck, a heavy ornate bracelet on each wrist.

"You don't get it?"

"I'm just sayin, why take the risk?"

He saw his boss's sinister smile in the rear view mirror. The car was parked in front of Buster's legitimate business, the Lion's Den Bar and Grille, on the Boulevard, a couple of blocks from the projects. A large neon sign above the door spelled the bar name in red cursive lettering. The big man stunk of aftershave. He turned, squeezing his fat belly past the steering wheel until he looked directly at Pabon. Surprisingly quick, his meaty fist punched him in the face. Jimmy held his nose, pain shooting into his brain. Wilfredo's mouth was wide open.

"So how about you mind your own fucking business from now on? How would that be? That be okay with you, Jimmy? I'm going inside and that backseat better not have a speck of blood on it when I come out."

Jimmy Pabon thought about capping Buster after that. He walked around for a couple of weeks with his nose bandaged. No one ever asked about it. They didn't have to. And Buster Alito never brought it up either, acting like nothing ever happened.

Jimmy knew he had made a poor choice. He should have tried harder to stay in touch with Rufus. He had thoughts of being a policeman, and a detective. But once Rufus wasn't around anymore and after he hooked up with Buster full time, he knew the reality. Especially after he got pinched three times, all for bullshit - petty gambling charges that Buster told him to plead to. He followed orders, Buster paying all the fines and lawyer's fees, with Jimmy ending up feeling like he owed him something.

"So where is he?" Rufus said.

"I don't know, Ru. He disappears every once in a while, sometimes a few days, sometimes a week or two. Until things are cool…you know what I'm talking about?"

There were a few moments of silence. Rufus didn't respond to Jimmy's last comments – a thinly veiled explanation of Wilfredo's main role in life – as an enforcer for Buster Alito. Rufus was too sharp to get drawn into a conversation about acts of violence that he'd rather not know about. If he did get specific information on a murder of serious assault he'd be obliged to follow it up, either himself or by referring it to the detective assigned to the case, which would be a huge waste of his time, because finding a witness willing to testify was becoming a rarity.

"Call when you hear from him."

"You asking a lot, Rufus."

"Yeah, I know that...but give me a call."

"Give me a safe number."

They walked to his car. He gave him the number he felt a hundred percent sure was safe – Sissy Kelley.

"Leave a message there – where to call you, or a time and place to meet."

Rufus drove back to the room he and McCoy had been using as an office for the last week, a spare bedroom in Rufus's girlfriend's house. It felt good to them, being close to the ocean, at least a mile away from the high-rise office towers and condos of downtown.

Anita, a tall willowy Cuban, let them meet there as long as they didn't interfere with her clients. Her brownstone had two apartments, one a few steps below street level, adjacent to the steps that led up to the main apartment. Rufus had promised her they would wait across the street, make sure no one would see them going in. Anita was a massage therapist, the legitimate kind she told him, but he always wondered. He didn't tell Anita that an informant would be meeting them. Dangerous game Rufus played, having Pam meet them at Anita's.

They waited for Pam to arrive, sitting by the casement windows, the pale orange curtains pulled back so they could see the street, each of them in a chair that looked like an orange saucer mounted on a wrought-iron frame. A bamboo coffee table covered with back issues of Cosmo sat between the chairs and a sofa with honey colored wood frame and pale green fabric with palm trees design.

Rufus was quiet, thinking that Dave was probably right - about not trusting Pam. But by that time Rufus had already been to bed with her, but wasn't about to admit that to Dave.

"There she is," Dave said.

"I'll get her."

Part Two

Chapter 24

Monday June 16th, 2008, 9:08 a.m.

Rufus was in the crosshairs of the police and a pit-bull of a prosecutor. In his confused state his only chance was to find out who killed Wanda and Fortune. He said as much to Jonah. But Jonah harbored beliefs that made him squirm, thoughts that maybe the cops and the A.G. were right to suspect his brother. Maybe he could be the killer.

He hadn't seen Rufus since Saturday. He thought of his antsy behavior of nearly fifty years ago, when Rufus couldn't make it through a whole day in school.

"You don't look too well," Jonah said.

"Sit down for Christ's sake, you're making me nervous."

He felt immediate relief from the verbal rebuke. It meant that Rufus was at least partially coherent. He sat and opened a fresh steno pad and waited for him to start talking. Rufus coughed several times then made a guttural sound, forcing phlegm from his throat. Then he stood and leaned over the terrace railing and spat. Not much boat traffic on the Sakonnet, just a lone barge stacked with blue and green containers, three high, being shoved up river by a red and black tug.

Jonah wondered, as he often did in recent months, if his brother actually recognized him. Rufus turned and sat down on the tan wicker chair, and began talking. Jonah sat on the matching chair, maneuvering it closer to the circular glass table, laying the pad there, before leaning back - trying to look relaxed. He found it hard to be relaxed around Rufus these days. He waited a few moments before saying anything.

"Go ahead…from where you left off Saturday."

"Who can fucking remember?"

"You were talking about you and Dave, in Narcotics."

"Yeah…back then the life of narcotics detectives could be treacherous. Before the days of crack or PCP, smack and coke, and the funny weed, was all we saw. Those days Narcotics Division kept tabs on the dealers that had balls enough to work in Rhode Island. My own New Netherland P.D. did next to nothing to prevent dealing."

On the surface, Patriarca and the bosses of the New York families were aligned. They had a prohibition against made guys dealing in junk. But anyone with half a brain knew that was bullshit. Wherever the most profits were that's where you'd find the mob. If Patriarca caught a guy dealing and he didn't sanction it, there was no appeal process – they'd be found in the weeds out on Dutch Island, or in a trunk at the airport...sometimes one of the fishermen pulled a body up in the net.

That's why that three hundred pound bag of shit, Buster Alito, and some of his guys were on the radar. A snitch told us Alito was sitting on a load...You don't want to write this down?"

"Don't worry about that, just keep talking."

"Me and Dave were in the Special Investigations Squad, the supposed elite of the Narcotics Bureau...all a big sham. Most of the dicks in the unit were real operators, had carte blanche to go anywhere. They'd make a few pinches to make things look legit, but no one ever bothered to check on the conviction rate. By the time the cases wound their way through the system, everyone got a piece of the pie - and the defendants got a walk.

Buster was careful, always looking for surveillance, getting his club and his bar swept for bugs or wires once a month. Not that he ever talked inside anyway. He learned that from John Gotti. They'd done time together in the sixties, when both were up and comers."

"Where'd he go wrong?" Jonah asked.

"He got greedy, let his guard down - trusted a neighborhood kid. Of course he didn't know the kid was my best snitch. Alito practically raised Jimmy Pabon since the age of twelve or thirteen. He trusted the kid more than he did his own shithead son, Little Buster. But like I said, I knew Jimmy even before him.

"When was this?"

"What?"

"When Alito had the big shipment coming in?"

"'81... The department was going through a shake up, with the Garabedian Commission making a lot of noise. And our sergeant was a money guy, had plenty of reason to worry. He didn't trust me and Dave and the feeling was mutual. In those days bosses in plainclothes details would leave a number where to reach them, in case something unusual happened. That in itself was pretty subjective, but with Sergeant Timmy Meldish the rule of thumb was – 'Who got shot?' He didn't want to be bothered with police work.

"We were staking out one of Alito's places on Thames Street, around the corner from Touro projects, when himself walks up to the car. We always tried to blend in, but the old sarge came parading down the street in his navy pinstriped Brooks Brother's suit, and a gray fedora he might have lifted off the set of the

Maltese Falcon. We're in my '64 Impala, the dark green one. Remember it? Had it tricked out with pom poms hanging from the mirror, a little dog with a bouncy head in the rear window. Anyway, we seen him, looked at each other - a "What the fuck is he doing here?" look. With partners you don't even have to speak half the time."

"Meldish climbs into the rear seat smelling like he just come from Saks Fifth Avenue – nauseating, some sweet expensive men's cologne."

What's up fellas?

Hey, sarge, good to see you. What brings you around?

Rufus my boy, how you doing?

Doing fine, how you doing?

On to anything?

Some junkie we think might be dealing out of his apartment. Possible he's been going to New Bedford to get his shit, bringing it back and cutting it here.

"That was total bullshit! But no way I'd let numb-nuts in on what we were looking at. I remember like it happened yesterday - not thirty years ago."

Heroin or coke?

Not sure yet.

What's troubling you, lad?

Nothing sarge, just surprised to see you.

"I glanced at Dave, in time to see his cratered face turn crimson. Dave wasn't one to give shit to a boss, but I figured -fuck this guy - he could care less about us or what we were doing, except for one thing – was there anything in it for him. Wouldn't be the first time he scored a guy behind our backs. We had to be careful; he was a sharp bastard, and a genuine tough guy. But far as I was concerned he's there for one reason, then sure enough, he comes out with it."

Listen fellas, I know you guys wouldn't cut me out of anything. Why I come up here is I made a nice score downtown, new pimp set up an operation, high-class call girls.

Forget it, Tim, we're not interested.

"Dave surprised me. Telling him we're not interested. No need for further explanation - Meldish knew we didn't take money."

"How'd he know?" Jonah said.

"How do you think? We knew how he operated and vice versa. Then he drops this on us."

Rufus, you missed my point. You guys know I'm in your corner and what's mine is yours, right? Nothing I'm asking you to do.

"We looked at each other, no words, just raised eyebrows. Meldish was laughing. He got out of the car without so much as a goodbye and we watched him disappear into traffic on Touro and Thames. We knocked off the surveillance;

decided we'd come back the next day with a different car. When we pulled into Touro District Headquarters' garage five rats descend on us, like we were last night's dinner."

Out of the car McCoy, Koufax!

"I recognized a sergeant who'd been Internal Affairs his whole career, one of the original guys from the old Chief's Confidential Squad, before there even was an I.A. Those guys were as hungry and greedy as the guys they chased."

What's this about?

"The sergeant weighed about two twenty-five, was well over six feet. He squeezed the upper half of his body into the back seat of our car. A lot of guys around the job called him "King Kong" Then he backed out, a fat envelope in his hand. You didn't have to write us a story - we knew we'd been set up. They kept us in separate rooms, on the thirteenth floor of Headquarters."

I want to see my delegate.

"After I said it, I'm thinking - a D.E.A. delegate wasn't going to do us a lot of good. The Detective's Endowment Association would get us a lawyer, but not the kind we needed. We needed a great damned lawyer."

"Later that night, Herb Reitman had those Internal Affairs guys sweating through their suits. Herb had a way of doing that to cops who thought nothing of trampling on the rights of his clients.

When he finished listing their assets –home, summer home, automobiles, savings accounts, brokerage accounts – explaining how easy it'd be to slap a lien to all of it, they were like gelded thoroughbreds.

He walked into the interrogation room, in his thousand-dollar gray pin-striped suit and glistening Italian loafers, says *let's go fellas.* I felt like giving him a hug."

Detective Koufax, Detective McCoy, you probably have important work to do, unlike these sorry excuses for public servants.

"We waited for him in the lobby while he completed some paperwork for the bonds. You wondering why we needed bonds – well, good as he was, we were still collars, would have to appear in court to answer the bogus charges. We left headquarters in Herb's chauffeured black Mercedes Limo."

Where to, Mr. Reitman?

Conte's, Frank, I think these fellows could use a libation.

"How'd the envelope get planted?" Jonah asked.

"Had to be Meldish. Dave and I talked about it, couldn't see any other way – they must have caught the sergeant dirty, flipped him, got him to stuff the envelope in the back seat. Either that or he came up with the idea, told the I.A. bums where we'd be, that they'd catch us dirty."

"What was in that envelope?" Jonah said.

"MRHP."

"MRHP?"

"Mutual race horse policy – numbers!"

"What happened next?"

"We were in front of Conte's, Frank, the driver, walked around to open the door, his blue sharkskin suit glimmering. He had to step around two Chinese peddlers selling dim sum, and the four or five customers lined up in front of the aluminum carts.

Herb Reitman always wanted payment for services rendered, but sometimes not in cash. He became the pre-eminent mob attorney in New Netherland by dealing in information, which in a certain way is what led to our demise in the New Netherland Police Department."

So what are you guys up to, that merits all this I.A. attention?

Damned if we know, Herb.

Rufus began to shiver, just slightly, but enough that Jonah noticed. He stood up, went into the kitchen and returned with a glass of water, asked him he wanted anything – tea, or a drink? Rufus didn't answer, just launched back into the story…kind of.

"What do you think? You think he gives two shits about me, or about Dave? …I got to meet Dave in an hour, we're going to stay on Alito, get him dirty, with a good package. He's moving keys, this prick, no way we let him operate like he owns the freaking city."

"Rufus, sure you don't want something to drink…a Makers?"

"Drink?"

"Yeah, or a juice, or coffee?"

He'd drifted off again, was totally in a different world. Jonah wondered what to do. Call an ambulance? Explain to another doctor that his brother was suffering from some sort of severe dementia? By the time they got to the hospital he might have returned to the present.

He excused himself, said he had to use the bathroom. Jonah felt grateful he didn't piss off the terrace. While he waited he wondered about Rufus and Herb Reitman. He'd been Rufus's lawyer for almost thirty years but Jonah couldn't help wondering about the relationship, because Reitman also represented Buster Alito. Talk about conflict of interest.

The toilet flushed. A few seconds later, the apartment door slammed. He hesitated a moment, got up and went to the door. By the time he opened it and looked into the hallway, the elevator door was closing. Did he delay getting to the door intentionally? Maybe he'd just had enough of Rufus.

Jonah felt convinced more than ever that Rufus had a serious mental problem, either Alzheimer's, or dementia; which made him think that whoever

Rufus had in mind as a suspect in the murders of Wanda Kelley and John Fortune was in grave danger with his brother wandering the streets of New Netherland. And thought about the likelihood that Rufus had it all wrong, and that his "suspect" could be totally innocent.

Chapter 25

November 18th, 1980, 7:05 p.m.

Marcel Petit sat in the hotel bar at the New Netherland Plaza smoking a European cigarette, holding it between the two first fingers on his right hand, palm face up. He stood out from the crowd - mostly tourists casually dressed, in ski jackets or bulky sweaters. He wore dark wool trousers and a cream-colored wool turtleneck. His olive skin was rough looking, probably from teenage acne. He looked slightly Asian and had a habit of squinting with his right eye. Several women were looking at him when Pam Stith walked into the bar. The room was all smoky mirrors and chrome, with jazz standards playing. She slid onto the stool next to him, smoothed her skirt and then crossed her legs.

"Can I buy you a drink?" Petit said.

"Of course," she said.

"Bartender."

After she got her vodka gimlet they spoke for a few minutes. She told him that she couldn't spend the night. He smiled, said that was no problem.

"Your fat friend told me to come meet you. What'd you have in mind?" she said.

"Why don't we have a drink in my suite, I'll call room service for something to eat."

The penthouse had three rooms, including a bathroom with a sunken tub. The living room windows looked out over Narragansett Bay and the New Netherland skyline. The furnishings were expensive looking, dark woods and oriental carpets. Several heavy gold frames with Renoir reproductions decorated one of the walls. A large screen television hung on another wall; and a stereo system built into a cabinet underneath was playing Stan Getz. The chandeliers were dimmed, leaving just enough light to navigate without tripping. Pam sat in one of two plush arm-chairs upholstered in dark red muted floral fabric, her legs pulled up under her, her head back on the cushion. Petit went behind the black marble bar, poured two Belvedere vodkas over ice.

He gave her her drink then sat on the matching couch. He took a long swallow and put his down on the glass coffee table.

"Do you like jazz?" he said.

"Jazz, blues, some rock and roll."

"What else do you like?"

"Sex, with the right person."

"Do you think that could be me?"

"Depends what you're like. If you the generous type, could be."

Pam wasn't at all prepared for Petit. Getting tied up and play-acting was one thing, but having scalding candle wax dripped onto the soft flesh of her breasts was horrifying and painful.

A couple of hours later she had had trouble walking from the suite to the elevator, her legs rubbery from a combination of pain and fear; worried that the burning wax would leave permanent scars. And even though she was there as a favor, she expected him to pay something. When she hailed a cab she had to count her money, make sure she had enough for the fare.

Bob Badway had introduced Marcel Petit to Vin Romandella. Badway hadn't even done a rudimentary background on him. He had no idea who Petit was, other than a convincingly bad man who had called the Commission office to volunteer to work as an informant. Badway got excited. But he didn't have the right kind of experience to properly evaluate, debrief and then handle someone like Petit. As a patrolman he'd often volunteered for inside duty, filling a variety of clerical roles for the precinct captain, was sometimes referred to by other cops as a "house mouse."

Marcel Petit was not a run-of-the-mill drug importer and seller. Francois Chiappe, the infamous head of the Unione Corse, the Corsican mafia, was his uncle. Chiappe was believed to be the mastermind behind the French Connection case, when NYPD had seized 97 kilos of pure heroin in 1962. At the time the authorities claimed they had put a big dent in the pipeline of heroin being imported into the U.S., but the seizure barely affected the narcotics trade. After the seizure Chiappe fled Corsica and then Marseille, to an estate in Argentina. He ran his criminal enterprise from there, largely with the help of his nephew Marcel, who effectively functioned as the C.E.O. of Chiappe's U.S. drug operations. After several years Petit sensed things going wrong and was seeking some insurance to insulate him from arrest and prosecution.

He told Badway he didn't want to approach the Drug Enforcement Agency, felt them untrustworthy. He'd read about the newly formed Garabedian Commission, decided to volunteer to work as an agent.

The timing couldn't have been better, or worse for Rufus and Dave. When Badway became Chief Investigator for the Special Commission on Police Corruption, the Garabedian Commission as it became known (named after the famed prosecutor Charlie Garabedian,) Badway's primary interest immediately became Rufus Koufax and Dave McCoy. He'd worked in Narcotics Division at the same time as them, and never trusted them. Never understood how they managed to develop such good cases, which almost always let to great arrests and seizures.

But they were in the dark about Badway, he told Jonah later on. Even though they didn't like each other, he never had a clue what the guy really thought about him and Dave. Jonah had covered a big murder trial when Romandella was a prosecutor, so he got access to the Commission files after they'd been disbanded. Even better, they went for a couple of dinners and Romandella filled Jonah in on stuff that never made it into reports, which is often more titillating. But he still never got Rufus to tell his version...till almost thirty years later. What the lawyer told Jonah about one particular meeting was especially interesting.

"What's this?" Romandella asked.

"Read them, then ask me," Badway said.

Badway had a flair for the dramatic. He got up and walked out, went over to talk to Sandy Cruz, to see if she'd have lunch with him. It didn't seem to bother him at all that she was twenty years younger...or that he had a wife and kids.

The next day Badway was in the Commission's conference room. He noticed the boxes that had been strewn about during his interview were gone. There were some Picasso and Dali reproductions in black frames, and brass floor lamps with cream color shades at each end of the room. Fluorescent lighting in panels in the drop ceiling also lit the room. Romandella had his feet up and was reading the *Tribune.* He'd removed his jacket and loosened his tie. Badway left his jacket on, waiting a few minutes before he broke the silence. He moved his chair a little closer to the table and cocked his head to one side, eyes squinting a little. Thick sandy brown hair that spilled onto his forehead gave him an almost boyish look.

"What'd you think?"

"About what?"

"About the articles and book?"

"Interesting."

"That's it?"

"What am I supposed to think?"

"That the guy is dirty. With what was in the book, and my experience with them, I don't think I've got to paint a picture for you."

The two articles dated back to the late 1960's, about an investigation conducted by the State Organized Crime Task Force. The mob got wind that there were wiretaps in a social club on Federal Hill in Providence, and "sources close to the investigation revealed, a New Netherland police officer was the leak." That was in the first article. In the second, Patrolman Rufus Koufax was named.

"Me and the Mob," published in 1978, was the autobiography of a cop named Roger Swensen, who was in Lewisburg Penitentiary doing life for murder. He got convicted on federal charges after the A.G.'s Office tried him twice, both trials ending in acquittals. The feds used the R.I.C.O. statute and made the murder of a mob informant one of the predicate charges. Swensen got an agent and a ghostwriter and told a fantastical tale that made for great reading. When Sergeant Bob Badway read it he became riveted on one part of the book, actually little more than a page, which said that Raymond Patriarca was Detective Rufus Koufax's godfather. It went on to describe the close relationship between Patriarca and Sheldon Koufax, dating back to the 1940's. Part of New Netherland's history in the first half of the twentieth century, were those quasi-criminal relationships, but for Jonah and Rufus it was merely family lore.

When Jonah first heard about his father, he and Rufus were having dinner at their cousin's house, with his parents and their mother. Lenny's father liked to drink and tell stories, sometimes got on a roll.

"Phil, enough with that," Aunt Paula said.

"With what?"

"With your cockamamie stories."

Their mother's sister was always protective. If she sensed her sister getting uncomfortable she'd go out of her way to make her feel better. Aunt Paula and Uncle Phil's apartment was the only place where they'd seen original art, by French Impressionist painters.

"All I'm saying is that Sheldon Koufax was a mensch, a man of his word. What's wrong with his sons hearing that?"

"Such a "mensch" betrays his wife?"

But Uncle Phil wasn't quite done. He sipped whiskey from a heavy crystal glass. His plate was empty except for the steak bone that looked like a feral animal had chewed it. He handed the plate to Aunt Paula and she and their mother carried stacks of dishes into the kitchen. He leaned toward Jonah and Rufus, Jonah watching to see what Rufus did. When his brother moved closer, so did he.

"A good man, your father…just didn't see eye to eye with your mother. It happens. But he loved the two of you, believe me."

He poured more whiskey from a square bottle with a black label with gold lettering. He lifted the glass and took a long swallow. Uncle Phil had no hair, just a thin border of white along his neck and around to the top of his ears. His blotchy scalp made the top of his head look like an unmarked map. He wore a white dress shirt, with triangular gold cufflinks, open at the collar. A large gold ring on his right index finger had some sort of crest.

"A stand up guy, Sheldon Koufax. Why the old man liked him, looked out for him."

"The old man?" Rufus said.

This was one of the things that made Jonah look up to Rufus. He could converse with an adult - ask a question if he didn't understand something. Jonah was terrified to ask or answer a question.

"Patriarca."

He watched Rufus nod. Later, at home, under the covers, he tried to explain who that was. Jonah remembered the word Godfather, so he knew they must have been talking about someone good.

In 1978, when Jonah read "Me and the Mob," he almost threw up. Then he got hysterical laughing. They hadn't seen Patriarca for years. Rufus was a rookie cop, him a stringer for the Tribune. They'd both met him at a holiday party up on the Hill, and exchanged a few words, Patriarca asking how their old man was. Then Rufus grabbed Jonah by the elbow and they walked out. That was it. Somehow, this party made the paper and the department got wind of Rufus being there. He took a two-day rip for associating with an organized crime figure. The hypocrisy was so thick in those days you could have used it to bury bodies.

"I read the book last night…what are we supposed to do with that?" Romandella said.

"Koufax is dirty," Badway said. "I watched how him and McCoy operated in Narcotics…always off doing their own thing. And the pinches they made just weren't possible without inside information."

"Isn't that what detectives are supposed to do, develop information?"

Badway turned red. He finally loosened his tie and took his suit jacket off. He went on talking, telling Romandella about his suspicions.

"Cheaters?" Romandella said.

"Illegal wires."

"Let's put this on hold, Sarge, we'll discuss it after the chief leaves."

The Chief of Internal Affairs was due any moment, for a meeting to discuss how the two agencies were going to keep the lines of communications open, as they both worked to uncover and ferret out corruption. More legerdemain. The command staff of the P.D., from the commissioner on down, had no interest in helping the newly formed commission, whose only mission was to humiliate the department. On the other end, Romandella and the other lawyers had been around long enough to realize that they'd get vacuous smiles from the chiefs of the New Netherland P.D., but nothing more.

"Whatever you say."

Romandella made notes on a yellow legal pad with a black Mont Blanc fountain pen. Every few seconds, he pressed a green blotter against the pad. Despite the blotter, fingers on both his hands had ink stains. He kept writing for a couple of minutes, until Badway interrupted.

"Could I ask you a favor?"

"What?"

"During the meeting could you not call me Sarge?"

"What should I call you?"

"Chief?"

Evidence or probable cause or reasonable suspicion weren't important factors when the Garabedian Commission opened their first official investigation As far as Badway was concerned he already had that. In the several weeks since he'd given Romandella the book and articles, he seldom missed a day of vilifying Rufus and Dave, making them sound like devils incarnate. After a while Romandella and the other lawyers began to believe what Badway was saying, as if there were actual evidence to support his suspicions. Even smart lawyers are sometimes susceptible to brainwashing by a devious cop.

Badway sat with Romandella and another one of his deputies, Carl Furillo, a tall patrician looking man of about fifty, who wore his navy blue Yale tie every day, and favored three-piece gray worsted suits. A dozen pages of telephone records were spread out on the table that they'd gotten through a subpoena to Rhode Island Bell for Rufus and Dave's home phones. The comparison between the two was stark. They went month by month, examining Dave McCoy's first, Furillo reading off the numbers and Badway copying the numbers onto three by five inch index cards, one card for each number dialed. They ended up with a stack of twenty cards. Badway noted how many times each number was called. When they got to Rufus's records they realized that he barely used the phone.

"How can that be, Bob, if he's such a big operator?" Romandella said.

"I don't know. I'm as surprised as you. Maybe he makes all his calls from work."

"Doesn't sound right. You said they're seldom in the office. Did we subpoena their work numbers?"

"The guys in the Division share four extensions between forty or fifty men. Impossible to know who's on which line when."

"When do we start surveillance?"

"Started a few days ago…there's teams on them right now."

"You didn't tell us that," Furillo said, glancing at Romandella.

"Didn't think I had to."

"Yes, you have to," Furillo said.

Badway waited for Romandella to say something, but he didn't.

"Anything else?" Badway said.

"That's all for now," Romandella said.

Badway walked out of the conference room and went to his office to get his jacket. On the way out he stopped to say goodbye to Sandy Cruz and confirmed their date for the next night, then walked to the elevator.

Sergeant Bob Badway liked to be called chief since he'd become chief investigator for the Garabedian Commission. He had Marcel Petit working for him, and Rufus and Dave McCoy had Pam Stith working for them. Badway didn't know of Pam Stith, and Rufus and Dave didn't know of Petit. It wouldn't have taken a genius to figure out that some sort of implosion or explosion was about to take place.

Months of headlines in the Tribune had reported on narcotics detectives who had made a routine of ripping off drug dealers; often stealing the drugs and selling it back to them or to their competition. And there were a series of federal indictments of officers as high as the rank of captain, who had received monthly payoffs to protect gambling operations throughout the city. The feds managed to turn one of the Mafioso, who provided a list of cops on the take. All of this caused the Mayor and the City Council to form the Commission, to show they were serious about rooting out corruption.

Sergeant Bob Badway was in some ways a natural for the commission job. He knew administration, record keeping and so forth. And he did know the rudimentaries of how to initiate an investigation, understood the necessity of developing a plan and having the right resources to carry it out. Romandella got the Police Commissioner to assign six of the best Internal Affairs investigators in the department to the commission.

Badway designated Detective Pedro Amoroso the team leader, in effect making him his assistant supervisor. Then he gave him and the other investigators their first assignment - to watch Rufus Koufax. He provided all the information he had: his last known address; the make, color and plate number of his car; and a few of the places he hung out. He had also told Amoroso to spend some time on Dave McCoy, but to make sure that Rufus was the main target.

Even though Badway knew the officers he'd recruited he did background investigations on each of them. He checked their personnel files for any record of complaints or allegations, and had each fill out a questionnaire that listed their assets and checked the answers against his own asset search. He checked bankruptcy filings and the state and federal court files for lawsuits. Every one of them passed muster. During one-on-one interviews he'd wondered how strong to be in the questioning, worried that he might eliminate some good prospect if he asked the wrong questions.

Badway went to a phone booth on a corner not far from the office, picked up the receiver, then let out a string of expletives. A wad of pink chewing gum was stuck to the earpiece. He walked into the next booth, gazed at the number printed in the middle of the black and chrome box, then dialed Amoroso's pager number. A gust of wind and some debris whirled at his feet. A few minutes later the phone rang.

"Badway."

"Sargento. We followed the R guy to a bar on Chafee Boulevard. He been in there for two hours."

"Good, stay on him."

"You want us to go past our shift?"

"Yes, put him to bed."

"Okay, boss."

A few minutes later Badway was on the east side of the Boulevard. Downtown New Netherland was a different city at night. The side streets were lit up with bright colored fluorescent signs advertising different ethnic restaurants and stores. There were gift and souvenir shops every twenty or thirty feet with dark skinned men and women pitching to tourists who came to the city for entertainment. For several blocks the entertainment strictly catered to adults. Women were usually dressed in very tight skirts more than half way up their thighs, and wore blouses that left little to the imagination. There were about a dozen small hotels with rooms rented by the hour, all of them with hanging neon signs over the door.

The cops that patrolled the District knew the players. If an unfamiliar girl or pimp showed up the local detectives got a call almost immediately. They'd take the information, including a good description; then make a visit as soon as possible. If the opportunity wasn't followed up on quickly the newcomer would end up belonging to someone else. And that's how it worked – certain pimps and prostitutes belonged to certain cops and detectives. On their end, the girls and their men liked to have a couple of uniform men and a detective or two on their payroll. That way, if another cop hassled them they'd drop a name and hopefully avoid an arrest.

A certain honor system prevailed and most of the cops and dicks didn't infringe on each other. Rufus and Dave really didn't care. If they caught someone dirty and the person started dropping names they'd look at each other and smile. The only currency that helped a pros or pimp out of a jam with them was information. After a while it became common knowledge on the street and in the warrens of the N.N.P.D., that if Rufus and Dave caught you, you were going in, unless you came up with some solid information.

Badway walked north, pondering his plans, while Amoroso and his team followed Rufus and Dave, hoping to catch them in a compromising or corrupt act. But Badway still had urges, had other things in mind.

He spotted a girl named Sylvia walking the Boulevard, peering in cars that stopped to admire her. She wore spiked silver heels and a matching metallic looking skirt, with a flimsy black blouse opened to the waist. Sylvia didn't have large breasts but it didn't matter. The mocha colored former model had beautiful red lips. Seconds after he spotted her Badway was right there.

160

They ended up at a hotel called the Shangri La, in a room on the second floor just over the hotel's large red neon blinking sign. She'd taken care of him in the way he liked and began to get dressed.

"Get your ass back in this bed," he said.

"No baby, I got to go out and earn or I'm in big trouble. You know what I'm talking about."

"Don't worry, I'll talk to him."

"You ain't gonna talk to nobody. All you gonna do is get off another time or two, keep me here for company, then I'm gonna get my ass whipped."

Badway laughed and pulled Sylvia back into bed. She tried resisting but only half-heartedly. They'd been together before and she knew Badway was capable of causing her way more trouble than a beating, so she stayed the night.

Chapter 26

June 16, 2008, 10:00 a.m.

Brito didn't ask for Falco as a partner. When he arrived at their squad three years ago McCoy asked Brito to try to work with him. He'd come from a quieter detective squad in the eastern half of the city that was known for its high per capita income and remarkably low crime rate, many of the homes secured behind gates.

Bill McCoy knew the backgrounds, the strengths and the weaknesses of his detectives. He'd learned to rely on Vernon Brito. Even though McCoy outranked him, Brito's longer experience was invaluable and he often deferred to the rotund detective. Around their squad he'd sometimes hear him referred to as "no ball of fire" or "an empty suit," but he ignored those comments as ignorant, or sometimes just blatant racism.

When Falco got transferred to Newport East precinct from uniform, he got promoted to detective shortly thereafter. Most cops and detectives believed he had a rabbi. In fact, he had compiled an outstanding arrest record. But once in the Newport East Squad he quickly developed a reputation for being abrasive. His new lieutenant had almost forty years in the job and had no trouble calling in a favor. Falco was transferred again, within a few weeks, to Newport West.

Brito wasn't thrilled when McCoy asked him to take him as a partner. In private moments he'd tell detectives close to him that Falco was a royal pain in the ass. Eventually that changed and the two formed a decent working relationship.

The lineup had been scheduled and rescheduled three times, partially because of the witness's reluctance and partially due to Rufus's antics. Since Herb Reitman got him out on bail he'd become hard to pin down. He'd bobbed and weaved all he could until Falco and Brito caught him coming out of Jimmy Shea's late Monday morning.

Shea's was a typical fish shack, a block from the water, with worn nets and different color marker buoys hanging off the outside walls, an old ship's wheel mounted on a concrete block about five feet from the entrance; and an avatar of Ahab, in a bright yellow slicker and rain hat, standing at the helm.

"We've been looking for you," Falco said.

"Couldn't have looked too hard, I'm easy to find."

"Get in the car."

Falco held the rear door of their four-door gray Ford open. Brito got in the driver's seat. A few people coming out from lunch stopped to see what was going on – two were longshoremen dressed in heavy wool outer shirts and jeans, and calf-high black rubber boots. The blond that stood between them looked like she'd fall if one of them moved aside.

"What for?"

"A ride to the A.G.'s office."

"Not unless you've got an arrest warrant we're not."

"Come on Rufus, don't be a ball-breaker. This is gonna happen whether you cooperate or not. Better you cooperate, no?" Falcone said.

"Tell me what we're doing."

"You gotta stand a lineup."

"I want my doctor there."

"What?"

"My doctor, he's gotta be there."

"You mean your lawyer."

"Yeah, yeah, you know what I mean…you trying to fuck with me, Falconi?"

"No problem Rufus…we'll notify him."

He got in the rear of the cruiser. Falco sat next to him and called McCoy to tell him they'd be there soon, asked him to call Francine Jurgenson and Herb Reitman.

Rufus stared out the window, deep in thought. My doctor, what the fuck was I thinking? I don't know what's wrong with me, but it's no joke, that's for damned sure. Either I do what Jonah says, go see a neurologist, or I eat the gun… but not till I nail the son of a bitch that done Sabrina…no, no, on, not her, Wanda, Wanda. And the cop…what's his name? The idiot, that caused all this. He'd still be alive if he'd listened to me…in a way I don't blame the guy. Where's a doofus like that gonna get a woman like her? …Wonder how ma's doing? Jonah said she wants to come home, but can't do that – she got nowhere to come home to. I gotta laugh… she wants me to apply to college…I'm barely passing half my subjects…subjects…no, no, no… what am I thinking?

"Where we going?"

"A.G.'s Office…you okay Rufus?"

"Yeah, I'm good…what's your name?"

"Vern Brito, man. We know each other thirty years."

"I know that…just fucking with you, Vern."

Brito and Falco looked at each other, their eyes speaking volumes, as if they weren't sure if he was putting on an act or not. Brito was having a hard time getting Falco to look at anyone else for the murders. He'd told him about the visit to North Andover, and about three other guys he'd tracked down in the city. He said they should be doing lineups with every one of Wanda's customers. But it was Falco's case, and Brito knew he could only do so much.

Lineups were conducted in New Netherland's sixty precincts sixty different ways. An operation order on it, O.O.#298/08, came out the year before, but the directive was poorly written and so ambiguous, leaving so many potential variables, that it seemed impossible for the department's hierarchy to control. The result was an inordinate number of overturned cases based on faulty eyewitness identifications. At any given time the city's corporation counsel was defending multiple lawsuits for wrongful convictions. They'd been paying out huge sums to settle the cases. At the same time the city and state didn't know where the revenues would come from to fund municipal pensions' and the schools, and public safety for that matter.

The Attorney General decided to start his own lineup process and tried to get his deputies to steer them into their building. They'd implemented sequential viewing, rather than standing the suspect alongside the fillers. Enough studies had shown that there were less false identifications using the sequential method. The detectives in N.N.P.D. didn't feel too warmly about any of it and did all they could to sabotage or at least make the process more difficult. Part of the A.G.'s solution was a man named Cortez Roberts.

The former professional heavyweight had supposedly sparred with Clay before he turned Muslim and changed his name to Ali. Roberts had a promising record and career until he ran afoul of the mob. He'd testified before the Kefauver committee on organized crime's influence in the boxing game, which effectively ended his professional career. Detectives were used to doing the intimidating but for most of them the tables were turned when they met the six-foot- five, ex-heavyweight.

"Detective Falco, you can stay back there with your partner while I get things going here. If I need your help I'll ask; heh heh,"

The nervous little giggle was disarming. People often inferred that Roberts was at least a little crazy. In fact, he wasn't crazy at all, but he was often a slight or insult away from unleashing a vicious jab or right cross.

"Miss Brown, please step up to the glass. When I turn the lights on inside and pull this curtain you're going to see six men enter the room, one at a time. We'll give you as much time as you need to look at each one. They won't be able to see us so don't worry. You'll notice a height scale on the wall in front of them so you'll be able to tell how tall they are. If you recognize anyone let me know, okay?"

When they picked her up to go to the lineup Falco almost didn't recognize her. She wore three-inch lime-green stilettos, a matching tight skirt, and a low-cut white blouse. She smelled of expensive perfume. Falco and Brito argued later over whether or not her straight brown hair was a wig.

"You sure they can't see out?"

"Positive."

Roberts pulled the brown curtain back. With the third man the witness made a funny sound, something like a yelp. She started to walk away from the glass. Roberts grabbed her arm.

"It's okay. He can't see a thing. Do you recognize him?"

"Yes, I do… But not from that day."

"Okay, we'll keep going."

On the drive home Cecelia Brown was non-communicative. Falco and Brito tried to get her to loosen up but the most they got out of her were one-word answers. She'd gotten them and Francine Jurgenson excited when she said to Cortez Roberts that she recognized Rufus. The room almost filled with their collective exhalations when she added – *but not from the murders.*

"Where do you know him from?" Jurgenson had asked.

"Ain't none of your business."

"It's very much my business."

"Says who?" Brown answered.

That put Francine Jurgenson on her heels. She knew very well she couldn't compel the witness to answer. Outside her office she'd asked Falco and Brito to try and get it out of her.

"Maybe she is holding back," Falco said.

"How do you mean?" Jurgenson said.

"Maybe she doesn't want to out and out lie, but is trying some stupid ploy. Maybe she's just afraid of him."

"See what you can get from her."

They drove to the front of 310 West 11th. She tried to open the door as soon as the car rolled to a stop but like all police vehicles used the inside handles of the rear doors were disabled.

"Let me the fuck out."

"Take it easy, Cecelia. Just a few more questions," Brito said.

"You got all you going to get from me. Now open the damn door."

Falco was out of the car standing by the front right bumper talking on his cell. They'd already agreed that Brito was more likely to get her to talk. Not only because they knew each other, but also because he had the edge with certain subjects.

"Come on Cecelia. Why you got to be that way? How about we go for a drink?"

"I don't want no drink right now, Brito. Not with you and him."

"How about later? I'll come back alone."

"I'll think about it…call me in a couple of hours."

Brito watched her climb the front steps of the building, go inside the vestibule off the lobby, and fish her keys from her white mesh pocketbook. Inside, she disappeared from view. He and Falco stood by the double-parked cruiser.

"How'd you do?" Falco said.

"I'll call her later. We'll see."

"What do you want to do?"

"Let's do another canvass. Some people we haven't reached yet...and we need to do the building across the street."

"We've done that one three times," Falco said.

"Doesn't hurt to do it once more, you never know who might have been peeking out their window...and maybe we'll run into the bongo player, the Melendez kid."

"Think he saw something?"

"He saw something...why do you think he's making himself so scarce?"

Chapter 27

Lieutenant William McCoy

A few years earlier Bill McCoy made lieutenant. The promotion ceremony took place at headquarters; flags and bagpipers, speeches, families all dressed up for a joyous celebration.

Rufus wasn't invited, but that didn't stop him from attending. He showed up dripping wet dressed in a yellow sailor's slicker. He spotted an old detective who got him past security.

A lieutenant at thirty-eight years of age was pretty damned good and Rufus figured no telling where the kid might end up. That was how they used to talk about him but he never even made the first jump to sergeant. I.A.D. and the Garabedian Commission made sure of that.

Rufus figured Dave McCoy would appreciate him being there. Dave's concave chest would have been puffed out on this day, being he practically raised the kid.

He sat in the auditorium, staring at all the sharply dressed chiefs and deputy commissioners on the dais. Being in headquarters and around all the pomp, he couldn't help thinking back forty years.

Rufus took the test for the P.D. as soon as he got out of the service, late winter of 1971. He scored high enough to get appointed during the summer of that year. He'd thought about other jobs, the State Police, or the Fire Department, but decided to try the N.N.P.D.

Several days after getting sworn in he and two hundred classmates at the Police Academy were pushed out the door into the field, replacing more experienced cops who were moved around to try and quell outbursts of violence that had become an expected part of summer.

His first day on post Rufus got approached by the local bookmaker, a tall black guy named Junior Walker (just like the singer,) who told him to get lost, said his customers were feeling intimidated.

They stood in front of a candy store on Aaron Lopez Avenue, one of the tougher streets in the city. Loud music, New Orleans jazz or Zydeco, was blasting from a speaker over the door. About fifteen or twenty people milled around in front of the candy store. Horns blared every few seconds, from cars and taxis double-parked on both sides.

"You joking?" Rufus said.

"No joke man…you getting my people nervous."

Rufus wasn't looking for trouble so he turned and walked ten or fifteen feet away, off to the side of the store.

"Ain't far enough man."

"Listen…"

"Ain't no listen my man. Let me explain something to you – all the plainclothesmen knows me, the precinct captain knows me, some of the chiefs knows me. Understand what I'm talking about?"

"I think so."

"I don't think you do. They all come around, every month …then again at Christmas, understand? I'm mother-fucking Santa in this precinct!"

"I get it."

"You better fucking get it, my man. Now take a fucking walk."

Rufus mumbled something, but didn't move an inch. The gambler looked down at him, a quizzical look, his head twisted to the side.

"What?"

"What" was half screamed. Rufus moved his lips again, seemed to be saying something.

"What the fuck you saying boy?" he said, more falsetto.

Rufus motioned with his right hand, asking him to come closer. The man took a step toward him, bent down. Rufus now spoke clearly in a staged whisper.

 "Go fuck yourself…my man."

The first car that responded to the *assist patrolman* from Central, found Rufus standing over the prone gambler, his nightstick raised like a torch, the man's hands in a defensive position. The other cops had all they could do to get Rufus away from him. A mini-riot erupted. A day later Rufus was sent back to the Academy, placed on administrative duties. The commanding officer of the Academy warned him any further trouble and he'd be terminated from the department.

Now he sat in the same building looking at other chiefs and commanders who in Rufus's estimation wouldn't make a pimple on a good cop's ass. At the end of the ceremony families and friends of the promotees milled about in the lobby outside the auditorium, the marble floors wet from the rain, the atmosphere steamy despite the air conditioning. Flashes went off every few seconds; children being held and passed around by men in sharp looking navy-blue uniforms with polished brass buttons and silver shields; and young wives and girlfriends in their best dresses and heavy make-up, flashing broad smiles. The cacophony of sounds was dominated by the cries and voices of babies and young children, an occasional scream from a frustrated mother.

"Bill, your uncle would be proud."

"Rufus!"

"He'd of been beaming."

"Thank you."

McCoy paused a moment, seeming at a loss for words, probably suppressing the urge to ask Rufus what he was doing there, but was too much of a gentleman to do that.

"Have you met my wife?" McCoy said.

After the niceties, and being invited and declining an invitation to join them for lunch, Rufus left headquarters and walked about a mile across town to his office. He checked his answering machine for messages, read the Tribune, made a couple of phone calls, and then put his feet on his desk and fell asleep.

A few years later, on Tuesday June 16th, 2008 he was in a world-class jam. At four in the afternoon he woke up in the same office, a half-empty bottle of Makers by his feet. He pissed in the sink in the back of the office, let the water run a few seconds then washed up and shaved. He'd eaten Mexican food the night before and his office stank.

He thought about Grunge for a while, then left and went to visit Darlene. He always gave her short notice. She lived and worked in one of the better parts of New Netherland, on Bellevue Avenue, down by the ocean. There were a few old mansions left from the eighteenth and nineteenth centuries. Her block was lined with old dark brownstones, built a bit later. He drove down Van Zandt Street, made a left on Huffman Place, where the trees formed an alee. Every forty feet or so, on each sidewalk, an old black iron lamppost stood, that at night lit up with gas flame. The homes on either side were three or four stories, most individually owned by people who either inherited old money, or some like Darlene, who made it on their own.

"You're late," she said.

"So sue me. You know traffic this time of day."

"What the fuck happened to your head?"

"Long story."

The black and blue was fading, being taken over by yellow and brown stains over his left eye. Darlene had a bemused look on her face. Her blond hair was over one shoulder of her dark blue satin blouse. A half smile showed just a glimpse of teeth, her lipstick faded to pale pink; her
legs were twisted up on the beige couch, white skirt halfway up her thighs.

"Why come here if you're not going to talk."

He'd been seeing her for over a year and still wasn't comfortable. Sometimes he thought he could trust her with anything, other times, he didn't feel so sure. But if he didn't tell her who was he gonna tell? McCoy? Falco or Brito? Sissy? His brother? He needed an escape valve, some place to let everything go.

He'd decided he would tell her about how often he seemed to be forgetting things, and of his frequent blackouts. He'd had them many times, but always connected to drinking. These were different. On a few occasions he'd found himself in places without any memory of how he'd gotten there. Like one day last week, on Atwells Avenue in Providence, in front of Marchesano's, one of the city's best Italian restaurants. Though he'd been there on a number of occasions, at two in the morning the place was closed. Rufus stood looking in the window.

"You alright sir?"

"Yes…I think so…why do you ask?"

"This place closes at one, so I was just wondering."

He patted the officer on the shoulder, an avuncular kind of tap, thanked him and walked away. An hour later he found a stub in his jacket pocket with the address of where his car was parked. He remembered none of it: driving to Providence, parking, where he'd gone. And worst of all, in his mind, he'd been dead sober.

The hour with Darlene went fast and he said more than he had expected…but he never mentioned the blackouts, or Wanda, or the murders. He left and went back to Newport West station. He sat in the back of his forest green Jaguar, a pair of Nikon 10X50 binoculars on the seat covered by the *Tribune*. Just after six Sergeant Herman Grunge left the station house.

He'd begun watching Grunge a day after the murders, quickly went to work with his handset, hooking on at different times to Grunge's home phone, the Rio's main number, and once to the Newport West main trunk line; which after two hours he realized was a waste of time – too many extensions in the precinct, would have had a better chance at a roulette wheel. Of course his investigation got interrupted by his incarceration as a material witness, and by the interrogations. He felt very disappointed in Bill McCoy, thought they had a good relationship, thought of him as a friend. But it became clear - Rufus was the main suspect in the double murder. There were more than a few times, just before or after his fuzzy episodes, what he'd come to call them -that he wondered himself whether he'd shot Fortune. Possible he thought, but he couldn't ever imagine, in any state of mind, hurting Wanda.

Grunge walked half a block to Broadway and boarded a New Netherland Surface Transit bus. The blue and white bus resembled a sleek high-speed locomotive. Rufus put his car in reverse, pulled out, trying to square the block in time to keep the bus in sight. It felt unseasonably warm and the streets were busier than usual with pedestrians. He felt uncertain he'd be able to spot him get off even if he did catch up.

He maneuvered around several double-parked cars then caught sight of the bus. He raced up the boulevard for a few blocks before hitting a wall of traffic. The blue and white was still in sight. He sat thinking more about Wanda. She had left clues – not only what she'd told Rufus, but notes in her phone book, cryptic, but enough to give him a place to start. Next to Grunge's name she wrote his phone number, and directly under that written in light ink, as if that was an extra layer of secrecy, she wrote – *young girl.*

When he read that he couldn't help thinking of him and Wanda. Barely sixteen when they started up, which he knew no one would understand. The off again/on again relationship was tempestuous. No question in Rufus's mind, if it had ever come to light he would have been locked up for statutory rape, branded a child molester. Sometimes he wondered if he didn't help push her into the life, but usually he'd rationalize that kind of thought away. He'd think - nobody would believe how we felt about each other.

Grunge got off the bus about a mile from the precinct. He wore black trousers and a rust colored knit shirt that looked two sizes too small. His hair was curly, mostly gray, like Wanda had described, but people still called him Red. Well over six feet, he had the sloping shoulders of a prizefighter.

Rufus left his car in a no-standing zone with the blinkers on, and tailed him on foot. He didn't have to go far. The Rio, on Moses Brown, was known for short stays. He tried following him into the lobby, to see if he could spot which floor he went to, but a tall, burly security guard put his hand up. Rufus saw Grunge get on one of the three elevators about forty feet away. The metal arrow over the door moved clockwise, stopped at one of the upper floors, but the dial was too far to see which one.

"Can I help you?" the guard said.

"Guy just came in looked like someone I used to work with…black pants, reddish gray hair. Where'd he go?"

"No idea."

He got a little smile out of Rosie Grier, but that's all he got. Good chance the guard would tell Grunge. Rufus wasn't worried about that, he figured if the guard gave him up it would be the start of Grunge feeling the squeeze – and that might lead to him making a mistake, perhaps, or hopefully, a fatal one.

Chapter 28

"**If** not for me, Jimmy Pabon might still be alive."

That's what Rufus had told him. Jonah Koufax continued typing his brother's story on his laptop. He'd made an outline on a two-by-four foot piece of oak-tag using a dark green erasable marker - a chronology of his brother's life and career. Every once in a while Jonah put something about himself in parentheses, and sat looking at the busy looking outline thinking – is that what my life has been, parenthetical? He thought back to a visit he'd made to their mother, about the same time in 1980 when Rufus's troubles were beginning to percolate.

When he began in the business, the politicos treated Jonah Koufax like a retard. Not that they'd out and out say anything, quite the contrary, they usually were fawningly polite, would regularly offer to buy coffee or pick up a lunch tab. Broad smiles, so wide that he could probably identify most of them from their dental records.

But once he broke his first big story the atmosphere changed, likely thinking - *he isn't as stupid as he looks*.

Jonah got his first sniff that something was far less than kosher in New Netherland city hall, from an unexpected source, their mother. They had just moved her into a retirement community in Portsmouth. For a month she did nothing but complain.

The sprawling pale red brick building was one story, with aluminum frame windows bordered by green plastic shutters. The owners had gone to great expense to landscape the ten- acre tract, giving it a park-like appearance. Oak and maple trees provided shade to benches along the blacktop paths that wove around the property. Several large fountains spouting water from Greek mythological figures, sat strategically in the center of wide expanses of lush lawns and rhododendrons, all of it eventually paid for by Medicare, so the owners spared little expense.

"It's about time you showed up," she said.

"I was here a few days ago."

"When did a week become a few days? Your brother comes almost every day."

Oddly, Rufus was better than Jonah about those things, keeping in touch, sending birthday cards. They sat in a common room with forty or fifty comfortable looking chairs, none matching. Nobody in the administration of the home was too worried about interior design - it was all about profits. And everyone there, or their families, or Medicare, was paying four grand a month.

They looked out at the Sakonnet River, past a low-rise development of Section-eight housing. A dozen or so boats were sailing east on a starboard tack, the wind blowing hard from the southwest, colorful genoas puffed out past their bows. The choppy seas made the river a surging torrent of blue, green and white. The sky was a mixture of blue and white, some of the clouds almost in the shape of luffing sails.

"I'll try to come more often."

"You stuck me in this place, it's the least you could do."

"Okay, Mom."

Jonah noticed his mother's normally jet-black hair hadn't been colored for some time, several inches of gray showing. And the hair was thinner, and hadn't been brushed or sprayed that day. Before he'd wheeled her out to the common room, he went to her dresser, picked up her brush, light brown thistles in a silver metal frame, turned and reached out with it.

"Gey avek…what the hell do you think you're doing?"

"I'll brush your hair a little, Mom."

"When I'm in the box, that's when you can brush…so what are you working on?"

He turned back, placing the brush back on the dresser, feeling a flush or embarrassment…or was it rejection? He noticed the dresser top didn't have much clutter, just a white cotton runner with a floral design; a few perfume bottles, and two silver framed photos – one of him; and one of Rufus in his rookie uniform.

"Nothing too exciting, routine city hall stuff."

"You should keep a diary, someday you'll write a book."

"Maybe."

"When, darling, when I'm in the ground? Get your brother to talk - he'll give you plenty to write about."

"Good luck with that."

Back in the large octagon shaped room, they sipped tea from brown cardboard cups that he'd gotten from a cart attended by a blond teenager in a white and pink striped dress. Most of the staff was black, which didn't thrill their mother. He glanced at the big screen TV, at Katherine Hepburn being interviewed by Dick Cavett. Hepburn laughed at something he'd asked. The sound was on but from across the room he couldn't make out the words.

"So, you're looking for a story?"

"Always looking."

She motioned with her head, toward a silver haired man in his eighties, who looked tall even sitting in the chair.

"See the one in the maroon silk robe, in the wheel chair?"

"Yes."

"The real Godfather."

"What?"

"Everyone thinks its Patriarca. Phooey, a thug! Dangerous, yes, but this one, he handles the big things…talks to the boys in New York."

"And you know this how?"

Music came on and Jonah recognized the quiz show tune, but couldn't identify the program. Almost in unison the whole room turned toward the forty-inch plasma screen on the west wall.

"You think Sheldon kept me in a garage? Before he ran off with his little chippy I went places with him, met people, had fun. Your father was a bum, but a loveable one - and he knew everybody."

A private nurse was by the patrician looking man's side, a Hispanic girl in a white uniform, shiny black hair in a bun.

"Who is he?"

"Fred Santini."

"The restaurateur?"

"Listen to him, restaurateur!"

"What else does he do?"

"He fixes things."

"Fixes things?"

"I have to paint you a picture? Why do you think Councilman Ciano is here every other day?"

And that was his lead. He began interviewing everyone that knew either of them. A month later, his bombastic editor called him in. The office had lots of furniture and two huge desks piled with books, magazines, newspapers, and correspondence. The walls were festooned with photographs of every famous New England politician of the last fifty years, and four presidents, all the pictures signed. A permanent smell of stale cigar smoke permeated the room. His boss lit up a fresh one as he walked in.

"You know what this is?"

He pointed with his cigar at that day's edition of the New Netherland Tribune. Jonah couldn't see the photo under the headline, but he didn't have to, he wrote the story.

"A hell of a good story?"

"It's a god-damned lawsuit for defamation unless you've got your ducks in a row!"

"The facts have been double, even triple-checked."

He smiled at his boss, a kind of come-hither type smile he liked to use to irritate him. The boss threw him out of his office...but the story ran the next day:

City Councilman and Mob Associate Being Investigated

After that he received wide berth in the chambers of city hall. You might have thought
the opposite, that young Jonah Koufax would have been blackballed. But the thing is, those
Machiavellian bastards believed very much in the tenet – keep your friends close and your
enemies closer.

Chapter 29

June 17th, 2008, 9:00 A.M.

Glass covered bookcases lined three walls of the office of the Chief of Detectives, with police memorabilia on half the shelves and spread around the office: models of patrol cars, headquarters or precinct buildings; helicopters and boats with the NNPD logo and motto – *To Protect and Serve.* Along the tops of the shelves that reached about two feet below the ceiling were rows of police hats of all shapes and sizes, almost all navy blue, gathered from departments around the country and the world. Wood plaques of different shapes and sizes with metal badges and plates with engraved inscriptions hung in between the shelves and behind his desk, on either side of the window.

His desk sat in front of a large bay window that had a few houseplants on the sill. Three comfortable looking green leather chairs with dark brown wooden arms and legs, were evenly spaced in front of the desk. On the glass top was a small wooden sign with a piece of golden brass, letters engraved in two rows: Robert J. Badway, Chief of Detectives. Two empty wooden baskets and the sign were the only things atop the desk. McCoy waited in one of the chairs while Badway read a report. Finally he looked up.

"What do we have on the double, Bill?"

"Not a lot, Chief. We've gone by the numbers: repeated canvasses of the building, interviewed everyone that knew the victims. The crime lab has two people on it full time, looking for DNA, prints, fibers, anything. We're looking at Fortune's arrest activity. And we're looking at every number she called or got a call from…We're also checking on all her customers, seeing if they alibi out."

Brito had undertaken that task without being asked or told. In fact, that was one of the things that occasionally made Bill McCoy question himself. He knew he'd developed pretty good management skills, was considered a good leader by most of his people, but as a detective, he seldom felt as technically competent nor as skilled as Brito or Falco, or for that matter, as Rufus Koufax.

"Anything else?"

"There's a truck driver Fortune pinched. That's how he met the other victim. But we ran the guy down, he's got an ironclad alibi according to his employer, was taking a haul out to Phoenix, was close to three thousand miles away."

Chief Badway walked around his office, alternately peering out the window, which overlooked Narragansett Bay, and examining the trivia on his bookshelves. His white dress-shirt was starched and he wore a maroon necktie with blue diagonal stripes. McCoy looked at the chief's black wingtips, thinking he could see himself in the reflection well enough to shave. He noticed his black socks were sheer, like ladies lingerie. Badway's normally sallow complexion was darker than usual, like he'd used a sun lamp. He let out a cough that McCoy thought was for affect.

"Does the lab have *anything*?"

"Like I said Chief, they've got two people on it, and it's a little early to expect anything. We had B.C.I. vacuum the place, if there's any trace evidence they'll find it."

"What about Koufax?

McCoy was waiting for that. The bad blood between Rufus and his old nemesis Bob Badway was no secret - at least amongst older detectives in the department. McCoy grew up hearing the stories about his uncle Dave and his "Jew" partner. That was how some of the McCoy family referred to Rufus after Dave's disappearance. McCoy was ambivalent about Rufus, didn't care one way or the other about him being a Jew. Though he didn't care for the man personally, he had a nagging respect for him, always felt the department had given him a bum rap, or certainly never proved anything definitively against him.

"We grilled him pretty good the date of occurrence, and the Assistant A.G. assigned called him in to her office. Based on his being at the scene, and admitting to having a confrontation with Patrolman Fortune a few days before the murders, we locked him up on a material witness order. He made bail couple of days later."

"What the hell was he doing there?"

"He knew the female victim real well, claimed she had called him to complain about getting shaken down by Fortune."

He paused, not sure whether to tell the rest, anticipating a bombastic response. Something made him hold back. Badway told McCoy to call him with any important developments, emphasizing the word directly, told him to ignore the chain of command.

He didn't tell Badway about canvassing the bus route that ran up Moses Brown. It was Rufus who had told McCoy that he just happened to spot Grunge boarding the blue and white, adding that maybe Falco and Brito ought to do a canvass. And McCoy certainly wasn't going to mention Grunge. He knew by now that the sergeant had worked for Badway for a couple of years.

Though he knew a lot of his uncle's history with Rufus, he only knew a little about Badway's relationship, if you could call it that, with the both of them. But he didn't know the entire history of Badway's ascension to Chief Investigator for the Garabedian Commission.

Bill McCoy left Chief Badway's office wondering – "what the hell is going on, what is all this about?"

Riding down in the elevator he pulled out his cell to look for messages. He couldn't get a signal. When he reached the garage he walked past Falco and Brito, went half way up the ramp to the street. The phone lit up, indicating three voicemails. He pressed the icon and listened: one was from his wife, another from his mistress, the third from his captain. He put the first two out of his mind, instead worried about what he'd say to Captain Baldassare. He'd kept his boss informed about developments but now he felt in a bad position. He'd been seen entering the Chief's office by about a dozen people and by the time he got back to his command, so would word of the visit. And he had to consider Falco and Brito, who he couldn't easily ask or expect to keep his visit secret.

"How'd it go, Lieu?" Falco said.

"Fine."

"What was it about?"

"He wanted to know if we're making progress...we making progress?"

"We'll be on Channel Ten, on Crime stoppers, day after tomorrow," Brito said.

"Maybe we'll catch a break."

"We got something from the lab, too," Falco said.

"What?"

"DNA...not Fortune's and not the girl's, got it from one of the glasses we took from the sink - male DNA, with about nine alleles. It's enough that if we get a match it would be in the half million to one range."

"Meaning what?"

"Meaning if we identify a person with that profile only about six hundred people in the country could possibly be a match."

"Doesn't sound so definite," McCoy said.

"We used to get excited if we matched a blood type. Even if it's not one in a hundred million, it's still damn good, definitely enough for an A.G. to present at trial. And it would give us a name, someone to focus on...and there's more."

"What?"

"Same DNA came up in semen in Wanda's vagina."

"Where do we go with this? I don't think we've ever used DNA in a case yet."

"We get saliva swabs from anyone that was at the apartment, any known individuals. We should start with Koufax, also any cops or detectives at the crime scene...always a possibility of contamination." Falco said.

Brito reached in his pocket and pulled out a bunch of white and cellophane rappers, the size for a toothbrush, and waved them around.

"What are those?" McCoy said.

"Swabs, we should get started right away," Brito said.

"Do every swinging dick that showed up at the scene, anyone else you can think of."

Brito handed one to McCoy. He looked at Falco's smiling face in the rearview mirror. They knew this could be an important step in identifying the killer. Even though they'd had zero experience with DNA every detective in the department had some knowledge of it. The department's Legal Division was lobbying in Providence to get the legislature to pass a law that made it part of the arrest process to collect DNA, just like they did prints.

"What if there's no match?"

"Then we hope CODIS, the federal data base, gives us a match. Not too many entries in there yet, maybe a couple of million," Falco said.

"I don't get why we don't collect samples just like we do fingerprints," Brito said.

"How about politics, and bleeding heart liberal assholes?" McCoy said.

Falco laughed. McCoy told them to drop him at the precinct. Before he got out of the car he told them:

"Someone on a bus might have seen something. I want you at the bus stop on Moses Brown, the one around the corner from the crime scene by ten, tomorrow morning. Talk to the driver and passengers. Make sure you have plenty of the fliers that Major Case made up. Maybe we'll get lucky."

"Ten-four, boss," Falco said. "By the way, Captain Baldassare called, wanted an update on the case."

"Why'd he call you?"

McCoy felt conflicted. He didn't like the captain bypassing him and going directly to his men. Then again Badway just asked him to do the same thing. Also, he felt just as happy not to have to see or hear from Baldassare, relieved him of having to lie, at the very least by omission.

"Probably because I worked for him on patrol," Falco said.

"Let me know what he says," McCoy said.

He watched them drive away before he went to his car. It was early to start, but after the meeting with Badway he needed a drink. He drove the few blocks to Kennedy's, hoping Jimmy Lane was behind the stick.

The life of a squad commander was great in some ways: interesting work, lots of freedom, at times total autonomy. But sometimes it felt just the opposite: daily tedium, hemmed in by the bureaucracy, and by the sometimes, onerous demands of bosses up the chain of command. And now he had the chief up his rear end, asking him to do an end-run around his supervisors, and report directly to him. There had to be more to this. Rufus might be able to give him a clue about what Badway was thinking. But he sure as hell couldn't talk to him.

"What's that?"

"Coffee."

"I wanted coffee I would have ordered it."

"You need it, and I'm not serving you anymore."

"You shitting me, Jimmy?"

"No sir. You were wasted when I walked in, no way you leave without drinking two cups."

McCoy's face had a look of disbelief. His last walk to the head he felt himself stagger, but he'd feel better when he hit the fresh air. A few minute walk to the car and he'd be fine. For Christ's sake he thought, this is embarrassing. He drank the damned coffee.

He sat in the car for maybe an hour, finishing up the second cup - on Redwood Boulevard, for a hundred years one of the city's main north-south arteries. Most of the city's commercial buildings had storefronts at street level, with offices or residences up to thirty stories high. The signs over the stores and stenciled in the windows looked the same from a distance/ but close up, most of them weren't in English. McCoy stared south, to the buildings that housed most of the banks and brokerage companies. Dwarfing those were Pell Towers, two sixty-story glass and steel buildings, which were another target for the Al Qaeda September 11th terrorists. Only because of a sharp-eyed New Netherland Bridge and Airport Authority cop, who'd stopped two Saudi men trying to board a flight, were those building spared. Unfortunately the officer was blown up along with the terrorists and several passengers when the two suicide bombers detonated hand grenades. But the officer was credited with saving two hundred other lives.

McCoy's house in Tiverton was a brick cape on Beach 39th Street. He sat at the kitchen table with a can of Budweiser in front of him, eating a sandwich made with remnants of a turkey, and slathered with mayonnaise. The whole trip home he'd thought about Wanda Kelley and Johnny Fortune, wondering if Rufus Koufax might have killed one or both of them. He couldn't figure out what his motive might have been, but on a good day he behaved weirdly, and was often impossible to figure out. And since the murders his behavior was totally off the wall.

My good buddy, Bill McCoy thought. The yellow telephone rang. It hung on the kitchen wall next to the basement door, under a calendar that his wife had gotten from the bank, of a girl sitting reading. He jumped out of the wooden dining chair to quiet the phone, afraid it would wake her and the kids.

"McCoy."

"Falco, Lieu. You got a minute?"

"Hey, the Falcon. What's up?"

"We got a little problem with your friend, Koufax."

"My uncle's friend."

"Yeah, whatever. The thing is we can't seem to find him."

"Why you looking for him?"

"For the swab, to get his DNA. We checked his usual haunts, his apartment and office, nowhere in sight."

"So, you'll find him tomorrow. Call it a night."

"Okay boss."

"Brito with you?"

"Sitting right here, want to talk to him?"

"No, thas awright."

He knew he'd slurred his words, was sure Falco picked up on it.

"Goodnight."

"Goodnight, Lieu."

The Falcon? He wondered, what the hell did I call him that for? He'd never used the nickname, at least not sober. Now he thought about calling Marie. She never turned him down. He could tell Ann he got called in on a case, suspicious death or some shit like that. Nothing too big that it would make the papers, nothing she could question him about the next day.

He stood up and went to the wall phone. A message board hung next to it, a chintzy little thing with a border of pink and white flowers and a message in cursive – *Love spoken here.* Shit! Then he thought about the phone in the bedroom – it'd be stupid to call – too risky. For some reason he didn't think of his cell...he poured a drink.

Something had pissed him off when he first got home - two Big Wheels in the driveway. He'd told Ann about that, to keep the drive clear. He had had to get out and move them and when he did he told himself, fuck that! The manicured lawn, the house with the orange tile roof was a block from the ocean - all bought with a hefty down payment, courtesy of Uncle Dave.

When he went to him, hat in hand, embarrassed to ask, Uncle Dave did everything he could to make it easy. Just the toothy smile on his skinny, cratered face made Bill McCoy melt. He loved the man.

"What do you need?"

"I'm trying to put about a hundred g's together, so the nut doesn't choke me. Anything you could help out with - I'll pay you back when I can."

"I'll send you a check. Two conditions: first, it's strictly between us... and second, no paying back."

"No, Uncle Dave, I couldn't..."

He raised his hand, stopped him mid-sentence. They'd each had four cans of beer, sitting on the rear deck of their first house. The deck was stained dark mahogany, with a tan patio table and chairs and umbrella in one corner. The hood of the gas barbecue was up. Smoke billowed upwards, an occasional flame, half a dozen hotdogs getting burned. The kids were on the lawn running in and out of a five-foot round plastic pool, screaming at each other.

"Don't get noivous!"

Then the big toothy grin - he wished Dave was still around, so he could ask him what to do. Sometimes McCoy felt like a fraud, like a kid himself, playing some kind of game of cowboys and Indians. A far cry from Uncle Dave and from Rufus, the scumbag he couldn't help admiring. He felt a slight relief with Dave being gone, would never want to face him if he found out about his own indiscretions. And it had become pretty common knowledge in the Detective Bureau about him and Marie St. Pierre.

Two days later, Friday June 19th at 9:30 in the morning, McCoy was in his office. He'd been waiting for Rufus for over an hour. He glanced at his Timex every few minutes, wondering what the hell was keeping him. He thought about what he'd say to him, how much of a hard time he'd give him, maybe tell him – who the fuck are you to keep me waiting? You're a private dick who spent six years in the job and escaped by the skin of your teeth, so don't you fucking dare disrespect me by wandering in here whenever the hell you feel like it. Or something like that.

When not running down other leads or information Falco and Brito had spent the last three days searching for Rufus. It didn't diminish their suspicions. Maybe Rufus was on the scene so quickly because he was the one who'd killed Fortune. Everyone thought of him as fully capable of killing, but then again, what could get him angry or crazy enough to almost decapitate Wanda.

McCoy and his detectives thought the DNA found in the semen in and around Wanda's vagina would give the answer, wondering if it would match Rufus's.

Rufus had freely admitted he'd had words with Fortune, said he'd actually smacked him around not too long ago. That definitely made him a viable suspect for that one.

The lab found nothing else in the search of trace evidence – hairs, fibers, or other liquids. One odd thing that nagged at the detectives was the orchid found on Wanda's dresser - not one of the cheap ones you'd buy in a grocery – but a rare African variety. It didn't fit. What would a close to down and out hooker be doing with an expensive rare orchid?

Chapter 30

June 20th, 2008, 3:35 p.m.

Falco and Brito were especially agitated after they'd watched and then confronted Rufus's old friend and attorney Herb Reitman a day earlier. He had been inside Conte's for about three hours, holding court with two young prosecutors who the week before had convicted Reitman's client in an organized crime case. Outside the restaurant the three of them were shaking hands and hugging. The prosecutors wore suits from J.C. Penney's or Macys. Reitman's Italian custom-made jacket draped over his shoulders, looked like it cost a few grand.

"Mr. Reitman, talk to you a minute?" Falco said.

"Two of my favorite detectives, what can I do for you?"

They could tell he'd had drinks, probably an expensive French wine. His chubby face had a wide grin, his hands held palms up.

"Have you seen Rufus Koufax lately?" Brito said.

"What's this about?"

"Have you seen him?" Falco said.

"You know I'd do anything to help you guys, but I repeat, what's this about? It didn't take a detective to discern his sarcastic tone. They weren't about to get a thing out of him.

"If you see him, ask him to give us a call," Falco said.

"Hey, I'll be sure to do that. Let me see, it's Brito and …"

"Falco," Falco said.

Reitman was screwing with him He'd cross-examined Falco on several occasions during preliminary hearings, and spoken with him on at least several other occasions. The detectives looked at each other, turned and walked away.

They barely got half a block away when gunshots rang out. They looked around, then at each other. River Avenue was one of the busiest east-west cross streets in New Netherland, a main shopping corridor of the city, stores lining each side of the avenue, peddlers scattered along the sidewalks. People ran frantically, from the other side of the street.

"It must be from across the street," Falco said.

Screams came from the crush of people trying to cross River, several pointing towards a store. Falco stopped a Jamaican man wearing a colorful Dashiki and a red fez.

"What's going on?"

"In the jewelry exchange, mon - they've got guns!"

They didn't ask for a description and the peddler wasn't hanging around to chat.

"Go that way, I'll walk into the entrance," Brito said.

"Maybe we'd better wait for uniforms to get here."

They didn't wait. Falco and Brito then separated to go around either end of a dark blue Dodge van in front of the exchange. The low pitch of sirens off in the distance indicated a call had gone out. Everything was happening in hyper speed, with barely time to converse, let alone carefully plan their next steps. Brito moved easily, confidently, while Falco's head jerked up and down, side to side, as if he might be able to see something to help them decide what to do next. Usually not reticent to act, now he hesitated slightly. He wanted to thwart the robbery, but he also wanted to wait for more back up. Brito on the other hand was workman like, and decisive.

"Might be a civilian in trouble, we have to at least look."

"I'll cover you."

Brito passed in front of the van. He looked at the driver, immediately realizing this was the getaway vehicle. The driver - shaved head, tattoos on his face, and pierced nose and lips, lifted a Remington double-barreled off the seat, swung it toward the windshield, the tip of the barrel striking the glass, and cracking it. Simultaneously, six or seven shots rang out.

"Get down Vernon!"

Falco ran toward the van when he heard the shots, saw Brito frozen in place, his Glock 9 pointed at the empty space where the windshield had been. Out of the corner of his eye Falco saw two figures coming out the front entrance of the jewelry exchange.

"Vernon, the entrance!"

Brito swung his arms like he were on a turret. Falco took cover behind a peddler's stand full of bootleg CD's and DVD's – hardly any cover at all.

"Freeze mother-fuckers or you're dead!"

By the time the first uniforms arrived the other robbers, both dressed in black, were on their bellies, rear cuffed. Black ski masks still concealed their faces. Falco and Brito stood, each with a foot on a back. The tattooed man was dead, lying across the front seat of the van.

A day later, on June 21st at 8:17 A.M., McCoy looked up, as Rufus knocked on the door, kind of incessantly.

"Hey, Billy, sorry I'm late."

"Good morning Rufus. Want coffee?"

"No thanks, not after eleven in the morning; will keep me up half the night."

McCoy looked at Rufus for a long moment, a quizzical look, as if he had no idea about their appointment. He didn't. And eleven in the morning? It was like

Rufus's internal clock was off by a few hours. If that were all that was wrong it wouldn't have been so bad.

Falco and Brito had been looking for Rufus for days, so McCoy probably presumed they'd finally found him, told him to come in. He stared at him looking pissed, wondering where he'd been hiding.

Rufus had too many garments on for a warm June day, in fact too many for any day. His gray herringbone blazer looked too small over two shirts - a white polo underneath, an open collared white dress shirt over it.

"The eye's healed pretty good," McCoy said.

He touched the scab over his left eye. He wore a Tag chronograph he'd bought at Tourneau Corner two years ago. He'd done well on a case of a missing teenage girl who'd run away to Miami Beach with her boyfriend. It took Rufus about three days to find the kids and the parents were stunned, not only that he found them so quickly but also that he didn't milk the job.   "Took a while," Rufus said, touching the eye again.

McCoy sipped from a Styrofoam cup, looking at Rufus, his office more cluttered than usual, stacks of reports and departmental orders scattered in no apparent order. Half of a breakfast roll wrapped in white paper sat between some reports, and an unopened FedEx envelope under the telephone.

"Where the fuck have you been?"

"What do you mean?"

"Falco and Brito have been looking for you for three days."

"I heard...they did some job yesterday."

Rufus was unshaven, his hair unbrushed. He kept rubbing the top of his head trying to make the few hairs stay flat, while the tufts on both sides stood straight out. Combined with his bizarre outfit, he looked ready to be institutionalized.

"Yeah, they sure did...Brito might be up for the Medal of Honor," McCoy said.

He moved some reports around his desk, picked up the half a roll; asked Rufus if he wanted it. When he said no he threw it in the dark green wastebasket; then stood, walked to the door and closed it.

"The guys want to ask you some more questions, about why you were at Wanda's."

"Christ's sake, Billy I told them everything, what more can they ask?"

"Do me a favor, Rufus, just answer their questions."

A few minutes later Rufus stood just inside the door to the squad. Callaghan, the big clerical man, came over with a dark blue N.N.P.D. mug in gold lettering, filled with steaming coffee. He handed it to Rufus, who looked at the half-uniformed cop, in dungarees and a wrinkled navy blue uniform shirt with his badge attached. He nodded and said thanks. Callaghan returned to his desk and continued banging away on the Smith Corona.

McCoy was probably the last squad commander in the city to allow his clerical man to use a typewriter. Callaghan didn't know it, nor did anyone else, but McCoy or his wife retyped all the reports at home. He came in early enough each day to plug his thumb-drive into the side of his computer and download the reports. About once a week he thought about the wasted time, but he didn't have the heart to see Callaghan dumped somewhere where they might abuse him, or even worse, force him to retire.

A large man the color of molasses, with captain's bars on the shoulders of his uniform jacket, walked past Callaghan. He stopped to stare at Rufus for a moment, then walked into McCoy's office and closed the door. A loud voice, not McCoy's, could be heard from inside the closed room. A few minutes later the captain stormed out. Ten minutes Rufus walked to the office door and saw McCoy staring out the window.

"Bill?"

"Sorry, Rufus, forgot about you."

"Who was that?"

"Captain Fields."

He said that the captain had taken a lot of heat at the COMPSTAT meeting at headquarters. The Chief of Detectives questioned Fields, relentlessly according to the captain, about the lack of progress on the Officer Fortune murder.

"Why the hell is he asking him about it…he knows I'm on top of it…and anyway, it's really got nothing to do with patrol."

Rufus leaned against the wall next to the door and stared at McCoy. McCoy stared back, could tell Rufus felt sorry for him. He knew he'd never be half the cop his uncle was and he was sure Rufus felt the same way.

"It's all changed, Rufus, the precinct C.O. is supreme now, has control over all resources, even detectives. Meantime, I've got to answer to two kings, the Chief of D. and this ball-breaker."

McCoy paused a moment, rubbed his face and looked at Rufus, who was frowning like he was holding something back. He didn't know what Rufus was thinking - about Benny Fields, and Johnny Fortune and Wanda, and that she had described Fields as an older white man with gray hair.

"Anyway, a cop was murdered - he ought to be on my ass… Rufus, as long as you're here, we're gonna take a DNA sample."

"That's a first. Not sure I agree, just on G.P.'s."

"Don't be a ball-breaker, Rufus, it's a formality we're going through with everyone who was at the scene."

"Yeah?"

"Yeah… and don't make me look bad in front of my men. No big deal, so don't turn it into one. Everyone's got to give it, even me."

A few minutes later Falco walked in. He had no jacket on and his fifteen shot Glock 9 hung upside down under his left armpit, wedged into a tan holster. A matching holder on his belt held two black metal clips with fifteen rounds in each. In his right hand was a swab kit. His hair was combed back - celebrity style - and his skin looked like it'd just been shaved and lotioned by a barber.

"Ready?" he said.

"Do what you gotta do…by the way, good job yesterday"

Falco grinned as he removed the white stick from the package. A half-inch at one end was surrounded with tiny white tiny bristles.

"Open your mouth, I'm gonna rub this on your gums."

He opened his mouth wide and Falco stepped forward and rubbed the bristles on his gums, then replaced the stick in the package. He took out a pen and wrote on the paper part KOUFAX.

"Thanks."

"Anything for you guys."

Falco walked out and Rufus looked up at Bill McCoy, a big grin on his face. McCoy responded with a quizzical look.

"What's funny, Rufus?"

"Funny? Nothin, nothin funny?...so what's the story on Grunge? I'm hearing more funny things about him."

"Like what?" McCoy said.

"Like he's half a freak…goes for young broads."

"Long as they're eighteen…"

"I'm talking younger."

"Never heard that."

"Wanda said there were two guys Fortune brought around, Grunge and another guy."

"You never gave us a name on the other guy, not even a description."

"She never gave one."

He swallowed hard, then stood and pulled his pants higher on his waist. He leaned forward and looked at Bill McCoy as he began to read a report.

"Where'd this guy work before?"

"Who?"

"Grunge."

"Up in the North, and downtown for a while, at headquarters."

"Where?"

"Chief of D's personnel officer, an inside guy."

"What happened?"

"I don't know."

"You guys even question him yet?"

McCoy looked at him but didn't answer for a few seconds. Rufus sat back down, didn't say anything for a few minutes. Finally, McCoy answered.

"Of course we did. He admits to getting laid, almost laughed about it, but claimed he hadn't seen her in several days."

"So he puts himself there."

"Yeah, but not that day."

"So what happens now? She's a known hooker, so he gets a total walk?"

"No, of course not. I.A. will draw up "charges and specifications," for conduct unbecoming, associating with a prostitute, shit like that."

"And?"

"And what? That's all we've got right now."

"You got to be shitting me Billy. This guy's a bon a fide head case. I don't know how he ever got on the job. You guys have to look harder at him."

"How do you know that?" McCoy asked.

"What?"

"That he's a head case."

"Do your homework, Billy, should take you about ten minutes to find that out. I hope
you guys aren't over your heads with this case. This is no ghettoside case... a robbery gone bad, an informant who got exposed, a domestic, a drug rip off - the usual shit."

"Okay, Rufus. I get what your saying...thanks for coming by."

When he got up to leave they shook hands. Then Rufus did something rare for him, he stepped closer, gave McCoy a hug.

"Sure, kid. Hey, let's have lunch in a couple of days."

"Sure, I'll let you know."

Bill McCoy was having trouble hiding his suspicions. Now he noticed for the first time that Rufus had on two shirts. Then Rufus did something really weird. He sat back down in the office chair and began to untie his shoes, got done and unbuckled his belt, then opened his pants, seemed ready to pull them down.

"Rufus, what the fuck are you doing?"

He felt his face flush, didn't like talking to him like that. Rufus pulled his pants up, retied his shoes. What do I say to him now, McCoy thought?

"Rufus?"

He turned and stood in the doorway, a look of despair now on his face.

"Yeah?"

"Do you need a ride home?"

Chapter 31

On the morning of November 20th, 1980 Marvin Mazur stared ahead blankly after Rufus and Dave left his office. Technically, the Narcotics Division fell under the organizational umbrella of the Detective Bureau. He went out on a limb, knew he ought to make a notification. But he didn't trust the Chief. He felt that at the very least the chief would notify the federal authorities and try and pass the case off to them. His mantra was well known: big cases big problems, little cases little problems. Mazur paced his office for about ten minutes before picking up the phone.

Three hours later he walked out of the gleaming-white Greek revival building that was City Hall. A six and a half foot black steel picket fence surrounded lush gardens and lawns, which in turn encircled the city's nerve center. At the entrance, a guard booth had two uniformed cops on-duty around the clock. There were enough spaces in the arced one hundred and twenty foot driveway to allow for the Mayor's car and about a six of his closest aides. Four spaces were held for visitors. Occasionally the drive got crowded, especially if there were delivery trucks, or a press conference. When Marvin Mazur came out of City Hall his department car was blocked by a FedEx van.

"Smitty, how long is that guy going to be?" Mazur said.

"Long as it takes."

Patrolman John Smith barked the answer. He had been at City Hall through five different Mayoral administrations and didn't care much about rank. The white haired officer was well past mandatory retirement age but none of the chiefs in the department administration were able to get him to retire. In fact, none of them ever brought it up.

Captain Mazur sat in his car thinking about the meeting he'd just had. His college roommate, Deputy Mayor Cliff Schlossberg, was a front-runner to take over his boss's job in two years. He'd promised Mazur that if that happened he intended to make him the Police Commissioner. Mazur had trouble believing that, couldn't conceive of jumping over the heads of about two hundred higher-ranking bosses in the department, though he didn't mind fantasizing.

Now, two of his men were on a case that could go wrong in a hundred different ways…one of the few times he agreed with the chief about "big cases." Schlossberg had listened for a half an hour before he said anything.

"You want my opinion?"

"That's why I'm here."

"You won't like it."

The office on the second floor of City Hall was less than fifty feet from the Mayor's. The façade of the two hundred year old building had recently been sandblasted and painted; and the offices redecorated with a mixture of period pieces, all sitting on plush burgundy carpeting. Schlossberg had an accumulation of knickknacks on top of his desk and lining a couple of the bookshelves. Stuff mostly made in China: miniature replicas of police cars, taxis, fire engines; mouse-sized stuffed animals, a ten-inch high model of the Twin Towers, one of the Empire State Building, and one of the Pell Towers, that though close to half the size of the New York sky-scrapers in real life, towered over everything else on his shelf.

Mazur had a pipe in his hand. Schlossberg was a health nut and abhorred smoking, so it remained unlit. He stared through his thick glasses at his friend, not sure what to say. Schlossberg had busied himself with a two-inch thick report. Mazur espied the title – "Alternatives to Addressing Sanitation Concerns in the Event of a Department Job Action." The city's Sanitation workers had been threatening to strike for the past year and with Christmas approaching the union leadership had ratcheted up the rhetoric. Mazur wondered if he'd made a mistake coming to City Hall.

"I want to hear it."

"Marv, if I were you I'd get those guys off that fucking case. From what you told me it's got nothing but headaches written all over it and with that freaking Garabedian Commission looming over the department, who knows what might happen."

"But your boss appointed them."

"Yeah, but it wasn't supposed to get this serious. It's an election year and the big man wanted some window-dressing to make him look tough on corruption. This guy Romandella actually thinks it's for real."

Mazur took his time returning to headquarters. He wandered the streets of Newport's Fifth Ward, one of New Netherland's last neighborhoods that hadn't been torn down or gentrified, or ravaged by drugs and crime. He stopped in front of the Liffey Pub, debated having a drink. He rarely drank on duty, but was feeling enormous pressure, what he imagined a heart attack victim might feel just before the full-blown infarction.

Three men were arguing on the sidewalk, all clearly intoxicated, all in blue and white Patriots jerseys, and each holding a pint mug spilling beer onto the sidewalk. The one closest to him, a dark skinned Hispanic man, dropped his. The beer and broken glass splattered across the sidewalk, some hitting Mazur's suit pants and shoes.

"Hey, I'm sorry man. Can I buy you a drink?"

"Don't worry about it."

The man began to insist. Mazur walked around the corner, saw another place he'd been meaning to try for a long time, with a small red neon sign over the entrance that said *Teds*. He looked at his watch, shrugged his shoulders and pulled open the heavy oak door. A few minutes later he took a long sip of his Ketel One martini. A silver haired man sitting next to him, dressed in a black turtleneck sweater and navy peacoat, said something, trying to strike up a conversation. Mazur stared at him, unresponsive, wondering where Rufus and Dave were.

On November 22, 1980 at five-thirty in the evening, Chief Investigator Bob Badway was in Conte's sipping a Stoly martini. The bar was full of detectives and Assistant Attorney Generals who'd just finished work. A half dozen secretaries and stenographers were seated at the thirty-foot bar. Van Morrison's "Brown Eyed Girl," was playing, barely audible in the din. Exhaust fans at either end hummed loudly. Badway watched the 25-inch TV hung from the ceiling at one end. Howard Cossell was somewhere on Bourbon Street talking about the fight between Duran and Leonard later that night. Badway couldn't hear but he kept watching.

Sandra Cruz walked in and several conversations stopped. A few male patrons said "Hi Sandy," talking over each other. She smiled at all of them then walked to the middle of the bar. Badway got up and slid his stool toward her. He squeezed next to her.

"Glad you made it."

"I shouldn't be here with you."

"Why is that?"

He ordered another martini from Knobby Walsh. The old prize fighter did a dance behind the bar, grabbing the shaker and bottle of Stoly's almost in one motion, filling it with ice and pouring the vodka, then splashing in a sniff of Vermouth. He shook it for half a minute, staring up at Cossell.

"Like maybe a thousand reasons," she said. "You're about twenty years older than me, and you're married…and maybe because we work together and our boss already said something."

"Romandella?"

"Who else?"

Badway was well aware of the age difference but felt sure she'd slept around, was certainly no virgin. He knew for a fact that she'd dated a deputy A.G. last year. That had raised a lot of eyebrows when things became hot and public.

"What'd he say?"

"That you had a reputation."

"You believe that shit?"

"Vodka Martini for the young lady," Knobby said.

He gave Badway a hard stare before taking a ten off the bar and turning to the register to make change. The cash register was brass colored with black keys, with white lettering and numerals. $5.50 popped up along the top in large black and white numerals. He placed the ten in a drawer, made change, turned and shoved it in the pile in front of Badway.

"Thanks, Knobby."

The bartender's blue eyes were cold. His muscled forearms had veins that looked like bluish ropes covered by wisps of white hair. He leaned on the bar an extra second or two then turned and walked away, to listen to an order from a drunken lawyer that, from the look on his face, he seemed to like even less than he did Badway. Sandy Cruz lifted the frosty cone-shaped glass carefully, and sipped, put it down, a smudge of red on the rim.

"Nice," she said.

"So what'd you say?"

She gave him a look. Badway's head swiveled while he spoke, as if he were expecting someone else or expecting something to happen. He had a nervous habit of constantly examining his surroundings, an exaggeration of the borderline paranoia most cops had. You could often pick out the men facing the door in restaurants.

"To Romandella?"

"Yeah."

"I told him thank you, but I could take care of my own self."

"You sound confident."

"You don't think I can?"

"We'll find out."

"Yes, we will," she said, taking a long sip, smiling afterwards.

Twenty minutes later, her martini was half gone. Badway waved to Knobby for another, too preoccupied to realize his pager was going off. The small gray plastic box was buried in the folds of his shirt that covered his spare tire, which seemed to grow larger every month.

Four hours later he finally realized Amoroso was trying to reach him. When they spoke he found out their team had observed Rufus meeting with a Spanish kid. They got a plate number but it came back to a leasing company, and they didn't stop the car to identify him.

"Why didn't you call earlier?" Badway said.

"I tried…you never answered the page."

"Spot him again make sure you identify him. That's exactly what we're looking for. In case this Marcel character doesn't come through for us, we'll need to go to plan "B"."

"Sorry we let it go."

"Me too."

Badway lay down next to Sandy Cruz. The mattress squeaked. Her perfume mixed weirdly with the smell of the cheap hotel room. A reproduction of a nautical scene hung on the wall over the headboard, and a worn-looking rattan table and dresser on the dirty linoleum floor. She'd fallen asleep, the most he got from his shoving and feeling - a slight moan. He rolled her over and forced his way in.

Chapter 32

June 23rd, 2008, 10:32 a.m.

Two men stood in the rain looking lost, apparently waiting for the New Netherland Surface Transit bus that was late, had been due at 10:20 a.m. Both were dressed in suits and ties and if not for the pounding rain they would have looked like detectives. Now they just looked like large drowned rats.

Josh Rosenblatt, unusually tall and slim, in a suit that looked two sizes too big, wore a yellow oxford shirt and loosely tied red tie. Despite holding an umbrella, he looked almost as wet as his partner, who had no hat or umbrella. Mo Maldonado was built close to the ground, and though he looked beyond drenched he didn't seem to care.

Major Case Squad's lieutenant had sent them to that corner. Their particular assignment this day was to conduct a canvass on the #12 bus that went south to north along Moses Brown Boulevard and ended at Aaron Lopez Way – the street in the north part of the city named after the eighteenth century merchant and slaver, one of the first Sephardic Jews to emigrate to New Netherland.

Bill McCoy had told Falco and Brito to join them, had said they needed to try and come up with another witness. Three weeks since the murders, still with no line on the killer, and no witness of any value. Cecelia Brown and the bongo drummer, Melendez, so far had been unwilling to make a positive ID.

The Major case men were in line behind eight other people. The one closest to them was a round medium skinned black man dressed in hip-hop clothes, wearing a lot of gold. His red umbrella kept hitting Rosenblatt in the shoulder. Behind the wannabe "rapper," were three high school aged girls, and behind them two women and two men all dressed for business. Most had umbrellas which made the relatively small group stretch to the curb on the next corner.

"What if they don't show?" Rosenblatt said.

"We do the canvass," Maldonado said.

"Shouldn't we wait?"

The dark-skinned Maldonado didn't bother answering. He'd been in Major Case for ten years and had a solid reputation, knew the streets. Rosenblatt had four years on the job and had just come to the unit from patrol, a contract from a chief who did a favor for an old friend. No one went out of the way to welcome him, Maldonado no exception.

The blue and white bus appeared out of the driving rain, the detectives ready to flag it down. No need, the driver stopped to discharge two passengers and pick up the waiting line. A dimly lit sign on the side of the bus advertised a recruiting drive for the New Netherland Fire Department, showing three firemen - one white one black and one Hispanic - dressed in navy blue uniforms and white helmets with the department logo.

Rosenblatt and Maldonado boarded the bus, stopped short when they saw Falco and Brito questioning passengers. They all got off at the last stop. Rosenblatt opened his wooden handled black umbrella. Falco and Brito opened theirs and the four detectives stood looking at each other, only Maldonado getting soaked.

"What are you guys doing?" he said.

"The canvass," Falco said.

"You got to be shitting me," Maldonado said. "We were standing out there half an hour waiting for you."

"Didn't you get our message?" Brito said.

"What message?"

"To meet at the start of the route. We've questioned every passenger that got on, so far nothing. You get anything at the bus stop?"

Falco, half grinning and half sneering, looked at Rosenblatt. Brito had been trying to get into Major Case for two years. When word got out that a guy off patrol had gotten one of the rare openings, it didn't sit well with a lot of detectives throughout the Bureau.

"No," Rosenblatt said.

"Why don't we go back to the precinct?" Falco said.

He'd ignored Rosenblatt turning to Maldonado. They all walked a half block on Aaron Lopez Way, got into Brito's car then drove to Newport West precinct, the only sound the squawk of the police radio.

Upstairs, Falco and Brito removed their raincoats and leaned their umbrellas in a corner near the door to the squad. They walked to the back of the squad room, past four detectives sitting at their desks, two on the phone and one typing a report. The other one, an unusually tall, heavy man about forty years of age, with a toothy grin, was doing a crossword. He stared at the four walking to the back, said to Maldonado "What the fuck happened to you?"

Maldonado ignored him. They got coffees then sat down in the interview room. The mood quickly changed.

"You mother-fuckers listen to me. You think you're going to fuck with us and get away with it you making a big fucking mistake. We was sent here to help you and if you not going to accept that then you better tell your boss to let the Chief of D know, cause I'm sure as shit going to let our boss know."

"Calm down, Mo. You got it wrong, we weren't fucking with you," Falco said.

"The fuck you weren't."

"Let's start over guys. We got a dead cop and there's no room for this bullshit. We were wrong…and it won't happen again," Brito said. "We've got a case to work."

Brito glared at his partner. Falco turned red, stood up knocking his chair over and left the room. Rosenblatt bent to pick it up but Maldonado put his arm out to stop him. He extended his arm to Brito and they shook hands.

Later, he and Falco briefed McCoy on the canvass.

"How'd it go?"

"We didn't find any witnesses," Brito said.

"Going to try it again?"

"We'll give it a few more tries…might do better now that the weather's changing."

Falco was uncharacteristically quiet. He and Brito hadn't spoken since the earlier exchange with the Major Case men.

"Get along okay with the Major Case guys?"

"No problem at all," Brito said.

McCoy's phone rang. He picked up the receiver, held it to his ear, waved a sign of dismissal at Brito and Falco.

The sun had come out but the streets were still wet and cars passing on Moses Brown sprayed pedestrians walking near the curb. Falco and Brito stood under the awning of a CVS, as if expecting more rain. Falco had taken his umbrella when they left the precinct.

"You didn't back me up, Vern."

"Back up your bullshit antics? No, I didn't…and don't expect me to. You're a good detective, Falco, but sometimes your head's in your ass. What did you think you were accomplishing? You were supposed to notify those guys, not leave them out in the rain."

"Fuck them - especially the Jew kid. Who the fuck is he to get your spot?"

"Don't worry about my spot, and what the fuck do you care anyway?"

"It's just not right, that's all."

Brito didn't say anything else, but clearly wasn't happy with Falco's reference to Rosenblatt. He wondered if he ever referred to him as a nigger. Then he forgot about it. He'd been around too long to worry about those things. As long as nothing was said to his face or in his presence he didn't care. They'd been in a deadly shooting three days ago and were entitled to at least two days off, but Falco didn't hesitate when Brito suggested they forgo that and keep working the case.

"We have to get Koufax back in. He's the key to this. He's the last one to see either of them alive, so it seems pretty likely he either knows more than he's saying…or maybe he's our murderer," Falco said.

Chapter 33

November 29, 1980, 2:00 p.m.

Marcel Petit smoked one cigarette after another waiting outside the Garabedian Commission office, the first time he'd been there since he called a couple of weeks earlier. He wore a black wool overcoat over his gray sharkskin suit, with a pink dress shirt open at the collar. The Commission offices were in a modern downtown eighteen-story glass and steel structure. He watched the entrance for twenty minutes before he went in. He had suggested to Chief Investigator Badway that they meet in a neutral place. Badway laughed, told him not to worry, the building had no police, in fact, no governmental agencies of any kind. He tried to impress the need for absolute secrecy but Badway seemed to ignore him.

"Yes, Mr. Petit, we've been expecting you. Please have a seat," Sandy Cruz said.

"Thank you."

He smiled politely, took a seat in the waiting room, picked up a copy of *Cosmopolitan* off the glass-topped coffee table and crossed his legs. Sandy Cruz opened the door to the rest of the suite, smiling as she glanced his way, before disappearing inside. Seething, he wondered if he'd made a mistake. Why does she know my name, and who is the "we," expecting me?

He thumbed through the magazine, stopped at an advertisement for perfume, looking at the face of a raven-haired model. When Sandy Cruz returned he glanced at her, and then back at the magazine, then back at her.

"Mr. Badway will see you now."

"Merci."

He placed the magazine in front of her, opened to the perfume ad, smiling warmly.

"I think you have another career, mademoiselle."

She smiled back, looking flushed, as he walked toward the door and met Bob Badway.

"This way," Badway said.

At the Commission conference room table were Vin Romandella and his two deputies. Now there are five people I have to worry about divulging my identity, Petit thought.

"Gentlemen, this is Mr. Petit. Mr. Petit, this is Vin Romandella, Carl Furillo, and Harris Wilson."

"Gentlemen," Petit said.

"Mr. Petit, Sergeant Badway says that you can deliver some corrupt policemen to us," Romandella said.

"I'm confident that I can be of assistance."

"Tell us about yourself. You're a French national and some sort of businessman?" Romandella said.

"Yes, a businessman. I specialize in facilitating imports and exports to and from my country… what you might call a "problem-shooter.""

Petit reached into his inside jacket pocket and removed a blue folder that held his passport. He slid it across to Romandella.

"A trouble-shooter," Wilson said.

"Yes, exactly, a trouble-shooter," Petit said.

"And you're French?" Romandella said.

"Corsican, but Oui, I believe that makes me French."

"Have you ever been convicted of a crime, or the subject of an investigation?" Wilson said.

"No, never convicted of anything. Subject of inquiries? That is impossible to say. In my world, I've met many, how would you say, colorful characters. Could that have caused someone to be interested in me? But of course…it is possible."

"Tell us how you think you could help us," Romandella said.

Petit explained that he'd been successful in Europe as an agent for different police agencies. They'd give him targets and he'd get the needed evidence.

For close to an hour Badway laid out a plan. Petit weighed in from time to time with suggestions. All three lawyers took notes, which made Petit feel more comfortable. He surmised it likely meant the room wasn't wired for sound or video. Still, he scanned the visible surfaces, casually going from floor to ceiling, looking for pinholes, examining the fixtures, still concentrating on the conversation while he did this, especially while Badway spoke. He felt uncertain about the policeman. Was he some type of chief, as he had introduced himself initially, or was he a mere sergeant, as the lawyer Romandella referred to him? No matter, he told himself, he'd use these men if necessary, in the event he ran into trouble with the American authorities.

"Tell us why you're doing this," Carl Furillo said.

"I would expect there'd be a reward, or finder's fee offered. For that and because I read of the establishment of your Commission and thought to myself, these must be most honorable people, the kind I would like to make an acquaintance with and help."

Petit told them that in his undercover work for European agencies he had travelled the world on assignments. He had plenty of experience with corrupt policemen and would have no trouble meeting and ensnaring one or more of them in New Netherland. All the Commission had to do was identify a likely target and he'd handle the rest.

"We would need tapes," Romandella said.

"Yes, of course. I will even provide my own equipment."

"No, we'll provide the equipment. Every time you record a conversation we want you to turn the tape over to Badway or one of his men, then they'll give you a fresh one."

"That is not my normal way of operating, but whatever works best for you."

"The tapes are never to be altered or even listened to. Once a meeting is over we want you to go to the pre-arranged location and turn the machine off. Then you'll turn the evidence over to Badway or one of his men," Romandella said.

"What is my code name?"

"Pick one," Badway said.

The other men at the table all looked at Badway. Petit saw this and hesitated before answering. He noticed that the man named Wilson had his hands folded together, was staring at his feet. Furillo stared at Badway. Four Styrofoam coffee cups were on the table along with a cardboard box containing pastries that no one had touched. A single yellow legal pad was in front of each of the lawyers. Furillo was making the most notes.

"Yes, why don't you do that," Romandella said.

"Very well. Refer to me as Chacal - in English is the Jackal."

Romandella frowned but didn't object. Badway stood up and walked to the windows that looked out toward Pell Justice. He seemed to be staring at something in the street. Then he told Petit about Rufus Koufax and Dave McCoy. The lawyers looked on but didn't interrupt as Badway gave him some background.

Before Petit left he lingered for a moment, shaking Sandy Cruz's hand, bowing politely. He rode the elevators to the lobby, went to the newsstand and bought a copy of *the Tribune*. The covering of snow on the sidewalks caused the streets to glisten, black and wet. He frowned when he felt the seep through his brown designer loafers, but still took up a position across the street, to wait for Miss Cruz to leave the building.

Several days later, on November 26th, 1980 Marcel Petit met Pam Stith and bedded her. He thought right away that she could be the right person to lure the policemen, Koufax and McCoy, into a trap. It would merely take some coordinating with Badway and his people to find out when and where the detectives would be working.

Petit also had successfully lured Sandy Cruz up to his room and was confident the young woman would be a help to him later on, though he wasn't sure exactly how. He showered, thinking about the beautiful black addict, when the telephone rang. He stepped out of the glass stall and grabbed one of the thick white towels with the Netherland Plaza logo, and wrapped himself in it. He walked across the plush carpet.

"Allo."

"This is Badway. Meet me in the lobby in half an hour."

"Half an hour, oui."

Petit stared at the phone. What an imbecile, he thought. Again he thought - I hope I
have not made a mistake throwing in with this Garabedian Commission.

He reminded himself that the machinations he went through with the Commission were merely insurance, that he had bigger things to worry about. In a certain way it felt like playing with children. The real challenge would soon happen in New York, where he would meet American mafia representatives - who seemed anxious to cement a new arrangement for the delivery of monthly shipments of heroin.

He'd become aware through his uncle, about a chasm between the Italian Mafia and their American born cousins. Chiappe positioned himself and was poised to take over much of the supply chain, which would in turn make Petit a very wealthy man. Petit fantasized about acquiring enough wealth to retire from the sordid smuggling business, to his home on the Spanish coast.

The policemen, McCoy and Koufax, no doubt thought they'd found a great informant in Pam Stith. Petit smiled every time he thought of how easy it was going, how simple it would be to lure and trap them.

Chapter 34

Tuesday June 24, 2008, 9:05 a.m.

Jonah Koufax's reputation sometimes got him into places other reporters rarely got to see and close to people who wouldn't give less accomplished newsmen the time of day. Buster Alito was doing life in the A.C.I., the Adult Correctional Institution, Rhode Island's state prison. He had been offered WITSEC, the Witness Protection Program, but had laughed in the faces of the Assistant United States Attorney and the F.B.I. agent who made the offer. He told Jonah they threatened him with everything from solitary to sending him to a joint in Alaska.

Herb Reitman had negotiated a deal with the A.G.'s Office and the U.S. Attorney. In exchange for Buster's testimony in thirteen murder cases, they'd let him plead to all the charges, and guarantee he'd do his time in the state facility. The agents and prosecutors thought Buster was signing his own death warrant. They didn't know that Reitman had brokered a deal with Raymond Patriarca first, promised him that Buster wouldn't testify against him or anyone else in "the family." Patriarca just nodded. Later he put the word out that Buster was under his protection – even better than WITSEC.

Two guards escorted him to Alito's two reconstructed cells. One was furnished in late twentieth century Italian, with a small gold brocade couch; and a stove, a refrigerator and microwave and a tiny round table and two chairs. The second cell had a bed with a heavy purple comforter, a TV, and stereo.

A pot with tomato sauce simmered on the stove, Italian sausage grilling in a pan next to it. Albert, the young tall black man with a slim muscular build was doing the cooking.

Jonah spent two hours getting all the information he could from Alito. Just before leaving he asked Albert when he'd be getting out. Buster had his arm around him and laughed, told Jonah they were both lifers. They seem happy, Jonah thought.

At home he poured a glass of merlot, sat at his antique cane desk, turned on the desk lamp and got the recorder ready. He looked out the window at the reflections of lights glistening on the river. He put the glass to his lips and sipped, kept the wine in his mouth for a few seconds before swallowing. Then he listened to the tape he'd made earlier of Joseph "Buster" Alito's version of the story. Then he read his notes from his brother's interviews. Then he began typing.

"Big man" was his code name. The other guy was "Corn," short for corned beef. Alito often called cops "corned beef and cabbage guys."

"What do you need?"

"Some guys are following me. Look into it, would ya?"

"You sure?"

"I think so. It's freaking annoying, you know what I mean? Cause all I do is go to work, run my bar, and come home, be with my family. You know what I'm saying?"

"I'll look into it."

"Hey, cump, thanks a lot. See if it's those freaking S.I.S. guys. I think they got the wrong idea about me, you know what I mean? I appreciate it. Come around, you get a drink on me, you hear?"

"Yes."

The call would cost him a lot more than a drink. If his source said no one was on him, it would cost a grand just for the effort. A few times he'd paid ten g's, to get someone off his tail. But the expense was well worth it. And every Christmas, for thirty years a fat envelope found its way into the cop's hands.

Alito walked back to the window, pulled the curtain back and waved, in case somebody was watching. Then he grabbed his crotch and shook it.

Tuesday had been a long day - a trip to the A.C.I., hours with Alito and his boyfriend, then back to the city for a meeting with his editor. He felt unusually fatigued.

Jonah was worried. He hadn't heard from in a long while. He conjured up all sorts of bad scenarios. He calmed himself by putting on a CD of the Boston Pops playing Hayden, and by pouring a generous scotch and planting himself on his terrace sofa, where he proceeded to fall asleep. Before he fell off his last thought, or really visualization, was of Rufus firing his gun.

Chapter 35

June 27th, 2008, 8:20 a.m.

Billy McCoy held the phone to his ear, mostly listening, a couple of times raising his right hand with his index finger extended. Brito motioned, asking in mime if he wanted them to leave. He shook his head no. A copy of the New Netherland Tribune lay opened on top of his desk. A blue and white Athena paper cup with a plastic lid was in his left hand. A darkly toasted sesame bagel, with cream cheese oozing out, sat on a sheet of waxed paper on top of some reports. McCoy shoved it toward them and then pointed. Both shook their heads no.

A horn blasted from somewhere up the street, and a radio car whelped its siren a couple of times. McCoy stood and turned to close the dark green casement window. He sat back down, now shaking his head at them.

"Listen, I've gotta go, I've got people in my office…yes, I understand…no, I won't forget…yes, I do…okay, goodbye."

He crashed the phone into its cradle, shook his head once more, removed the lid from the coffee and took a sip.

"God damned shit's lukewarm."

Brito and Falco looked at each other then at the cup. Their normally fastidious lieutenant, who looked like it'd been a couple of days since he'd shaved. He had stains on his shirt, and his pants looked like they'd been on the closet floor.

"Want us to come back, lieu?" Brito asked.

"No, I'm good."

He'd been sleeping in the precinct dormitory for several nights, since his wife had given him an ultimatum. She'd found Marie St. Pierre's phone number on the last cell phone bill. After ruminating over it for several days, wondering how she could find out who, the frequently dialed number was listed to, she got her courage up and called. Detective St. Pierre answered the way she always did – "St. Pierre!" Ann McCoy hung up but Marie recognized the number, and immediately called Bill McCoy. She told him everything she'd done, then told him to pack his bags.

But he didn't get the reception he'd expected from the beautiful and sexually skilled Detective St. Pierre, ergo, he ended up living like a skell in the precinct dormitory. Even though he tried to keep it secret, Brito and Falco had figured it out. They knew of the "secret" affair with Marie St. Pierre, as did most of their co-workers.

"So let me get this straight – you want to run two more lineups, one with Grunge and another with Rufus."

"Yes," Falco said.

"You agree, Vern?"

"Yes...I guess so."

"And the A.G.'s Office?"

"Who gives a shit, lieu? We'll put the case together and give them the package. That Jurgenson broad is on the phone every day asking for updates, but she's got thirty other cases so it's not too hard to fend her off," Falco said.

"And you like this witness...what's the kid's name, Rodriguez?"

"Melendez...we won't know till he's in front of the glass again, but Vern did a good job with him."

"You still like Rufus for this?"

"Half like," Brito, said. "Could be the other guy...or anyone else. But the M.E. found Rufus's semen in her vagina - a good DNA profile."

"But he's been banging her for years."

"You running interference for him, boss?" Falco said.

"What?"

"Don't get pissed, Lieu...but it's well known you guys go way back."

Brito's brown skin turned more reddish. McCoy was out of his chair standing over Falco, his right index finger inches away from his chest. Falco's mouth was contorted into a disgusted expression, as if he might say – you gonna hit me? But he didn't say anything.

"Get out of my office!"

Faclo and Brito both stood up.

"Vern, stay here, I want to talk to you."

Ten minutes later Brito asked Falco to meet him outside the station house. It was a thick muggy day, heavy rains forecast, and it felt like the heavens might open any second. They stood opposite the entrance, in front of the precinct parking lot.

"You're a good detective, Al, but sometimes you behave like a first-class asshole."

"Is that right?"

"That's right. You'll be lucky if the lieutenant doesn't look to have you transferred."

"Fuck him. He won't do shit. The fucking guy's been carrying on behind his wife's back and he's gonna have me transferred? I'll drop a dime on him, he tries anything like that."

Brito grabbed Falco's wrist and when he tried to wrest free he twisted outwards. He'd used the old wrist lock a hundred times on recalcitrant prisoners, but never on another cop. Falco let out a gasp, trying to stifle a scream.

"You do that, I'll be looking for you."

Brito walked to the station house, leaving Falco holding his right wrist with his left hand. A cop named Geraghty walked over and asked if everything was okay.

"Mind your own fucking business, Kevin," Falco said.

The lanky officer walked away shaking his head.

Chapter 36

June 28th, 2008, 9:40 a.m.

Rufus got the word from his brother that McCoy wanted to see him again. Though he'd had little trouble avoiding Falco and Brito, he found it difficult turning down Billy McCoy; as if it were an act of disloyalty to Dave. So he found himself again in the lieutenant's office, rambling on about 1980, which was a lot easier than remembering the events of yesterday. In the last week he'd been keeping meticulous notes, which he read every morning, along with his to-do lists. That was how he held it together…or at least he thought he did.

Assistant Attorney General Francine Jurgenson called while Rufus was sitting in front of McCoy. She told Bill McCoy to place him under arrest. McCoy asked if he could call back in a few minutes, hung up before she answered. He excused himself, told Rufus he'd be right back.

Falco and Brito had arrived, were talking to a woman dressed in a black and orange dashiki. It had something to do with a missing child, but it turned out her baby was twenty-three years old. McCoy asked them to see him in his office afterwards.

When he walked back in, Rufus was snoring, his head cocked to the left side, drool making its way down his jaw, onto his shirt. A few minutes later Falco appeared in the doorway and McCoy waved for him to wait outside. He stepped out again without waking Rufus.

"What was that?" McCoy asked.

"Her son's got emotional problems, hasn't been home for a few days," Brito said.

"Who doesn't," Falco said.

Said like an afterthought, which would have meant nothing if he hadn't stared right at his lieutenant when he said it.

"I've got to call Jurgenson back…she just called, said to place Rufus under arrest.""

"Okay!" Falco said.

"Not so fast. I've got to talk to her, find out on what basis…look at the poor bastard in there, doesn't look like he could fight his way out of a paper bag, let alone kill someone."

McCoy made the call, from an extension on the other side of the squad room. A few minutes later he hung up and walked toward Brito and Falco, a frown on his face, nodding yes.

Falco grabbed Rufus by the shoulder of his black and gray hounds-tooth sport coat – the exact kind Falco was wearing -and helped him up. He twisted one arm behind his back, placed one cuff on, then did the same with the other. Rufus kept blinking, twisting his head around, looking from one to the other; not saying a word.

"Rufus, you're under arrest for the murders of Wanda Kelley and John Fortune. You have a right to remain silent. If you give up the right…" Falco said, before he got cut off.

"I know my rights, shmendrik!"

Then Falco said to no one in particular, "I'll bring him downstairs…get him printed on the live-scan."

An hour later, McCoy entered the interview room. He had on light brown slacks and a white dress shirt with the top button open and no tie. His dark brown sport jacket was draped over his right arm, as if he were going somewhere. He must have picked up his dry cleaning that morning, because except for forgetting to shave, he looked more like himself.

"Stand up, Rufus, I'll take the cuffs off."

"About time. What's Falco's problem…he think I'll slither through the bars?"

"I'll speak to him."

"Prick needs more than talk."

"You ready to talk to me?"

"What is this, good guy – bad guy? Your uncle and me practically invented that."

"This has gone on long enough, Rufus." McCoy paused for what seemed like a day to Rufus. "You killed Wanda and Johnny Fortune, I know it and you know it - time to give it up."

Rufus felt droplets form on his skull and forehead. He'd just gotten his hair cut short, eschewing the come-over he'd had for years. He had on a light blue v-neck cotton sweater and gray lightweight wool trousers, with his hound's-tooth jacket and cordovan shoes. Falco had removed the laces earlier. Now he sat staring down, wondering what was next, hoping they'd called Reitman like he'd asked. He looked at McCoy.

"You got to be crazy Billy. Anyway, you think if I did it, you could get me to give it up?"

He had half a grin on his face, kept staring at McCoy, who stared back.

Five hours later they both looked worn. They took bathroom breaks every hour or two, and twice, McCoy left for five minutes; Rufus guessing to tell Francine Jurgenson this was going to take a while.

"Rufus, let's forget Wanda and Fortune for now. Tell me about the Corsican connection case. What happened that made you leave the job?"

"Uncle Dave must have told you?"

"He told me the public story. Tell me what really happened."

He couldn't help grinning. He thought of telling him to see Jonah, that he knew the whole story.

"It's all about Alito."

"Buster Alito?"

"It's all connected. You know - six degrees of separation, except it's only two or three here in the Ocean State."

McCoy watched him brushing the top of his head, as if there were hairs there.

"Bad things began to happen. We had this surveillance going, from information we were getting from our new C.I., and at the same time I'm trying to get Jimmy Pabon to give up something on Alito…then his scumbag friend goes and kills two niggers, excuse me, African Americans."

"It took the dicks a while to identify Jimmy's pal Wilfredo Colon in the bodega murders. By the way, that case broke because of Brito."

"What was the story with the informant?"

"I'll get to that…So Colon and Jimmy got themselves into a jackpot. Colon? Stone psycho - bad as they come."

He asked for more coffee and something to eat. McCoy returned twenty minutes later with a brown paper bag with two bagels wrapped in foil and four cups of coffee. Rufus was thinking of different things, about what he should say, what he shouldn't. Like about him and Pam. Part of him wanted to tell that and another part was a little embarrassed. Getting involved with an informant was strictly bush league. But would he do it again? In a heartbeat he told himself. He'd never had a woman like her before that, or since. Blah, blah, blah... what the fuck's it all mean? Does he tell him or not? And does he tell Billy McCoy that he's a nihilist, had convinced himself of that a long time ago. That it's all bullshit, that nothing really matters. But if that's true why not tell him the whole damned thing, right? And why the hell is he so hell-bent on catching Wanda's killer if nothing matters?

Anyway, he's going to see Pam later, like they'd arranged? Pam? No, the other one. He shoved his hands in his pockets, looking for a note, a scrap of paper, something to help him…

Billy McCoy sipped coffee, looking at him, listening to him talk, as if he, Rufus, were alone in the room.

"You okay, Rufus?"

"Am I okay? What do you think? Am I okay?"

"Let's get back to the story -what happened next?"

"I turned Buster Alito."

"What?"

"That's right."

"How?"

"Easy. We knew we were being followed, your uncle verified that. But we thought it was Internal Affairs - which wasn't such a big deal to us. We always figured that since we weren't on the take, we had nothing to worry about. Talk about a mistake.

So we keep working the wire on the Frenchman, pick up just enough – first the connection to wiseguys in New York City. We give that to your uncle's old friend Culhane, in the Intelligence Division in Manhattan. That worked out good for them. Little did we know him and his sergeant, another Jew no less, were better at cheaters than us.

Next thing you know the whole thing is going to shit. First off, Pabon's hooked up with that murdering little savage, Colon, and the two of them are working for Buster Alito. So let me tell you…things with good intentions could *go to hell in hand-basket* real fast."

"So how'd you turn Alito?" McCoy said.

"Give me a little leverage, I could turn anyone in those days - sometimes not all the way, but enough to get a tidbit every once in a while. What a lot of your dicks have forgotten, you know what I'm saying? …They don't realize that you don't usually get the whole story from one source, sometimes you piece it together from a few of them…Anyway, a guy like Buster was never gonna roll completely, not for me anyway. The Feds had RICO, life sentences to hold over their heads. That's how they got Sammy the Bull to turn, and Little Al, and the handsome guy, what's his name, was with the Gambinos."

"Did you register Alito with the department?"

"You gotta be kidding. I did that, he gets whacked and I go back to patrol, forthwith. Nah, I had a ton of informants the department never knew about. Register? Forget about it."

"What'd you promise Alito and, what'd he give you?" McCoy said.

"I should probably be talking to a lawyer now, but I figure the statute has run, no?"

He looked at Francine Jurgenson. She'd walked in a few minutes earlier, in a pale green business suit with a tight fitting skirt, and beige high-heels. The small room stunk of Chanel Number Five, which lost some of its appeal when it mixed with the combined body odors of three men. She uncrossed her legs and walked to the window, straining to open it wider. Brito got up and helped her.

"Thank you."

"You're welcome."

"Should I continue?" Rufus said.

"Yes," she said.

"What you've got to understand is that we did some things in those days that'd probably get us pinched today."

He paused for a long few seconds shaking his head a few times, as if to say *I can't believe I'm doing this.*

"Me and Dave made a three kilo seizure two months before, off of a Dominican kid. Guy was just a mule, no big deal, so when it came to vouchering the shit one kilo seemed like plenty and it left me a lot to play around with. I'm not prescient, but when Alito came on to the radar those extra two kilos came in very handy. By the way, your uncle wanted no part of that. He followed a pretty strict moral code, but had kind of a *live and let live* attitude as far as I went."

McCoy, Brito and Jurgenson stared at him, each with looks that said *I can't believe what I'm hearing.*

"We were in Special Investigations by then, then a few weeks later, in the middle of all the confusion, we got assigned to the Attorney General's Office Squad - the best detective assignment in the department…and there were more than a few feathers ruffled over that. The thing was, the Chief of Detectives didn't quite know what to do with us. We'd shaken the department to its core when we volunteered to testify before the commission. The Corsican Connection case eventually falls apart, the Attorney General himself demanded an independent investigation, and the Mayor joined the chorus. The new Commission, the Garabedians, was on the verge of collapsing before us, with that nincompoop Badway leading them down the garden path to oblivion. Romandella tried to salvage it, made us key witnesses. Us volunteering drove Badway up a wall. He thought he'd get us dirty, make us rats."

"Weren't you?" McCoy said.

"What?"

"What you said…rats?"

"Absolutely not! A rat's a guy's caught and rolls over to save his ass. We might have done a few things to advance a case, but we never took money off of anyone. In the end the Corsican case was being compared to the French Connection. Almost as much drugs seized and like the French Connection, every ounce of the hundred keys disappeared."

Rufus thought - what the fuck can they do about it now? It's ancient history and if they wanted to know about it, why not? Anyway, he had to get out of here soon, had to go meet Pam, told her he'd help her out…wait, wait, wait…he stood up, walked toward the door…who's this kid think he is, that he's gonna stop me?

"Sit back down, Rufus," Bill McCoy said.

"What's your name?"

"…Billy McCoy, Rufus…Dave's nephew."

"You're looking at me funny…think I didn't know that? I know you, Billy."

Rufus sat down, everyone else squirming, quizzical looks on their faces, like a collective thought of *what do we do with this guy?*

"So we spot Alito closing his joint - the Lion's Den. It's three in the morning. He gets into his Caddy and we follow him to the edge of the city. He stops for a light, I get out and walk up to his window - scare the shit out of him. He thinks he's getting whacked. I show him the tin, not that it's necessary - he knows me very well. I see the relief on his face… when he realizes who it is. I tell you, I thought about that, about how easy it would be to whack a guy like him…Anyway, I walk around the car, get in and tell him to drive. Dave follows us. We end up in Sachuest Park, my favorite meeting spot…where I give him the proposal."

The room was now quiet, like a funeral parlor lounge. Francine Jurgenson had crossed and uncrossed her legs about a dozen times. Brito barely moved, no expression on his face. And McCoy looked like he'd been hearing a confession to J.F.K.'s assassination.

"Then what?" McCoy said.

"You really wanna know? …Yeah, I know you do, but you're not getting another thing until you let me out of here. I gotta know that you're on the right track, that you're gonna stop wasting time on me and go after whoever killed them kids. You can't keep this bullshit up – pick me up, let me go, pick me up, let me go. Know what I'm saying?"

"I'm not authorized to do that…and you're not in a position to make those kinds of demands," Francine Jurgenson said.

Rufus stood up, looked at all of them, and smiled. He waited a full minute before he said:

"I didn't kill anybody and you've got no evidence to prove I did. I don't know where this is coming from, who's the real push here, but I'll tell you this: you get nothing more until you come to your collective senses. I want a lawyer!"

They released Rufus an hour later. Brito handed him a brown manila envelope. He tore it open and emptied onto the wood table outside the interview room. His wallet fell out, some loose change, a silver Swiss Army pocketknife, a black and silver Parker T-Ball Jotter pen, a small notebook (which Rufus presumed they'd copied,) his cell, and a gold money clip, which held a quarter inch thick wad of bills. He removed the bills and counted them, $178.

"It's been real, Brito."

Chapter 37

July 25th, 2008, 6:22 a.m.

It was a warm summer day, predicted to hit the high nineties. Rufus looked at the cream colored Bose clock radio. The alarm had gone off – a song called *Take a Bow* was playing, he heard "it's over now," but couldn't make out any of Rihanna's other words, just that one phrase playing over and over in his head.

He had an appointment in a little more than two hours to see a cardiologist. When his doctor told him his E.K.G. showed abnormalities, it felt like a death sentence. Dr. Seinfeld said he shouldn't jump to conclusions. He didn't know if his face turned white but it had felt that way.

He swung his legs over the side of the bed, pushed himself to a half upright position, grabbed the edge of the mattress and sat up. He felt around for his slippers, didn't like walking barefoot. The housekeeper his brother hired to come in one day a week did a nice job keeping the place clean, but he still felt squeamish. The tall young Jamaican woman had high cheekbones and long shapely legs. It bothered him that he never once got aroused, in fact wasn't the least bit interested in her. Should he mention that to Dr. Seinfeld? Should he be on some kind of hormone therapy, or maybe try the little blue pills? But then what? End up with his brother losing a good housekeeper? He went on thinking about his lost libido, which of course only made him more depressed.

Jonah had insisted he talk to Seinfeld about a neurological referral. Rufus thought his short-term memory had improved a bit since he'd basically moved in full-time. Jonah agreed, told Rufus living with someone else must have something to do with it.

He stayed under the hot water until he saw all the remnants of the soap spiral down the drain. Then he pushed the black and white vertical striped canvas curtain to one side, stepped out and grabbed for the thick white towel. For the first time that day he thought of Billy McCoy. After he finished with the heart guy at Miriam Hospital he'd call McCoy, tell him he'd meet him, for lunch. Close to two months since the murders - if something didn't happen soon the case would soon be officially categorized as cold. Rufus really didn't care about that, in fact it might work in his favor if Falco and Brito got assigned to a different case.

He turned on the Today Show, sat on the yellow and blue striped wing chair next to the dresser and put his shoes on. Matt Lauer and Meredith Vieira were talking about Obama - something to do with foreign policy. Lauer mentioned Hillary Clinton. He muted the television, looked at his cordovan wingtips that he'd had for fifteen years, highly polished but cracking in several places on the sides.

Soft and comfortable - he hated the thought of breaking in new ones. He looked at the worn black and white photograph in the silver frame in the middle of the dresser. Their mother smiling; dressed in a suit and high heels, with her somber looking little boy, seven or eight, head cocked to one side, her arm around his shoulder; an innocent looking kid, in a horizontal striped polo shirt and short pants, with black high tops. Rufus stared for a couple of minutes before putting the framed photo back in its place. He remembered something she frequently said when she got older – *where does the time go?* Yeah, what the fuck happened?

He went to the closet, picked out gray trousers and a navy blazer, laid them carefully on the bed. Then he leaned against the mattress, lifted his left leg and pushed it into the pants leg. His shoe got stuck around the knee of the pants and he struggled to push it through. Then he tried the opposite leg, this time pointing his foot and pushing harder. That shoe became lodged in the pants leg, below the knee, and he couldn't push it through, nor could he pull it back out. Then he fell.

About ten minutes later, after he'd stopped crying, he shimmied over to the bamboo desk in one corner of the room, saw a pair of scissors, managed to reach them, and began cutting carefully along the seam, until he finally freed his foot. Then he returned to the closet to pick out another pair of pants.

He pushed the button of the one-cup coffee maker, the kind that flips the little container out when the brewing is done. He stayed there, watching the coffee brew, waiting for the flip. Before he left he sat down at his laptop, brought up the *Tribune*, skimming the paper for the latest local news. When he got done he wrote a note for Jasmine, with some instructions. He often did that, even though he rarely had anything significant to say. He left the note on the kitchen table under an acrylic salt shaker shaped like a pyramid, sandwiched a ten between the shaker and his instructions.

Rufus followed Grunge every chance he had, meaning when Falco and Brito weren't in his rearview. A few times he'd hooked up to his home phone, once tried the main precinct trunk line, and did the Rio's twice; but so far he hadn't gotten too much. It was about this time when the word *fiberoptics* came to him. Then he wondered – is that why I'm not getting anywhere? Are the old disintegrating wires I've been hooking up to dead? But he'd heard some conversations. Hadn't he?

He dialed Jonah's number at the Tribune.

"Where are you?" Jonah said.

"None of your freaking business," he said. "But listen, do me a favor."

"What?"

"Rent me a car. I need to switch cars while these idiots keep following me."

"Wouldn't that be like aiding and abetting? ...Anyway, did you forget? I don't have a license, never drove a car in my life."

"All right, forget it, I've got another plan."

Another plan? Rufus thought as soon as he'd said it – plan? I couldn't plan a picnic! When they worked together, Dave did all the planning, while Rufus lived by his wits. Planning something long-term or complicated just wasn't his thing, maybe why he'd had limited success as a private dick for the last thirty or so years.

Rufus hadn't been wild about the idea of talking into a tape recorder but Jonah talked him into it, said that he, Rufus, owed it to Dave McCoy to finish what he'd started. So he did. Jonah listened to recordings of Rufus's recollections about the Corsican, and of Bob Badway and the Garabedian Commission. He'd also asked him to record everything he recalled about Wanda and Johnny Fortune.

They sat surrounded by houseplants, sitting on cane chairs with comfortable cushions covered in waterproof fabric with tropical scenes.

"It just happened a few weeks ago. What's the point?"

"The point is you might have left something out."

"Like what? Like I forgot to tell you I killed them?"

"Funny!"

"Come on, we gotta get out of here. I'm afraid after thirty-five years I'm starting to wear out my welcome with the beautiful spic."

"Who?"

"Anita."

"Ruf, we're at my house…you've been living here a month…and why are you talking like that all of sudden? Our whole lives I never heard you use that language."

"What language?"

"Spic, nigger…like all of a sudden you've become a racist."

He sat staring back, a benign thoughtful look on his face. He sipped some coffee then put the mug down on the bamboo end table.

"What can I tell you?"

He continued staring at Jonah for a few seconds then stood up, walked into the spare bedroom, closing the door behind him. Jonah heard things crashing to the floor, the sound of something breaking. He got worried, but was afraid to knock, to interrupt the tirade. And he felt an odd sense of relief, in the absence of the sound of a gunshot.

Later, sitting in the park next to Trader Stadium, they watched a pickup basketball game - three on three, shirts and skins. The "shirts" wore loose fitting tanks, two Celtics and one L.A. with Kobe's number. They were outclassed by, a "skin." That kid looked like Rondo, the Celtic point guard. A crowd had gathered along the chain link fence so the guy with the aluminum hotdog cart pushed it to a bench nearby.

"Up to you what you put on the tapes, but it couldn't hurt. Up to you if you do it at all."

"That's a pretty stupid comment, brother. How would you know whether it could hurt me or not until you hear what it is?"

Jonah didn't answer. The question came just as a "skin" made a behind-the-back pass as he drove toward the basket. "Kobe" caught it in mid-air, sweat spraying off of him, continuing to climb until his head was level with the rim, and let the ball roll from his fingers, through the hoop - like a fragile gift.

Four days later Jonah got a FedEx envelope with his P.O. Box as the return address. He was surprised to see two micro cassettes fall out; no note, just the little tapes. He removed an old Pearlcorder from his desk, the size of a pack of cigarettes, put fresh Duracell's in. In the kitchen he sat on a bar stool at the counter, turned up the track lighting, pushed the play button and began listening.

Chapter 38

Billy McCoy was number eight on the captain's list. The promotion was almost a guarantee, he just had to get by the oral board next week, and get a good recommendation from Chief of Detectives Badway. That shouldn't be a problem, he'd told himself - as long as he left his suspicions on the Fortune-Kelley murders simmering, didn't turn up the heat. He thought about waiting to get made before he took his next step in the case. But captain meant a whole new assignment. And he worried about who would follow up on what he had pieced together.

Falco and Brito had actually come up with it. They didn't know it - but if his theory was right, they'd gotten very close to breaking the case wide open. If he told them what he knew, it would all become clear, but his career would be in the shitter. A few weeks earlier it had all jelled. He'd had dinner with Rufus at Morton's Steak House, the one by the pier in the lower part of the city. McCoy always felt a little conflicted when he had a meal with Rufus. Something like when you had a girl you wanted to break up with, but couldn't give up the sex. McCoy was hooked on Rufus's stories and history.

"How'd you make out?" McCoy said.

"Good, Doc said I'm in good shape for the shape I'm in."

"Very funny...ticker's okay?"

"No, it's not okay. But I'm sure as shit not gonna do what he said."

"You're killing me with suspense."

"I'm a good candidate for a transplant."

"What kind?"

"What kind? A heart!"

"Rough news."

"He says I could get a couple more years out of this one, I watch myself."

"Doesn't look like you're watching yourself."

Rufus sliced his two-inch thick slab of porterhouse, taking large bites, followed by a few well-done thick-cut fries, every few minutes gulping Jack Daniels.

"What good's living you can't indulge yourself once in a while? I've had a good run."

He took another piece of steak, chewed it for what seemed to McCoy to be two or three minutes then took some more Jack.

"What do your boys have on Wanda and Fortune?"

"Not much?"

"You freaking guys think you're too smart, is the problem. You bother to ask, I could help you break it...and you might want to suggest that they quit wasting time following me."

Bill McCoy stayed quiet. Of course he knew that Rufus remained Falco and Brito's number one suspect.

"You okay to drive?"

"I'm good, Ruf!"

They shook hands in front of the restaurant and said goodnight, McCoy half staggering to his car. He got behind the wheel, put the container of coffee in the holder between the front seats, then started it up. Pulling away from the curb he sensed his right rear tire needed air. Then he heard Rufus yelling after him. He pressed the brake, the car screeched and stopped. Rufus approached the driver's door.

"Move over, I'm gonna drive you home."

McCoy didn't argue, he got out, walked around to the passenger's side and got in; Rufus sliding into the driver's seat. He moved the seat forward half a foot then adjusted the rear-view mirror.

McCoy never noticed that Rufus had made a couple of wrong turns. They kept talking, Rufus made a few u-turns to try and correct himself.

"Rufus, you're beginning to make sense – about what happened to Uncle Dave. That freaking Garabedian Commission was a total sham."

"Of course."

When Rufus didn't respond, he turned the police radio back on, listened for a couple of minutes, but in the half-hour they'd been driving things had gone dead. Close to his house he began to talk about something that seemed to get Rufus a little nervous.

"How many cheaters you work, Ruf?

"Think I kept count?

"Just curious, five, ten? Did you always have one going?"

"No. A few times we threw one on a guy's phone - if we had no shot at a legal one, wasn't enough p.c. for a court order."

"I worked a few in Narcotics."

"With orders?"

"Absolutely!"

"Back in the day we didn't always bother with paper. If it meant a very bad man kept walking the streets...what would you do?"

McCoy paused, trying to gauge what Rufus wanted to hear. What would put him more at ease? He laughed to himself...then took a deep breath and shook his head, side-to-side like drunks sometimes do.

"You'd get jammed up pretty good, if you got caught."

They approached a flashing yellow signal atop a wooden barrier that had a sign – *single lane ahead.* The car slowed quickly to a few miles an hour. McCoy took a quick breath after he'd slammed his hands on the dash.

"No one ever got caught. Everyone knew the score - judges, prosecutors, even the defense bar."

"They all accepted it?"

"A hundred per cent…until me and your uncle got grabbed by the commission. That's what led to our downfall…but at least I survived…even though it took years for anyone in the job to talk to me...after I testified."

Rufus paused, staring at Bill McCoy, who all of a sudden didn't feel so drunk.

"We found ourselves in the jackpot, big time. And the pressure got to your uncle. No matter how much I told him they'd never get enough to lock us up, and that once we testified we'd be protected… well, he just couldn't do it, all the pressure just got to him."

Rufus slowed the car and pulled close to the curb. McCoy got out and walked up the driveway, a few kids' toys blocking the way. He kicked at one of them. Rufus got out and followed him up the drive, as McCoy fumbled with the key at the front door.

"What the fuck you doing?"

"Coming in to use the head, then call a car service. I can't drive your department car."

He paused a moment or two, looking at Rufus and past him, with a thousand yard stare.

"You'll sleep over…no freaking car service out here."

The brown recliner was pushed back and his feet were a few feet off the ground. McCoy looked at the holes in his black cotton socks - his toes popping through. They heard his wife moving around upstairs.

Rufus was close to falling asleep in the chair when McCoy said to follow him into the smaller room off the den, his home office. He sat down, pushed the button on the Dell. It took a couple of minutes for the machine to reboot. He put his head down, resting it on his arms while Rufus stood there, before he flopped into an easy chair a few feet away. He'd wanted to show Rufus something on the laptop but they both fell asleep.

The next morning, just past sunrise, Rufus stumbled up the carpeted stairs. McCoy and his wife were at the round kitchen table, eating heavily buttered English Muffins, sipping steaming hot coffee.

"Remember Rufus, Annie?"

"Yeah, I remember him. What are you doing here?"

"Nice to see you, too, Mrs. McCoy."

"Fuck off…and get your ass out of our house."

"Hey, Annie, stow it – he's our guest."

She looked like she'd slept in her clothes, had on a wrinkled dungaree skirt that covered her knees, a sea-green sweatshirt with a white Leprechaun logo over her left breast. The sweatshirt was loose, looked like she had no bra on - uneven bulges, the left higher than the right. Her blond hair was shoulder length and unbrushed. She hadn't bothered with makeup. She'd eschewed doing much since allowing Billy McCoy to come home. He'd promised the affair was over.

Rufus asked to use the bathroom, right off the kitchen. When the door closed McCoy threw his arms in the air in a gesture of frustration. Then he pulled out some folded papers from his inside jacket pocket.

"What's that?"

"Notes."

"Was you really with Rufus?"

"I told you that."

"I'm just asking."

"You're always just asking. It's getting a little old."

Then he thought of the story he'd told Rufus last night, feeling a combination of shame and regret, wondering why he'd told him about the first time he cheated.

He had a foot post in midtown, not too far from Pell Justice. About ten at night, all the businesses shut down on that part of Broadway. An ash-blond, maybe thirty or thirty-five, pulled to the curb, the top of her pink Bonneville down. She'd stopped right under one of the brown iron streetlights that flickered with gas flames. The city had installed them to give an historic look to Broadway. She flashed a smile, and he smiled back.

"Can I help you?"

"Where's there a car wash around here?"

"At this hour?"

"I need it, bad."

The way she said *need it* and the way she parted her lips in half a smile, showing just a little enamel, was plenty of signal. And that was that.

"You going to work?"

"Yes."

"You could take an emergency day."

"I've got things to do, and I've got to drive Rufus in anyway."

"Rufus, you want an English Muffin, some coffee?"

"Thanks."

She sliced the muffin with a fork, popped it in the toaster, reached up and took a blue mug off a hook under the cabinets.

"Sugar, cream?"

"Black, please."

She placed a steaming mug it in front of him then gave him a pat on the shoulder and half a smile. He got a close look, was surprised to see braces.

"Take your pants off."

"What?"

"Take your freaking pants off, I'll sew them…you look like a freaking bum."

Rufus apparently hadn't notice the gaping hole in his left knee. Before they left she invited him back for dinner. The woman must be bi-polar or some shit like that, McCoy thought.

She reached across the table and stroked McCoy's hand. His skin looked the same as it always had, freckled, the back of his hand covered with a fuzz of pale brown hair, with bluish veins cutting through the middle, a couple of secondary ones forming a border on the outside. Anne's hands had the look of an older woman, the skin beginning to look loose and a little bit leathery.

"We'll have time to catch up tomorrow."

McCoy bent over, gave her a kiss and started for the kitchen door with Rufus right behind him. She reminded him of the index cards. He came back, took them from the table and thanked her. Rufus was in the car when McCoy got in. He handed him his keys.

Then he turned on the dome light, took out his spiral notebook and began to make notes. The police radio was blaring, something about an armed robbery twenty minutes in the past on Chafee, just west of Moses Brown. Rufus looked at the gray box with the red and green light. McCoy reached and turned the dial on the right side to the off position. He pulled out of the driveway and headed towards the city.

Rufus got out around the corner from Jonah's building. He leaned in the passenger's window to thank McCoy, in time to see him reaching in his right jacket pocket.

"Thanks for this, Rufus."

"Don't mention it kid…wasn't doing me any good."

McCoy waved the red phone book – as if to say I've got what I need. It had taken him a while to get over being furious at Rufus for withholding the book, but then once he'd thought about it, he began to wonder whether they'd all been wrong about him. In a certain way, McCoy was more confused than ever.

Every week Rufus visited Sissy Kelley with a bag of groceries, and every week he heard the same song and dance – "Rufus, when you gonna find who killed, Wanda?"

Of course, he had a good idea who it was, but couldn't figure out what to do. He'd often sit in Harry's Downtown, the fancy joint his late friend Harry Ross had opened, sip whiskey from nine or ten till closing, mostly thinking of the case. Or he'd wake up in the middle of the night, a vivid image of Wanda tied to the bed posts, head hanging, blood spattered all over. He'd be shaking, would stumble to the kitchen and pour himself two more fingers of Makers.

He thought about dinner with Billy McCoy, when he'd given him the red phone book, turning to the page with Bob Badway's name and poking his forefinger at it.

Part 3

Chapter 39

Monday July 27th, 2008, 8:05 a.m.

Falco and Brito plodded ahead with the investigation. However, Falco was constantly on his partner about Lieutenant Bill McCoy's close relationship with Rufus Koufax, expressing concern that their boss might be less than enthusiastic about going after Rufus. Brito wasn't overly sympathetic about that theory, but even he admitted he felt uneasy. But they both agreed that McCoy also seemed to be caving to pressure from headquarters.

And as far as Rufus went, they fully agreed that he'd gotten weirder. They'd watched him on numerous occasions during the almost eight weeks since the murders, at first unsure if his antics were intended to confuse them. Recently he put that idea to rest.

They'd been getting to Jonah's place by seven, plenty of time to set up surveillance. They knew the comings and goings of most of the building's residents by then. Working people left between eight and eight-thirty, a few others, like Mrs. Minifee, took their dogs out and walked up to the Strand, the ribbon of walkway that overlooked the water. School-aged children in the building left by seven thirty.

This day they arrived about 8:05 a.m., set up a half block from the entrance, a few minutes before Rufus walked out. The sun was still low in the sky, visible through the trees and shrubbery that lined both sides of the Strand.

A naked man roaming the streets of the city wasn't unprecedented. Most big cities experienced emotionally disturbed people in various states of undress from time to time. Rufus carried a brown paper shopping bag in his right hand that appeared to be full of papers of some sort, a few sheets blowing off the top and then along the sidewalk. In his left hand he carried a pair of swimming goggles. The detectives looked at each other, eyebrows arched, then looked back at Rufus as he walked up the thirty gray stone steps to the Strand. He stopped for a second, looked down at what might have been broken glass, took a step to the left, over a six-inch curved rail and into a flower bed of white and lavender impatiens, before stepping back onto the steps. They got out after a few seconds, deciding it didn't matter at that point if they blew their cover. They lost sight of him for a few moments, their vision blocked by the thick vegetation on either side of the stone stairs. When they reached the promenade they saw him, on the other side of the black iron four-foot railing at the water's edge, swinging the bag, just before he let it fly into the water. Then he quickly donned the goggles and dove off the ledge, at least twenty feet above the water's surface.

The cops of the Harbor Unit that retrieved him from the river reported that he said that it was a warm day and he felt like taking a swim. They just scooped him out of the water and covered him with a couple of blankets until they met a patrol unit at the nearest pier. The psych ward at New Netherland General held him for observation for not quite twenty-four hours. When Falco and Brito checked the hospital logs they found out that his brother Jonah came to pick him up the next morning. Falco tried to sweet-talk a nurse into seeing the psychiatric report but all she'd said to him was "no dice, that's confidential."

Falco and Brito felt they'd exhausted almost all of the leads they got from their appearance on Crime Stoppers a month earlier. Most of it amounted to a waste of several days but one was intriguing, a tipster who said to watch the Rio: *you'll eventually see a tall middle-aged red-haired guy…he knows all about the double murder.* The detective who took the call said she couldn't get any more out of the caller, no name, no further description, or how the caller came across the information. When the detective tried to give the caller a code name to use in case the man became eligible for a reward, he hung up.

Falco was about to throw it on the pile of vague and useless calls that typically came in to Crime Stoppers, but the lieutenant in command, an old-timer named Charlie McManus, talked them out of it.

"I'd check out the hotel," McManus said.

"Sounds pretty vague, lieutenant," Falco said.

McManus was gray haired, had the remnants of freckles that now mostly looked like age spots. He wore suits to work but took the jacket off when he got there and didn't put it back on until he left, even when he got called to a chief's office. He hadn't been a street cop or detective for the last fifteen years, but McManus lived in New Netherland, on Quimby Avenue, in the house he grew up in.

"It's specific enough. And we are talking about the murder of a cop."

Falco and Brito were in a small office, designed for visiting detectives who either manned the hotline, or used the space to work their case, unencumbered by the often busy and frenetic life in a precinct detective squad. There were two gray metal desks, two beige console telephones with multiple extensions, and two white Apple desktop computers, the type with the entire works built into the pedestal. Gray industrial grade carpet covered the floor.

"Thanks, lieu," Falco said.

"You're welcome."

McManus walked back into the large room that was the operations center for the unit, which had about a dozen detectives at their desks, most of them on the phone, a few typing reports, and one large black haired detective reclining in his chair - doing a crossword. Falco and Brito looked through the open door as McManus walked by him.

"You believe that guy, telling us how to work our case, then walks by Reed and says nothing," Falco said.

"Not your business," Brito said.

Later that night, at 11 p.m., five hours past the end of their tour, they sat on Moses Brown watching a lot of traffic in and out of the Rio. Brito had walked across the street three times in two hours, to use the bathroom in a seedy bar called the Last Chance. His shoes were soggy and made noise when he walked. Falco was bone dry. A light steady rain made watching more difficult.

"I think we oughta go," Falco said.

"Let's give it till midnight," Brito said.

"It's a fucking waste of time."

"You worried about overtime?"

Their overtime hadn't been pre-approved, the latest brainy order to come out of the chief's office – any detective overtime required pre-approval by a squad supervisor and someone at a command level, a captain or above. It didn't matter whether it was a high profile murder, a rape, or a grand larceny – every case was treated the same. Brito often reminded Falco, that not so long ago detectives didn't get paid overtime; that they'd do the extra work just out of a sense of pride and duty.

Forty minutes later Brito had to piss again. Falco, who was twenty-five years younger and fifty pounds lighter, watched as his rotund partner swung his legs to get out.

"It ain't normal to piss this much."

Brito slammed the door, walked to the rear of the dark gray Crown Victoria and stepped off the curb. At the same moment a tall muscular man with graying red hair came out the door of the Last Chance, lighted a cigarette and stood in front smoking. The façade of the bar was an imitation of an old western saloon, including swinging oak doors that led to a vestibule with a cigarette machine, an old pew that looked like it came from a turn-of-the-century train station, and a sign in three-inch letters that said *you must be 21 to enter.*

Brito hesitated, seeming undecided if he should cross the street and risk being spotted or get back into the car, pretty sure the guy he'd seen was Herman Grunge. He crossed the street and entered the hotel.

"Can I use your bathroom?"

The six-foot-four security guard looked down at Brito, sizing him up. Brito considered showing the tin, decided not to. He was the same "Rosie Grier" look-a-like that had denied access to Rufus weeks earlier.

"Down the hall to the left of the front desk, ask the clerk for the key."

"Thanks."

An effeminate blond haired man dressed in a white shirt and narrow dark-purple tie gave him the key. He walked into a corridor off the lobby, the floor covered with worn carpet with floral designs. The walls had faded dull wallpaper of a beach scene, a palm tree every few feet, with blue ocean and skies in the background. Before he entered the bathroom he glanced toward the front entrance, in time to see Grunge enter the hotel.

Five minutes later he opened the car door.

"You see who went in?" Falco said.

Brito moved a *Tribune* and a greasy brown paper bag with a half-eaten grilled cheese and bacon sandwich off the seat, opening the top of the bag, then peering in. He threw it on the floor then sat down.

"Grunge."

A moment later a loud crack on Brito's window made them both jump. Brito lowered the window. A woman leaned on the door looking in, and they'd agree later, that from what was visible, she'd already seen her best days. Her upper arms were flabby and mottled, and her face full of wrinkles, despite the pancake make-up. Her clothes looked like they'd been plucked from a dumpster.

"You guys know Rufus?"

"Who wants to know?" Brito said.

"Don't go hard ass on me...you know him?"

"Maybe."

"Yeah, you know him...I could tell from your faces."

"So what do you know about Rufus?" Falco said, half-leaning toward Brito and the woman.

"Know everything."

They looked at each other with matching cynical frowns. Falco got out, walked around to the curb and opened the rear door. She got in.

"How bout you take a ride with us?"

"How bout you kiss my ass?"

The car was already rolling, Falco stopping at the red signal at the next corner.

"We want to hear what you have to say," Brito said.

He had reached in his pocket and pulled a couple of bills out. He stretched his arm across the front seat to show them to her.

"We'll buy you dinner."

"Y'all all right, you know that?"

She grabbed the bills and stuffed them into her green plastic purse.

A few minutes later, around the corner from the Rio, the sallow skinned woman fished in her purse. Her lips were puffy, covered with too much lipstick. She came out with a crushed business card and handed it to Brito. He read it – *Rufus Koufax, Licensed Private Detective.*

"You tell him his old friend said hello, wanted to know where the fuck he went to."

"We'll tell him next time we see him," Brito said.

She got out of the car, stood unsteadily next to Brito's open window.

"Tell Rufus, Sabrina said hi, tell him his…"

They never heard the last words, and never gave her another thought.

An hour and a half later Grunge left the Rio, walking back toward the station house, carrying a blue and white golf umbrella. At Newport West he walked into the vacant lot next to the precinct and got into his brand new gray Lexus. They decided not to follow him.

"Nice car," Falco said.

"Very nice," Brito said.

They returned to the Rio, arguing about what to do next. Their partnership was never very warm but since this case it'd become close to icy. Falco sometimes wondered if Brito was a slug, whether his best days as a detective were long behind him. He'd changed his attitude a bit after the jewelry store shootout, had had to admit to himself that Vern Brito did a great job. In fact, not a day went by when Falco didn't feel regrets that it wasn't him who took the guy out. Even though Falco had performed admirably, he'd never shot anyone, never even discharged his weapon. He sometimes wondered what it would be like.

Outside the Rio they continued to disagree over whether to go interview the woman Grunge had visited upstairs.

"What if she tips him off?" Brito said.

"We don't even know who she is. Isn't it a little premature to be worrying about that?"

"I don't like it – it's too risky."

"And how about if the broad is up there injured, close to death? What if we're on the right guy and he did it again?"

Faclo's confident authoritative tone was effective with the desk clerk, too. He told them the room number and the name of the girl, who had the room for another two hours. But he balked when Falco asked for the key.

"I couldn't possibly do that without permission."

"I'm giving you permission," Falco said. "Anyway, you don't give it to us we're going to kick the door in...and I can't imagine your boss would be too pleased about that."

The clerk accompanied them upstairs and opened the door then rushed back to his desk. Doris Randall wasn't wearing much. Her gray robe was made of some sort of thin synthetic fabric with a two-inch border of purple trim. She held it closed with her left hand, smoking with her right. Her right eye was swollen – practically closed – and even with her dark skin, it had already discolored into several shades of blue and black.

"Never seen the man before and if you showed me a thousand pictures, ten thousand, wouldn't ever be able to pick him out."

She inhaled deeply, held the smoke a few seconds then let it come out of her mouth and nose. Her head shook slightly from side to side, her good eye watery. She wouldn't look at either of them, even Brito, who she'd met ten years ago when he worked vice. The room reeked of stale smoke and cheap perfume, despite the one window over the washbasin being wide open.

"All right, so you refuse to identify him. Tell us what happened," Brito said.

"You know what happened. Two of you ain't cherries...specially you Brito."

"Don't assume what we know, sweetheart. Assume we don't know shit and just tell us the details," Falco said.

"You right about that," she said.

"About what?" Falco said.

"You don't know shit."

Later, after Brito reminded Falco they hadn't eaten yet, they went back to the only place open that time of night. Goldberg's was half-crowded, even at 10:30 p.m. Brito inhaled deeply as they approached the deli counter.

"Two dogs, with the works," Brito said.

"Same for me."

The round Russian man moved in slow motion, his white apron heavily stained, evidence of many hours behind the counter. His hand opened and he placed four buns across, from his fingertips to the heel, and it looked like he could have held one more.

At a table in the rear, Brito sat facing the door, one of the things he wouldn't relinquish to Falco. Several times he had remarked: "What good is it? You're too big and slow to do anything even if you did see something happen." It didn't faze Brito, he always faced the door.

"She's lying you know," Falco said.

"Of course she's lying. Can you blame her?"

"This guy is going to do it again."

241

"Beat up a whore?"

"Kill again."

"It's a long way from assault to murder, and we ain't there yet," Brito said. "And since when did you change your mind about who the killer is?"

Falco had a mouthful of bun and frank, and mustard at the corners of his mouth that he blotted at with a napkin. He ignored the question. Brito had finished his franks, was picking at the French-fries.

"What's our next step?"

"Keep watching.... I want to take another look at her customer, the one in Massachusetts. And we just can't forget the other guy, can't take him out of the running."

"Rufus?"

"That's right."

"I'm surprised," Falco said.

"Why's that?"

"Thought you went way back, were friends at one time."

"We were – bad friends."

Chapter 40

Friday July 31, 2008, 6:15 p.m.

Since Monday, when he took his swim, Rufus did nothing but sleep, watch TV, and take walks on the Strand. He actually began to act more like his old self. Jonah came home from a long day at the paper. He'd recently been appointed to a position on the editorial board, which he had mixed feelings about. Though certainly an honor, he also felt it a sign that his career as a journeyman reporter was changing. Rufus told Jonah he planned to meet McCoy and his detectives for dinner.

"Are you nuts?"

"I know what I'm doing."

"Maybe…but do they? You should talk to Reitman first."

Unusually cool for July, the Traders had a twilight double-header scheduled, but a storm speeding across the Midwest had curved toward New England, which didn't bode well for baseball fans. The Yankees were visiting; the Traders sandwiched in second place between them and Boston, the three teams a game apart.

They met at Bishops Diner, on the edge of Newport, under the shadow of a huge housing development called Aquidneck City, planned by Robert Moses, the master builder, from New York. He had built most of the expressways, beaches, parks, and housing developments during the fifties and sixties. Aquidneck City was an almost exact replica of Co-op City in the Bronx, and neither one of the massive developments had lived up to expectations. Rufus was there at six, the first to arrive. He waited fifteen minutes for McCoy and his men to arrive.

"Your uncle and me were being set up, we knew that from jump street…but we didn't know we were about to get into a squeeze play. Once we reached out for help in New York - that was the beginning of the end. The truth is, I got a little mad at Dave for that. He vouched for those bums and in the end their bullshit scam helped get us in the jackpot."

Rufus stood up to go to the bathroom, brushed crumbs off of his shirt. McCoy looked like his head was spinning, and Rufus hadn't even gotten into specifics. When Rufus returned he had a wide grin.

"How you doing, Brito?"

"Okay, how you doing?"

"We'll see in a while."

The burly detective stared at him. Brito had on brown wool trousers and a short-sleeved light-blue shirt with a loosely tied brown necktie. He smiled and looked at his lieutenant.

"Not much of a conversationalist, this Brito," Rufus said.

He'd gone to the head to change the tape. Jonah had told him - "if you have to meet them at least wire yourself up". Rufus thought that was a splendid idea and told him so, said, "truth is - I'm a wireman at heart."

In the tiny diner bathroom he'd dropped the mini-cassette on the tile floor and bent to retrieve it. When he went to stand he cracked the back of his head on the sink, holding on to the tape in his left hand, grabbing the sink with his right to steady himself. He stayed like that for a minute or two, then pulled a paper towel from the dispenser and put it on back of his head. There was just enough blood to make him and the sink look a mess. He finished changing the tape, switched the recorder back to the on position and slipped it into his jacket pocket. He cleaned the back of his head with a wet towel, ran the water in the sink and did the best he could to clean that.

"What the fuck happened, Rufus?" McCoy said.

"What?"

"Your shirts full of blood."

He looked down, frowning at the stains, which he hadn't noticed in the bathroom.

"Nothing - little accident in the head."

"What is it with you and bathrooms?"

"What are you talking about?"

As if he had no idea what Bill McCoy was referring to...as if the assault in Kennedy's of several weeks ago never happened. Rufus stared at McCoy, then at Brito, beginning to wonder if Jonah had been right, that maybe this was a mistake.

"Go on, Rufus, finish the story," McCoy said.

"Finish the story...would take all our lifetimes to finish the story."

"Anyone else want more coffee?"

The waitress didn't wait for an answer, just began to pour. The three of them - Rufus, McCoy and Brito - didn't say anything while she served them. She put the pot down in the next booth, began to clear away their dirty dishes, stacking three plates in her right hand and sweeping the table for used napkins and butter containers with her left. She put those with the coffee pot, a wet rag appearing in her hand that she cleaned the table top with. The three of them sat with their cups raised to chest level.

"I'd hire her," Rufus said.

Rufus paused, took a sip of coffee, then slid out and went to the bathroom again. He returned a couple of minutes later and McCoy and Brito looked frozen, like they hadn't even sipped their coffees. He slid into the booth, picked up his cup and smiled at them.

"Beautiful day, no?"

"Rufus... tell us about Fortune and Wanda?" McCoy said.

Rufus paused for a long time. He took several gulps until his mug was empty, made a show of wiping the corners of his mouth, and folded the napkin into its original shape; looking from McCoy to Brito and back again.

"You guys are detectives – figure it out."

"Don't be like that," McCoy said.

"We're meeting at the P.C's office tomorrow, I'll tell you then, so I don't have to repeat myself."

McCoy and Brito looked at each other, bewildered, one probably waiting for the other to ask what the hell Rufus was talking about. He smiled for a second or two, slid from the booth and walked out of the diner.

Chapter 41

November 29, 1980, 6:55 a.m.

For ten minutes Rufus stared at the algae covered fish tank that he'd ignored lately, listened to the air pump, watching the bubbles coming out of the tiny helmeted deep sea diver, guppies and tetras circling. He walked into his bedroom and took his Smith and Wesson out of the top drawer, swinging the holster over his left shoulder, the leather strap over his right. It was 6:55 A.M., still dark outside due to threatening clouds.

"Where you going?" Anita said.

"To meet Dave."

"Be careful."

He bent over, pulled the flowered green comforter down, gave her a kiss on the cheek and left the apartment, not sure how he felt about Anita anymore. He couldn't get his mind off of Pam Stith – they'd been together three times and he'd never had sex like that. Anita was skilled at certain things, but Pam? Each time they'd been together they'd make love twice within a few hours. And even though Pam was a junkie; (and their informant,) it didn't discourage him. He felt bothered by all of it, but couldn't seem to help himself.

By the time he turned the corner and headed toward his car – he made it a habit to park a few blocks away from Anita's - he thought about the final touches he'd taken care of yesterday. They had the pen register in place, set up in a room he'd borrowed near the Netherland Plaza. The machine could be visited daily, or every couple of days if they actually used it as a pen, merely had to retrieve the numbers called from Marcel Petit's room. But that's not what Rufus and Dave had in mind when they got authorization from the A.G.'s Office to install the device. They planned to listen to as many of Petit's conversations as they could, get a handle on who he might be meeting. The conversion of a pen register to an actual wiretap was simple – and totally illegal. In fact, they could be charged with a felony if they got caught. But they often took risks and they had no trouble rationalizing their actions – they were going after a very bad man.

The pen register was a newer model, housed in a silver metal attaché case. A spool of white paper fed into one end of the device, came out the other. A call triggered the mechanism making it jump to life, ticking sounds that corresponded to the number dialed. Simultaneously, a small screen lighted up in bright green with black background, showing the number being called. An incoming call created a different sound, the screen merely read "incoming." A plug in the rear was labeled "input."

They sat at the coffee table for nine hours before the machine made a sound. At 5:10 p.m. the clattering caused Rufus to drop the book from his hands, *the Day of the Jackal*, by Frederick Forsyth. Dave put down his crossword, looked at his partner expectantly then picked up the headphones. The call took less than one minute.

The suite the manager at the Netherland Marriot provided was usually taken by visiting celebrities. The entire room was furnished in French provincial dark woods, with artwork in wide gilded gold frames hanging on each wall.

They'd had no trouble finding the terminals in the huge gray metal box in the basement. The only difficulty was that the stuccoed corridor was, used by the kitchen and dining room staff. When they first located it they both took deep breaths of the kitchen odors - a combination of sauces and freshly baked French bread.

The light on the Tandberg recorder attached to the pen was green. As soon as they heard the pen kick in, the reel-to-reel tape began to move. They'd argued about the need for taping, Rufus saying why waste the time, and that it could be evidence against them if ever found? McCoy prevailed, saying they could destroy the tapes later, said they couldn't be sure to get the essence of each conversation as it came in, that they might have to listen to it several times or more to get the meaning.

Dave McCoy grabbed the headphones off the coffee table, placed them over his ears.

He looked at Rufus and smiled, shaking his head yes. When the call ended he finished writing on the "line sheet" they'd prepared, as if it were a legal wire.

I   *Hallo.*
O   *We'd like to meet you.*
I   *When?*
O   *Tomorrow.*
I   *Where?*
O   *By us, at the place I told you about.*
I   *Goodbye then.*

Rufus listened to the conversation several times, as if he were going to will more out of the tape. Dave watched him maneuvering the Tandberg levers to rewind and advance, replaying the conversation. After a minute he raised his hand. Rufus removed the headphones, dragging the comb-over from the center of his head, using his left hand to smooth it back in place.

"What?" Rufus said.

"You'll wear out the tape."

"What's the difference? We're never going to use it again."

He and Dave looked at each other and Rufus smiled.

"Well?" Dave said.

"We've got a case. All we have to do is tail this frog and see who he meets with."

"Is that all?"

Then they both smiled, not giving a thought to the fact that they'd just committed a crime.

The dicks from New York were just like Rufus and Dave - could smell a good case from a mile away. Detective Mickey Culhane of the N.Y.P.D. had once worked with Dave on a case involving untaxed cigarettes. Dave convinced Rufus that Culhane was the go-to guy in New York City, could be trusted to follow up on any leads they gave him. But Rufus worried, told Dave that he'd seen him get fooled before.

After intercepting the call between Petit and the unknown caller they followed him the next day to New York City. The meet took place out in the open in Penn Station and lasted all of two minutes. The man who Petit met looked good to Rufus and Dave, so they had to make a decision. Petit seemed prepared to board a train right back to Rhode Island. Rufus and Dave followed the other man.

They didn't get too far with the well built John Travolta look alike. He wore a black leather jacket and black turtleneck. On the escalator up to the Eighth Avenue exit he removed a comb from his back pocket and ran it through his hair. He got onto the street, waved to someone, then walked past a hotdog and pretzel vendor and climbed into a waiting green Buick LeSabre. They got the plate number and Dave called his New York contact. They met later that day, at the Old Town on East 18th off of Broadway, maybe the oldest bar in the city, catering to a lot of show business types; and actors working as waiters or waitresses. They took a table in the back, next to the men's room.

"We'll get right on it," Mickey Culhane said.

Sergeant Andy Melnick sat not saying much. All four detectives had pints of Guinness in front of them. Culhane, a skinny gray haired man who wore a thin tie and a suit a size too small, said that they knew the driver and owner of the car, a bodyguard-chauffer for Johnny Boy DePietro, a made man in the Luchesse crime family. Melnick said he was involved with smack and coke. They didn't have DePietro's pager number so that spiked Culhane's interest when Dave gave it to him. Melnick was an overweight man in his fifties whose suit looked off the rack. He sat silently.

"What you want us to do?" Culhane said.

Dave had told Rufus again, that he trusted Culhane. Rufus continued to caution him not to give up too much information, to just let the New York guys see what they could find on their own. Then Dave gave up the name, and then the pager number. Rufus was steaming, but then again, after thinking about it for a few minutes, he figured, how could they expect help and not at least give them that much?

Rufus and Dave found out that the New York detectives had been after DiPietro and his uncle for years. It made them wonder how good the New York dicks actually were. Culhane and Melnick were assigned to the organized crime unit of the N.Y.P.D.'s Intelligence Division, its sole responsibility to investigate the Mafia.

"We'd like you to tail him. If you get a whiff that something's happening, call us. We'll be doing the same on the Frenchman," Rufus said.

Rufus heard from Culhane two days later. He said he and Melnick had put Johnny Boy to bed two nights in a row. The night before they'd followed him to the Sherry Netherland, on Fifth Avenue opposite Central Park. Between there and the Plaza Hotel, a block away, at the southeast end of Central Park, there's always dozens of yellow cabs, some horse drawn hansom cabs, and peddlers with metal pushcarts selling roasted chestnuts or large soft pretzels. Sidewalk Santas rang their bells every fifty or hundred feet, and thousands of pedestrians, in town for Christmas shopping or shows, milled around as if they had nowhere to go.

Culhane said he and Melnick shit a brick when a guy named Stepney showed up, one of the major black dealers in the city, controlled most of Harlem and the Bronx. Melnick, despite his sloppy attire, could pass for a middle-aged Frenchman, had a neatly trimmed black and gray beard and navy blue beret. He went into the hotel, stayed inside less than a minute, spun around and came out.

"He didn't want to push it. He got close enough to confirm the meet," Culhane said.

Rufus thanked him, said he'd get back to him if they got anything more. He didn't tell Culhane anything about Dave McCoy - that nobody had heard from him for twenty-four hours.

On December 2, 1980 at 7:03 a.m. Rufus was still at Anita's, feeling certain Pam would be calling him. He sat by the window looking through a gap in the sheer green curtains. Cars passed and he'd follow them with his eyes, try and see if they looked like department vehicles, or even worse, Feds, who were the easiest to spot. They always drove late model American mid-sized cars that looked like they'd just been washed. His pager went off. He went to Anita's phone, which sat on top of the Yellow Pages, on a wrought iron table with a multi-colored ceramic tile top.

Dave's wife told Rufus they'd planned go to a movie last night, and he was going to spend the next afternoon with Billy, who'd graduated Providence College last June. She added Billy had been studying for the test for the department, and that Dave tried to talk him out of it. He'd been encouraging him to go on to law school, or teach, do anything other than be a cop. Rufus listened patiently. Of course he knew everything she told him - Dave had several times expressed concerns to Rufus that his nephew might not be strong enough to stay out of the muck. Rufus and Dave had each other. He'd often told Jonah that if he had to go it alone he might not have resisted the pressure. Jonah didn't believe that, but Rufus had always sworn that it was Dave who had kept him honest. Now Dave was missing.

Dave McCoy was a confirmed bachelor when he met Clare Howe. Then he went to pieces. He found her looks and sweet voice hard to resist. She'd had a few roles in "B movies" after college, but like most young actors, she finally moved on to a more predictable career - as a parochial school teacher.

They lived in her apartment on Vanderbilt Circle, not far from the Cliff Walk in Newport. That part of Newport had been all large one-family homes and townhouses - before the city gave way to the developers. Soon there was little left to see other than skyscrapers and huge apartment complexes. Her third floor apartment on the circle had a partial view of the ocean and if you went to the roof deck at sunset you'd see a great skyline, with the blue waters of the bay in the foreground.

When Rufus showed up at their house to ask if she'd heard from Dave, Clare began to cry. He walked her to the couch. She collapsed into the khaki colored cushions, continuing to weep. He sat next to her, put his hand on her shoulder, asked if Dave had said anything.

"Nothing – but I knew he was bothered by something."

"Why?"

"Billy had called, left a message for him to call back. He said he couldn't, he'd call tomorrow…and you know how much he loves that kid."

Rufus felt a spark of reassurance when she used the present tense to refer to Dave, even though he realized she knew less than he did, that her confidence that he'd be back soon was not based on anything but raw hope. She went to the glass-topped bar and poured herself a scotch.

"Yes, I do. What else Clare, did he say anything else, do anything unusual?"

"Before we went to bed he said he wanted to get away for a few days, asked me if I'd mind. I told him of course not, but you know Dave, Rufus. Get away? He could barely drag himself out of New Netherland. I'd tried to get him to go to Trinity Rep up in Providence a couple of times, but he'd always tell me to go with a friend, to have a good time."

Rufus always felt that that comment about "getting away for a few days" might have been important, could have indicated that Dave did just that – got away, was still alive somewhere. But in his heart of hearts, he knew it was a real long shot.

"Rufus, want a drink?"

"Too early, honey…what else did he say?"

"Nothing really. I said be careful Davey. He gave me a kiss, grabbed me and pulled me close. He never did that, Rufus."

He could almost read Clare's mind. He wondered if she had sensed it would be the last time they'd see each other. Rufus knew what was bothering Dave. They'd both been prepped by Romandella and the other lawyers the day before, and were due to testify tomorrow. Dave had said to him – "I don't think I can do it, Ruf."

The next day, Rufus went to visit her an hour before he was due at the commission. When she opened the door he almost didn't recognize her. He leaned over kissed her on the cheek. Her face was puffy, her eyes all red, hair stiff and uncombed. He explained to her where he was going, told her that's probably why Dave disappeared. Clare got a disgusted look on her face, looked at Rufus with disdain. He expected it.

The police pound is the cemetery for unclaimed stolen and abandoned cars; situated on ten acres that bordered the landfill that New Netherland had turned into a mountain, with grass growing up the sides. Roads encircled the mound, with dirty white garbage trucks going up with their loads and coming down empty. The odors of rotting garbage wafted off the mountain, a feasting ground for seabirds.

Dave McCoy's yellow 1973 Plymouth Duster, fenders dented on both sides, rust bleeding through, sat on the edge of one of the many rows, of shells of squeezed together cars. Little space was left to walk around. Another day and Rufus would have had to beg to get the newest wrecks moved to allow him to get to the Duster.

Once he got inside he took out his flashlight and went over the glove box, looked under the seats, in the visors, ripped at the roof fabric. He looked in the trunk, removed the spare tire. Nothing. Then he looked down, spotted something under the gas pedal. He made sure nobody was nearby, reached down and picked up a small yellow envelope, slipped the safe-deposit-box key that was inside it, into his right trouser pocket.

He thought about it on the ride back into midtown. He had enough to do, trying to find out what happened to Dave; now he had an extra mystery.

Chapter 42

Tuesday August 5th, 2008, 4:00 p.m.

Rufus was getting on Jonah's nerves; living in his apartment, eating his food, and then telling him how to proceed with his own journalistic investigation. On top of that, Rufus had become obsessed with the Taliban, followed the news incessantly, often quoting Anderson Cooper or some other TV personality covering the wars in Iraq and Afghanistan. He watched Al Jazeera even more than he did CNN, which seemed to increase his agitation. He'd also become increasingly self-aggrandizing, given to outbursts, which included exclamations like *they ought to send me over there - I'd wipe them out in a month.* In reality, Jonah felt uncertain about his brother's war record in Vietnam, for no reason he could identify to himself.

Between spoonfuls of cereal Rufus looked at him and said they ought to visit their mother. Jonah had trouble dissuading him. Rufus said the doctor had told him yesterday, that she had a month to live at the outside. Jonah humored him, said they'd definitely go tomorrow. The trouble was, she'd been dead thirty years.

McCoy met Falco and Brito in a diner on Moses Brown Boulevard. All of them were exhausted and listless as they ate. McCoy had lied - told Jurgenson that he didn't have more than they already knew, but added that he'd work on Rufus some more in the morning.

"What do we really have, Lieu?" Falco said.

"Not much."

"Must be something the Feds can charge him with."

"You really want to go there, Al? I thought you were hot on Grunge now."

A waitress came over, a black woman with skin the color of onyx, which shined in some places on her arms. In a pleasant southern twang, she asked if they'd like coffee. They all said yes. When she returned they began to place their food order, interrupted when Falco asked her where the regular waitress was, the one who usually served them. She'd been working there for almost ten years, she said. He laughed, said he must have been thinking of another diner. The look on her face was directed at Brito, which could have interpreted to mean *how can you work with this asshole?*

"I'm not locked on to anyone anymore," Falco said.

"Since when?" Brito said.

Brito finished his coffee, placed the empty mug on the table and took his steno pad from his jacket's left inside breast pocket, opened to a blank page and wrote the day and date.

"You finish checking alibis of Wanda's customers, everyone from the phone records?" McCoy said.

As if they wanted to avoid, or at least change the subject, Falco and Brito didn't immediately respond. McCoy let it sink in for a while, allowing his detectives to ponder the question.

"They're all pretty solid...except my friend up in Massachusetts," Brito said.

"What's up with him?"

"Lawyer never produced him for questioning, or a DNA sample. He keeps cancelling appointments."

"Can we compel him to come in, get an interstate subpoena?"

"Talked to Jurgenson about it, but she must have put it on the bottom of her to-do list. If it doesn't involve Rufus it's hard to get her attention."

A few minutes later McCoy stood outside the diner thinking about what he had: an Assistant A.G. with tunnel vision; an Attorney General who wouldn't make a move unless it gave him some advantage in his run for governor; and his own boss, the Chief of Detectives, who McCoy had questions about, more than he was likely to answer. He'd been around long enough to understand that no one in the state was terribly interested in uncovering corruption. He felt Badway was capable of a lot, but had trouble believing what had recently been suggested.

Rufus Koufax had fingered Bob Badway, the Chief of Detectives of the New Netherland Police Department for Wanda's murder. In addition to finding plenty of reasons to dismiss out of hand his outlandish assertion, it was entirely possible Rufus was trying to deflect attention away from himself. And of course Bill McCoy also knew Rufus had an ax to grind. McCoy stepped out of the way as a family of six Chinese people exited the diner. He looked at them and at their reflections in the glass and chrome of the diner's façade. A fourteen year old girl held the door for what looked to be her parents and grandparents, and then for perhaps an older brother; a sixteen year old who wore blue jeans and a white tee, pants hanging down his ass, his crack half exposed, his brilliant black hair worn in a long ponytail tight to his scalp. He gave McCoy a dirty look. He ignored it, waited until the family had cleared the entrance then walked back inside.

"About Badway...I left the A.G. in the dark for obvious reasons. No way Rufus's allegation remains secret in her office. If we have any chance of nailing this bastard it has to stay with the three of us."

Brito and Falco nodded, both looking grave. Their boss stood up again and went to the bathroom. The diner was brightly lit and noisy, and several people had to say excuse me to get by. He tried the locked door, stepped to the side, and began pacing in place. A large man in denim dark-blue bib overalls and a light-blue gabardine shirt unlocked the door and came out. McCoy went in, paused a second, then flushed the feces left floating in the bowl. He barely got his zipper down in time. A couple of minutes in the tiny room seemed interminable.

"Did he offer anything solid, any proof?" Falco said.

"This book."

McCoy removed the red phone book from his inside jacket pocket. Brito's and Falco's eyes widened.

"What is it?" Falco said.

"Phone book... Wanda's."

"Son of a bitch," Brito said.

"What's in it?" Falco said.

"Badway's name...and Grunge's."

"Not much proof," Brito said.

"Place to start," McCoy said.

"We should pinch him for tampering, or withholding evidence," Falco said.

Falco was a great tail man. He'd spent six years in the Narcotics Division, on a surveillance team that did nothing but follow people. No case responsibilities, no other duties, just stay with targets. Tedious work - like eating the same thing for breakfast every day of your life - but it paid off. It often took them longer than the field teams liked, but there never was a time they didn't eventually put their subjects down, put them to bed; eventually they'd get their whole pattern.

His partner Brito was more like the average squad detective - couldn't follow a guy if his life depended on it. Not without getting made. But Brito knew how to interview people, how to develop information; and how to put a case together that would stand up in court.

When McCoy told them what he wanted to do, he thought that they were probably thinking - this doesn't seem impossible, it seems insane.

"I want you to follow Badway. From the time he leaves headquarters at night until he puts the lights out," he said.

"This is nuts," Brito said. "You want us to follow the chief?"

"What do we know about him? You have his address, what cars the family drives?" Falco said.

"Here's the address. It's in Westerly, one of the big homes overlooking the water. And he only uses his department car."

"We'll have trouble getting near the house. Westerly cops will be all over us if we sit there too long," Falco said.

"See how it goes. Most important thing, to state the obvious - don't get made."

"Why are we doing this?" Brito said.

"What if he and Grunge are in some way involved in Wanda Kelley's and Fortune's murder?"

"Just seems a stretch," Falco said.

"Take a look at the back page. There's a bunch of names and numbers scribbled there you may recognize."

They ordered more coffee. Brito asked the waitress for an apple turnover.

"Want it hot?"

"Please."

She spun on her rubber-soled shoes making a squeaking sound, walked behind the counter and slid a glass door open to reach the turnover. Brito watched her put it into a microwave and press a few buttons.

"They're department numbers," Falco said.

"Right," McCoy said. "Read the names."

"Red and captain. Doesn't say chief," Falco said.

"Wanda Kelley was servicing Fortune. Then he introduced his sergeant - Grunge. Then Grunge brings around the boss he's been closest to for over thirty years - Badway. But Badway uses the name Benny Fields."

"How ...?" Brito began to say.

"Koufax," McCoy said.

"Not exactly incontrovertible evidence," Falco said.

"We've got their cell records. There are calls back and forth - Badway to Grunge, Grunge to Wanda. All the times correspond."

McCoy shoved a sheath of records across the table. Brito picked them up just as the waitress reappeared.

"Here you go, honey."

"Thank you."

"How'd you get these?" Falco said.

"Never mind."

"So what do you think we get by following him?" Falco said.

"You have a better idea? You want to pick him up and bring him in for questioning?"

Brito and Falco both gave McCoy a funny look – because their lieutenant wasn't usually given to sarcasm.

Back at his office, McCoy made an effort to go over some of the other reports that kept increasing the pile in his in-basket. He shuffled through a few of them then flung them back on the pile. He'd been ignoring the normal caseload that came into the squad every day, relying on his two sergeants to handle most of that.

He got up from his desk, walked to the window and looked at a shiny steel tanker truck on its way to deliver fuel to a storage depot near the Bay. He smelled the fumes, closed the window and walked back to his desk. His Glock, in its holster, sagged off the left side of his belt. He almost fell into the worn looking desk chair. His eyes were closing while he thought of the conversation of less than an hour ago.

McCoy's eyes opened. He shook his head from side to side then pulled the center drawer of his metal desk, found it hard to open. It made a sound like fingernails on a blackboard. He reached in looking for the small red telephone book he'd examined a hundred times, then remembered he no longer had it.

They set up outside headquarters at about four in the afternoon. Three hours later Badway drove his freshly washed dark blue Crown Victoria out of the garage and headed north on Broadway. One of the perks chiefs in N.N.P.D. enjoyed was having one of the limited duty cops who manned the headquarters garage wash and vacuum their cars every day. Once, a cop protested that wasn't in his job description. A couple of weeks later he got transferred to the gas pumps at one of the department refueling depots.

Falco drove and Brito sat in the back, next to Falco's wood box that he'd made in his basement workshop; highly polished oak with brass hinges and hasp. It contained a pair of Bausch and Lomb 10X50 binoculars, a 35 Millimeter Nikon digital camera with a high definition telephoto lens, a pair of old style Motorola walkie-talkies, several blank steno pads, a package of No-Doz, a few cans of a super caffeinated drink, and a quart jug with a wide opening.

"Slide down in the seat a little more," Falco said.

"Bad for my back."

"For Christ's sake."

"This better?"

He looked in the rear-view mirror, didn't see anything. Brito was on his back with his legs bent. He stayed that way for forty minutes, until Falco stopped, told him to sit up.

"Where are we?" Brito said.

"Federal Hill."

"What's he doing?"

"He pulled up to valet parking at Antica Roma."

"That makes no sense...a Patriarca joint and he's being this obvious?"

"Too bad he knows both of us. I'd love to know who he's meeting with," Falco said.

"You hungry?"

"Why?"

"I'm going in."

"Are you crazy? He's sure to spot you."

"Doesn't matter…I lived up here for ten years, they know me, it will look perfectly normal."

Brito also reminded him that he'd been on the job in Providence for a few years before joining the New Netherland P.D.

He ordered a glass of Chianti and two veal parmagiana sandwiches to go, sat and sipped his wine, looking around the crowded bar. The tables in the back room seemed full. All the waiters at Antica dressed the same - black trousers, white shirts with narrow black ties, and black and gold vests. There was constant motion, trays loaded down with steaming dishes moving out of the kitchen. The din of conversations mixed with music, from speakers hung at either end of the bar - mostly Frank Sinatra, Placido Domingo, Dean Martin, or Mel Torme'. All the patrons looked Italian. Some glanced at Brito, the only black person in the place, but he didn't acknowledge, just sat sipping his wine.

Twenty-five minutes later the bartender, a short beefy man with several bad scars on his face, dropped a brown bag in front of Brito. They knew each other but rarely said much.

"How's it going, Brito?"

"Good. What do I owe you?"

"Twenty-one fifty."

"Pricey sandwiches."

"You're forgetting the wine."

"Right."

He dropped a twenty and a five on the bar, told him to keep the change. As he swung his legs around to get up he saw Chief Badway staring at him. The fiftyish blond woman he was speaking to was behind a half-door at the coatroom; but he never took his eyes off of Brito. As he walked toward the front door he nodded at his chief. All he got back was an icy stare.

At 10:30 P.M. Badway exited with the blond hatcheck girl. He nodded to the parking attendant, who went running off. The couple stood under the restaurant's awning exchanging a few strokes and kisses. A minute or two later the attendant pulled the department car up to the front, jumped out and ran around to open the passenger door. Badway began to argue with the woman.

"What do we do?" Falco said.

"Follow him," Brito said.

"But he already made you."

"Look at him, he's boxed. They're probably arguing about who's driving."

"He won't let her drive a department vehicle," Falco said.

A moment later Badway slid into the passenger's seat. Blondie walked casually around the car and got behind the wheel of the Crown Vic, a big smile on her face. The parking attendant was grinning, as well.

The surveillance was easy - 95 south, then 138 back towards New Netherland. They got off the highway just short of the bridges, ended up on a deserted street in Saunderstown. Falco pulled the car to the side of the road, told Brito he'd walk into the small street the couple had turned into. As he walked out of sight Brito went to turn the radio on. Before he reached the knob he heard a gunshot.

Badway and the Antica hatcheck girl had a thirty-year relationship. Every time he told his wife he'd be staying at headquarters he'd actually stayed with Nicole Starr. She had once looked like a star, now was just an aging blond with too many roots. When she called the police to report the suicide, the responding officers had to call a second ambulance for the grieving mistress. Then the shit hit the fan.

Chapter 43

Friday August 8th, 2008

Billy McCoy hadn't slept more than four hours a night for several days. The suicide of Bob Badway had set off wild speculation at two city halls, in the ranks of every one of the thirty-nine Rhode Island police departments, at Capitol Hill, on Federal Hill and on the front pages of the Providence Journal and the New Netherland Tribune. The unanswered question - what could have motivated the chief to take his own life?

McCoy's face was covered with stubble and his clothes were wrinkled. He tried to sort out what Francine Jurgenson was saying, about getting the Feds involved. She looked even sharper than usual, had removed her suit jacket after he walked in, the two top buttons of her white blouse open. A gold medallion hung from a thin gold chain, lying flat on her tanned chest, nestled between her breasts. Her blouse was tucked into the suit's tight fitting gray glen-plaid skirt. He looked out the window, past a stack of light brown law books, the titles in bright gold lettering on black background.

Three diplomas, all in black frames, hung on the wall behind her desk. The window to her right had a dead houseplant on it, and a couple of open greeting cards standing next to each other. He wondered what the occasion was, who sent them, but didn't ask.

"Tell me again."

"Koufax is a first class prick, in addition to being a murderer. The only way we get him to come clean is to hold the RICO hammer over his head."

"We gave him our word," he said.

"Bullshit, McCoy! Our word if he told the whole story. He hasn't come close to doing that. He's falling back on the statute of limitations for all his admitted corruption. So now we tell him there is no statute under the federal racketeering laws, see how tough he is then."

"I'm not sure you're right on that."

"What's the difference? He's not going to know that!"

She gave him an icy stare. He shifted in his chair, looking down at the old Oriental that reached to the edge of his chair. He examined the frayed worn light-brown fringe, the strands tangled, going in different directions.

McCoy knew the law, not from school, but more from a self-study program. Ever since he'd attended the police academy, he'd made a point of keeping up with court decisions that affected the police. This wasn't the first time he'd questioned a prosecutor, and Francine Jurgenson's reaction was the same sort of *how dare you…you're not a lawyer* response he usually got.

His body language displayed all the signs of someone with something to hide. He hadn't yet told her about the red phone book, or his suspicions about Badway. Since the chief was dead, he worried that if he voiced his suspicions now, it would look contrived.

The Tribune didn't get a full report before the paper went to press, but enough for a banner headline and a brief story:

N.N.P.D. Chief of Detectives is Dead

Chief of Detectives Robert Badway, a legendary New Netherland policeman, was found shot to death on a quiet street in Saunderstown last night. Early speculation amongst high- ranking members of the department suggests that the chief may have died at his own hand, and so forth,

McCoy wanted to vomit when he read the phrase *legendary New Netherland policeman.* He wondered if Badway did the *Dutch Act* over the murders, or if he merely got shook when he saw Brito, and if it was the just enough to push him over the edge. And for McCoy, all of it was now complicated by last night. Barely over Marie St. Pierre – now he'd complicated his life even more.

"You don't seem yourself. Come over tonight, we'll get you feeling good again."

"I don't think so."

Her voice changed, from syrupy and seductive back to a jackhammer punching concrete, her face looking sort of lop-sided. Jurgenson normally had a beautiful mouth, full shapely lips. But now they were twisted, the right side of her mouth an inch higher than the left.

"Fine - but either way, this prick is mine. I'm taking him down."

"We've already had one suicide."

"Not my problem."

She had to be wondering if he'd referred to his Uncle Dave or to the chief, but it didn't seem to faze her either way. He regretted more and more that he'd agreed to dinner last night. After his second Martini he had no chance. Though later on the booze had seriously hampered his performance. He didn't say anything about it and she didn't either. He'd wondered whether or not she even cared.

He waited for the next question, stomach churning, like it did as a child, when his father interrogated him for some youthful indiscretion.

"I want to go talk to him," she said.

"We'll have to go to his house, hope we catch him home."

"What the hell are you talking about?"

Her eyes widened and McCoy saw her cheeks and forehead turn crimson.

"He's been awfully hard to find lately. Brito and Falco haven't seen him in a while."

"That mother-fucker!"

"...What do you want to do?" he said.

"What I want to do is drop a cinder block on his head. What I'll settle for is finding him and dropping this RICO warrant on him."

"Shouldn't we let the Bureau handle that?"

"Fuck the F.B.I., McCoy...you going soft on me?"

They stared at each other for a few seconds, McCoy wondering - is that double entendre? He thought he sensed an expression of regret on her face, that maybe she felt sorry she made the remark, double entendre or not.

They left Pell Justice and drove to Rufus's house. His old girlfriend Anita was there. She said she hadn't seen him since early in the morning, said that he'd left and didn't say anything.

"He took both his guns. He never did that before."

She said it to McCoy, acting like Francine Jurgenson was invisible. The orange cat in her arms made low purring sounds, squirming every few seconds to have its belly stroked. He looked at the cat hairs that covered Anita's brown blouse, felt himself about to sneeze. He thanked her and they left.

Obviously Rufus intended to exact his revenge soon, McCoy thought. So does that mean he didn't do it, that we'd wasted our time looking at him? Or is he just that fucked up, doesn't have much of a grasp on reality...and maybe he is the killer? McCoy asked himself the same questions over and over, which didn't help him get any answers. Quite the contrary, it made him feel like he wasn't too far from falling into Rufus's state of mind.

Sitting in his car, before pulling away from the curb in front of Anita's, he told Francine Jurgenson that Rufus had called the other night. He'd admitted to McCoy that he'd been banging Wanda for years; from the age of sixteen, until she got fucked up on junk. He said they'd kept it from Sissy, said that even though Wanda had plenty to resent her mother for, she didn't have the heart to hurt her that way.

Rufus had told McCoy he didn't waste time psychoanalyzing himself. He said all he wanted now was to settle the score...then they could do anything they wanted to him. 'But you'll have to catch me first,' he'd added. If he did do something he certainly wasn't going to march in and surrender. McCoy thought.

"What else, Bill?" Jurgenson said.

He could sense the steam coming off of her, felt grateful she didn't ask the obvious, why he didn't tell her all this sooner. A dozen school kids, carrying book bags, horsing around, walked up the tree-lined street in their direction.

"He knows Grunge is no pushover. He's convinced he's either the killer or knows who is… said he'd get the truth out of him…they'd both gone to Wanda to get a free piece – Badway gave his name as Benny Fields. Rufus says he'll get it out of Grunge…then do what he has to do."

"Keep going."

"He also said he knew Falco and Brito were looking for him, they'd called Jonah half a dozen times in the last two days. We figured the best way to find him would be to stay on Grunge… they've already gone to him, told him his life's in danger."

"What else haven't you told me?"

"That's about it."

Rufus did say more to McCoy. He described how he could sit on a location and piss in a jar for twenty-four, forty-eight hours if he had to. Said all he needed was binoculars, a camera, granola bars, couple of sandwiches, a few cans of Coke, and a bottle of Makers; he's good to go.

Jurgenson thought she had a smoking gun with Rufus's DNA showing up inside Wanda. McCoy was concerned - didn't know what was true, didn't know what to think.

But the certitude of Francine Jurgenson along with some circumstantial stuff that Falco and Brito could fill in – there wasn't much question Rufus was about to get arrested and charged with murder.

McCoy dropped Jurgenson at her office, then drove through the city, checked out obvious hangouts like Kennedy's, Conte's, Shea's, and Harry's Downtown; hoping to find Rufus.

He cursed every minute or so, stuck near the entrance to the Bay Bridge Tunnel. Directly in front of him was a stainless steel tanker, flashers going. McCoy couldn't tell what was in front of it. He was just as unsure about what was ahead in his own life.

"What are you going to do?"

"Don't worry about it," Rufus said.

"Right now you can probably beat any charges they try and whip up and throw at you, but not if you do something crazy."

"It's not crazy baby brother. It's perfectly sane and reasonable the way I see it. Those bastards used that kid like a piece of meat…killed her when she threatened to turn them in. And to tie up loose ends they killed Fortune, too. In my book there's only one reasonable thing to do… I'm gonna take care of Grunge."

"You're acting like judge, jury and executioner, Ruf…and you haven't even heard the evidence, let alone give the accused his day in court."

After a long pause, Rufus leaned over on his knees looking down at the black water of the Sakonnet. Several couples sat on other benches along the Strand, twenty feet away the voices nothing more than murmurs.

"You've been a good brother," Rufus said.

"You too."

"How come you never told me about yourself," he said.

"What?"

"You know what. You think it would have mattered? It wouldn't have, and it don't now."

"How long have you known?"

"You shitting me?" he said.

Rufus broke into his gravelly laugh. His teeth had gotten longer, the gaps wider, and were no longer very white. Years of dissolute living had taken their toll.

"Little brother starts trying on ma's underwear, playing with make-up, it don't take a shrink – or a detective - to figure it out."

He smiled again, looked up at Jonah's red face.

"Anything you want me to do?"

"There's an account in the Cayman Islands, substantial amount. The account number and password are written on a piece of paper, hidden in my first-edition of Lonesome Dove, page one thousand. The power of attorney is in the middle drawer of my desk, gives you full authority. Anything happens to me, get the money – half for you; divide the rest between Sissy and Anita. Kapish?"

"Can't talk you out of this can I?"

"Not a chance."

The next day was searing, like the sun was a few miles away. Jonah didn't ask what he'd done the night before, where he'd gone, and Rufus didn't volunteer anything. He had on a freshly pressed gray suit, cordovan brogues, with no laces. They flopped around on his feet and he had to shuffle to keep them from falling off. Despite the clean clothes, he looked homeless. Standing next to Jonah, who wore a blue and white seersucker summer-suit with a light blue Brooks Brothers shirt and pale pink paisley tie, made Rufus look a sad figure. Behind them were plate glass windows of the Ocean State Cafeteria, at the Pell Towers, hundreds of people inside the huge breakfast and lunch emporium, known for their fresh baked goods. Every time one of the doors opened, which was frequently, the smell of country cooking spilled out. A queue at the south entrance spilled around the corner onto the Boulevard.

A short time later, back at Jonah's, blue haired Mrs. Minifee walked her buff-colored miniature bull dogs by the curb, talking to them like children, looking up in time to see Rufus and Jonah walk into the building. Rufus carried his shoes in his hands. They passed a neighbor, a middle-aged Jamaican man with jet-black skin, dressed in a tan linen suit and sea-green tee shirt. He smiled and said hello to Jonah, then gave Rufus a withering suspicious look.

Later Jonah went out with a list: shoelaces, a roll of Duck Tape, a package of double-C batteries, a dozen Granola Bars (cinnamon) three quart-size Tupper Ware containers, a two gallon gas can, a pair of work gloves, and two rolls of quarters. He wondered about all of it but didn't ask questions.

Chapter 44

Just before daybreak he did something he hadn't done in years. He spread a quilted mover's blanket in the sand at the old Second Beach (for the last twenty years called Smuggler's Cove.) The beach was a natural wonder, an almost perfect half-mile arc of white sand, the water bordered on each side by rocky shores. The small waves were perfectly formed. The sun began to appear over the rocks to the east and a red-tailed hawk circled over a reedy marsh adjacent to the beach.

Rufus put a folding chair atop the blanket, removed his shoes and socks, took off his tan windbreaker and felt the breeze against his bare shoulders and arms. He sat in his ribbed Hanes undershirt and light gray wool pants, looking at the water, trying to remember the last time he'd gone in the ocean. He thought it might have been at Sandhill Cove with Dave and his little nephew, Billy, well over thirty years ago, just before their last case began.

Billy! He'd call his mom later, see if she wanted him to bring him back to the beach, maybe do a little fishing later, off the Van Zandt pier. He'd have to hit Walmart first, pick up one of those little packaged rod and reels sets, just right for a boy his age…but what was his age? Ten, eleven?…That can't be right…hadn't he seen him recently…kid looked older…was wearing regular clothes…what the hell am I thinking?

Jonah wanted to stop him, but the only thing he could imagine accomplishing was getting him locked up again, or maybe even killed. He decided the best thing he could do was to sit and wait for him to call. Anyway, Rufus said he'd dumped his cell into the Sakonnet, bought an untraceable disposable phone. He'd *gone to ground* and there didn't seem to be a thing anyone could do about it.

Gone to ground… like the LRRP missions he used to talk about – long-range reconnaissance patrols, that Rufus claimed he'd performed in Vietnam. He had no reason to disbelieve him, he'd been away long enough back in the sixties, but something always nagged at him, made him a little skeptical. Maybe because whenever Jonah tried to elicit some details out of him he'd either walk away or change the subject. And there was no easy way to check it out. What was he going to do, write to the Pentagon, or wherever one writes to, ask for his brother's military records?

Jonas felt conflicted about the murders. Rufus did have motive for Johnny Fortune…but who knows after that? He didn't want to believe his brother capable

of committing a heinous double murder, but sometimes he faltered, would say -
"why not?" Then he'd spend hours hating himself for harboring the thought.

Rufus wondered, how much of his life was spent below street level, in dark
dank basements that smelled of the lives that people wanted to leave behind? He
found a broken folding chair and dragged it over to the junction box, placed the
headphones on then dialed the number on his cell. He put it on top of the chair
began to slide the clips up and down the terminals until he heard the ringing. It
took only a few seconds to find the right pair. He disconnected, grateful no one had
answered. Now he just had to be patient. He sat for three hours before he heard an
outgoing call. His mind wasn't in a much better place than it had been at breakfast
with Jonah. But, something kept him grounded now, maybe his sense of purpose.

Out   *Hello.*
In   *You okay?*
Out   *I think so.*
In   *We could help you out...if you need a long vacation.*
Out   *I'm going back to work.*
In   *When?*
Out   *Tomorrow.*
In   *That's good.*

He turned off the recorder when the call ended. The conversation he'd
intercepted didn't reveal much, but to Rufus it spoke volumes. How much more
did he really need?

Either way, he said to himself, both were bad actors, much worse than street
criminals, most of whom were nothing more than victims themselves. But these
two were supposed to stand for something.

He disconnected the wires from the junction box, rolled them up and stuffed
them in the large duffel bag containing the rest of his equipment. It was army-
green canvas about four feet long, that he lifted by the strap in the middle. He
climbed the steps outside the basement, when he got onto the street, felt relieved to
find no one in front of the building. A block away the red fluorescent sign above
the Lion's Den blinked, as if it were about to be snuffed out. Heaving, greedy for
air, he walked to his car, threw the bag into the trunk, got in and drove back toward
Jonah's.

He typed out a transcript of the imagined conversation, took half an hour to
do less than two minutes of talk. He also did a version of line sheets – a
chronology of the calls he was convinced he'd listened to, the dates and times, who
was the inside party who was out, a one line summary of the call, and even who the
intercepting "officer" was. Then he looked at it wondering, why bother?

If Brito and Falco, or Billy McCoy had been observing Rufus, they'd have known quickly that he was totally delusional. None of the calls he'd imagined took place. In fact, the junction box he "tapped" into had been dead for years, replaced long ago by more modern fiber-optic cables.

"You want a scoop – I'm giving you one. Badway's gonna retire this week."

"What are you talking about?" Jonah said.

"I got him by the short hairs, got the leverage I been looking for…tapes, photographs, the whole enchilada!"

"Ruf, Badway is dead."

Jonah just stared at his brother, realized that even though everyone in the city of New Netherland knew, and even though they, Jonah and Rufus had discussed the suicide a few days before, right now, Rufus seemed to have no clue that Badway was dead. And in his mind, the conversation he imagined he'd intercepted was between Alito and Badway. And in his mind it was 1981!

Jonah sat on the terrace looking out at the river, early morning and the sky looked threatening, dark clouds enveloping the few light gray ones, with a smell of rain in the air. He looked at the editorial page of the Tribune while drinking green tea. The tall frosted glass had the monogram *JK*. A lemon wedge floated on top, a clear plastic straw reaching a few inches up from the rim. He put it down on the round glass table in front of the terracotta planter that held his African orchids. At page 200 of a biography about Cary Grant, he'd just begun to feel relaxed. The phone rang and he debated a moment whether to answer.

"Hello?"

"It's McCoy."

"What can I do for you lieutenant?"

"Have you heard from your brother? I need to talk to him."

"I wish I could help you. But I haven't heard from him in days… and I think he's ditched his cell."

"If he doesn't give up soon I can't promise this will end well."

"Is that a veiled threat?"

"Listen, I know him almost my whole life and I don't want to see him get hurt."

Jonah Koufax wrestled with how much to tell McCoy He knew that Rufus would be mad as hell, but as he weighed it, he thought the lieutenant and his guys were probably in more danger than his brother, who had very little to lose.

"I probably shouldn't be telling you this, but…my brother might only have a few weeks to live. My advice Bill, work another case for a while."

There was a long pause, Jonah trying to remember the last time he'd seen Bill McCoy. He first met him when he worked as a detective in the Highjack Squad, about twenty years ago. McCoy impressed him the first time he laid eyes on him and nothing had changed as he advanced in rank and assignment. He thought maybe he should say something more, that maybe using the word advice didn't go over well.

"Thanks," McCoy said.

"You're welcome."

Jonah went into his bedroom and got the dark red accordion file with all his notes out of the right hand drawer. He thumbed through the third steno pad to the part he'd just thought of, wanted to refresh his memory of what Rufus had said in more lucid moments. Then he tossed the book across the room, feeling disgusted, thinking of two words he'd heard someone use during a lecture on writing memoir: *morally reprehensible.*

Chapter 45

Saturday August 16th, 2008, 11:05 a.m.

McCoy, Falco and Brito were a step behind Rufus. They'd been on him for several weeks, working late into the night with only a couple of days off to recoup. Each of them could sense that something was about to happen. Rufus followed Grunge, who was now on duty at Newport West. Rufus was in his car, a block from the station house. Then McCoy decided to send them home. They'd protested, but he insisted, saying he'd cover him until morning. They'd discussed getting other detectives involved, but then all agreed less was better in this case.

Chief Badway was dead and the Detective Bureau was temporarily under the command of a former Internal Affairs chief, Sidney Sachson, a merciless investigator of corruption, widely loathed throughout the department. That didn't bother McCoy. In fact, he respected Sachson. But he didn't want to answer any questions about the double murder case, about Rufus, or about Uncle Dave. Sachson was a thirty-five year veteran, who had to be well versed on the Corsican Connection episode.

Badway's suicide bothered McCoy a lot. He now wondered if Rufus was exactly right when he'd told him either Badway or Grunge did it, or maybe both. He thought about the phone calls: Badway to Grunge, Grunge to Wanda, Wanda to Rufus - and Fortune's calls to Wanda. When they examined the records they found that Johnny "Mis" Fortune was hooked, had called her at least once a day for a month.

The last night Bill McCoy was with Rufus he finally got the whole story out of him, about how the Corsican, Petit, ended up double crossing the Garabedian Commission. The prosecutors and investigators were more than embarrassed. In fact, the episode led to the dismantling of the Commission - which stalled Badway's plans and ambitions for about ten years.

Marcel Petit didn't exactly fit in, in the Lion's Den. He had to be the only Frenchman ever to sit at the bar, and certainly the only drug dealer with the capacity to import and distribute hundreds of pounds of heroin or cocaine.

He'd gotten Buster Alito to agree to purchase ten kilos of cocaine. Both men had sufficient bona fides in the criminal world. On November 30th, 1980 at 11:05 a.m. Alito put a call into a twenty-four hour laundromat on Federal Hill.

I   *Tell the old man I have to see him.*
O   *Que es?*
O   *Big man.*

274

The person on the other end just hung up.

Rufus looked at Dave, who sat with headphones covering his ears, plugged into a box like contraption made of wood and brass, with two large reels that held a quarter inch wide white paper tape. The machine had an inked needle that hit the moving paper that fed out from a four inch spool as many times as the digit being dialed, then left a space. At the end of each call a line was drawn across the tape, to delineate it from the next number dialed. Counting the dots on the paper would reveal the seven or ten digit number. Rufus and Dave and a few others knew how to make the "pen" even more valuable. It took mere seconds to convert the box into a full-fledged wiretap.

Rufus was reading the sport section of the Tribune, McCoy the crossword. They had a room in the Essex House, on upper Broadway, that usually rented for a couple of hundred a night. The room had gotten messy, with some used paper coffee cups scattered on the counter of the brown marble bar of the hotel room Rufus had "borrowed;" and the coffee table was covered with their equipment: the pen register, a Sony cassette deck, yellow pads, and index cards. They treated it like a "plant," as if it were a legitimate wiretap.

Rufus had met Vinnie Hawkes in the Intelligence Division, spent a year as his partner, long enough for Hawkes to realize Rufus was all thumbs. That's when Gunshannon replaced Rufus, but there were no hard feelings. Rufus was more of a street man, had felt claustrophobic and frustrated in his assignment at Intel. But he learned just enough to make him dangerous – someone who thought little of invading a suspect's privacy.

When he left Intelligence he went to work with Dave McCoy in Narcotics. McCoy was a lot easier to get along with, though years later, over drinks with Billy McCoy, Rufus complained that his uncle was too straight, wouldn't do what had to be done to go after certain targets.

"What things?" Bill McCoy said.

"Things," Rufus said.

That was all he got out of him then, but McCoy had been around long enough by then to know what he'd alluded to.

"I think we're gonna need help," Rufus said.

"Who?" Dave said.

"Hawkes?"

"Then I'm out."

"Why?"

Dave McCoy finished his second hotdog from the corner street vendor. Rufus was about to go talk to his brother, about searching the Tribune archives for any information on their targets.

"Go on a phone without an order...never gonna do that with someone else knowing, Rufus."

Dave had a line he wouldn't cross. He used to tell Rufus: "Do something illegal - best if you're the only one that knows. Not your brother, or rabbi, or girlfriend. Understand what I'm saying? You and me's another story...but let's hope we're never tested."

The equipment jumped to life again. Rufus grabbed the headphones this time, put them over his ears. Sitting in a sleeveless undershirt, he slid a yellow pad in front of him.

I   *Yeah.*
O   *Old man will meet you.*
I   *When?*
O   *Tomorrow...where he go for coffee.*
I   *Bye.*

They knew where Patriarca went for coffee every morning – everyone did. It'd been reported enough times in the *Providence Journal.* At 8 A.M. Alito's Cadillac pulled up in front of the café. He got out, lumbered to the front entrance, turned and looked around. He didn't seem to notice the dark gray van half-a-block away, with two detectives in the rear, taking photographs with a Nikon F2 with a 300 mm telephoto lens.

A day later, (two days day before Rufus and Dave got grabbed by the Garabedians,) Alito showed up at a pre-arranged meeting place, with two suitcases filled with tens, twenties and hundreds, wrapped in paper bands. Each packet held ten thousand dollars, a hundred and fifty packets in each suitcase. Petit had convinced Alito to forget about fronting half; they'd do the whole deal.

Petit stood opposite a McDonald's on upper Broadway. He wore his brown leather jacket, gray trousers and a beige turtleneck, chain-smoking European cigarettes which he dropped at his feet, crushing them out with the toe of his shoe. There were at least fifteen butts on the ground. A tall black man dressed in an Army field jacket, carrying a clipboard and silver coin holder, walked towards him, stopping to stare. Petit stared back, then the cab driver turned and crossed the street, walked into the Golden Arches. Three teenagers dressed in black jeans, black boots, and heavily quilted winter jackets, laughing hysterically and pushing and shoving each other, followed the cab driver inside.

A few minutes later the fat gangster lifted the trunk lid of his Cadillac, showed Petit a large suitcase. Alito wore a white double-breasted raincoat, dark-brown pants over tan cowboy boots. Petit leaned in examining the piles of money. Two young men stood twenty feet away from the car, one short, the other tall.

"I presume those gentlemen are with you," Petit said.

He reached into the inside pocket of his jacket. Alito took a step backwards, his eyes widening. The Frenchman removed a pack of cigarettes, shook one loose, put it between his teeth, grinning. He held the pack out to Alito who shook his head. He reached in his raincoat, removed and stuffed an unlit eight-inch cigar into his mouth.

"You presume correct," Alito said.

Everything was being recorded on a concealed Nagra recorder. The flat rectangular metal case, about the size of a thin paperback, was taped to Petit's back, the wire with the mike at the end, running around his body, taped to his solar plexus. Badway and his men had attached the wire, tested it to make sure it could pick up conversation through his clothes.

Petit and Alito crossed Broadway. At four in the morning ordinarily there'd be a couple of N.N.P.D. radio cars in the area but Alito had made a call, made sure no uniform cops would be nearby on this evening. A man dressed in a gray sharkskin suit, royal blue dress shirt and a black wool overcoat, got out of a station wagon, walked to the rear gate and swung it open. His wavy black and gray hair shined under the streetlight. He lifted a cover off one of the heavy cardboard boxes in the back of the wagon.

Alito nodded his approval and shook Petit's hand. Petit got a quizzical look on his face, held by Alito's grip.

"Something wrong?" Petit said.

"We need to test a sample."

"Not necessary…I'm easy to find, and just like your people would not tolerate a betrayal, neither would mine."

"Petit nodded to the man in gray sharkskin who then walked over and handed the station wagon keys to Alito. Alito in turn handed his Cadillac keys to Petit. He thanked Alito and crossed the street. In a few seconds the Cadillac was a block away, driving north on Broadway. Alito's men, Pabon and Shorty stood by, as if awaiting instructions.

Alito drove the station wagon south on Broadway. A few moments later, cars with sirens blasting, red roof lights spinning, came from every direction. Unmarked and marked cruisers surrounded the wood paneled wagon. Alito had his hands on the dashboard and Badway and his men and the other officers that got him out of the car would later report that the Mafioso had a disgusted look on his face. One of Badway's men, Pedro Amoroso, was dressed in a gray sharkskin suit.

Several detectives from the Commission were assigned to pick up Petit, to veil the fact that he'd been working as an agent - but the Corsican was nowhere to be found. Later, the abandoned Cadillac was found, the backup Nagra recorder in the glove box - without a tape.

"Who found the car?"

"Jogger who runs here every morning."

"Has anyone touched it?"

"No sarge, the instructions were clear, just locate it and notify headquarters. My partner and I been here two hours, waiting."

The officer was young, large and athletic looking, with a military haircut. His partner was a woman who looked like she should be wearing a tie. The car was half buried in weeds on a road near Sachuest Point, snow covering the shoulders of the road, remnants of a storm several days earlier. Over the roof, and past the sea grass that covered the dunes, the horizon of Little Compton could be seen, but just barely, the high-rise public housing shrouded in clouds.

"We'll wait for crime scene to get here to process the car, then you can impound it for evidence."

"Ten-four, boss."

Badway walked away shaking his head.

Petit had removed the Nagra tape and likely tossed it into Narragansett Bay. He removed the suitcase with the money, abandoning the Cadillac in the weeds. He walked close to a mile, to the north part of the city where he hailed a taxi.

At the entrance to Ninety-Five he told the driver to enter the highway and head for T.F. Green Airport in Warwick.

Petit had gotten away with $350,000 of "buy money" used to purchase the ten kilos of pure heroin. Badway had persuaded Romandella into agreeing to use what amounted to the Commission's entire annual budget for the operation.

The story ran for weeks in the Tribune. The articles made it appear like the entire Narcotics Division of New Netherland PD was dirty. Of course, that wasn't entirely true. The mirror story happened ten years earlier in N.Y.P.D., with their Narco guys, especially their Special Investigations Unit. A newspaperman named Daley wrote a book about it – *Prince of the City*. Then they made a movie. A decade later, less than two hundred miles away, same scenario - cops getting locked up, going to the can, a few eating their guns.

The Garabedian Commission had for a short time, looked like knights in shining armor. Badway led the charge and reveled in the publicity surrounding the commission's phenomenal success in exposing corruption, and there were almost daily pronouncements about the new NNPD, whose culture would be forever changed.

At a press conference at headquarters, Charlie Garabedian and Vin Romandella were flanking Commissioner Martin D. Lynch, who spoke from behind a mahogany podium:

These arrests mark the end of an era, one that most of us thought was well behind us. I will not tolerate this type of corruption nor will this department allow criminals posing as police officers to tarnish the reputations of the good men and women of this department. Now, I turn the moment over to Deputy Commissioner Romandella for some remarks.

As Commissioner Lynch stepped aside several photographers captured him sneering at Romandella as he took the podium. By the end of his prepared speech everyone in attendance was fairly convinced that all was well in the metropolis of New Netherland. Romandella was even being touted as a possible replacement for Lynch; but other rumors said he was on borrowed time, and unlikely to survive this scandal.

No one speculated on the behind the scenes activities of Rufus Koufax and Dave McCoy, which of course were entirely illegal, and their influence on the entire episode.

A few days later, when things had quieted down, Rufus threw a copy of a tape that captured a salacious conversation between the deputy mayor and a call girl, onto Romandella's desk. At the same time he volunteered himself and Dave to appear as witnesses before the commission – which Rufus knew was what caused Dave McCoy to disappear.

Chapter 46

Rufus had been watching the decaying hotel for a day-and-a-half confident that Grunge would eventually show at the brothel he'd been shaking down for years. He'd advised McCoy weeks ago to stake the place out, but he seemed disinterested, which told Rufus that he'd put his stock in Falco's cockamamie theory - that Rufus was the killer. Rufus understood that being at the scene and being the last known person to speak to Wanda, and his semen being present in her, all added up to making him an excellent suspect.

Every day he'd wake up thinking about it, as if it were a continuation of a dream. Wanda's dead body remained vivid in his mind, blood and deep cuts into her flesh included. He'd remember stepping over Fortune's body and would try to put himself back a little further, try to recall the events that led to him being there, but he felt stuck at the scene. Then he'd begin to wonder, if it were possible he'd killed them. There was no kidding himself - his mind was all fucked up. So maybe Falco was right, maybe Rufus was in fact a murderer.

When he'd told McCoy about erasing the grease board notation on Wanda's refrigerator, *BG 617* – even that didn't spark much reaction. Rufus found out Butch was Grunge's nickname and assumed *BG* stood for Butch Grunge, and that the numbers were a partial plate number, or some other thing Wanda must have noticed. He never figured it out, though.

He expected Billy McCoy to go a little nuts, or to at least threaten him with a tampering with evidence charge…but nothing. Rufus figured he'd worn him down with his weird behavior.

Quite a few residents rented single rooms at the Rio. The price, between a hundred and a hundred and fifty a week, depended on a private bathroom. Either way, the accommodations were at best primitive and sadly there were more than a few families that had no better choice, the private rooms being a step up from a homeless shelter. On a hot August night, people in the poorer parts of the city sat out on rooftops or fire escapes. He'd been in the place quite a few times and Rufus recalled the smells of decaying food and musty wallpaper.

He had the four car windows open and a supply of ice in a blue plastic cooler with bottles of water on the passenger seat. A two-gallon dark green plastic bucket sat on the floor in front of the cooler, a tattered gray towel over it in a futile effort to hide the stench of urine.

He'd stripped down to his sleeveless Hanes, rolls of flesh bulging at his waist, more fat than muscle on his upper chest and arms. It helped him blend into the neighborhood. He kept the radio loud enough for passersby to hear Salsa music. Every half hour or so he got out to stretch, always with a beer in his hand, that no one realized was empty. He hadn't shaved in a couple of days, looking every bit like a sixty something dirty old man.

Grunge walked to the front of the hotel wearing khakis and a light blue short-sleeved shirt outside his pants. At 7:30 in the evening he climbed the few concrete steps without looking around. Rufus waited about twenty minutes, Grunge somewhere inside doing who knew what...perhaps victimizing another woman. He readied himself, slid into his shoulder holster, grimacing from pain in his right shoulder. He'd been diagnosed with osteoarthritis, had laughed at the orthopedist who had suggested a shoulder replacement, told him he didn't think he'd be around long enough to justify going through that. He looked behind him at the navy blue Kevlar vest with Velcro straps, reached back and got it in his hand, but then let it drop.

The clerk on the other side of the bulletproof enclosure looked surprised. He knew Rufus but it had been years since they'd seen each other. The three hundred pound man had thinning silver hair and matching stubble on his face. He smiled, his teeth more yellow than white.

"Where the fuck you been Rufus?"

"Open up, Henry."

The fat man pressed a buzzer, releasing the locked door. Rufus stepped inside and into the small office.

"Where's Grunge?"

"Who?"

"The red-headed sergeant."

"He ain't too red these days."

He wheezed, laughing at his own joke, brought up some phlegm, turned on his stool and spat into a dark green wastebasket. The glass enclosure had papers taped on either side of the clerk: a license from the city, a rate chart, some advertisements from local eateries, and several wanted posters from Crime stoppers - that the police department required short-stay hotels to post.

"What room's he in?"

"You know I can't tell you that...wouldn't give you up neither."

It took just seconds for him to change his mind, to violate his privacy code. Rufus could talk or threaten his way past an obstacle better than almost anyone else. He winked and thanked him, turned grim again, told him to keep his hands off the phone. The man grimaced then whined something in protest.

Room 622 was on the right side of a long hallway with a window facing the back of a row of stores. The fire escape at the end reminded Rufus that the rooms had none, so no danger of Grunge fleeing. This was the showdown he'd dreamed about and planned. But now, he still felt uncertain - just take it a step at a time, see how Grunge reacted, he told himself.

He faced the door, looking to his right and left to see if anyone was in the hallway. A dim bare bulb was almost directly over his head, another thirty feet away. He lifted his left arm, the one that still worked reasonably well. He couldn't reach the bulb. Then he listened at the door while looking around, trying to figure out how to douse the lights, so he wouldn't be an easy target when the room door opened.

He returned from a utility closet with a broom, lifted the handle from the middle, poking at the bulb furthest from the door, shattering it easily, making almost no noise. Bits of the glass showered onto his head and shoulders. He bent and shook off loose fragments.

In front of 622 he did the same thing, but when the bulb broke it made a muffled exploding noise. He quickly stepped to the left, pulling his revolver from the shoulder holster. At the same time he banged on the door with his left fist screaming "Grunge…come on out!" For a few seconds there was no response, so he repeated the banging and the shout, this time saying, "Grunge, get out here, it's over!"

"Who's there?"

"Rufus Koufax!"

"Fuck you, Rufus. You better get the fuck out of here before I call nine one one."

"They're already on the way, Grunge. Come on out…your best chance is to talk to me first."

"I don't know what the fuck you're talking about. Piss off!"

Rufus knew that in a way Grunge was right, that this whole scene didn't make sense. He was trying to decide what to say next when the hallway erupted in gunfire and the old wood door splintered in about eight places. The smell of burnt powder poured into the hall.

Rufus walked to the front of the door, turning to face it, lifted his left leg and crashed it in. He slid to his left in a half crouch, firing at the silhouette that was Herman Grunge. Then total silence.

He moved forward, stopping just past the door jam, feeling with his left hand for the light switch. He slid his fingers along the wall, found the switch and turned on the overhead light. He looked at Grunge's legs, one crossed over the other. How did that happen? Not the first time he'd seen a dead person in that position. He glanced to his right, noticed the thin salmon colored bed spread hanging off the end of the bed, then saw the contours of another body on its back – long slim legs, boney hips, and a chest that barely protruded. A moist dark outline on the sheets surrounded her from the shoulders down to the waist. The young woman was dead.

Too late Rufus thought, always too late. If you asked him right then he would have said that. But he certainly wasn't quoted in the Tribune the next day. The article was perfunctory at best.

Yesterday, a blazing gun battle at the Rio Hotel, one of the last remnants of the seedy downtown establishments that thrived a couple of decades ago, left an N.N.P.D. police sergeant dead in the aftermath of the shootout, and the other, a former member of the New Netherland Police Department, Rufus Koufax, who left the department under a cloud of suspicion in 1981, unharmed. The deceased was a highly decorated sergeant named Herman Grunge. Also, a still unidentified young woman, whom police estimate to be between fifteen and twenty years of age, was found stabbed to death in the room.

Detectives are trying to sort out the details of what occurred on the sixth floor of the hotel, but right now all they would disclose is that it may have been a domestic quarrel, and said that the matter is under investigation. Interviews of several hotel employees revealed that Sergeant Grunge was a frequent visitor to the establishment. One of the employees, who asked not to be identified, said that he thought that the old detective looked familiar. When asked to elaborate he refused further comment.

Later that day, in police headquarters McCoy met with acting Chief of Detectives Sidney Sachson. He explained why they intended to close the double murder case with *exceptional clearance.*

"My men liked Grunge for this all along. We just couldn't get enough to satisfy the A.G.'s Office."

"And now?"

"Well, it all fits. With the other dead girl, it's the same M.O. Nearly cut her head off …the same way he did the Kelley girl."

"Any forensic evidence, DNA, prints?" Sachson said.

"A ton at the Rio, and from Wanda Kelley's place. It all fits."

"I know, you said that."

McCoy walked out feeling uncertain and not at all sure that he'd convinced Chief Sachson. Then he wondered about what Rufus said, whether Badway had in fact visited Wanda and was shaking her down for sex, along with Grunge.

Chapter 47

Monday August 19th, 2008

Weather wise, Monday was a *perfect* day for a lawyer from Massachusetts to travel to New Netherland with his client. Despite predictions for a storm traveling out of the south, it had blown out to sea and the skies were vivid light blue, with wisps of cirrus clouds creating a border. It had taken almost six weeks of persistent calling by Vernon Brito to finally get Howard Felder to bring his client Bob Gilbride to New Netherland for questioning. Brito explained that he just needed to tie up loose ends. He knew a lawyer like Felder wouldn't mind that for a couple of reasons. First, Gilbride was just one of a number of Wanda's customers, all of whom by now were breathing a sigh of relief, with the announcement by the N.N.P.D. that the murders were solved, both perpetrators deceased, and the citizens of New Netherland resting easier. The second reason - at $400 an hour it would be a good payday.

Brito hadn't told anyone what he'd planned to do; in fact he wasn't too sure himself. As despicable as Herman Grunge and Bob Badway were, he felt certain they probably didn't murder Wanda Kelley or Johnny Fortune. He'd told Falco what he thought and then told Lieutenant McCoy the same. Falco laughed and walked out of the squad, but McCoy sat in silence, looking stunned. Brito waited for him to say something but he didn't utter a word, so he just got up and left the office.

"Would you like coffee?"

"Sure, I wouldn't mind," Felder, said.

"Yes, thanks," Gilbride said.

Felder was Brooks Brothers all the way: navy pin striped suit, pale blue button down shirt, red and gray striped tie, cordovan tassel loafers. Gilbride wore a pair of camel colored cotton trousers, a pink Izod polo, and dark brown Sperry Rand boat shoes with white bottoms. He looked totally relaxed.

"I take it black, please," Gilbride said.

"I'll be right back."

Brito returned to the interview room with two cups of steaming coffee in white ceramic mugs with the navy blue and gold NNPD logo. He placed them at the edge of the table.

"Hey, I'm sorry about that, let me get some paper towels."

Some of the coffee had spilled onto Gilbride's trousers. He looked a little flustered. Felder had an annoyed look on his jowly face. Brito walked out. And even though the public gets almost 24 -7 on police procedure from Dateline or

CNN, or from C.S.I., people still often don't get the small nuances or tactics available to a detective.

"What an idiot," Felder said.

His client remained mute, but smiled, nodding in agreement. Brito, in the adjoining room with McCoy and Falco - watched the monitor. Even though they'd expressed skepticism, he wanted them to observe the entire interview.

"Here's some towels...so sorry about that."

Vernon Brito then squeezed Gilbride, between his neck and his right shoulder. He saw him wince. After that the whole tone of the interview changed. Brito never moved more than a foot from Gilbride's face, his right leg slid between the suspect's legs, his knee almost touching his crotch. The whole time he recited a long preamble of Gilbride's history, leaving Wanda's client believing the old detective new more about him than he did about himself.

An hour later, Felder appeared ashen when Brito put handcuffs on Gilbride. His client on the other hand, looked relieved, as if all his problems were over. And in a certain way that was true. They marched him out of the precinct, put him into the back of their unmarked cruiser, for the ride to Pell Justice. They'd process him at Central Booking, lodge him in the Dungeon, and draw up the murder complaint.

Bill McCoy called Chief Sachson, then Francine Erickson. No need to do much else. The city of New Netherland had a very efficient, albeit informal, system of communications. But he did make one more call.

"It's Bill McCoy."

"Hello lieutenant, what can I do for you?"

"How's Rufus?"

"Good as can be expected," Jonah said "Brain surgery is never a walk in the park."

There were so many loose ends, but Jonah had decided he'd learned as much as he wanted to, and that there were some things about his brother he'd just as soon not know. Like the safe deposit box in the Cayman Islands. He'd found the account number where Rufus said it would be – in his first edition of Lonesome Dove. But when he inquired at the bank they didn't seem to know of any such account number, in fact, the young woman told him that their numbers were configured very differently from the one he gave. So Jonah just let it go.

"Let's meet for a drink...I've got a story to tell you," Billy McCoy said.

The end